Suddenly, Justin pushed Janelle away. He stared at her, dark brows drawn together in a deep scowl. His eyes were hard and cold.

"Well, whatever it is you want this time, my dear, you evidently want it very badly, enough to tolerate . . . no, better than that, to respond to my kisses. You're a very good actress when you need to be."

Janelle was so stunned she could hardly find her voice. Only moments ago this grim-faced stranger had aroused her as no other man had ever done. Tears sparkled on her lashes as she turned away from him.

"Wait," he commanded. "I won't allow myself to play the fool for you again. You may stay at Delacroix only so long as you don't try any of your tricks. I won't throw you out. After all, I did love you once."

"Excellent! An unforgettable hero and heroine, an ending that touched my heart—I couldn't put it down."

—Kat Martin, author of *Lover's Gold*

Yesterday's Passion

CHERYL BIGGS

CORNERSTONE USED BOOKS
28 S. VILLA AVE. - VILLA PARK, IL
630-832-1020
HOURS MON-FRI...10 TO 7 SAT...9-5

HarperPaperbacks
A Division of HarperCollinsPublishers

If you purchased this book without a cover, you should
be aware that this book is stolen property. It was
reported as "unsold and destroyed" to the publisher
and neither the author nor the publisher has received
any payment for this "stripped book."

This is a work of fiction. The characters, incidents, and
dialogues are products of the author's imagination and are
not to be construed as real. Any resemblance to actual
events or persons, living or dead, is entirely coincidental.

Harper Paperbacks *A Division of* HarperCollins*Publishers*
               10 East 53rd Street, New York, N.Y. 10022

Copyright © 1991 by Cheryl Biggs
All rights reserved. No part of this book may be used or
reproduced in any manner whatsoever without written
permission of the publisher, except in the case of brief
quotations embodied in critical articles and reviews. For
information address HarperCollins*Publishers,*
10 East 53rd Street, New York, N.Y. 10022.

Cover illustration by Jim Griffin

First printing: December 1991

Printed in the United States of America

HarperPaperbacks and colophon are trademarks of
HarperCollins*Publishers*

10 9 8 7 6 5 4 3 2 1

This book is dedicated with love to:

My Dad, for all his unfailing support
and patience;

My Mom, for her continual encouragement
and for passing on her love of a good book;

My children, Chantel, Ken, and Stacy,
who always believed in their mom's dream;

and to my husband, Jack, my best friend, my
lover, and above all . . . my hero.

Prologue

Delacroix Plantation
New Orleans, Louisiana
April 18, 1856

THE GREEN RIDING HAT TUMBLED ACROSS THE ground, hastened on its journey by an afternoon breeze. A giant cypress tree, several roots twisting atop bare earth, brought the hat to an abrupt halt. The stiff velvet brim caught in a crevice at the tree's base, the tulle trim snagging on rough bark and settling on the hat's crown, obscuring it from sight.

Moments later, black riding boots followed nearly the same path the hat had just skipped over. The soles of the boots were caked with mud, one heel bearing just a hint of red stain. From beneath a hooded cape, eyes luminous with hatred scanned the landscape. For nearly an hour the cloaked figure searched between the trees and shrubs of Bayou Tejue, several times passing near, yet never seeing the bit of velvet and lace.

Sara Janei had laughed, taunting and teasing mercilessly as always, ever so confident in herself, but at that final moment, fear had flashed into her eyes. As the knife swept through the air, its blade a gleaming reflection of the sun, she had realized too late her mistake. The sharpened steel had struck savagely, and she had fallen to the ground, motionless among tall blades of swaying grass. Her taunting laughter no longer filled the quiet grove, and her beautiful green eyes would never again look at the cloaked figure with contempt and scorn.

The black waters of the lush bayou proved a good burial ground, one that gave up no trace of its victims. Now, only the hat remained.

At the swamp's edge, hood-shaded eyes swept the landscape one last time before turning to where two horses stood tethered to a small bush. The killer mounted the large gray gelding, the cloak thrown back with a flourish as a gloved hand reached for the reins of the small mare standing alongside. The other hand pulled at the cloak's hood, lowering it further to veil a smiling face from the noonday sun. The mare had to be disposed of, too, but that would have to wait until later.

Chapter one

Delacroix Plantation
New Orleans, Louisiana
June 18, 1991

A PRICKLING SENSATION CREPT UP JANELLE'S
spine as Cathy Delacroix's car rounded a sharp curve in
the old River Road, which ran alongside the Mississippi.
Motioning for her friend to pull over, Janelle threw the
car door open and scrambled out when the sleek Cor-
vette rolled to a stop. Without a backward glance, she
ran across the road and disappeared into an overgrowth
of vines and trees that lined both sides of the narrow
highway. A few feet beyond the road's edge a set of tall,
rusted iron gates stood in her path. Janelle stood and
stared at the scene beyond.

Weeds grew in thick patches over the entry drive and
spiraling vines of kudzu ivy trailed over everything that
stood upright. At the end of the long drive was the
hollow hulk of an old plantation house, framed and partially obscured by two giant live oak trees, their gnarled,
twisted branches draped heavily with thick curtains of
gray Spanish moss. Sunlight filtered through the trees
creating a brief illusion of beauty. The weather-beaten
front door stood ajar, and above it a fanlight window
held only a few jagged shards of glass. Six Tuscan
pillars lined the sagging gallery, their white paint long
ago worn away, patches of red brick exposed in several
places. Wild ivy entwined the girth of the two center

pillars, threatening to enwreath them forever in greenness, and window shutters hung crooked, precariously
dangling from their few remaining hinges. The house
seemed steeped in loneliness, as if waiting for yesterday
to return.

"It shouldn't look like this!" Janelle whispered. She
closed her eyes and shook her head, as if to clear it of
the scene before her. Thick waves of auburn hair curled
over her shoulders.

Cathy caught up with Janelle. "What's the matter? Are
you okay?" she asked.

Janelle turned away from the gate. Her green eyes
that were usually vibrant with life, were now blank
and unfocused. Without a word, she walked back to
the car.

Worriedly, Cathy trailed after her. She'd shared a
dorm room at the University of Nevada with Janelle
Torrance for the past two years, and now the two were
more like sisters than friends. Never in all that time had
she seen Janelle act so strangely.

She didn't respond to any of Cathy's questions, and
for the remainder of the ride to the plantation, stared
straight ahead as if in a trance.

Steering the car between the iron gates of Delacroix
Plantation, Cathy heard Janelle's quick intake of breath
and felt her tense as the house came into view.

It sat atop a small rise. Several giant live oaks stood
to one side of the magnificent structure, their widespread branches dripping with long strands of gray
moss that resembled shrouds of lacy cobwebs as they
swayed with the afternoon breeze. Eight sparkling white
Corinthian columns lined the front of the mansion, the
center four flanking a set of gracefully curved entry
steps and supporting a huge white portico which shaded
the entrance. Forest green shutters adorned every tall
window, and both the first- and second-story galleries

were trimmed with an exquisitely carved white balustrade.

Janelle gazed at the house as though mesmerized. She'd been looking forward to coming to Delacroix ever since the sudden death of her parents in a car accident three months before. Cathy had helped her through the ordeal, and the invitation to Louisiana seemed just what she needed to pull her out of her depression. But rather than the excitement she'd anticipated upon her arrival, a strange loneliness filled her.

The car rolled slowly over the oyster-shelled drive, and suddenly, the scene before Janelle began to blur and dim, as if shrouded by a heavy, dark fog. For a few brief seconds she saw, not a beautiful old plantation house, but dark woods and stagnant swamps. She felt the cloak of death surrounding her. Unseen eyes seemed to glare at her. Invisible fingers tightened about her throat.

She wasn't aware that she'd screamed until she turned to see Cathy's startled gaze.

Cathy slammed on the brakes. "Janelle," she said, "what the hell is the matter with you?"

"I . . . I don't know." She looked back out at the landscape, normal now, and began to breathe easier. "I'm all right now. It was just some weird hallucination, I guess." She smiled weakly in an effort to satisfy Cathy. "I'm all right, Cath, really."

Unconvinced, but not knowing what else to do, Cathy restarted the engine.

Janelle let her head drop back against the car seat and closed her eyes, but her mind found no rest. The flight from Reno had taken over six hours, and on her arrival in New Orleans, Cathy insisted they stop for lunch in the French Quarter. Everything had been fine at first. After parking the car, Cathy led her through the throng of tourists that crowded Royal Street and through a dimly lit porte cochere. At its end, a maître d' showed them to a table in the center of a huge courtyard where the air was filled with the aromatic scent of wisteria that clung to one pale pink wall, and vines of greenery wrapped around wires stretched overhead to create a living roof.

Midway through their lunch a rather rotund man dressed in a white tuxedo, balancing two glasses of champagne in one hand, a bottle in the other, weaved his way toward their table.

"Ah, my favorite cousin," he exclaimed, kissing Cathy's cheek and setting down the glasses. "And this must be the beautiful best friend, Janelle, I have heard so much about." He smiled widely, and brown eyes twinkled with amusement and warmth. "You look somehow very familiar to me, my dear." He kissed Janelle's hand.

"This is my cousin, Gerard," Cathy said to Janelle. "He's the owner of this place, and a terrible flirt."

Janelle laughed.

"Maybe you saw a picture of someone who looks like her in one of those history books you're always reading," Cathy suggested. "Gerard is a genealogy nut. He's always researching our family tree."

Gerard shrugged, but continued to frown thoughtfully. "Perhaps, *chère*, perhaps."

After lunch, they stopped at a small boutique where Cathy had earlier ordered a dress. Enthralled by the scenery, Janelle remained outside, admiring the old buildings with their galleries of delicate lacy ironwork and plaster walls of pink, green, orange, and brown mellowed with age, each structure nestled against another to line the narrow streets and alleyways. The exotic flavor of the Vieux Carré was like no other she'd experienced. It had a timelessness to it, even though surrounded by skyscrapers and other evidence of the twentieth century, and thronged with loud, gaily dressed tourists, its aura of days long past remained strong.

High overhead the afternoon sun blazed, creating waves of sultry air. Yet Janelle felt suddenly cold. Everything blurred. Rubbing her eyes, she looked back at the street and nearly fainted in shock.

A horse-drawn carriage rumbled past, its giant wheels clattering loudly as it swerved to pass a slowly moving work wagon laden with bales of cotton. Vendors pushing two-wheeled carts, women with large baskets balanced on their heads, and men on horseback all jostled for space to move about the narrow roadway. Several small children knelt on the street, laughing delightedly as a tiny, crudely made sailboat floated in the dirty stagnant water of a narrow trench that ran between the road's edge and the bricked banquette. Women dressed in long skirts, their widths taking up half the walkway, strolled by, parasols shading them from the afternoon sun.

And then, as suddenly as the scene had come to life before her, it was gone, and Janelle was left wondering if she'd drunk too much champagne at lunch, or left her senses back in Nevada.

But now it had happened again.

"Hey, I'd almost given up on you two," a deep voice called out when Cathy and Janelle entered the house.

Janelle looked up to see Cathy's brother Paul coming toward them. In appearance he was almost the exact opposite of his fair sister. A mass of dark hair framed a square, olive-complexioned face, but the blue-gray eyes surrounded by thick black lashes were the same as Cathy's.

"So, Janelle, welcome to our humble home." He took her hand and placed it on his arm. "Cath, Mom and Dad are out, but they'll be back in time for dinner." He glanced over his shoulder at the servant who approached. "Carter, take Miss Torrance's things up to the gold room. I'm going to give her a tour of the house."

"Paul . . ." Cathy began.

"It's okay, Cath, I'd love it," Janelle interjected, suddenly realizing she meant it. She smiled up at Paul.

"So, obviously this is the foyer." He threw out his other arm in a sweeping gesture of exaggerated presentation.

"It's just like I . . . imagined," Janelle stammered. She'd been about to say *remembered.* Now where did that come from? she wondered. How could she remember something she'd never seen before?

Overhead hung one of the largest and most elegant crystal chandeliers she'd ever laid eyes on. At least three hundred flame-shaped bulbs lined the three-tiered fixture, each bulb surrounded by small, delicately scalloped crystal bowls, and beneath each hung four teardrop-shaped prisms. The bright rays of late afternoon sun streamed in through a fanlight window above the door, the yellow haze reflecting a rainbow of color upon each crystal prism and softening the starkly contrasting tiles of black and white marble that covered the floor.

But by the time Paul had escorted her through the house, and they'd wound their way about the massive garden with its mazelike paths, Janelle felt exhausted. It was all she could do just to get through dinner without yawning. Finally Saundra Delacroix, Cathy's mother, suggested Janelle retire for the night, stating they could all have a nice, long visit together in the morning.

Closing the door behind her as she entered her room, Janelle smiled. The soft yellow coverlet on the huge canopy bed had been turned down, and the sight filled her with sadness. It was something her mother used to do whenever she was home from school. She let her gaze travel over the large room. The furnishings were original to the house, which had been in Cathy's family since 1824, the year it was built. An ornate lamp, its amber glass shade dangling with crystal teardrops, sat atop a small wooden chest beside the bed, casting a warm yellowish glow over the room and enriching the faded gold damask drapes and flowered wallpaper. The grate of a white Italian marble fireplace stood bare, but she could see it was more ornamental than necessary. For the sake of modern convenience, all the oil lamps and chandeliers had been electrified, heating and air conditioning installed, and dressing rooms converted into bathrooms.

Janelle shivered. She'd never been to Delacroix before, or to Louisiana for that matter, yet she had the distinct impression that everything in this room, in this house, was familiar.

"Morning, miss, what are you doing up so early?" An old black man stood in the bright kitchen. Thick white hair framed his face. "I ain't even heard our old rooster crow more'n twice this morning," he said, a tremor evident in his raspy voice, one gnarled and bony hand clutching the sinktop to help support his ancient and hunched body. He watched her steadily, his eyes sad and weary, as if old beyond time itself. "My name's Tano. I'm the butler here."

Janelle smiled and moved toward the stove where a pot of coffee sat steaming. There was something disturbing about him, she thought, something she didn't understand that caused a torrent of emotion to swell in her throat, and brought tears to the back of her eyelids. "It's nice to meet you, Tano," she said in an uneven voice. "My name's Janelle Torrance."

"Yes, I know. Are you all right, Miss Janelle? You look kinda tired."

She leaned her back against the stove. "Yes, thank you, Tano. I . . . I didn't sleep very well, probably jet lag. I just wanted some coffee to get me going, you know, and I think I'll take a quick walk before everyone gets up. Maybe some fresh air will perk me up a bit."

"Miss Janelle, you sure it's the right time to be going out there? I mean, looks like a storm brewing. It's going to be raining pretty soon."

Janelle frowned. "Rain? But it looks so sunny outside. Oh, wait, I get it, you're talking about those little flash storms the South gets in the summer, right? Two minutes of rain and then back to sizzling heat?" She continued before he could answer. "Don't worry, Tano, I won't go far."

The old man seemed to want to continue their conversation, but Janelle made for the back door with a quick wave and was outside before he could say anything further.

Moving aimlessly from one path to another, the sun warming her shoulders, she found the garden's lush beauty exhilarating. Louisiana was so different from Nevada, where everything was sagebrush and wild grasses. The morning air, already sultry and warm, was full of the heady fragrance of blooming jasmine, magnolia, camellia and other flowers she couldn't put names to. In some areas the manicured foliage grew so high and thick it blocked the light of the sun from the path, while in other areas it curved inwards, fashioning small alcoves of greenery that surrounded a marble bench or statue. One path led to another and another, crisscrossing, curving around the shrubberies, branching off in different directions, and winding over small knolls or low dips in the land. Janelle found the gardens enchanting, unaware of the changes taking place overhead, of the slow and steady transformation of sun to clouds, of blue skies to gray.

Suddenly the air filled with deep rolls of thunder and a streak of lightning cut jaggedly across the swiftly darkening sky. Startled, Janelle instantly turned back, attempting to retrace her footsteps. Rain began to fall heavily and the narrow path quickly became a sticky quagmire of mud. Within seconds Janelle realized, to her horror, she was lost.

Another flash of lightning ripped across the sky, illuminating her surroundings. She was no longer in the lush gardens and manicured hedges, but an overgrown, scraggly part of the estate. Waist-high weeds fought for space between long-neglected shrubbery and half-dead trees. Unsheared curtains of moss hung heavily from brittle branches, and the path was so littered with broken tree limbs and leaves it was nearly indistinguishable from the overgrowth. Janelle shivered; her light robe offered no protection from the rain.

"Damn, why do these things always happen to me?" She was torn between irritation at getting herself into this mess, fear that she'd be lost for hours, and embarrassment at the thought of returning to Delacroix looking like a drowned rat.

Moving carefully along the path, she strained to see into the darkness, searching for the lights of the house. She pushed a wet, moss-laden branch from her path, and almost fell into the weeds when another streak of lightning flashed. It struck a nearby tree, and splinters of bark flew through the air.

Abruptly, there was a lull in the storm. The rain turned to a light mist, the sky quieted, and the clouds parted slightly. It was then she saw it, a wrought-iron fence alongside the path, its metal spears covered with rust. Weeds and wild ivy entwined about the thin bars as if attempting to hide them from view. Janelle followed the length of fence for several yards and came to a gate standing open at an awkward angle, a top hinge having long ago given up its struggle to keep the two united.

She took a step forward and paused to listen. The only sound that broke the deathly quiet was the soft sucking noise her slippers made in the mud whenever she moved. Janelle looked about warily, and then turned to enter the enclosure.

A hundred feet inside the fence stood a tall oak tree, sheets of moss hanging from its widespread branches hiding the trunk and interior area of the enclosure from view. She brushed aside the prickly gray curtain and stepped within its folds. A feeling of apprehension swept over her as the musky smell of wet earth and long-dead foliage assaulted her nostrils. It was as if she had entered a large room, the moss serving as walls, the tree's thick leaves overhead acting as a roof, allowing only faint streams of light to penetrate. All around her, in every direction, were tombstones, old and crumbling, some having toppled to rest face down.

One gravestone near the base of the huge tree caught her attention as it cast a soft, pinkish hue into the darkness. Without volition, Janelle moved toward it and bent down to read its inscription, but in the darkness the letters formed only a dim blur. Brushing her fingertips over the face of the marble letter by letter, Janelle was able to make out the name—Sara Janei Delacroix.

She whispered it aloud, and shivered. When she tried to pull back, she found she couldn't move, her fingers held to the engraved letters by an unknown force.

The sky split open in renewed violence, lashing out with unrelenting fury. Thunder crashed, lightning streaked across the sky in blinding arcs, and sheets of rain whipped the air. She huddled next to the pink tombstone as moss slashed at her face, its sharp spears scratching her skin. The wind tore at the silk robe and whipped her hair about. Suddenly, the cold, wet ground beneath her shifted. Janelle clutched at the stone.

Then, as quickly as it had erupted, the storm ceased. The dark clouds parted and the golden rays of the sun burst through, bathing the landscape in a flood of light. Janelle blinked rapidly. Her fingers were free of the force that had held them to the pink stone. She moved to place her hands on the marble's curved top as leverage to rise to her feet, and found only air. The tombstone was gone. The earth was covered with a thick, rich covering of grass, its surface smooth and unbroken.

She scrambled to her feet. Every tombstone stood upright, the grass was a well-manicured carpet of emerald lushness, and the moss that hung from the tree was cut high above the ground. On trembling legs she moved toward the small wrought-iron gate, now hanging straight and erect on its hinges. The thin black bars glistened in the sunlight, no longer rusted or concealed by overgrown weeds and clinging vines.

Janelle shut her eyes and rubbed at the lids with the tips of her fingers. She was hallucinating again. Her brain was playing tricks on her. Grief was causing her to fantasize, to see things that weren't there. She reopened her eyes. Everything remained the same. The tombstone was gone, the grass was lush and green, the fence appeared almost brand-new.

Grabbing up the skirt of her robe, Janelle dashed toward the open gate and ran down the narrow path. Everything was different now. Or was it? Had she only imagined the dead trees and shrubs? The pink tombstone?

Tears streaked her face as she hurried through the maze of garden, tripping over a slight rise in the path, snagging her robe when she moved too near a rose bush, and stubbing her toes as she paused, looking about for direction. Her hands and knees were bruised and bleeding from numerous falls, her arms scored from pushing at branches as she cut corners too hurriedly in her haste to try yet another path. Several yards farther, when she rounded the corner of a tall hedge, the Delacroix mansion came into view.

"Oh, thank heavens," Janelle muttered breathlessly. She stared up at the house in relief, yet at the same time she felt a faint, unexplainable sense of apprehension.

A door on the rear gallery stood open. Janelle stumbled toward it and grasped the door's knob, but her weak legs buckled. She collapsed and fell across the threshold. A piercing scream filled the air and the world began to blur, spinning crazily, until a blanket of darkness closed in about her, and erased the throbbing pain in her leaden limbs.

Chapter two

"MARIE, WHAT'S GOING ON IN H . . . OH, GOOD Lord, Sara Janei! Janei, can you hear me?" He knelt and took her hand in his. It was cold and clammy, but he felt a pulse. Weak and slightly erratic, but definitely there.

Dark auburn-tipped lashes weakly fluttered open and gold-flecked emerald eyes met icy gray for a brief moment. Then, too exhausted to fight the blackness swelling up around her again, Janelle allowed herself to slip back into the dark void.

"Damn!" He turned away and smashed his fist against the doorjamb. The servants fidgeted uneasily at their master's anger and began to disperse. A few cast dark looks of resentment at the unconscious woman. They knew only too well what the appearance of the prone figure meant to the calm of everyday life at Delacroix.

Sighing in resignation, Justin Delacroix pivoted and lifted her into his arms, but when he stood, found his path into the house blocked.

Marie was stationed in the doorway, arms crossed over ample breasts, lips set in firm determination. She shook her head. "Justin, you listen to me. You can't bring that woman back into this house. It ain't right. We done had enough of her trouble."

He remained silent, and with despair she recognized his answer in the flinty glare of his eyes. He was determined. Knowing she dare not speak further, Marie moved aside.

"Bring hot water and towels," Justin said brusquely over his shoulder as he brushed past and moved toward the staircase. "And send someone to town for the doctor."

For a brief, gut-wrenching moment, he debated carrying her to the master bedroom they had shared so briefly. She felt small and cold in his arms. He glanced down into her face, a picture of innocence in peaceful repose, and wished for the hundredth time things had turned out differently for them. Why had it all gone so wrong? Then, remembering her betrayal, his heart quickly closed against those insidious feelings. With determined steps he moved to her bedroom door and pushed it open with his foot, the force slamming it against the wall. The room was musty and dank, having been closed since the day she'd disappeared.

He hesitated at the threshold. Justin had vowed months ago never to set foot across this doorway again. Swearing under his breath, he moved into the room. With gentle movements he put her down in the center of the large, canopied bed and then sat on its edge, staring bleakly down at her. Emotions he'd thought long dead came to life as he reached a hand to her cold cheek. Her skin was darker than he remembered, not the pale alabaster Janei was so proud of. His fingers slid slowly across her soft flesh to the small hollow of her throat. Skin smooth as satin spread beneath his hand, and a damp tendril of dark hair coiled on her breast like a silken rope.

"Why, Janei?" he whispered, stroking her skin with his thumb. "Why did you do it?" A sudden flash of arousal surged through him and he recoiled at the feeling, immediately rejecting it. He had been without a woman for several months, since long before her disappearance, and even though she had returned, nothing between them would change. He knew that.

Memories of the torment and sorrow she'd brought to Delacroix swept over him, and his feelings of tenderness struggled with a rush of bitterness. With unconscious effort, his fingers began to press down, feeling the faint resistance of her neck muscles beneath his tightening grasp.

"I just don't understand you at all, Justin," Marie grumbled as she entered the room, her arms draped with towels, liniment, and a bowl of steaming water.

Startled into realization of his actions, and more than a little horrified, Justin quickly drew his hand back and moved to stand before a window.

"She's my wife," he said softly, wishing the words were true. Sara Janei had never been his wife, at least not the wife he'd wanted, the wife he'd dreamed of.

Marie shook her head in disgust. "Wife? This woman ain't never acted like no decent wife, flirting and flaunting herself at everything that wears pants. Got in trouble again most likely, and comes dragging back here so we can take care of her. Oughtta throw her out, that's what!" She began stripping the wet and torn nightclothes from Janelle's limp body and tossed them on the floor, dabbing none too gently at the many cuts and scratches covering her arms and legs.

"Nevertheless, Marie, she is my wife." He stared out at the rain-washed night, wondering where she had been, and wishing in cold anger that she had never come back.

It was well after the dinner hour when the doctor finally arrived with apologies for not coming sooner. The child he had been delivering had seemed determined to make his grand entrance into the world feet first.

"I'll wait for you in the study," Justin said.

Dr. Theo Allard merely nodded, and hastened to follow a silent and frowning Marie up the stairs.

Less than thirty minutes later he entered the study to find Justin slouched in a huge wing chair before the fireplace. The crackling flames created the only light in the room.

"There doesn't seem to be anything seriously wrong with her, Justin, mainly cuts and bruises. She's had a pretty good shock too, I'd say, and she is completely exhausted. What in heaven's name happened?"

Justin studied the drink in his hand for several long moments, finally he answered. "I don't really know, Theo. She's been gone for over two months. I assumed she had run off with someone." He looked up and saw the startled expression of his close friend.

Though the same age as Justin, a balding pate, thin, wiry body, and small, square glasses perched on the end of his beaklike nose caused Theo Allard to look at least ten years older than his actual twenty-nine years.

Justin's lips twisted derisively. "You of all people know our marriage was a fraud. The only thing Sara Janei wanted was money and position, and marrying me gave her both."

Theo nodded. He had often wondered how his good friend had fallen under the spell of the stunning, but supposedly immoral Sara Janei Chevillon. It had not exactly been a match made in heaven.

"I loved her, Theo," Justin said, as if he'd read the man's thoughts.

Theo Allard merely nodded again, and moved to a wide cabinet set against the wall to pour himself a brandy.

Justin fell silent, his mind in the past. Though he and Sara Janei had been married only six months, and it still hurt to admit it, he had acknowledged to himself only hours after their wedding ceremony that it had been a mistake, a grave one. All his hopes and dreams for a peaceful and fulfilling family life had been quickly dashed by the reality of what his new wife really was. But he had stubbornly continued to try, striving to make their marriage work, though even that effort had lasted only a short time. By the time she'd run off, they had been barely civil to each other.

"What are you going to do now?" Theo asked, pulling Justin from his memories.

He shrugged, but didn't answer.

Theo downed the last of his drink, set the glass on a table next to his chair and rose. "Well, I'd best be going. Got two more babies back in town just waiting to be born. I'll be back in a few days to check up on Sara. He picked up his bag, moved toward the door, and hesitated. He had never seen Justin this bitter and depressed before. Slipping quietly out of the room, Theo softly cursed the woman who had so scarred his friend in such a brief span of time.

When Janelle awoke, the bedroom was in almost complete darkness. Heavy velvet curtains shuttered the sunlight; only a thin stream of yellow peeked through the slightly parted seams of the thick fabric.

Was it still morning?

She felt so tired, as if she hadn't slept for a week. Then she remembered the storm.

Her gaze traveled to the canopy overhead and she breathed a sigh of relief. This was her room at Delacroix. It had all been a nightmare, nothing more. Rising to a sitting position, Janelle felt pains shoot through what seemed like every aching muscle in her body. She stared at the cuts and scratches that covered her hands and arms, and when she threw back the covers, confirmed that her legs and feet were badly bruised and cut.

She had been lost in the garden. The terror and panic, the sudden storm and old graveyard—it had all been real. Janelle slipped clumsily from the bed, and her attention was caught by her reflection in the mirrored armoire. Someone had combed her hair into a single braid that now draped over one shoulder, and she was dressed in a long nightgown of white batiste, the neckline embroidered with tiny yellow and orange flowers.

It was not one of hers.

She turned to move away from the bed and caught sight of her own nightgown and robe lying draped over a chair next to the bed. Janelle picked up the sheer material, and looked at the dirt-smudged, ragged silk that had once been a beautiful gown. A small vial fell from the torn pocket of the robe to land softly on the thick carpet at her feet. She stared down at the antihistamine, and then let the gown fall.

Janelle moved slowly toward the adjoining bathroom. With shaky hands, she pushed the door open and gasped at the sight of the interior. She shook her head as if to clear it, and looked back again. The room remained the same.

"Oh, my God, what's going on?" Instead of the gleaming yellow porcelain bathtub, an ugly green tin tub sat in the corner, and where a marble sink should have been, there was a small walnut table with an ornately decorated bowl and pitcher set beneath an oval mirror. Candles stood in holders on each side of the mirror. The toilet was completely gone. In its place stood a hideous wooden chair with a boxed-in bottom.

Turning away, Janelle stumbled against the doorjamb, stopping to catch her breath as a jolt of fresh pain streaked through her bruised arm. She hadn't noticed any changes in the bedroom, but then, there had been no reason to look for any. She forced herself to picture it as it had been upon her arrival. Was that really only yesterday?

The canopy and bedspread were a heavy gold silk trimmed with lace and ruffles. Yesterday they had been pale yellow, and plain. And there was a canopy of mosquito netting pulled partially around the bed that she knew hadn't been there before. But the light in the room was too dim to see everything clearly. Moving to the table beside the bed, she reached beneath the glass shade to flip the lamp's switch to a brighter level, and quickly snatched her fingers back as they touched hot glass instead of the small brass switch. On closer inspection, the reason for the faint light became obvious. The lamp was aglow with a live flame rather than a light bulb, yet she was sure it was the same lamp. The amber shade, dangling thin crystals, ornate brass feet, all were exactly as she remembered; but last night she had read before falling asleep, and there *had* been a light bulb. Then she noticed the paperback novel she had laid beside the lamp was gone. In its place was a thin magazine, the name *Godey's Lady's Book* printed across its front page.

With trembling fingers she picked up the magazine and stared at its cover, a drawing of two women in monstrous hoopskirts standing beside a man who reminded Janelle of Sherlock Holmes. She recognized the name Godey's from her history class, but the magazine looked brand-new. The date, February, 1856, printed in the top corner, fairly jumped off the page at her. As if scorched by fire, her fingers lost their grasp of the magazine and it fell to the floor at her feet.

She went to the window and pushed the heavy curtains aside. The room was instantly immersed in light. Drawing a deep breath, she turned slowly to look at the bedroom again. On the wall near the entry door, where last night there had been a wall heater, there was now only a continuing pattern of rose-and-ribbon wallpaper.

"This is crazy," Janelle mumbled, determined not to panic.

The thought of just staying in her room until this whole madness went away had a cowardly appeal to it, but she had to dress and find Cathy. However, when she opened the doors of the armoire, her fingers froze on the door handles. Dozens of satin-covered hangers held beautiful, old-fashioned, floor-length gowns in every color and fabric imaginable. Taffeta, silk, satin, brocade, organdy, and muslin gowns crowded against one another, creating a rainbow of brightness, and to the far right side of the closet hung petticoats, pantalettes, camisoles, hoopskirts, and several torturous-looking corsets. With a gasp, Janelle hurriedly shut the armoire doors as though she could make the incredible contents disappear by the mere act.

Where were her clothes? What did all of this mean? The room? The old-fashioned gowns? The magazine? The cuts and bruises on her body?

Pressing a hand to her chest as if to slow the racing beat of her heart, she felt the thin links of a chain around her neck. Janelle's fingers closed around the small bejeweled locket hanging from the delicate strand of gold. She lifted it to the light, slipped a fingernail between its edges, and flipped the cover open.

The time flashed from the face of the small digital watch. "Well, at least one thing hasn't changed," she muttered softly, closing the locket and clutching it tightly in her palm as though it were a lifeline. It had been a present from her parents for her twenty-first birthday. Working with her father in his horse clinic, Janelle was constantly breaking her wristwatch, so her mother had taken the locket, an heirloom handed down through her own family, to a local jeweler and had the tiny watch installed inside its casing. The small teardrop-shaped ruby embedded in the gold cover of the locket caught the light, the circle of minute diamonds that surrounded the ruby picking up its red sparkle.

A thin robe, the same embroidered batiste as the gown she wore, lay draped across a nearby chair. It wasn't hers either, but at this point she didn't care. Janelle slipped quickly into the flowing wrap and left the room, but at the top of the staircase, she hesitated.

In the foyer below the elaborate crystal chandelier, though exactly as she remembered, now had thick candles wedged into each sconce instead of delicate flicker bulbs. The fanlight window above the entry door was ablaze with morning sun. When Janelle had toured the house yesterday with Cathy's brother, Paul, he had proudly pointed to a cracked pane in the fanlight. In 1862, he'd explained, Confederate troops had been quartered at Delacroix when the Union Army invaded New Orleans. A skirmish broke out, shots were fired, and one hit the fanlight window's wooden frame, cracking the glass. It had never been replaced.

The window was now perfect. There was no trace of a crack, and the foyer's black-and-white marble floor held no sign of the gouged scars where Paul said a drunken Union soldier had ridden his horse after the skirmish.

Nausea swept over Janelle, and the room began to fade into a blur. She grabbed the banister quickly, determined not to faint. Moving slowly, she began to descend the stairs, but had gone only two steps when she heard voices, raised in anger, directly below. Hastily she retraced her steps, flattening herself against a hallway wall.

There was no reason for panic, except for the conviction that she was not quite ready to face the owner of that deep, rich voice. Not until some sense could be made out of what was happening. She couldn't see the speakers, but their words were loud enough to be heard throughout the entire house.

"Justin, you gotta get rid of her, that's all. You know she ain't no good. You two was only married three months before she disappeared and she was flitting all over with other men the whole time. I don't want her here no more, no sir. She's evil. She just gonna—"

"Damn it, Marie, can you really think I do not know all that? But I cannot throw her out, and you know that, too."

"She ain't done nothing but bring trouble to this house, and she'll bring more now, you mark my words, Justin. More trouble, that's what her coming back means. More trouble!"

Peering around the corner Janelle saw that the woman had moved into her line of vision; she walked toward the entry door, and tossed a small black bundle out onto the porch.

"And that's another thing," the woman said over her shoulder, "that dumb dog of hers, he don't want nothing to do with her since she come back. He's been staying in the kitchen all the time, and he's always under my feet." She slammed the door, and turned back, giving Janelle a clear view of her.

She was a heavyset black woman, about fifty years old, with a body so big and round that her floor-length red skirt seemed to sway whenever she moved, making it appear as if she floated across the floor rather than walked. The fleshy face was smooth, and her cheeks glowed with a rosy tinge. Her hair was covered by a brightly colored *tignon,* and huge gold loop earrings dangled from each ear lobe.

From within the parlor came the low, drawling voice. "What do you mean, Cinder will not go near her? They've always been inseparable. That dog pined for days after she disappeared."

Something about that voice plucked at Janelle's heart-strings, and she wished perversely that he would show himself. At the same time, something within her shied away from seeing the face that went with the deep voice.

"Well, he ain't pining no more," the large woman retorted, still standing at the open door. "I tried to put him in her room this morning and he started growling and run out, right back down to my kitchen. Dumb dog finally showing some sense. Now you gotta do the same. You get rid of her, and this time make sure you do it right, and permanent." There was a note of finality about the last sentence.

"Marie, stop trying to nag me. It's not going to do any good. I do not know what is the matter with Cinder, he's probably just confused. But he will come around. As for Sara Janei, just be patient."

There were muffled footsteps, and then Janelle saw him appear beside the black woman, wrapping an arm around her shoulders and squeezing gently. He stood with his back to the staircase, but then the woman moved away from the circle of his arm, and turned to stare up at him. They stood in profile before the open door, the golden rays of the morning sun streaming in around them and suffusing the foyer in a pale yellow haze.

It was hard to judge from this angle, but Janelle suspected he was at least six feet tall or more, standing a good foot or so above the woman beside him. A white linen shirt stretched tightly across wide shoulders, rippling muscles easily visible beneath the thin material. Something about him stirred in her memory, a nagging familiarity that she couldn't quite place. Even at this distance she could discern an incredible strength about him, an ambience of masculinity and darkness like none she'd ever recognized before. It was frightening, and yet mesmerizing.

"I want Sara Janei out of here as much as you do, Marie, but we have to be careful. I will find a way, I promise."

"Humph! Don't you go trying to sweet talk me, Justin Delacroix. You was supposed to get rid of that woman long ago, and look, she's right back here. I ain't gonna stand for her uppity ways no more either, no sir. You find a way to get her out of here, or I'll fix her for good myself." Her words were set with hard determination. "Don't be letting her fool you again." She turned and walked from the foyer before he could respond.

Janelle waited until she saw the man called Justin leave by the front door before moving from her hiding place.

Janelle crept down the wide staircase, determined to find an answer to what was happening. She peeked first into the dining and music rooms and found them same as she remembered, but on entering the parlor, her throat knotted.

She moved across the room on shaking legs. A life-sized portrait of the man who had just been in the foyer hung above the fireplace. One part of Janelle's mind registered the insolent virility of the starkly attractive figure in the portrait, while the other desperately refused to acknowledge the surge of familiarity and desire welling up in her. How could a man she didn't know, and had never seen before, have such a profound effect on her?

The artist had purposely painted him in shadows, shades of gray and blue sharply etching the patrician yet hawkish features, and darkening the high cheekbones and long nose with its flaring nostrils. Sleek black hair crowned a head poised with the cool arrogance and ruthlessness of a Spanish conquistador.

There was something frighteningly male and cruel about this man, and yet the artist had captured something else, too. Shining within the depths of those steel gray eyes was a gentleness and an intense passion for life and love.

But it was the woman in the portrait who caused Janelle's heart to pound violently. Unlike her dark partner, the woman in the painting was vibrantly depicted in hues of blinding gold, red, and white. She wore a gown of shimmering white material, the plunging bodice embroidered with clustered rows of tiny red and gold leaves that dripped in a thin line to her waist and sprinkled the massive folds of the widely hooped skirt. The woman's dark auburn hair was pulled back and arranged in elaborate curls on the crown of her head, long ringlets shimmering with red highlights cascading over one bare ivory shoulder. Her green eyes flecked with gold seemed to dance with a haughty mischief as she smiled alluringly at her audience. Even with the swirling curls piled on top of her head, the woman barely reached the shoulder of the swarthy figure standing alongside who had a proprietary arm around her slender waist, a tangible stamp of intimacy and ownership.

Janelle felt as if she were looking into a mirror, her resemblance was so exact.

"Oh, dear Lord," she said softly. How could this be?

After a long moment of staring in disbelief, she tore her gaze from the portrait and looked at the small brass plaque affixed to the frame.

Justin and Sara Janei Delacroix, 1856

A tumult of emotions swept through her: fear, anger, panic, bewilderment. Was it possible she had gone a hundred and thirty-five years into the past?

Without warning, another thought struck her. They thought *she* was Sara Janei Delacroix!

She laid her head against the fireplace mantle and closed her eyes. Could this still be part of a nightmare? Or had her grief over her parents' death caused her to lose her mind? To hallucinate?

There had to be a logical explanation. Everyone knew there was no such thing as time travel. The past was dead . . . wasn't it? Opening her eyes, Janelle moved away from the mantle and looked again at her surroundings, and up at the painting. The dark face still towered above that of the woman who looked exactly like Janelle. This was no nightmare of sleep, but one come alive.

Suddenly the hair on the back of her neck felt as if it were standing on end. She whirled around.

Justin Delacroix stood in the doorway.

As their eyes met she shivered. Every harsh, unyielding line of him resonated with rage, and it was directed unerringly at her. The look of cold contempt in his eyes chilled her blood, yet at the same time she found herself searingly aware of an incredible aura of virility and force surrounding him. Perhaps too aware. Here was no portrait in oil. In no way had that glimpse of him earlier in the foyer, or the painting, prepared her for this man of flesh and blood, nor for her own reactions to him.

The veiled darkness captured by the artist on canvas surrounded the real man. Gray eyes, glacial with fury and scorn, held none of the gentleness or passion she had envisioned in the portrait. But something else had been added. Slashing across one side of the chiseled face, marring the aristocratic handsomeness, was a jagged white scar, its ugly presence giving him an air of malevolence. It began at the corner of his left eye, raked its way in a wide arc over one high cheekbone, sliced through the once perfectly formed lips and ended bluntly just above the curve of his square chin.

Janelle felt herself pale. Though she was aware that he had moved into the room, closing the distance between them, she could not tear her gaze away from his. Her shoulders pressed against the mantle, and she felt the cool touch of the white marble at her back through the thin nightgown. Slowly a feeling of compassion swept over her and Janelle had the insane urge to reach out and run her fingers lightly over the puckered flesh, to comfort him against the barbarity that had caused the wound. The world of reason and caution fell away, leaving her on the threshold of a new world, one dominated by this man, by the sheer awareness of him.

He stood directly before her, and Janelle sensed the coiled power in his tall frame. Thick, muscular shoulders and arms were evident beneath the crisp white linen shirt, the open collar accentuating a wide chest which tapered dramatically to a slim waist. Long legs were encased in snug-fitting black trousers, held taut by thin leather straps that ran beneath the sole of each highly polished boot. His hands clenched into tight fists as he stared down at her, and unconsciously she tried to back away again, but the fireplace at her back prevented any further retreat. His towering form, looming so close, was stifling, a raw and savage presence that shattered her feeble defenses. Yet his voice, a low purring drawl, was controlled, made much more frightening by his quiet scorn.

Mere inches separated them. Justin lifted a hand to her face, his fingers softly brushing over her cheek, a caressing touch she had not expected. For just a brief instant, warmth flashed into his eyes.

"Why, Janei?" he asked, his voice barely above a whisper.

Janelle stared up at him, her mind racing for understanding. Ja-nay? she thought. Who was Ja-nay? Then she remembered. Sara Janei, his wife. "No." She shook her head. "You've got to listen to me, I'm not . . ."

But his patience was short-lived, the flames of his fury too well fanned to allow him to listen to her denials.

"Where have you been for the past two months, Janei?" he demanded, his eyes, cold and hard again, narrowing as he glared down at her.

"But, I'm not who you th . . ."

"I do not know what kind of scheme you have in mind this time, but whatever it is, be warned, it will not work. Not this time. I will not be tricked again. It may have taken me longer than some, but I have finally awakened to what you are—a whore. A most refined one, I'm sure, but a whore just the same." His rage chilled the air as he continued, his face only inches from hers, etched with bitterness, even as his low, smoky voice lashed at her. "Why did you come back, Janei? Why couldn't you have remained dead?"

"But, if you'll just listen . . ."

His voice cut mercilessly across her words. "Get out, Janei. Get out of this house while you still can, or I will not be responsible for what happens to you, do you understand?"

Spinning on his heel he stalked from the room and crossed the foyer. The front door closed behind him with a brutal finality.

Chapter three

IT HAD HAPPENED, JUST AS SHE'D SAID IT would. Long ago, when he'd been just a boy, and she'd been a very old, but still regal, lady, she had told Tano the story for the first time, swearing him to secrecy. She repeated it to him every year thereafter, almost like a ritual, engraving it upon his memory. He kept his promise and never told anyone, but he had never been quite sure if he really believed her story. Now, finally, he would satisfy that last thread of doubt. Then he would see to the things she'd asked him to do.

The house was filled with the soft echo of steady tapping as raindrops slapped against the outer walls. Old cypress shutters, latched over the windows, rattled and strained against their hinges as the wind whipped and tore at them. Entering the breakfast room, Cathy cringed slightly as a wave of thunder rumbled across the sky, and reverberated loudly through the halls of Delacroix.

"Cathy, don't tell me you're still afraid of a little summer storm?" Leland Delacroix teased his daughter. He pulled her chair from the table and leaned over to lightly brush his lips across her cheek as she sat down.

Her brother Paul laughed. "She's probably just practicing her clinging vine act for when the guys start coming around."

"Well, big brother, you should know, aren't most of your girlfriends little wilting Southern flowers?" she said.

"All right, truce, truce." Saundra Delacroix smiled at her children as she seated herself.

Looking at her parents and brother, Cathy suddenly thought of how much she'd missed them while away at school. When she remembered Janelle's recent loss, she also realized how lucky she was to have them.

"Cathy, dear, where's your friend this morning?" Saundra asked. "We didn't get to talk to her much last night. Won't she be joining us for breakfast?"

"I thought she was already downstairs, Mom. I peeked into her room on my way down, but she wasn't there, so I figured she beat me to breakfast. Nancy," Cathy said, addressing an elderly maid who entered the room carrying a dish of steaming sausages, "have you seen Janelle this morning?"

"Yes, ma'am, I saw her a couple of hours ago in the garden."

"A couple of hours ago? What was she doing in the garden so early?" Cathy felt a ripple of alarm. After witnessing Janelle's unusual behavior yesterday, Cathy had been deeply concerned about her friend, but when she'd tried to talk to her just before retiring to bed, Janelle had brushed aside her worry, assuring her it was merely fatigue, or overexcitement.

"I don't rightly know, Miss Cathy," the maid answered. "I was just getting to the house this morning and passed her on the back terrace."

"You didn't see her come back in, Nancy?" Saundra asked, a faint hint of disquiet in her usually tranquil voice. The flash of anxiety in her daughter's eyes had not gone unnoticed.

"No, ma'am, but I was busy getting breakfast and all, and wasn't really paying no mind. You want I should check her room?"

"Why don't you check all the upstairs rooms, Nancy, and get a couple of the other maids to look through the rest of the house, too. Oh, and please check her bath, perhaps she dozed off in a hot tub."

As they waited for the maid's return, the wind howled through the trees and lashed at draping sheets of moss, sending the prickly tendrils into a dancing frenzy and slamming rain against the walls of the house. Wave after wave of thunder reverberated through the rooms, and frequent cracks of lightning flashed between the jalousies of the window shutters.

Some minutes later, Nancy reported having found no trace of Janelle in the house.

"Janelle's out in that storm somewhere." Cathy ran to the window.

Paul moved to his father's side. "She's right, Dad. Janelle's obviously outside, and by the sound of this storm, it's going to get a lot worse before it gets better. We need to find her." He glanced at his sister before continuing. "Crazy thing, a storm like this coming in June. Summer storms aren't usually so harsh."

Leland nodded. "You're right, son, we need to find her as quickly as possible. I hope she's found shelter from this onslaught somewhere on the grounds." He didn't want to think of the other possibilities. Delacroix Plantation was made up of a vast expanse, quite a bit of it still wild and untended. With the sudden darkness of a storm, and the pounding rain, there were a dozen or more ways a person could become seriously injured, especially if she didn't know her way around the property.

Leland turned to his wife. "Saundra, Paul and I are going outside for a look around. Why don't you and Cathy check the house again."

In the kitchen, they noticed Tano standing at the open back door, silently staring out into the storm's blackness.

"Tano, have you seen Cathy's friend this morning?" Leland asked as he grabbed two rain slickers from a small closet near the door. "It seems she went out early this morning and hasn't returned."

"Yes, sir, I was in the kitchen here when she left, but I ain't seen her come back," the old man answered. Preoccupied in gearing up for the foul weather outside, neither man noticed the odd look of satisfaction on the lined brown face.

Paul moved to stand at the door. "Could you get us a couple of flashlights? It's kind of dark out there."

Tano did as requested, muttering, "Ain't no use going out there, no sir. She's gone, just like she said."

Leland threw the old servant a quizzical glance, but not having clearly heard his words, paid him no further attention.

Tano returned to stand at the doorway after they'd left, and watched Leland and Paul disappear into the storm. The orb of light each carried grew dimmer as they moved farther from the house. Only when they were completely out of sight did Tano allow a smile to form on his lips.

A moment later, the old man drew a rain cape around his own shoulders and left the house. He did not carry a flashlight; he didn't need one. After ninety-two years, he knew every inch of Delacroix earth, and he knew where he was going. A decided advantage over Leland and Paul.

He moved as quickly through the gardens as his weak, old legs would allow. The storm had begun to quiet, rain turning to a fine mist, the wind barely a whisper through the trees. The sun slipped from behind a passing black cloud and soft rays of light filtered over the garden. Louisiana's hard clay ground had turned to a sticky mud, making each step heavier as the saturated earth clung to Tano's shoes. When he walked beneath a tree, a wet branch slapped at his face and strands of heavy, rain-sodden moss slid across his uncovered head. A shiver ran up his spine. The rain cape kept him dry, but not warm.

Reaching the old iron fence, Tano felt a sharp tug at his heart. His eyes filled with tears as his tired gaze swept over the neglected graveyard. An overgrowth of weeds and vines partially hid the marble monuments of death in the small enclosure as if attempting to shroud them in greenness and life.

After she'd died, he had never come back here. Now he knew it had all been true. It happened, just as his mistress had said it would.

Hours later, after a futile search by the two Delacroix men, Saundra summoned the sheriff. Within a short time, a half dozen policemen were scouring the plantation grounds, looking beneath every tree and bush. An hour later, several more arrived. They swarmed everywhere, yelling orders, asking questions, trampling over manicured gardens and poking into every room and corner of the house and outbuildings, and even going through the cars.

It seemed obvious that Janelle had not planned to leave. Her luggage and belongings were in her room, untouched, and how far could a woman go, the police reasoned, in her nightgown and robe?

Paul insisted on joining the sheriff's search party. It was nearing the end of morning, five hours since Janelle had left the kitchen to stroll the gardens, and so far they had turned up nothing to indicate her whereabouts.

He made his way along a path almost obscured by weeds and dried brush. The voices of the other searchers were becoming faint as he moved farther into an overgrowth of forgotten grounds. Paul came to a fence, and a sudden stirring of memory jogged him. He realized where he was at the same moment he saw Tano.

The old man kneeled against a pink marble tombstone, his arms draped around it as if hugging the cold stone to his breast. Stunned, Paul knelt down beside him, and wrapped his arms around the elderly servant's frail body. Tano sagged weakly in the younger man's arms, his breathing labored and feverish.

"Mr. Paul, it was true, it was all true," he whispered hoarsely, a serene smile creasing his face as he looked up at Paul. "She's gone now, back to where she belong. Just like she always said."

Something about the old man's contented manner and that beatific smile moved Paul. He tried to ease Tano into a more comfortable position. For a moment he heard strong, erratic heartbeats, and wondered dazedly whether they were his or Tano's.

He wrapped an arm around the old man's back, holding the other bony hand in his own after draping Tano's thin arm around his shoulder. "Who's gone?"

"Miss Sara, she went back like she told me she would."

"Tano, I don't know what you're talking about, but I've got to get you to the house before you catch your death out here. You're sopping wet! What on earth are you doing in the old cemetery anyway?" The two men rose together, and Paul was alarmed by how light the older man felt.

"Wait, wait, Mr. Paul. Her shoes," Tano croaked as they turned to leave. "Please, Miss Sara's shoes, she forgot them." He pointed to a mud-splattered pair of silk mule slippers that lay at the base of the tombstone, half-hidden by tall grass and weeds.

A sharp hiss escaped Paul's mouth at the sight. He scooped up the slippers, tucking them under his arm and urged the old man into motion. Fear gripped Paul as they stumbled along the path. He didn't know what had happened to Janelle, but whatever it was, he had a feeling that Tano's mumblings held the answer. Surely those were Janelle's slippers!

Chapter four

JANELLE FINALLY TURNED FROM THE EMPTY
doorway. There was no rationalizing away Justin Delacroix; he was no dream, no gray specter come to haunt
her from the depths of a nightmare. No, Justin Delacroix
was definitely very much alive . . . in 1856.

The confrontation had taken less than five minutes in
all, and yet, to Janelle, it had seemed to go on forever. At
first, his touch, so gentle and caring, and the intense look
of longing in his eyes had surprised her, moved her, so
that she had been unprepared for the sudden onslaught
of anger that erupted only seconds later. His words had
been cruel and cutting, and still echoed in her mind. The
bitterness he clearly felt toward the woman who was his
wife had now been transferred, its force directed solely
at Janelle, whom he believed to be Sara Janei. Though
glad to be relieved of his presence, she somehow felt
more alone than ever.

Her gaze returned to the portrait, but it was the face
of the woman, Sara Janei Delacroix, that Janelle's eyes
focused on. "Where are you?" she whispered softly. "Why
do I look so much like you?"

She noticed the tiny locket lying against the woman's
pale skin, just above the plunging décolleté of her gown.

A thin veil of perspiration covered Janelle's forehead. She looked again at the all-too-familiar locket. Embedded in the small gold oval was a teardrop ruby surrounded by ten tiny diamonds. With trembling fingers Janelle lifted her own locket from beneath the nightgown's neckline, staring in wonder from one to the other. They were identical.

How could she and Sara Janei both have the same necklace? Or was it the same one? What had happened to the woman in the portrait? It was obvious that her husband had been only too glad to be rid of her, but why? What had Sara Janei done to deserve such scorn from him? The reasons behind Justin Delacroix's hostility toward his wife were not as important now as the damning question that succeeded it, and sent Janelle's heart racing madly. What did he plan to do now that he believed Janelle was his wife, and thought she had returned?

What if the woman herself returned? Where would that leave Janelle, with her fantastic story of time travel?

Her mind felt as if it would explode. So many questions, and so few answers. She longed for Cathy, for the security of their friendship, for all the familiarity and support they'd shared. She shook off the poignant thought. It wasn't going to do her any good to wallow in self-pity.

Whatever had happened to Sara Janei, Janelle knew that while she was trapped in this nightmare, she must be extremely careful of everyone. If necessary, she would pretend to be Sara Janei, there was no other way. No one would believe the truth. Above all, she had to try to return to her own time.

That was the first order of the day, she decided, to get to the cemetery. That had to be the way back home.

Without further hesitation, Janelle slipped from the house and down the shallow steps that led to the garden. The sun was warm on her shoulders, but she didn't notice. She had one thing in mind now, and one thing only. The cemetery.

Janelle hurried through the rose garden. It looked nearly the same as she remembered. She quickened her pace, almost running through the tall maze of boxwood hedge and giant oaks.

Suddenly the thick growth of foliage gave way to an open field, and Janelle stopped. There had been no open field before, merely more shrubs and trees.

She heard whistling, then a soft, melodic humming. A few yards away, several blacks were bent over amidst the waist-high growth of tobacco, tilling the ground around each young plant.

Despair engulfed her and she turned to retrace her steps. She'd just have to try again later.

Back in the house, Janelle decided to orient herself to her surroundings. She started with the downstairs rooms.

The servants seemed more than willing to ignore her, hastening from each room upon her entry, their eyes downcast, hands fidgeting nervously with aprons or dust rags as they scurried away. She attempted to speak with one black maid who was polishing silverware in the dining room, but gave up in exasperation when the woman became paralyzed by fear.

Could she ever get used to the idea that these people were slaves? And what kind of person was this Sara Janei that she instilled such obvious terror in the servants, and violence in her husband?

Janelle entered what she remembered to be the kitchen, only to discover it had turned into nothing more than counters and brick ovens for keeping previously prepared food warm.

She spied a bowl of fruit on the table and gratefully grabbed an apple.

Weary and depressed, she retreated to her bedroom. Sara Janei's daintily decorated room did not seem to hold any evidence of her husband's belongings, much less his overwhelming personality. It took Janelle only a moment to discover why.

A door was set into the far wall of the room. Tentatively, unconsciously holding her breath, Janelle approached the door, grasped the knob, and turned. She saw a spacious chamber that had an unmistakable, powerfully masculine force stamped on the elegant furnishings. Stepping back quickly she slammed the door shut, cutting off sight of the darkish room.

Hours passed unnoticed as she sat before the window in her room, thinking. Until she found a way to get home, she would have to cope with the world she'd been thrown into, a world where even the simple things in life had changed.

As the day passed the house had grown uncomfortably warm and stuffy, but there was no such thing as air-conditioning, merely wooden fans hanging from the ceiling of each room that only moved when someone stood in the corner and continually pulled a rope attached to it. And clothes! She couldn't just slip into a pair of jeans and a T-shirt; they didn't exist. And what would she do about her hair? The faithful electric rollers she'd used every morning for as long as she could remember were now only a vision of things to come, along with cars, instant coffee, electricity, and indoor plumbing. Had the circumstances been different, she could have been amused by the lack of modern conveniences; as it was, it only depressed her more.

She turned to look out the window, finding the small field that had prevented her access to the cemetery. The workers were still there, but now another figure caught her attention. A tall man with black hair and strong, broad shoulders.

"Oh, if only I could get back to my own time before having to confront him again," she said softly. The thought of facing Justin Delacroix again caused her pulse to quicken, but this time, Janelle realized with shock, a thread of excitement mingled with the fear.

On the horizon the sun was slowly sinking from sight, its fading light projecting a pinkish glow over the treetops. There was a knock on her door and a young girl, no more than fourteen, entered. She grinned shyly as she waited to be acknowledged.

Janelle smiled, and the girl took a step forward. "I'm here to help you get ready for dinner now, Miss Sara."

"Oh . . . I can manage," Janelle answered after a moment of staring at the girl in confusion. It was going to prove hard answering to someone else's name, and being waited on hand and foot, but maybe she wouldn't be here long enough to get used to it.

"But Miss Sara, I always help you get dressed. Is you mad at me for something?" The child, who stood wringing her hands together, seemed ready to burst into tears.

"No, no. I'm sorry," Janelle stammered quickly. A feeling of guilt flooded her as she recognized fear in the girl's eyes. The young maid was very pretty, her skin the color of a dark night, but she was obviously also very self-conscious.

Janelle rose, ignoring the pain in her legs at the movement, and moved toward the ugly bathroom, closing the door behind her and leaning heavily against it. She didn't even know the girl's name, and she was obviously Sara Janei's personal servant. How was she ever going to do this? That same question had been repeating itself in her mind all day.

"Miss Sara, you need any help?" the young maid called out.

Janelle jumped away from the door. "Huh, no, I'm fine. I'll be out in a minute."

An elaborately painted bowl and a pitcher filled with water sat on a marble-topped table. Janelle poured the water into the deep bowl, slipped her hands into the cool liquid, and splashed it on her face. It helped, but only slightly.

Back in the bedroom she saw that the girl had opened the large armoire, and was busily laying petticoats and underthings across a chair. At Janelle's approach, the maid looked up and seemed to cower slightly.

"Miss Sara, I shoulda asked if you wanted your supper up here in your room, being you don't feel good and all. You want me to fetch you a tray?"

"No, thank you, I'm fine," Janelle answered, a bit puzzled at the girl's statement until realizing with a start that she had spent the entire day in nightgown and robe. With a spurt of horror she also realized she'd been out on the grounds in that same flimsy attire.

"Do you want me to pick a dress for you, Miss Sara?" the girl asked, a huge smile lighting her face at the thought.

"Yes, please, select something especially pretty," Janelle answered. She would need all the help she could get in her next confrontation with Justin Delacroix and was relieved not to have to venture a guess as to which dress would be appropriate for dinner.

The maid stretched her arm toward Janelle. "Here's your stockings, Miss Sara."

Janelle took the proffered stockings, staring at the thick, white fabric and trying not to look as if she didn't know what she was doing. How was she supposed to keep them up?

"And your garters," the girl added. She reached into a drawer of the armoire and pulled out a pair of ivory satin garters.

Janelle stifled the sigh of relief that welled within her throat and relaxed, but found deliverance only momentary. She was almost horrified when she looked back up after donning the stockings to see the servant holding a huge baggy pair of pantalettes. She bit her lip so as not to laugh. Without the drawstring at the waist, she could have fit two more people into the ruffled breeches. Next came a beribboned camisole, similar to some she had seen in stores in her own time, but the corset the maid wrapped around Janelle's ribs was definitely from the dark ages. The torturous garment's stiff ribbings cut into her flesh and the tight binding almost prohibited normal breathing. For a few seconds after the thing was securely in place, Janelle felt lightheaded and gasped for air, all the while afraid she was going to faint.

"This is archaic," Janelle muttered. She looked at the young girl and groaned. She was waiting patiently for Janelle to turn around, a huge hoopskirt held ready to add to the other trappings already engulfing Janelle's body.

Next came a ruffle-edged petticoat, and then, finally, the dress, a beautiful pale pink silk, the skirt made up of large flounces of draped material and lace, accentuated by a velvet sash of dark rose at the waist. The scooped neckline was quite a bit more revealing than Janelle felt comfortable with, but there was no helping that, she could only feel thankful that she and Sara Janei were the same size, although the dress was a little snug around the waist.

By the time she'd finished dressing, she felt as if she'd struggled into more layers of clothing than she ever dreamed a body could hold.

Sitting at the dressing table, she watched in the mirror while the maid took the long braid of auburn hair in her hands and began to brush the strands vigorously and pin them in large swirls atop her head. As the girl deftly worked at turning the dark mane into a massive chignon of curls, Janelle tried to figure out a way to discover her name without it appearing strange that she didn't already know it.

"What else do you do around here, I mean, besides helping me?" she finally asked, hoping to lead the maid into some kind of conversation about herself. She saw a helpless look of confusion crease the girl's brow. "Away from the main house, I mean," she added.

"I don't know what you mean, Miss Sara," the girl stammered, her dark gaze on Janelle's hair.

"Well, do you have a boyfriend? A beau? Someone special?"

"Yes. Miss Sara. If Michie Justin says . . ."

"Michie? Why do you call him that?" Janelle asked before she could stop herself.

The maid was clearly puzzled. "Michie Justin don't like to be called master. Never did. Long time ago he told all of us to call him michie. Said it means mister in that fancy language he uses sometimes."

"French?"

"Yes, ma'am. That's it. French." She pinned another curl into place.

"And so you do have a beau," Jannelle said, leading the conversation back to her original question.

"Oh, yes, ma'am. Big Toby. We're planning on getting hitched. That is, if it's all right with Michie Justin." A smile lit her face at the mention of Toby and their marriage plans.

"That's wonderful, but why would you think Justin might not approve?"

"Well, there's been some talk about Michie selling off some of the menfolk, and Toby, he's one of the best workers. Big and strong. He'd bring lotsa money, so he'd most likely be first to go. Can't get hitched if Toby's sold off." Every trace of the bright smile and happiness that Janelle had seen on the girl's face a moment ago was now replaced by anguish.

Janelle had forgotten about that aspect of this era. The old South she had read of in history books possessed many beautiful and gracious customs. Selling off slaves, many times separating families forever, was not one of them.

"Why would your people believe talk like that? Has Justin done it before, sold some of you?" she asked hesitantly, hoping that her question didn't sound entirely ignorant. She really knew nothing at all about Justin Delacroix. He was an enigma to her, a puzzle whose missing pieces she must find and put into place, if she remained here. The only thing Janelle could be sure of about him at the moment was that his real wife was missing, though no one was aware of that now besides herself, and Sara Janei.

"Oh, no, Miss Sara," the girl was answering. "Michie Justin been real good to us, never sold nobody that I remember, but talk is, things is changing. Some folks even thinks there's going to be fighting."

"But that won't be for about four years yet," Janelle blurted. She groaned silently. Damn, she'd done it again.

"How you know that, Miss Sara?" the girl drew away nervously.

"Oh, uh, just a guess. After all, no one wants to rush into a war," Janelle said inanely, wondering how convincing her words were.

"Miss Sara, you all right?" the girl asked, noticing Janelle's thoughtful frown.

"Um, yes," she muttered. "Let's talk about something more pleasant. When do you plan on getting married? And what does Toby call you? Any special names?"

"No, no special name, Miss Sara. He just calls me Callie, same as everybody else."

Finally, the girl's name. Now if she could just get a little more information out of her. "Callie, I get the feeling that Marie doesn't like me. Do you know why?"

"Oh, Mama's all right, Miss Sara." Callie's gaze dropped, then fixed itself upon Janelle's hair again. "She's just used to being a mama to Michie Justin, since his own mama and papa died of the fever. Mama still cries every now and then when she thinks of Miss Felicity dying. Her and Michie Justin were twins, but Mama says Miss Felicity was just too tiny a little thing to fight off that old yellow jack. Course, you probably know all that, and I was just a baby then, so I don't remember them none. Must be more'n ten years now, but Mama don't mean nothing against you, Miss Sara," Callie added. Again Janelle noticed a flicker of fear come into the girl's eyes. "Well, I's done with your hair. You best get yourself downstairs now, Michie Justin's waiting on you, most probably."

Standing, Janelle gave herself an appraising glance in a tall cheval mirror that stood in the corner of the room. There, staring back out at her, was the very vision of the woman in the portrait downstairs.

Determined to ignore the trembling the glance in the mirror had caused, Janelle hurriedly left the room and made her way down the wide hallway toward the stairs. She felt as if she had a giant lampshade propped about her waist, the hoop cage swaying about her legs with each step.

"I'd better not get too close to any of the furniture with this thing on," she mumbled, and then came around the corner of the hall to the landing and stopped, staring in horror at the stairs. "How do I get down those?"

With a handful of skirt in one hand, Janelle clung to the banister railing with the other and slowly, with extreme care, made her way down the stairs. She summoned all her courage and entered the dining room. Justin was already seated at the head of the long table. As he looked up, their eyes met for a brief moment, but his attention quickly returned to the glass of wine he had been about to lift to his lips.

At least she didn't have to guess where to sit. There was only one other place setting, at the opposite end of the table from where Justin sat. He was obviously intent on ignoring her.

She watched him from beneath slightly lowered lashes. Janelle had to admit, the man was terribly handsome in a dark, brooding way. But the jagged scar, cruelly outlined by the soft candlelight, gave a sinister air to his appearance and underscored the barely leashed anger in his glinting gray eyes. His broad shoulders strained within the confines of a gray dinner jacket and his ruffled white shirt was topped by a striped silk cravat, its gray and black fabric shimmering in the glow of the yellow flames. The set of his jaw as he stared at the deep red liquid in his glass was hard and unrelenting. Yet she had seen the flash of warmth, the trace of, was it longing? in his eyes earlier, when he'd confronted her in the parlor, and again, when he'd looked up just a moment ago at her entrance into the dining room. For some reason she did not understand herself, that brief glimpse into his soul pulled at her, more than his anger and scorn scared her away.

Two maids scurried in and out of the dining room with platters of food. Justin nodded his acceptance on each entrée as it was set before him on the table; he wasted no words or attention on Janelle.

Finally, when all the food had been served and the maids gone from the room, his cool gaze flickered over her. Suddenly Janelle was very aware of the pink gown's plunging neckline and the thin strand of pearls Callie had fastened around her neck, the opaque beads resting just above her bosom. The necklace watch had been put away, along with the small vial of antihistamine she'd discovered in the pocket of her torn and dirt-stained robe. After much thought, she had hidden them in a small space between the back of the armoire and the wall, beneath the rug's edge. She couldn't take the risk of anyone opening the tiny covers of the locket to reveal the digital watch inside. No explanation in the world could reason that away, or the plastic vial, for that matter. She looked away from Justin and then back again. His eyes were still on her, both seductively appraising, and coldly contemptuous.

Janelle flushed and quickly lowered her gaze. Looking at the food the maid had piled on her plate, she realized with surprise that she had no appetite. She wished her dress wasn't so lowcut and revealing. She wished she was anywhere, any time but here and now. But most of all, she wished she could think of something to say. For the moment, at least, she was stuck here, in this man's time, in his house, and forced by circumstances to pretend to be his wife. And where in heaven's name was his wife?

If she were to survive this ordeal, at least until she found a way to get back to her own time, she would have to do everything possible to discover the truth, and that meant trying to create a degree of communication with Justin Delacroix. Whether he wanted it or not.

But her attempts at conversation drew no response. Justin's manner seemed hardened and impenetrable. Finally, after bearing his silence for as long as she could, angry with herself as much as with him, Janelle rose to leave the room.

"Sit down, Janei," Justin ordered.

His steel gray gaze moved slowly over every inch of her face. Janelle clenched her hands together within the folds of her gown, afraid that he had guessed the truth, that he knew she wasn't Sara Janei. Though she'd tried to tell him earlier, now she knew that had been a mistake.

"I assumed you wished to be alone," she said, keeping her tone neutral.

"It is a little late for that, isn't it?" He leaned back in the chair, and shadows drew across his hawkish face. His voice, low and silky, sent shivers up her arms. "Tell me, Janei, where have you been all this time? In town with one of your dandies?"

Janelle stared at him, stunned, her mind racing for a response, any response! What could she tell him? "I was . . . I went . . ." she couldn't think!

His burning gaze held hers shackled, prisoner to his. Suddenly she was all too aware of him, of his raw masculine power and strength, in a way she had never been with anyone.

He shook his head. "Never mind, Janei, I'd rather not hear your lies. But you can tell me one thing, how do you find your handiwork on my face since it has healed? Amusing? Or repulsive?"

"My handiwork?" She didn't understand until his fingers moved to trace lightly the scar on his cheek. Then she knew, and the startling realization brought forth a tumult of emotion. Shock, and horror hit her like a physical blow.

Sara Janei was responsible for the ragged line that branded him forever. How could she have done that to him? And why? In no way did it detract from his virility or presence. If anything, it made him dangerously intriguing. Her senses stirred and without thought, or conscious effort, Janelle moved to sit in the chair beside him, placing a hand on his arm, her green eyes stricken yet sincere. She had to keep up the pretense, at least for a while, but in this instance, at least, it was not hard. "Justin, I am sorry. You must believe that." She licked suddenly dried lips. His closeness and the mere touch seared and charged her, the muscles of his arm like sleek bands of iron beneath her fingertips. "Can we try to behave amicably with one another? At least that?"

Her apology came as a shock to him, and her question as a surprise, but whatever degree of composure he lost, he regained just as rapidly. Taking her hand in his, Justin gently stroked the top of her fingers with his thumb. There was something different about her, but he couldn't quite discern what it was, and that irrationally made him angrier than her words. God, how he wanted to believe her, but he had tried too many times in the past to trust her, and she had always betrayed him. Damn her lies! Damn her beautiful face!

And she was beautiful, more so it seemed than any other time he had beheld her. The light touch of her hand on his arm had been gentle, those slender fingers so soft and warm within his. He noticed the way the candlelight caused the red highlights of her hair to sparkle, and how the flickering flames gave her skin a golden glow, so different from the sickly white pallor she had fanatically protected before. He looked into her eyes and became almost hypnotized by the golden flecks that seemed to dance there. Justin felt an involuntary tightening in his loins that pushed further at his already taut control. He hadn't desired her since a few weeks after their wedding ceremony, so why now? What was it about her that had him wishing things could be different between them? That it could be the way it had been before they'd married, that it could be the way he'd dreamed it would always be.

Cursing his weakness, Justin's voice was edged in steel when he responded. "Just what is it you really want, Janei? You did not come back here because you want to be friends, and we both know you do not love me, so what is it? Money? Delacroix Plantation? What?" He felt a twinge of remorse as those emerald eyes, only a moment ago filled with compassion, became shuttered at his cold words.

Raising her chin proudly, Janelle forced herself to maintain the pretense. "I told you, Justin, I just want to forget the past. Can't we at least try?" She wanted desperately to pull her hand away, but didn't dare. Her fingers were swallowed in his larger hand, a hand that could easily break hers, yet she felt certain could also be infinitely gentle.

"Do you think you can just say you are sorry, and we will start all over as if nothing ever happened? As if you have never been little more than a whore throughout our brief attempt at marriage?" he asked icily.

She flinched then, and tried to pull her hand away. His grip tightened, almost crushing Janelle's fingers as his cold eyes mocked her futile effort to escape him. Then casually, insolently, he released her.

"Justin, I'm not after anything, I swear. I just want us to talk, to be civil to each other. Can't we do that?" She knew she sounded nothing like Sara Janei; it was obvious by the look on his face, and her heart skipped a beat in fearful anticipation.

He tried to conceal his surprise. He'd expected Sara Janei to fly into her usual theatrics. Instead, she stared at him in defiance and fear. Her words hung between them. The voice was the same, soft and somewhat throaty, though the short clipped way of talking sounded so alien coming from her lips. But Justin noticed something else too, something he couldn't quite comprehend. Could it be pain? Had the sting of his words at last penetrated that heartless persona Sara Janei had affected after their marriage?

A small spark of hope gleamed to life within the dark, walled-off confines of his heart, but he quickly banked it down. He refused to allow it to grow, fearful of the consequences if he trusted her yet another time. Forcing himself to remember the past, to remember her treachery, there was suddenly the taste of bile in his throat. He had to get away from her, now. He was too wretchedly aware of her, of her shimmering eyes staring beseechingly into his, of her lush body so tantalizing and golden in the soft pink silk gown. Rising, he walked to the window. "I've waited a long time to hear you say you were sorry, Janei, but I am afraid it is too late."

She moved to stand before him; compassion edged her voice. "It's never too late to be friends, Justin."

As their eyes met he found himself flooded with desire, a need to take her so intense it swept all caution and past hurt from his heart. Passion surged through him, swift and consuming, slacking the rein on his tightly controlled self-restraint. His sudden movement gave Janelle no warning. Justin's mouth came down on hers, warm and possessive. His arms slid around her waist, crushing her against his hard length, almost forcing the breath from her lungs.

Shock ran through Janelle and she made a sound of protest deep within her throat, reaching up to push at his arms, but Justin's embrace only tightened, his hand warm upon the bare flesh of her back. Suddenly a surge of heat leapt to life in the pit of Janelle's stomach, exploding in great force and sending searing trails of flame to every fiber of her body. His tongue caressed the soft corners of her lips, and then forced them apart, darting into the dark, sweet cavern of her mouth.

His mouth came down over hers, arousing, inciting, devouring, and possessing. He brought her to the very precipice of passion, and she began to tremble in fierce hunger.

A moan of pleasure she was helpless to prevent sprang from Janelle's lips. Justin covered her throat with kisses, his warm lips moving slowly, causing a shiver of reaction that sent tingling ripples across her overheated skin. She shuddered, adrift in mindless pleasure, all thought of danger and resistance forgotten. Their bodies were molded together, and she could feel the aroused hardness of him pressing against her stomach as his lips blazed a provocative path to the soft curve of breasts revealed by the low décolletage of the pink gown. Her head fell back in delight; her hands clutched his broad shoulders.

It was a nameless need that was both torment and joy, and it centered on his lips upon her breast. She was lost in a maelstrom of passion as he pressed kisses over the exposed swells, his tongue touching her sensitized flesh.

Justin drew her against him tightly, the heat and strength of his thighs searing through the voluminous folds of the silk gown. Flushed with overwhelming need, she brushed her hands through his jet black hair, then more boldly, more needful, stroked the tight cords of his nape, the width of his back. His scent, his power, his body enfolded her and she gasped when he took her lips again in a savage, intoxicating kiss, his tongue twining and dueling with hers. Sweet, molten pleasure surged again and again within her.

She arched her body closer to his, hips swaying against him, the ache of desire growing unbearable. Janelle no longer thought to escape his lovemaking. She was struggling with the passions he had awakened in her, and with the undeniable longing to be possessed by him.

Suddenly Justin pushed her away, the movement so abrupt and savage Janelle stumbled and almost fell to the floor.

Turning away, he once again fought the flow of desire that throbbed within him, silently calling himself every kind of fool for nearly falling so willingly, and easily, into her trap. His hands clenched into fists at his side as he willed his body into a cool control and turned to glare at Janelle.

Her mind still swimming in a world of dreamy sensuality, of newly awakened emotions, Janelle stared back at him in bewilderment, unable to comprehend his suddenly violent action.

"Well, whatever it is you want this time, Janei, you evidently want it very badly, enough even to tolerate—no, better than that, to respond to, my kisses. You are a very good actress when you need to be."

Despite his biting sarcasm, Justin was very much aware that the joke had been on him. With unerring concentration he fought to regain control of the passion that burned at his soul, his very senses still aflame with the feel of her in his arms, the sweet taste of her on his lips. Even now he felt a tightening at the sight of her bruised mouth and desire-darkened eyes. She had tasted of wine and honey, and the faint scent of her jasmine cologne still clung to him. Her response had been a stimulant like none he had ever known, not even when he'd fallen in love with her beguiling facade. He found himself lost in his desire, the need to lose himself within her almost overwhelming. How could she have penetrated his control so easily, when he had thought all his feelings for her had died? Yet with just one touch she had sent his barriers crumbling, and ignited a need in him stronger than any he had ever felt. Filled with self-contempt, Justin withdrew with chilled indifference, a veil of disdain clouding the steely gray eyes.

Janelle was so stunned she could hardly find her voice. Justin Delacroix had aroused her, both physically and emotionally, to a height of passion she had never known before. She had wanted him, desired nothing more than to be taken by him, but, once sure he could have her, Justin had brutally discarded her as if proving to himself she was the whore he accused her of being. Yet even now, in the face of his derision, she could not shake off his touch, or the feel of his lips on hers. Already he had left his mark on her, a mark that could not be erased.

"How could you?" she said, the constriction of her throat muscles causing the words to be no more than a broken whisper.

"I wanted to see exactly how far you would go to get whatever it is you want this time, Janei, but I think maybe I have not really found out yet," he answered, his words followed by a low, scornful laugh. But even as he spoke, his heart was twisting into a knot of regret, his loneliness growing.

Tears sparkled on her lashes. Humiliation dulled her green eyes as she turned away from him abruptly.

"Janei, wait," he commanded, and she paused without turning. "I will not allow myself to play the fool over you again. You may stay at Delacroix only so long as you cause me no trouble or embarrassment. Is that understood?"

She winced at the distaste evident in his words as he continued.

"I will not throw you out, Janei. After all, I did love you, once."

Chapter five

THE HOUSE WAS SILENT AT LAST. SLIPPING INTO the hallway and holding the batiste robe tightly wrapped around her, Janelle hurried down the hallway toward the stairs.

She made it through the rose garden, past the maze of hedges, and across the field of young tobacco plants, all the while holding her breath, afraid her absence from the house had been discovered. Then she saw it, the small cemetery. Not overgrown with weeds and vines, neglected, as she'd seen it the first time, but landscaped and cared for as it had been after the storm, after whatever force pulled her back to this time had left her here. The gate opened easily on silent, well-oiled hinges, and Janelle stepped through, her gaze scanning the dark landscape for the pink tombstone. But as she'd feared, it wasn't there.

Panic began to tremble to life within her. What was she to do now? Would it work without the tombstone? She had to try. Rushing across the dew-covered ground, Janelle located the spot where she thought the stone should have been.

She prayed, she begged the heavens, pleading with the forces that had brought her here to help her, but nothing happened. The night remained still, the faint sounds of the small animals and birds that lived in the nearby foliage continued peacefully, undisturbed.

The next morning the click of a door being shut and the soft rustling of skirts brought Janelle out of a deep slumber. She tensed, wondering who would dare enter her dorm room, and then with a flood of despair remembered where she was, and her late-night sojourn to the cemetery.

Suddenly Callie pulled open the heavy drapes and a bright stream of sunlight filled the room. "Good morning, Miss Sara," she called merrily, bustling about pouring warm water into a washbowl and laying out fresh towels. "I fetched some water so you can wash, and I'll pick out a pretty dress for you to wear. It's going to be a real hot day, so I'm gonna lay out one of those fluffy kind of dresses you like."

Thoroughly awake now, Janelle sat up and yawned. "Callie, is Justin already downstairs?"

"Oh, he's already gone, Miss Sara."

"Gone? Gone where?"

"Why, he's riding the fields like always, Miss Sara."

"Hurry then and help me get ready. I need to talk to him." She began to munch hastily on one of the apple muffins Callie had brought with the coffee tray, while at the same time wrestling to get into the cumbersome pantalettes.

Callie exchanged the yellow poplin gown she'd laid out for a lightweight tan riding habit trimmed with a rich brown velvet, then turned back to help Janelle secure the corset she was struggling to fasten about her ribcage. Callie pulled on the strings.

"Ouch!" Janelle said. "I feel like a trussed-up Thanksgiving turkey." The stays of the corset bit into her flesh and forced Janelle's back to remain ramrod straight, while the long skirt and petticoat severely hampered her ability to move with any speed without falling flat on her face.

"Why would any sensible woman wear one of these things?" she mumbled to herself.

Callie's head jerked up in surprise. "Why, it ain't proper not to wear a corset, Miss Sara."

To Janelle's relief, she discovered that the awkward hoopskirt was not necessary with a riding habit. At least she didn't have to worry about getting onto the horse with that thing bouncing around her legs. She considered not wearing the corset, and the thought proved too inviting to ignore. While Callie rummaged through the armoire in search of Sara Janei's riding boots, Janelle hurried into the dressing room. She tore off the jacket and blouse of the habit and yanked at the strings of the corset. In seconds she had the horrid thing off and hidden behind the commode and had dressed again. The blouse was a little snug, but at least she could breathe. She re-entered the bedroom just as Callie emerged from the armoire.

Sitting on the settee, Janelle clenched her teeth together when Callie pushed one of Sara Janei's ankle-top, high-button riding shoes onto her foot. The shoes were too short, and too narrow, but she had no choice, unless she wanted to go barefoot, and she knew that would really raise some eyebrows.

"Boy, what I wouldn't give for a pair of jeans, a T-shirt, and my tennies," she grumbled.

"What're you talking about, Miss Sara? What's them things?"

"Clothes, Callie, sensible, comfortable clothes. Oh, but how can I explain?" Janelle threw up her hands in frustration. She might as well do something about the situation, she decided. Who knew how long she'd be stuck here. "Callie, can you get me a pair of Justin's pants, and an old shirt? Oh, and some thread and a needle?"

The girl nodded.

"Good. This afternoon we'll make an outfit I can breathe in."

Entering the stable some minutes later, Janelle was glad to see that Justin had not left yet. He was just preparing to mount the most beautiful black stallion she had ever seen. The huge beast pawed the earth and shook his head, whipping long silken strands of mane through the air as Justin tightened the cinch around the animal's belly. The horse started at her approach and reared on his hind legs, snorting his displeasure. A young black groom yanked on the reins in an attempt to control him.

"Damn it, Janei, don't sneak up on Tobar that way! You know how edgy he can be," Justin said sharply. "You could have gotten Sammy trampled."

Sammy kept his eyes averted, the look on his face clearly indicating he would rather be anywhere else than here during his master's and mistress's argument.

"I'm sorry, Justin. I just thought perhaps we could ride together this morning." Janelle had to bite her lip to keep from screaming at him. The man was infuriating. She had not *sneaked* up on his precious horse; she had merely walked into the stable. Could she help it if the animal spooked so easily? Even as she raged silently at his unfair reproof, she could not control the leap of her heart as she watched him.

Justin was dressed in tight-fitting riding trousers, the snug pants clearly defining every muscle and line of his long, sinewy thighs. A crisp white linen shirt, open at the neck, emphasized the broad shoulders and bronze skin, contrasting strikingly with the short black strands of hair that curled raggedly below his throat. A lightweight brown jacket was thrown casually over Tobar's saddle.

He stared at her, a measuring look in his eyes. Suspicion laced his answer. "Why, Janei? You never enjoyed riding with me before. Why now? Besides," he continued before she could respond, "Duchess is gone. Since you did not see fit to bring her back with you, what will you ride?"

"I'm sure you can choose a suitable mount for me. It seems there are plenty available," she answered, assuming Duchess had been Sara Janei's horse. "It's been quite awhile since I've ridden, Justin, and I'd really enjoy it. Besides, it's such a beautiful morning."

"I do not have time for a leisurely ride today, Janei," he snapped, moving to mount the large stallion. Wariness of her was something he found a necessity, yet he could not quite help the small thread of hope that stubbornly lingered in his heart, refusing to be vanquished. But memory of the past, of what she'd done, always helped. It brought back the anger, and made dealing with her easier.

"Leisurely or not, I would like to go," Janelle insisted, her tone causing him to look back, bridled anger glinting from the slate gray eyes.

"Sammy, saddle Lady," Justin ordered curtly. "And tell Marie neither Janei or I will be here for the midday meal. We will be riding over to the Foucheaus."

"Oh, I thought we were just going to ride around the fields," Janelle said quickly, fear overtaking her at the thought of meeting someone else who knew the real Sara Janei. She'd never be able to pull that off. What would she say?

"I told you I had things to do. Gilbert has just gotten back from Baton Rouge, and I want to see what news he brought. Anyway, you always enjoy going to Melody's, it gives you an opportunity to needle away at her." His eyes were mocking and full of contempt.

She was trapped. Without arousing suspicion there was no way to get out of accompanying him now, especially since she'd made such a point of wanting to go riding. It had been a crazy idea in the first place, riding off into the countryside with him alone. He could be dangerous. Hadn't he proven his dislike of her already? Even if it wasn't really her, but Sara Janei he disliked, Justin had shown he could be brutal and cold. Certainly not the type of man she envisioned falling in love with. Love? Where had that thought come from? No, she couldn't think like that, it was insane. But Janelle couldn't help remembering the feel of his lips upon hers, his arms crushing their bodies together, and an unaccustomed tightness began to swell in her breast. She turned away from him as her breath quickened.

"I'll wait for you outside, Janei." He led Tobar toward the open door.

"Oh, no!" she said. Sammy was placing a sidesaddle on the back of a small chestnut mare. She realized belatedly that women rode sidesaddle now, and Sara Janei had probably been an expert. Janelle felt a moment of panic: she would be lucky if she even knew how to mount the horrid thing, let alone stay on it once the horse began to move.

"Justin, I want to try riding with a saddle like yours, if you don't mind," she said hesitantly.

"Like mine? You want to ride astride like a man?" Disbelief flashed across his lean face.

"Well, I just thought I'd like to try it. You don't realize how really uncomfortable those contraptions are." She pointed to the sidesaddle. "Would you mind terribly?"

He ordered Sammy to mount one of his other saddles on Lady. Though he did not want to admit it, Justin felt something stir in him at her apparent happiness at the simple change of saddle. It was considered highly scandalous for a woman to ride astride, but then he knew Sara Janei had never worried about what other people thought of her behavior. He wondered wryly why she had never complained before.

They did not set out for the Foucheaus immediately, but rode about the grounds of Delacroix for over an hour first. The overseer, a stout, weathered man with a surly face, joined them immediately on their appearance in the fields. She'd heard Justin refer to the man earlier as Stephan O'Roarke. He sidled his horse up next to Justin's. His movement forced Janelle to ride behind them on the narrow trail, and when the man turned to nod a silent greeting in her direction, she was shocked to see a leering grin on his unshaven face. The two men dismounted frequently, checking and discussing the crops, fingering the soil, and conversing with several of the workers. The overseer stayed with them until they approached the edge of the cultivated land. Janelle hadn't minded, though. She'd found herself enjoying the scenes of living history spread out before her. Only it wasn't history now, she reminded herself, it was real, and she was a part of it.

The rows of cotton plants in bloom and ready for harvest seemed endless, their white tufts giving the horizon the illusion of being covered with snow, while the hot July sun blazed overhead. Here and there a group of field slaves worked over the plants, deftly plucking the tufts from the prickly vines and filling the sacks they carried slung over their backs.

The overseer's presence had rendered any conversation between Janelle and Justin impossible, but when he rode away, Justin reined in the stallion and turned to face her. "Are you not afraid of getting too much sun, Janei? Where is your parasol?" He had been waiting for her to complain of the sun and heat, and perhaps demand they return to the house.

She smiled, thankful that Justin was in the habit of calling his wife by her middle name. It was much closer to her own, and easier to respond to. "I love the sun, Justin," she said, tossing her head to rid her shoulders of the wave of auburn curls. She realized too late those words would never have crossed Sara Janei's lips. Hadn't she read somewhere that women used to avoid the sun, keeping their skin as white as the cotton they'd just ridden past?

Her remark surprised him, but he chose to ignore it. "Fine. I just hope you and Melody can at least be civil to one another this time." He watched her carefully while waiting for a reply.

Janelle nodded, wondering what problem was between Melody whoever-she-was and Sara Janei.

After a few initial attempts at conversation and getting only cryptic answers in return, Janelle gave up and rode the remainder of the way to the Foucheau plantation in silence.

But she couldn't ignore Justin's presence and found her attention constantly drawn to him as he rode ahead of her at an easy gait. He hadn't worn a hat, and his sable hair gleamed in the bright light; several wayward strands at the base of his neck curled over the edge of the white collar. The late morning sun seemed to gild him in amber rays as if caressing a cherished lover, and the burnished look it gave him caused her breath to catch in her throat. It would be so easy to become involved with him, she thought. Already he had affected her in ways no other man ever had. But she had to resist, to remind herself to be wary of him.

The Foucheau house came into view. Although not as grand or imposing as Delacroix, it was beautiful in its own right. Thin, square pillars and airy galleries graced the two-storied front, and a rainbow of flowering shrubs hugged the base of the structure in a ruffle of dazzling pink, red and white.

They were shown into the parlor, a small room done in blue and white, while a servant went in search of Gilbert and Melody Foucheau. Janelle moved about the room restlessly, finally deciding to stand near a window in the corner, out of the immediate sight of anyone entering. There she would be better able to judge their reaction to her presence, and to act accordingly.

Gilbert Foucheau sauntered easily into the room, alone, and Janelle's first reaction to him was one of distaste. As she hung back watching him greet Justin she perceived an air of pompousness about him. Gilbert was a thin man, several inches shorter than Justin. He wore a dark brown cutaway coat adorned with huge gold buttons and a yellow silk cravat at his throat. The bright color only accentuated the sallowness of his olive skin. Brown hair prematurely gray at the temples fluffed in tight curls about a face whose too-sharp features and dark brown eyes gave him the look of a ferret.

"Good morning, Justin, sorry I kept you waiting. So many things to do, you know, when one travels as much as I do. Of course, I enjoy it, do not misunderstand. I thoroughly relish being a representative of our parish. Always have been rather outspoken, haven't I?"

The two men shook hands. Then Gilbert noticed Janelle. "Sara? But I thought . . ." He moved beside her quickly and took her hand. His lips brushed across the top of her fingers. "It is so good to see you again, my dear. Caleb did not announce your presence. I had no idea you were here."

"Good morning, Gilbert," she said softly, uncomfortable when his lips lingered a few seconds too long on her hand. She felt an onrush of total dislike the moment their gaze met. She couldn't explain it, other than that she found him too slick, too urbane, and too familiar.

"Gilbert." Justin diverted their host's attention from Janelle. "I rode over this morning mainly to inquire if you had brought any news back from Baton Rouge?"

Gilbert gestured for them to be seated, and then joined them. "Yes, yes, but damnation, Justin, it is not at all good. Senator Sumner has been left almost crippled from that attack on him by our good Congressman Brooks from South Carolina, the dolt! It has positively ruined any chance our delegates had of obtaining an audience with the president," Gilbert Foucheau said angrily, his easy-going countenance darkening.

"I was afraid of that when I heard of the attack. There seems to be a lot of support for our hot-headed Congressman Brooks, but I fear overall it will prove to be a disaster for the Southern states. Anything else?" In contrast to Gilbert's volatile reaction, Justin was calm, and Janelle guessed he was already thinking of the future consequences. She remained quiet, wondering why Gilbert wasn't more curious about where Sara Janei had been for the past two months. Or was it that he already knew?

"The only good thing I heard was that horrid scoundrel John Brown is dead," Gilbert said. "After he attacked all those folks up in Kansas, some place called Pottawatomie Creek or some confounded Indian name like that, they sent a posse after him. Cornered him in a canyon and had it out. He managed to get away, but word is he left a lot of blood behind. They don't figure he could have gotten far, though. At least we won't be hearing from him again."

"But John Brown was hanged after the assault at Harper's Ferry," Janelle blurted out, then stared in horror at a stunned Justin. There was no calling the statement back; it echoed in the air. Gilbert frowned as though he felt women had no place in a discussion of politics, but Justin was regarding her intently, speculatively. Stuttering an excuse, Janelle turned and hurried out through the open French doors. How could she have been so stupid? She would have to watch her words more carefully.

She paced the wide gallery for a while before the two men joined her. During that time Janelle had managed to calm down and begin wondering why Melody Foucheau had not yet appeared.

"Gilbert insists we have lemonade and cakes with them before riding back to Delacroix," Justin said as he came to stand beside her. He cupped her elbow with his hand and gently, but firmly, directed her back inside.

The three were already seated when Melody entered the room. When she saw Janelle, her face took on a sickly pallor. She clutched at the door handle, and took a deep breath. A smile was frozen on her lips. "Sara, how nice of you to call, but I thought you were ... traveling."

"I decided to come home," Janelle answered, not knowing what else to say. Was that the excuse Justin had given to their friends?

She tried to be casual in her assessment of the other woman. There was no question of Melody Foucheau's exquisite porcelain beauty. Pale blond hair was swept into a large chignon at her nape, and her skin was almost as white as the crisp lace that trimmed the bodice of her gown. Beneath a short, turned-up nose were perfectly formed heart-shaped lips. They curved upward now, but the smile did not reach Melody's eyes, which were the blue of a New England sky in January, and just as frigid. Beautiful and cold, Janelle thought.

Melody smiled almost pityingly at Justin, then, having regained her composure, walked gracefully into the parlor, her gown of Venetian blue silk swirling around her petite figure. She took a seat opposite Janelle on a twin settee, and Janelle found herself tensing at the woman's oddly fierce, and blatant, scrutiny.

Did Melody suspect she was not Sara Janei? How close were the two women? From what Justin had said earlier, Janelle suspected they weren't the best of friends. In fact, he had implied the opposite, but that did not mean they didn't know each other well.

"Have you seen Antoine since your return, Sara?" Melody asked, too sweetly.

"Uh, no, I haven't," she stammered. This was exactly what she had been afraid of. She didn't know who in the world Antoine was, but out of the corner of her eye she saw Gilbert stiffen.

"Sara, don't tell me you've been neglecting one of your dearest friends? Why, the man hasn't been himself since you left so abruptly. He's missed you terribly," Melody cooed.

"We all did, Sara." At this remark from Gilbert, Melody's lips tightened, and something not unlike pain flickered in her blue eyes before she averted her gaze.

Before Janelle could respond, Justin interceded. "Antoine enjoys a rather sordid reputation, Melody, as you well know. He is not a friend of either Sara Janei's or mine, only an annoying acquaintance."

Melody moved closer to Gilbert, placing a proprietorial hand on his thigh. "Well, perhaps he had better be informed of that, Justin. You may not be aware of it, but Antoine has been quite free in expressing his warm feelings for Sara Janei all over the Vieux Carré for some time now," she said in seeming sincerity.

"Melody, for God's sake," Gilbert interrupted hotly, "Antoine is one of the best *maîtres d'armes* in New Orleans. Are you trying to get Justin killed?" He laughed forcefully as though to dismiss Melody's words, but Janelle felt the undercurrents in the room like live wires.

"Of course not, darling," Melody smiled. "I only thought Justin should know what is being said. After all, it is *his* wife everyone is talking about."

"Thank you for your concern, Melody, but I rarely, if ever, pay attention to common gossip," Justin drawled, his cool, dispassionate voice an instant source of security for Janelle.

His defense offered her a degree of comfort. She turned toward him, and for just a second, the hard line of his lips softened, and as her gaze met his, the icy brilliance of his eyes warmed.

Melody stood and walked around the sofa, coming to stand behind her husband. She placed her hands upon his shoulders, caressing them lightly, but her gaze never wavered from Janelle. "You are quite right, Justin, of course, but don't forget, sometimes rumors have their origin in fact." She smiled, her eyes challenging and full of spite.

Chapter six

CALLIE BUSIED HERSELF AT THE ARMOIRE, RE-hanging the green gingham dress she had removed earlier, and returning the petticoats and hoop cage to their hooks. But, try as she might, she couldn't control her nervousness and kept throwing fearful glances over her shoulder at Janelle, who refused to wear the clothes Callie had laid out.

"Actually, Callie, this came out a lot better than I expected," Janelle said. She tied a black sash around her waist. She was trying her best to sound happy, but the mood was forced. She had been unable to get back to the cemetery during the daylight hours, and so had tried again during the night. Again nothing had happened.

She turned to look in the mirror. Everything had required extensive altering, and Justin's trousers had needed shortening. The shirt cuffs had been done away with completely, the material cut high above the elbow and folded over several times. To satisfy propriety Janelle cut off the legs of a pair of pantalettes so that she could wear them under the altered pants. Callie's eyes had opened even wider at that maneuver but she said nothing when her mistress proclaimed them "panties."

"Miss Sara, you sure you want to go out like that? I mean, it just ain't proper for a lady."

Janelle steeled herself not to smile. "I'll be fine, Callie. I'm used to dressing like this." Oh, blast, why had she said that? She hurried to cover up. "Anyway, all those petticoats are just too heavy in this heat."

"But Miss Sara, you ain't even got on no proper underthings," Callie wailed. Fear overrode the good sense that normally kept her opinions from being put into words. Sara Janei had been acting strangely ever since her return, but most of the time it was a welcome change. She was so much more pleasant, actually treating Callie as if she liked her, but this outfit could ruin everything. It was Justin's reaction that Callie feared.

Janelle laughed softly, unable to help herself. "Callie, stop being such an old worrywart. I've got a camisole under my shirt and panties under the trousers. That's surely enough to consider me decent, even if I don't have on a dress. If not, well, tough tiddles!"

Settling down in front of the dressing table, Janelle secured her thick hair in a ponytail, using a white satin ribbon which she tied into a large, droopy bow. A few shorter strands of hair hung loose to curl sassily here and there. Satisfied with the result, she stood, bid Callie good morning, and left the room.

At the entrance to the dining room, Janelle summoned her courage, forced a smile to her lips, and entered. The room was empty. Several serving bowls sat on the sideboard, but only one place setting remained on the table—hers. Suddenly the door to the kitchen swung open and a tiny black dog tripped into the room. It looked like nothing more than a mass of moving hair, the curly tresses on its head gathered into a tuft and secured with a blue ribbon, allowing view of a pointy little snout and big brown eyes. The dog stopped dead in its tracks at spotting Janelle. Crouching low to the floor, eyes narrowed, it yapped twice and then took another step toward her, a low growl filling the little throat.

"Cinder, what's the matter with you? Dumb dog," Marie grumbled, waddling into the room. She looked from the growling dog to Janelle. A cold glint of suspicion flickered in her eyes.

"Oh, uh, I guess I've been away too long, he doesn't seem to recognize me," Janelle offered weakly. A flash of memory brought back the conversation she'd overheard between Justin and Marie concerning Sara Janei's dog, and the black bundle that had been tossed out onto the gallery that day. The dog certainly wasn't doing her any favors. Somehow she'd have to find a way to make friends with the little monster, and soon.

"What's that you got on?" Marie demanded, staring at Janelle's makeshift trousers.

"Oh, I altered a pair of Justin's pants and a shirt to fit me," she answered, forcing a light laugh.

"Ain't proper."

Janelle fought to keep the smile on her face. "I know it's not really proper, Marie, but all those petticoats are just too heavy to wear in this heat. Anyway, I wanted to go riding with Justin and this outfit is much more suitable for that than all those billowing skirts."

"Humph! Ain't proper," Marie repeated. She turned to leave the room.

"Marie, wait, please. Has Justin already gone out?"

Janelle hadn't seen him since their return from the Foucheaus the previous day. He'd mumbled something about the fields and hadn't returned to the house until late evening, after she'd finally gone to bed. He also hadn't mentioned anything about her blunder concerning John Brown, but she'd seen the questions, the confusion in his eyes whenever he'd looked at her since.

The housekeeper turned back, a smug smile on her face. "Yes, ma'am. Lotsa work to do round here. Don't expect him back much before dinnertime." She disappeared through the swinging door.

Janelle didn't remember Cinder's presence until she took a step toward the sideboard and the dog snarled, his eyes following her every movement. She placed an extra piece of bacon on her plate. If she had to bribe the little monster into making friends with her, that's what she would do. But half an hour later Janelle gave up. She had crumbled the bacon into small pieces and placed them on a napkin on the floor, but Cinder wouldn't come near it. All he would do was watch, growl, occasionally bark, and act as if he thought she was trying to poison him. She made several attempts to win him over, but all she received for her trouble was a tiny mouthful of sharp teeth snapping at her fingers. Cursing softly, she rose to leave, totally frustrated by what she considered a five-pound, ill-tempered, miserable little beast.

"Fine, then forget it!" she muttered to the dog.

In the foyer, she tried to decide what, if anything, could be done with her day that would be constructive since Justin was already gone. The house seemed unnaturally quiet. She wandered through the downstairs rooms, but saw no one. She was especially surprised to find the warming kitchen also empty, but as she skirted the wide plank table that sat in the center of the room, and approached the back door, she heard laughter and singing coming from outside.

Stepping onto the back gallery she decided the sounds were coming from a small brick cottage set several dozen feet from the right rear wing of the house. The doors and windows of the cottage were opened wide and wisps of dark smoke curled skyward from the chimney. Next to the front door, several black women stood in a circle, their bodies bent over huge metal cauldrons of steaming water as they stirred the contents with wooden paddles. The women kept up a constant stream of animated chatter, arms waving in the air, fingers pointing, heads thrown back in laughter. A small black child knelt next to one of the women, poking a stick at the flames beneath the huge pots and occasionally adding another log to the fire.

The women noticed Janelle descend the steps of the gallery and move toward the cottage, and their talking abruptly ceased. Without so much as a glance in her direction, they offered murmured acknowledgment of her greeting. Even the child shied away, scooting across the ground to hide behind the wide folds of his mother's skirt.

Inside the cottage, Marie, Callie, and a half dozen other women were busily preparing food for the main house. Except for Callie, who smiled shyly when she saw Janelle enter, the response inside was the same as she'd received from the women outside. Conversation ceased, eyes were lowered, and only solemn mumbles were given in answer to her now forced cheerful greeting.

Only Marie spoke directly to Janelle. The big woman looked up from the wide table upon which she had been kneading a massive lump of dough, her eyes cold and unforgiving. Placing the dough in a large bowl, her movements insolently slow, Marie wiped her flour-covered hands on the wide muslin apron that draped around her immense frame like a tent. "You want something, Miss Sara? Looking for Callie, maybe?" Her tone was polite, but the coolness that laced it was clearly definable.

The other women had stopped work at Marie's acknowledgment of Janelle's presence. They watched in silence, their bodies tense, as if witnessing two combatants facing off.

"No, Marie, thank you. I was just curious to know where everyone was. The house seemed so empty."

"Well, now you know." The housekeeper sniffed. "We got lotsa food to be fixin', so if there ain't nothing you want, we'll get back to work."

"Yes, you do that. I didn't mean to interrupt you," Janelle said softly, hastily retreating from the strained atmosphere. She returned to the main house, quickly confirmed that she was, indeed, alone, except for a maid in the dining room who was washing the tall windows.

Hurrying upstairs, she entered her bedroom and went directly to the door that connected her room with Justin's. She knocked and nervously waited for a response. When none came, Janelle entered. There she found the stamp of Justin Delacroix almost overwhelming. The furniture was massive and thick, the wood a dark, highly polished walnut. Folds of burgundy and muted gold brocade hung from the corners of a large tester bed, the fabric matching that of the heavy drapes which had been pulled away from the windows and secured to the wainscoting by gold hooks. The wooden floors were bare except for several floral area rugs, the sunlight filtering through sheer lace window panels giving the oak planks a rich glow. Near the hall entry door was a large, rather austere Jacobean desk.

Gooseflesh covered Janelle's skin as she forced herself to sit at the desk. She didn't really know what she was looking for, anything that could give her some insight into Justin's feelings, into the man himself. If nothing else, she had to find out if he had anything to do with Sara Janei's disappearance.

The drawers of his desk were unlocked. The first and second drawers held only writing supplies, account sheets, and old receipts. The third held several thin ledgers. Briefly skimming through them she found they were dated and itemized listings of all the household expenditures at Delacroix for the past two years. She noticed that the outpouring of money had practically tripled after Justin's marriage. There were numerous entries to dressmakers, milliners, shoemakers, perfumeries, and jewelers.

That made her stop and think. If Sara Janei was so fond of material possessions, would she have willingly left without the beautiful gowns still in her armoire, and the jewelry in the case sitting on the dressing table?

In the fourth drawer Janelle discovered more than she had dared hope to find—a leather journal with Justin's initials embossed on the cover. With trembling fingers she laid the journal open on the desktop and hastily flipped the pages to the last entry. Justin's words practically jumped off the page and Janelle's heart began to pound rapidly as she read.

Something is very, very wrong. Janei is so different. There is something strange about her, yet I cannot seem to discern exactly what it is that bothers me. She seems unsure of herself, even vulnerable at times, so unlike the Sara Janei I married. Her mannerisms are different too, even her voice has changed. She has a clipped accent now, rather than the languid drawl I had come to dread listening to as she complained. There is only one explanation, yet I know that is impossible.

Her hands shook so badly it took several attempts to accomplish the simple task of turning back a few pages. She stopped at an entry dated April 15, 1856.

I could have killed her this morning. She was out all night again, and I know she was with one of them. I just do not know which one. But does it really matter? There are so many. I told her I would not put up with her vulgar habits any longer, but she laughed. Does Sara Janei think I will merely stand by and meekly accept whatever she does? She seems to feed off the attentions of these other men. How could I have been such a blind fool? I should have listened to her brother, Bernard, when he tried to warn me of what she was really like. Sara Janei has made a laughingstock of me and scandalized my name. I must find a way to be rid of her . . . permanently.

The book dropped from Janelle's hands. She couldn't read any more. The realization of just how desperately she'd wanted to find something that would prove him innocent suddenly swept over her.

Why did she feel so let down? So disappointed? How could she feel this way over a man who had shown her nothing but disdain, who rejected every attempt she made at friendship, whose sheer contempt for the wife he believed her to be shone in his eyes every time he looked at her?

Then Janelle remembered his kiss, and the way it felt to be in his arms. Justin Delacroix had sparked a response in her that could not be ignored, and yet she knew now she must deny it, for her own salvation. She shoved the journal back into the drawer and rushed from the room, craving fresh air, open skies, and a little time to think and plan.

She encountered Marie near the back door. "I . . . I'm going for a walk," Janelle mumbled, not slowing her pace.

The black woman's stare held nothing but distrust as she watched Janelle pass, but she remained silent. Cinder, hugging the hem of Marie's skirt, growled softly, made a threatening lunge toward Janelle as she hurried by, and then scrambled back behind the voluminous folds of material.

In the barn, Janelle looked around for Sammy, but the groom was nowhere to be seen. Grabbing a bridle from the storage room, she walked directly to Lady's stall. Janelle had grown up on a ranch and owned a horse all her life; there wasn't anything anyone could tell her about the animals that she didn't already know. Once she had even entertained the notion of following in her father's footsteps and becoming a veterinarian, but in spite of her love for animals, her heart just wasn't in it. Long before she had entered college, she realized her true goal in life—to fall in love, marry, raise a house full of children and a stable full of prize-winning horses.

Absorbed in memories of her dead parents, of college, of Cathy, she rode aimlessly, looking at scenery but not really seeing it. She came upon the acres of cotton she and Justin had ridden through the day before on their way to the Foucheaus.

The overseer saw Janelle's approach and was about to yell out a warning of trespassing when he recognized her. Stephan O'Roarke's mouth gaped at the sight of her in men's clothing. With her hair tied back and one of Justin's wide-brimmed black hats shading her face, the mistress of Delacroix had been mistaken for a man. O'Roarke urged his horse in her direction and then just as quickly reined back. She looked preoccupied, and he knew all too well what her temper tantrums could be like. He wanted no part of that.

Short, dirty fingers snatched the well-chewed stub of cigar from the corner of his mouth and a wide grin split his unshaven face. She'd come to him again when she was ready. He tipped his hat in Janelle's direction when she passed by.

The field hands stole furtive glances, their curiosity piqued by her outlandish choice of attire.

Leaving the wide expanse of cotton field, Janelle crossed a dirt clearing and entered a field of sugar cane. The blue-green stalks were well over eight feet in height, but not yet ready for harvest. The path between the tall stalks was narrow, and several times Janelle found the sun completely blocked from sight by the thick leaves. Emerging from the cane field, she crossed an open meadow and guided Lady through a copse of pecan trees, their thin, spearlike leaves hanging in thick clusters. She came upon a creek meandering crookedly between several small knolls. The banks were dotted with lushly blooming wildflowers and a lone live oak, the moss draped from one of its gnarled branches tickling the surface of the slowly moving water.

She tied Lady's reins to a nearby bush, leaving enough slack so that she could graze, and sat down at the creek's edge. She pulled her legs up, arms crossed on knees to act as a pillow for her chin, and stared up at the sky. An occasional haze of cloud broke the wide expanse of blue and the bright sun, blazing mercilessly, was almost directly overhead. The scene was peaceful, almost hypnotic in its tranquillity. She remembered riding like this on her parents' ranch. Everything had been so simple then.

Closing her eyes, Janelle pictured Glen Torrance riding beside her, his big paint gelding occasionally nuzzling the neck of her smaller Appaloosa mare. Janelle and her father had ridden together every morning until she left home to live at school. Sometimes her mother had joined them, but usually she stayed behind, always having breakfast waiting upon their return.

But nothing was simple now. Her whole life had been turned inside out and upside down, and she didn't know what to do about it, or if anything could be done. All she could do was muddle through each day, and be on her guard.

Janelle was so lost in her thoughts, she did not hear the soft rustle of long grass being pushed aside by approaching riding boots. A second later, she started when she saw another face floating beside the blurry reflection of her own image in the water.

Gilbert Foucheau stood behind her.

"Gilbert, you startled me! I didn't hear you."

"Sorry, *chérie,* but I was not sure it was even you. What is this nonsense you are wearing?"

"I . . . I just wanted something more comfortable to ride in. All those skirts are so cumbersome." She tried to make her voice sound casual. "What are you doing here?"

"You must have known I would come to you, *mon amie,"* he said, his voice deep and husky as he lowered himself to sit beside her.

Janelle leaned away, every muscle in her body tensing. A moment ago she had been relieved to see him, now she found herself apprehensive of his closeness, of the intimacy of his words. She looked into his eyes, recognized the raw lust, and made a hasty move to get to her feet.

His reaction was swift. Long, slender hands gripped her shoulders, forcing her to face him, his thin fingers biting into her flesh. "What is it, Sara? You seem not so happy to see me."

Janelle sensed that her only hope was to stall him. "I didn't really expect you today, Gilbert, that's all. Now, I really must go. There are things I must see to." She tried to turn away but his hands did not release her. She stiffened in panic.

"Do not toy with me, Sara. It is not necessary." His mouth came down on hers, warm and possessive as his weight forced her back to the ground.

Shock held Janelle immobile, leaving her momentarily vulnerable. His hand pulled at her shirt and slipped beneath the crisp linen; only the thin camisole was between his grasping, hot fingers and her bare flesh. A shudder of revulsion coursed through her as his fingers moved to cup her breast and his hardness pushed against her thigh. She twisted beneath his weight, dragging her lips away. Still pinioned to the ground within his embrace Janelle hid her head against Gilbert's shoulder so he would not see the disgust mirrored in her eyes. Sara Janei had obviously welcomed his embraces, but that was one part of this impersonation Janelle knew she could not carry out. She groped to find the right words, those he would believe.

"Gilbert, please, not here. Someone might come by," she whispered, moving a hand slowly across his shoulder. "Please, Gilbert, I need time. There are things you do not know, things I must do before we can be together again."

"What things, Sara?" he drawled. Gilbert shifted slightly, which released her from his weight, but not his grasp. "You of all people should know I do not like to wait."

"Trust me, Gilbert, it will not be long." Janelle forced herself to brush her lips across his.

"All right, I will wait for you to get a message to me, through Nessa, as always." He stood, staring down at her for a long moment before turning to walk back to where his horse stood tethered near Lady. "Do not take too long, *chère*. I am an impatient man, as you know."

Janelle hadn't realized she'd been holding her breath until Gilbert walked away. For long moments after he left she remained beside the creek, knees drawn up tightly, her face hidden within folded arms as she fought to control the revulsion his touch had roused. When she finally looked up, her attention was drawn to a small knoll several hundred feet beyond the opposite edge of the creek. A large gray horse stood poised upon the knoll's crest, his heavily muscled body motionless, the rider mounted on his back watching Janelle.

The sun was behind them, silhouetting horse and rider against the brightness, making recognition impossible. Janelle turned quickly to see Gilbert far off in the distance behind her, riding toward his home. She shivered. So, they had been watched, and whoever it was did not seem concerned that Janelle knew it.

She turned her attention back to the figure on the hillside and saw the big horse being urged into movement. A cape flared around the rider, and the sun caught and glistened off the red satin lining. With a growing sense of unease Janelle got to her feet, watching the rider disappear into the distance. Who was it? Who had watched them? What if Justin were to be told of the incident with Gilbert today? He would believe it to be another clandestine meeting of Sara's with one of her lovers. This one with his best friend! Then again, she thought despairingly, it could have been Justin watching them.

The ride back to the house seemed endless. Justin's huge stallion was grazing in the corral so Janelle realized with a start that he'd already returned.

Peering around the open doorway from the foyer she saw him seated behind a large walnut desk, a sheaf of papers spread out in front of him. Backing away, she turned toward the stairs and ran headlong into Marie, who stood glaring at her, hands on hips.

In a movement swift for a woman so big, Marie sidestepped Janelle and quietly closed the library door. "You missed the midday meal. You want I should send a tray up to your room?" Her words were deliberate, almost surly.

"Uh, not just now, Marie, thank you," Janelle answered, uncomfortable under the woman's hostile glare.

In her bedroom, Janelle was ready to do nothing more than relax when an idea popped into her head. She hurried to the small writing desk that sat near the window. If Justin kept a journal, why wouldn't his wife?

The small cubbyhole drawers held odds and ends; inks, quills, wax, and a sealing stamp with SJ carved on it. There were only two good-sized drawers, and the first held nothing but writing paper. The second seemed a hodgepodge of plain junk. Janelle was just about to close it in frustration when she noticed the length of the drawer. It was shorter than the other, and by quite a bit. Poking at the back board she realized it was a fake, a thin piece of wood wedged into the drawer to look like the end piece. Wrapping her fingers over the top she pushed on it with the heel of her hand and it fell forward.

"Now we're getting somewhere," she said in excitement.

Behind the fake end piece Janelle discovered a small stack of daguerreotypes and tintypes tied together with a yellow ribbon. Excited at her find, she pulled the ribbon loose and spread the pictures atop the desk. There were ten in all. Two were of women, the rest were men. Janelle picked one up. It was a tintype of a man about thirty years old. He had a pleasant-looking face, and somehow, it seemed oddly familiar, which she knew was insane. Turning it over she read the name written on the back; Bernard. She put it aside and looked at the next, another man, but much younger, maybe twenty-one or two, and devilishly handsome. The name on the back of the picture said Robert Etienne, and beneath the name was printed *1854*. She quickly examined the other pictures. Half an hour later, having found nothing more in the desk, Janelle returned the daguerreotypes and tintypes to the drawer, disappointed not to have found Sara Janei's diary. She'd look for it again, later.

She lay down on the high tester bed, her head sinking into the down-filled pillow, her body luxuriating in the softness of the mattress. Tension crept out of her limbs in slow degrees. A picture of Gilbert Foucheau flashed into her mind and she stiffened. However was she going to handle that situation? She could, of course, tell Justin the truth, in a direct, commonsense fashion.

She suspected strongly, however, that Justin would believe it was another of his wife's tricks. From what little Janelle had discovered about Sara Janei, she had no question in her mind that the woman had been devious and self-centered. What other unpleasantries was she destined to find out while masquerading as the missing woman?

Forcing the worrisome thoughts from her mind, she ordered herself to relax. The knotted ribbon at the nape of her neck pressed uncomfortably into the hollow at the base of her skull. She untied the ribbon, shook her long hair free, and leaned across the bed to place the thin strand of silk on a nearby table. As her weight shifted on the mattress, Janelle heard a low growl coming from under the bed.

Cinder! No sooner had the thought registered than the tiny black dog darted from beneath the bed ruffle. He scurried around the room, yipping loudly, and stopped every few seconds to crouch in her direction, as if preparing to attack.

He had to be put out of the room. Wearily Janelle pushed the covers aside and swung her legs from the bed. Just as her feet touched the soft carpet, Cinder lunged toward her unprotected toes.

Chapter seven

"WHAT'S KEEPING THAT DOCTOR?" PAUL GRUM-
bled, his eyes anxious with worry.

It had been two hours since he'd found Tano and carried him back to the house, and the old man's condition
seemed to be worsening with each passing minute. No
matter how many blankets they piled on his thin frame,
Tano remained cold to the touch, yet beads of perspiration dotted his forehead. His breathing was shallow
and ragged, and a wheezing sound had developed in
his chest in the last half hour.

Paul couldn't conceive of Delacroix without Tano.
The old man had been a fixture at the plantation for
so many years, having already been considered ancient
when Paul was born. Tano had watched four generations of Delacroix grow up; it seemed unthinkable that
his presence could vanish from the scene.

"Here he is," Leland announced, turning from the window. The door opened and Dr. Kyle Donovan entered.
He moved directly toward Tano and kneeled down
beside the sofa. He flung the covers from the old
man's fragile body and loosened the front of his
shirt.

"How did he get like this, Leland?" Donovan asked.

"He was caught in a flash storm," Paul said. "By the time I found him he was drenched. I had to carry him back to the house. He passed out on me."

"It's a wonder he didn't die on you." Donovan pulled a stethoscope from the bag he'd set on the floor. "I don't know if his body can take this kind of abuse. It already looks like he's developing a pretty good case of pneumonia."

Paul bristled at Kyle's words. "Well, we didn't send him out there, you know."

"Pipe down, Paul, I didn't say you did." He brushed a lock of blond hair from his forehead and placed the stethoscope on Tano's chest.

The examination was brief. When he finally stood and turned toward the family, the doctor's expression gave them all further cause for alarm. "He should be in the hospital."

"No," Saundra said. "He wouldn't want that. If he woke up in a hospital, he'd be terrified. Please, Kyle, we'll care for him here. Just tell us what we need to do."

Kyle sighed in exasperation. Many of the older residents of the parish felt that way, viewing hospitals not as a place of healing, but as a place of death. "Watch him closely, Saundra, very closely. I'm going to give him a shot of penicillin and write a couple of prescriptions. Get them filled right away. I'll also get an oxygen tent out here. Other than that, we'll just have to wait it out, and pray."

"What are the odds?" Leland looked down at Tano's still form, remembering all the times during his childhood that the faithful old man had been there for him.

"I wish I could say it was good, Leland, but I don't know. He's old and he's tired. If Tano has the will to live, he might pull through. If not, nothing short of a miracle can save him."

A feeling of helplessness invaded the household. By the fourth day of Janelle's disappearance, Tano's condition seemed to stabilize. It didn't get any better, and it didn't get any worse.

Cathy's nerves were strung taut. First Janelle, now Tano. She stayed by the windows, as if she expected Janelle to walk in at any moment.

The sheriff came by frequently, but he had nothing concrete to report. He'd wired the police in Reno and Carson City, Nevada, and they were on the watch for Janelle, but so far they'd come up empty-handed, too.

The Carson City police had driven out to Janelle's parents' ranch, but the new owners hadn't heard from Janelle since they'd signed the final settlement papers; the rancher who'd bought her horses hadn't heard anything from her either. The university was closed for the summer, but the office clerk promised to alert the authorities if Janelle called or came by the dorm.

Despair settled over Delacroix, and everyone agreed it was as if Janelle Torrance had dropped off the face of the earth.

Kyle Donovan returned on the fifth day and gave Tano a complete examination.

"How is he, Kyle?" Leland asked. Kyle seemed more puzzled, and that worried Leland. He'd thought Tano was getting better, but from the look on the doctor's face, Leland wasn't so sure anymore.

"I don't know. I just don't know. He's got me stumped. His breathing's normal, the wheezing in his chest has cleared, his pulse rate is good, and his heartbeat is steady and strong. All his vital signs are normal." He turned and replaced a vial in his bag, then looked back at Leland. "Hell, his signs are so normal he should be up doing a jig right now, not lying there comatose. I'm going to run some tests on this blood sample, but if I don't get an answer, I'll have to insist he be brought to the hospital." He shook his head. "Right now I'd say there's absolutely no reason why Tano isn't awake. He's obviously just not ready."

"But how can that be? I mean, have you ever seen this kind of thing before?"

"Not myself, but I've heard about cases like this. Theoretically a coma can be self-induced. We don't know why, or how. Anyway, my guess is that he'll come around when he's good and ready, and not before."

"Is there anything we can do?" Paul asked, having walked into the room during the middle of Donovan's conversation.

"Wait," Kyle said, and shrugged. "That's all anyone can do now."

"That seems to be the standard answer for everything these days." Paul led the other two men across the foyer to the parlor.

"Any word on the girl yet?" Kyle asked. He accepted the drink Paul offered and sat down.

"No, nothing," Leland said. "It's as if she walked out the back door and disappeared into thin air. There's not a clue. Cathy's a mess. She practically lives in her room. Can't sleep, doesn't eat worth a damn. When she does go outside, all she does is walk the gardens and visit that damn grave where Paul found Tano."

"I'll look in on her before I go."

"Have you seen the papers, Kyle?" Paul interjected. He handed several newspapers to the doctor.

"Murder in the Bayou?" Kyle said, appalled at the papers' headlines. "Voodoo Curse, True or False? Has Passion Led to Murder in the Swamps of Delacroix? Where the hell do they come up with this stuff?"

"In their dreams probably, who knows?" Paul said angrily. "The stories themselves are okay, it's the damn headlines that are so outlandish and aggravating."

"Do they have any reason to be calling it murder?" Kyle asked.

"No, but it obviously makes a better story."

"Well, hopefully we'll hear something soon. I'd like to go up and see Cathy now. Maybe I can give her something to help her get some sleep."

Kyle spent the next hour talking with Cathy in her room. He felt strongly that she was not only in shock, but punishing herself both emotionally and physically for having invited Janelle to New Orleans in the first place. And he was right.

"This isn't your fault, Cathy," Kyle insisted, his voice quiet and soothing. "You couldn't have known this would happen when you invited her here."

"But if I hadn't invited her, it wouldn't have happened. Don't you see?"

"You don't know that. Maybe it would have, somewhere else."

"If I just knew what happened," she said softly, wiping at her eyes. "Is she dead, alive, hurt somewhere, kidnapped, what?"

"Cathy, stop assuming all the blame for whatever's happened. You've got to pull yourself together. Look at you!" He sounded angry. He was angry.

She started at the tone of his voice, surprised.

"Cathy, your family needs you. I need—" He stopped himself, knowing this was the wrong time.

But she'd caught his words, recognized the look in his eyes and warmed to it.

Even in her distraught state, Cathy was a beautiful woman, and Kyle Donovan was not immune to that fact. Several years ahead of her and Paul in school, he had watched her grow up, a pretty and popular teenager. Kyle had never approached her, never asked for a date. His parents weren't rich; they were just ordinary working people, and he'd always felt

Cathy was out of his league, but maybe that wasn't so anymore.

He vowed then that when things were better, Cathy Delacroix would be in his arms, but not because she was in need of consolation.

"I'm going to prescribe some tranquilizers to help you relax, Cathy," he said, his voice full of betraying emotion. "And I want you to start eating. Have I got your word on that?"

She nodded, a slight smile curving her lips for the first time in days.

Returning downstairs, Kyle saw that the sheriff had arrived, but the news he was relaying to Paul was anything but favorable.

"We heard back from the police in Reno," the sheriff said. "Seems Janelle Torrance broke up with her fiancé a few months back, called off their wedding. Rumor is that the young man took it pretty bad. Made some threats, harassed her some till she called the police on him. Something real curious though," the sheriff added, placing his hat back on his head. "Seems her ex-fiancé is now living in New Orleans. We've already been to his place, but he's away. Neighbor says he went on a fishing trip, but doesn't know where."

Chapter eight

JANELLE CAME INSTANTLY AWAKE, SENSES alert, eyes wide.

Sudden knowledge that she was not alone washed over her. She remained still. The bedroom was dark, but for a thin beam of moonlight streaming in through a breach in the closed draperies. She took a deep breath, summoned up what little courage she could find, and turned toward the end of the bed.

Watery brown eyes met hers and she smiled in relief. The mop of black hair bounded happily across the bed, his miniature paws almost disappearing into the folds of the thick coverlet. A blue silk ribbon on the little dog's head, meant to hold the hair away from his face, had loosened, allowing the tuft to hang askew over one ear. Cinder now looked to be sporting a lopsided ponytail. His tiny pink tongue darted out and kissed her.

"Cinder, you scared me half to death, you little imp!" She picked up the five-pound bundle of hair and energy and hugged him. Janelle had spent a long time on the bedroom floor the previous evening coaxing, cajoling, teasing, and begging the pint-sized terror into being her friend. She had given up half her dinner to the poodle, along with a glass of milk and a shoe for chewing. With each offering, coupled with endless flattery, Cinder's guard against her had softened. Finally, nearing midnight, they had come to terms. Now she had at least one friend in the big house.

As dawn crept over the horizon, Callie entered the room.

"Miss Sara, let me help you with them things." Callie rushed to Janelle's side who was awkwardly trying to arrange the cumbersome petticoats beneath the skirt of a blue silk dress. "Why didn't you call for me? And what you doing up so early, anyways?"

"I wanted to make sure I caught Justin this morning before he leaves," Janelle explained, holding her arms out while Callie straightened the huge hoopskirt. "I've barely seen anything of him for two days now, since we rode over to the Foucheaus. He hasn't gone out already, has he?"

She felt relieved when Callie shook her head no. Janelle wanted to look especially good at the breakfast table this morning. She hoped it would aid her plan to get Justin to talk. The more information she could gather on Sara Janei, the better Janelle would feel about her impersonation of the woman. She had to do it without arousing Justin's suspicions, and figured a little extra attention paid to her physical attributes wouldn't hurt.

She glanced out the window as Callie fidgeted with the hem of her petticoats. The field by the cemetery was again alive with workers. She'd already been back there twice and nothing had happened, and getting back there during the morning hours had proved impossible.

"Hurry, Callie," Janelle said, turning her attention back to the girl. "I don't want to miss Justin."

"Oh, you gots time, Miss Sara. Mama ain't done with getting breakfast ready yet, and Michie Justin was just going down the stairs when I was coming up."

Moments later, after allowing Callie to tie her thick

auburn hair at the nape of her neck, Janelle left the room, her spirits higher than they had been in days. Janelle carefully descended the stairs. She was beginning to get the hang of maneuvering the stairs within the confines of the petticoats and crinoline, but she was still far from confident.

Suddenly nervous, she paused at the open door to the dining room. Justin stood before a window at the opposite wall, his back to her. One booted foot rested on a small stool, his arm leaning on the raised thigh, a steaming cup of coffee in the other hand. He seemed to be in deep thought, his gaze fixed on the entrance drive. She stood quietly, watching him.

"Good morning, Justin." She forced herself to smile as she entered and moved directly to the table.

He turned at the sound of her voice, surprised he had not heard her approach. A flicker of warmth flashed into his eyes, but it disappeared so quickly Janelle found herself uncertain it had really been there at all.

"You are up quite early this morning," he said stiffly, moving to pull out her chair.

He was close enough that his warm breath fanned the auburn curls at her temples. His gaze roamed over her, taking note of the rapid rise and fall of her chest, the plunging neckline of blue silk that revealed firm swells of flesh, and the delicate curve of her bare shoulders.

He seemed to find no need to break the tense silence between them, or to vanquish the tension that hung in the air like a dark shadow. He waited several moments for her to reply, and all the while his glaring eyes raked insultingly over her body.

"No rendezvous today, Janei?"

Shaking with suppressed anger at his insolence, and striving to remain calm, Janelle finally found her voice. "No, I have no rendezvous planned. I thought, since it was such a lovely day, I'd join you in a ride, but obviously you are not in the mood." She took a deep breath, her hands clenched into fists at her sides. She'd been totally unprepared for the turbulent force of desire that had begun to course through her veins at his nearness. She wanted to reach out to him, and at the same time longed to slap his face.

He turned and took his own chair. "I have a meeting of the Coalition this morning, Janei. I have no time for rides," he said brusquely.

Coalition? What Coalition? She gathered it was something Sara Janei was well aware of. She blinked rapidly several times, fidgeting with the napkin in her lap, painfully aware of his intense gaze upon her. "Well, perhaps I'll ride alone then," she said, tilting her chin upwards as she glared back at him.

"Yes, I rather thought you would." Justin's face tightened and his deep voice was suddenly edged with contempt.

"If you'd rather I not . . ."

"Since when does it matter what I prefer? Go wherever and whenever you like, Janei. And with whom, for that matter," he added pointedly.

Janelle persisted. "Justin, please, I've asked you several times to consider forgiving my past transgressions and at least try for an amicable relationship between us. If you cannot forgive, can you at least put your contempt for me aside for a while?" Her voice held a faint quaver, alerting him to her nervousness. "I'll stay around the house today. Perhaps we can ride together tomorrow."

His face was devoid of expression, a mask concealing all emotion. Whatever he was thinking or feeling at her words he kept carefully hidden behind the bland expression. Janelle had offered to stay near the house to appease him, but judging from the look on his face she realized it obviously had not.

Was there any way to win with this man? On impulse

she reached across the table and placed a hand on his, the gesture meant only to assure him of her sincerity. Justin immediately jerked his hand from under hers, gray eyes narrowing in suspicion. The dark emotions emanating from him were paradoxically a physical blow and a magnetic current which drew her inexorably to him, even as she fought an intense desire to flee.

Justin Delacroix was a danger to her, if not physically, then emotionally. Yet, though she feared him, the urge to feel the savage possession of his body taking hers, to know the ecstasy of surrender to him, all of those newly awakened, stirring emotions were becoming harder to ignore, and to resist.

Nor was Justin immune to the sensual attraction between them. Her words had pulled at him, made him want to believe her yet again, but he held back, remembering Sara Janei's betrayals. A hunger, as devastatingly fierce as any he had ever known, stirred within him as he looked at her. His features darkened with passion, the onslaught of desire from his traitorous thoughts threatening to overwhelm him. The power she wielded over his senses enraged him. Infuriated at what he considered his own weakness, he pushed his chair away from the table, toppling it over in his haste to rise and leave her.

"I have to go into town tomorrow," he said hoarsely. "If you like you can accompany me, but I warn you, I will be busy all day with business. I will not be able to entertain you, Janei. You'll be on your own. Then again," he added derisively, "maybe it is not such a good idea. If my business is not satisfactorily concluded by day's end, I may decide to stay over at the hotel. As it is the season, there is a very good chance they may only be able to accommodate with one suite. Think about it, Janei, after all, would you really want to share a room with me? Your own husband?"

New Orleans. The Vieux Carré. The mere thought of

it charged her with excitement. She'd have a chance to experience the French Quarter, to relish the sights and sounds of New Orleans in 1856.

Before she had time to say anything, Justin turned on his heel and strode from the room without a backward glance. Beneath his breath he uttered a steady stream of oaths, calling himself every kind of fool for allowing her to accompany him into town. He hadn't meant to do it, but somehow, looking down into those depthless green eyes, he had not been able to help himself.

Janelle refused to dwell on Justin's disdainful words, or the warring tide of emotion that threatened to capture them both in its wake. Instead, she decided to enjoy the day, and make plans for her trip into New Orleans.

After eating, she left the dining room, and with no purpose to her day now, wandered idly around the house. She paused in the parlor to flip through the pages of a book of poems, but the stiff English prose didn't grasp her attention. Bored, she searched out Cinder to take him for a walk through the grounds, but changed her mind when she finally found him. He was snoring loudly, his tiny black body sprawled lazily in the center of a yellow chair in the music room.

Laughing softly, Janelle left the house alone. She roamed the manicured grounds, attempting to talk to an old black man tending a rosebush near the front gallery, but he proved no great communicator. His grunts of acknowledgment soon became exasperating and she gave up yet another futile search for companionship.

The sound of wheels on the shell-covered drive drew her attention. Half a dozen carriages moved down the curving entry toward the house, and she watched them in fascination, recognizing several models from her visits to the Western museums around her hometown. In the lead was a surrey, two rows of seats only half full. Next came what she thought was a victoria, named for the queen herself. Two passengers sat in the hooded compartment behind a driver who was perched high above them. Several plain buggies followed, and a landau brought up the rear. Janelle assumed all to be members of the Coalition Justin had mentioned, whatever it was.

Aimlessly, Janelle wandered about the grounds. At the stable she plucked an apple from one of the trees in the garden and gave it to Lady, who was enjoying a day in the open corral. The little mare nuzzled Janelle's shoulder appreciatively and then burrowed her nose into the folds of Janelle's skirt in search of another hidden morsel.

Next to the stables was a carriage house, but it was closed up tight. To the left of it was a *garçonnière,* the apartment for single male guests of the plantation. Suddenly she was swept up in a rush of homesickness, remembering how she'd toured the gardens with Paul, and he'd explained that the *garçonnière* was now his apartment. Janelle quickly banished the feeling, scoffing at herself. She couldn't be homesick. With the death of her parents, she didn't have a home any longer. But she did miss her friends. Farther along the path a bouquet of scents filled the warm air. Every plant in the garden seemed in bloom, each competing with the others to dominate the air with sweet fragrance. Then she thought of the cemetery. She had all day to herself now. Maybe she could find another way to get to it besides going through the fields where the slaves were working.

She hesitated. Did she really want to go back there? To find a way to leave this Delacroix, to leave Justin?

It was too dangerous to care for Justin. He was a man completely alien to her own time. With Sara Janei's mysterious disappearance there was also the possibility that Justin was a murderer. She didn't want to believe that, but she had to at least consider it. She had to find out if she could return to her own time. If she went to the graveyard during the daylight hours, and stood beneath the oak tree where the pink tombstone had been, would it happen again?

Taking care that no one saw her, Janelle made her way around the wide fields where the workers were. She searched for over an hour, until she stepped around a copse of tall oleanders and saw the small black wrought-iron fence. The black bars gleamed in the morning sun. Everything was well cared for, not at all like it had been the morning she'd stumbled into the small graveyard seeking shelter from the sudden storm. Now all the tombstones stood upright, the grass around them well trimmed; some even had flowers at their base.

She moved to where she knew the pink tombstone had been, the ground now smooth and unturned. Whose gravesite would it really be? Janelle wondered. Would Sara Janei return to Delacroix and live out her life with Justin? Would Justin find his wife's body somewhere and bring it back here for burial? Or was it Janelle's grave? Was she destined to spend the rest of her life here on Delacroix, with Justin, forever pretending to be Sara Janei? Had it been her own grave she'd stumbled onto? Is that why she was here? She had to know.

Janelle knelt down, running her fingers through the short green blades of grass that covered the ground. It was smooth and lush, cool to the touch, the earth in that spot unbroken. Nothing happened. The sky remained quiet, the air still. She felt nothing unusual. No tremors or sensations of déjà vu, no fear, no apprehension . . . nothing.

Then abruptly shadows crept over the cemetery and the air took on a chill. Janelle's heart jumped and began a frantic pounding within her chest. It was happening again. Closing her eyes she dug her fingers into the soft dirt. Any minute now the rain would come, the air would fill with the crashing sounds of thunder and jagged streaks of lightning would rip through the darkened sky.

But rather than rain and cold, she felt warmth spread across her shoulders. Janelle opened her eyes and saw the sun slowly reclaiming the earth. Feeling strangely lightheaded, she rose on wobbly legs and, stepping from the cover of the tree, looked up at the peaceful sky. A lone puff of white cloud slowly drifted beside the blazing sun.

Had it worked? She looked about. The grounds were still carefully manicured. The tombstones all erect. At the wide cotton field she stopped. The field was alive with workers, and their soft chanting filled the air, crooning voices blending together in harmony.

She had been gone from the house for nearly an hour, but as she approached the front drive Janelle saw the visiting carriages still gathered in the shade of a nearby tree. The liveried black drivers sat in a circle on the ground a few feet from the vehicles, engaged in a card game. Nearing the house, she heard voices, several raised in anger. Curious, Janelle stopped near the window of Justin's study and listened to the heated words. The men seemed to be arguing over shipping costs and a tax that was soon to be levied on all exported freight. Cotton and sugarcane, two of the South's main exports, were to be taxed more heavily than anything else. Janelle decided that Justin's meeting would probably be going on for some time yet.

She knew she should be more upset at the outcome of her visit to the cemetery, but for some reason she was at a loss to explain even to herself, she wasn't.

She walked past the stables and continued on a narrow path that led through a grove of pines and into what at first glance looked like a foreign civilization. Then she realized she was staring at the slave quarters. The tract consisted of six rows of wooden cottages, approximately a dozen structures in each row. Except for the first three cabins, which were built of brick, they were all identical; plain whitewashed wood planking for walls, a door set squarely in the middle of the front wall, a window opening on each side with shutters but no glass, and a brick chimney on the rear wall opposite the front door. Each cottage had a small, covered veranda-type porch attached to the front. Some had squares of raw muslin on the windows, crudely fashioned into curtains. The three brick structures were much sturdier and more elaborate.

Stepping up to the door of the first one she knocked and the door swung open at her touch. She peered inside, and found it empty. It was a hospital, of sorts. There were six cots positioned against one wall, a dressing screen in the corner and another beside a large table in the center of the room. A small desk near the door held a variety of medical books, an array of primitive-looking instruments hung on a wall near the fireplace, and a tall cabinet with glass doors stood near the window.

Leaving the small hospital, Janelle moved past the other two cabins. They were obviously residences, and clearly more adequate in creature comforts than their wooden counterparts.

She moved down a wide path that ran between the center row of cottages. Though she had witnessed that Justin treated his slaves well, and they in turn seemed to hold him in high regard, the thought of one man owning another distressed her. She walked on.

Near the last cottage she came across the people who were either too old or too young to work the fields or house. A gathering of elderly women sat in a semicircle, their chairs situated to catch the shade of a giant oak, their attention divided between the sewing in their laps and the group of toddlers playing nearby.

Remaining out of sight beside one of the cabins, Janelle watched as one child, a diminutive little girl with huge almond-shaped black eyes, led the other children in some sort of game. The child had an air of dominating authority. She strutted around the tree, issuing orders for the other children to follow.

But it was the hat sitting on her head like an over-sized helmet that caught Janelle's attention. It was obviously very expensive, too much so to be a slave child's plaything. Janelle guessed it could only have belonged to one person—Sara Janei. From what she had heard about Sara Janei so far, she couldn't believe the missing woman would have given anything to a slave child, let alone an expensive hat. Cautiously, Janelle approached the children.

"Hello, there," she called softly, bending down to their level.

The silence that followed her simple greeting was almost deafening. Every eye turned toward her, but no one spoke. Just when she was about to try another greeting, most of the children abandoned their game and scattered. Only the little girl with the hat and two toddlers who could barely walk did not flee.

The girl stared at Janelle, chin lifted high. Stubborn defiance shone from the child's wide black eyes.

"Morning, Miss Sara," she squeaked, trying desperately to sound brave. She curtsied low, holding her ragged hem out wide in her small fingers and then stood upright, waiting for whatever was to come.

Janelle smiled. She could empathize with the tiny figure whose fragile courage was most undoubtedly held together by nothing more than sheer stubborn will. She realized after a moment that the child's bravado was being severely undermined by her silence and hurried to speak. "Well, it seems I'm at a disadvantage today. You know my name, but I don't know yours."

The child swallowed hard. "Tansy. My name's Tansy."

"That's a very pretty name, Tansy." She could feel the watchful eyes of the old women and other children on her back. The air all around was still. No one dared move. Janelle could imagine that Sara Janei had rarely come to the slave quarters. She could almost feel their terror as they held their breath and waited for her wrath to explode. Well, she mused, they were in for a surprise . . . a pleasant one. She turned and waved to the old women, putting a wide smile on her face as she did. It was almost too difficult to keep that smile when she wanted to chuckle at their expressions of sheer amazement.

Janelle turned back to Tansy. "Who taught you to curtsy so nicely, Tansy?"

"*Tante* Marie. She says I have to learn my manners like a real lady."

"Well, you're doing very nicely. That's a beautiful hat you have there. May I ask where you got it, Tansy?"

"I found it," the child declared defensively, her back stiffening instantly.

"Oh, how lucky for you!" Janelle cried, clapping her hands together and trying to sound cheerful. "Where did you find such a wonderful treasure?"

The child relaxed at once. "In the swamp. It was stuck between a tree's feet and was all dirty. Sammy done cleaned it for me and said I could keep it." Her bottom lip began to tremble. Tears welled in the big dark eyes and threatened to spill down her cheeks. She put up a valiant fight to stop them, sucking her lower lip between her teeth.

"Of course you can keep it, Tansy. My mother always told me, finders keepers, losers weepers, right?" Janelle's heart swelled at the huge smile that swept over the child's face. "Now, can you tell me exactly where this place is that you found the hat?"

"Nah, but Sammy can, Miss Sara. He was with me. All I know is we was way out past the cane fields. Mama don't let me go out to the fields by myself. That's why Sammy took me." Her bottom lip began to quiver again. "Is it your hat, Miss Sara?"

"Yes, Tansy, but I want you to have it now. It looks so nice on you. I just wanted to know where I lost it so I won't lose anything else there." She hoped the words sounded convincing enough to at least satisfy the inquisitive mind of a small child.

"Oh, well, Sammy takes me there lotsa times, Miss Sara. He knows right where we was. You ask him, he'll tell you."

"Thank you, Tansy, you've been a real big help to me. I'll see you again, all right?" Impulsively Janelle leaned forward and lightly kissed the child's cheek. A gasp rose from the direction where the elderly women sat, their eyes wide with shock.

Janelle was unaware of yet another set of eyes watching the scene in the slave quarter, eyes that blazed with hatred. A large gray gelding stood motionless beside the brick hospital cottage, its caped rider intent on the two figures at the opposite end of the row. As Janelle stood, the animal was urged into movement, its huge head rising in the air, thick neck muscles flexing in readiness as his reins were pulled to the side, guiding him toward the dense foliage nearby. Within seconds, horse and rider disappeared within the greenery. No one had even witnessed their presence.

Janelle knew she had to go to the swamp where Tansy claimed to have found the hat. It would mean breaking her word to Justin about staying close to the house, but he was busy with his meeting. If she hurried, with any kind of luck, she'd be back before his friends left and he would never know she'd been gone. She hated the thought of traipsing around a swamp grove and riding a horse in the beautiful silk gown, but it would be too risky to return to the house to change clothes.

Sammy was in the stable area when she entered, and while he saddled Lady, and explained where he had found the hat, Janelle slipped into the shadows of an empty stall and quickly shed the cumbersome hoopskirt.

"Sure hope you ain't ma . . . mad, Miss Sara. I . . . I didn't even think about it being your hat. The way it was all torn and dirty, and all, I jus . . . just figured no one would want it, no how," he stammered, clearly afraid she was angry.

"It's all right, Sammy. Tansy is welcome to the hat. I didn't want it anymore anyway." She smiled at his obvious relief.

"You want I should go with you, show you where it was?"

"No, I'll find it. Just help me up. I can't see the stirrup with all this material around my legs."

She knew she didn't look very ladylike, riding astride with her dress and petticoats bunched up around her legs and billowing out over her hips.

As she rode toward the area Sammy had directed her to, visions of alligator-infested lagoons, snakes writhing through murky waters, and leeches buried in the mud just waiting to cling to her skin, filled Janelle with dread.

A moment later, arriving at her destination, she released her breath, unaware she'd been holding it.

Bayou Tejue, as Sammy had called it, was not half as large or as ominous looking as she'd expected. A grove of cypress trees stood at the far end of the open meadow. The trees were immense, many standing well over a hundred and fifty feet tall, their girth looking five to ten feet. Wildflowers sprouted up all around the edge of the area, bright red, blue, pink, and yellow blossoms providing a splash of color. Three magnolia trees grew at one end of the grove, their glossy dark leaves a magnificent contrast to the large, waxlike white flowers sitting delicately upon each limb, their petals spread wide to receive the sun. The strong sweet essence of magnolia blooms permeated the air.

A feeling of uneasiness crept over Janelle at the silence in the bayou. It was unnatural, almost eerie in its stillness. Even the birds had grown quiet. She guided Lady cautiously through the tall grass surrounding the swamp grove, finally dismounted and tied the reins to a chestnut sapling. Janelle picked her way about the grove's edge, inspecting the ground carefully. It was almost too much to hope that anything else of significance would be found. The place seemed untouched, as if it had never been visited by any other human. She moved toward the swamp, pausing to admire the pale pink petals of a water lily floating on the murky surface. To her right she saw that there was a narrow strip of land leading into the depths of the swamp grove.

Suddenly, Janelle no longer wanted to enter the dank marsh. Fear swept over her, and turned her blood cold. There were snakes in there, she knew it. She'd always been terrified of snakes; their slithering bodies gave her the creeps. She'd taken a failing mark in one of her high school science classes for refusing to hold a harmless twelve-inch garter snake. Her skin crawled just thinking of it. The water rippled and she thought of alligators, their beady little eyes watching her, just waiting to attack. Were there alligators in Louisiana? Or crocodiles?

"Cripes, does it make any difference?" she said to herself. "One's just as bad as the other."

Lifting the heavy skirts high, she made her way along the meager slice of earth, the blackness of the stagnant water only inches from her feet. A slimy moss covered the ground along the sides of the path and down to the water's edge. Several times she saw the water move, a swishing of activity as if something swam just below the dark surface. Janelle bit her lip, resisting the compulsion to turn back.

"Sara Janei, for God's sake, where are you?" A vision of a woman who looked very much like herself, dancing the night away in San Francisco, or lounging comfortably in a beautiful drawing room, popped into her mind. She pushed it away, sensing with a deep, inexplicable certainty that was not the missing woman's fate. "If you're in here, Sara, there's probably nothing I or anyone else can do for you now. Why am I even in here? I must be crazy, that's why!" She kept talking to herself; it was the only way she could retain a modicum of calmness, keep her mind from giving in to the fear that she was fighting to keep under control.

The path curved between two closely growing cypress trees whose trunks were half-submerged in the water. They grew so close together that she had to climb over them to continue following the path. Her right foot securely on the ground, the other still wedged in the crevice of the trees' trunks, Janelle felt a soft, invisible veil wrap around her face. She screamed and clawed at it. Something large and black dropped on her arm and began crawling across her flesh. In a blind terror, she brushed frantically at the spider, sending it flying through the air. The small hairy body landed with a soft plop on top of the water. At almost the same instant, a frog leapt from the swamp's black depths; its tongue snatched the helpless spider and pulled it below the surface.

Wispy trails of cobweb clung to her arms and hair. She had dropped her skirts while fending off the spider, and now the material lay limp around her feet, the heavy hem quickly soaking up muddy water. Staring down at the horridly stained fabric, hopelessly beyond repair now, her attention was drawn to a faint sparkle in the mire at the water's edge. Janelle bent down, and submerged her fingers into the muck to get at the small piece of metal. Lifting it from the water she stood to examine the object cradled in the palm of her hand. It was a tiny gold locket, identical to her own. The initials *SJ* were delicately engraved on the back jacket. A thin chain, its clasp broken, dangled from the locket.

She slid her thumbnail between the gold jackets and forced them apart. A miniature daguerreotype was secured to the inside of one jacket. Though slightly blurred by water stains and mud, it was still obvious that the man in the portrait was quite handsome in a classically Greek god sort of way. Dark hair cascaded over his forehead in large ringlets, and thick lashes framed eyes that seemed to be alive with laughter. It was clearly not Sara Janei's husband, and no one Janelle recognized . . . yet.

No, that was wrong. She did recognize him. His picture had been in Sara Janei's drawer. Robert, that was his name. But why would Sara Janei have his picture in her locket?

A loud cracking sound cleaved the air, followed by a sharp whizzing close to her head, and Janelle jumped, whipping around and nearly loosing her balance. Slivers of wood from a nearby tree flew all around her.

A second crack split the air.

Janelle threw herself to the ground, her breath coming in heavy gasps, heart racing madly. After a moment of stunned confusion she'd recognized the sound. Someone was shooting at her!

After a while, she got to her feet, although she kept her body crouched low to the ground. She listened for the sounds of someone approaching, but heard nothing. Keeping herself bent over, Janelle ran along the narrow path, heedless now of the dangers from nature she'd feared so intensely only a short time before. At the moment she felt this animal was far more dangerous than any she could encounter in the swamp. This one had a gun.

Chapter nine

JANELLE TRIPPED OVER A FALLEN TREE AND grit-filled water splattered across her face. The long, auburn-tinged hair fell loose from its ribbon and spilled around her shoulders. The bodice of her dress was covered with mud.

More shots pierced the air, shattering the silence. Her breath labored, Janelle thrashed her way through the grove of cypress, disregarding any attempt now to stay on the path. Galvanized by stark, sheer panic, her only thought was to get away. Fear had left her disoriented; she didn't know which direction led out of the grove and which led deeper into its darkness.

She stumbled, her feet sinking in the quagmire, ooze clinging to the hem of her dress and weighing it down. She heard the explosive sound of another bullet being fired; the deadly projectile slashed through the skirt of her dress and hit the stump of a cypress tree only inches away. Swerving in a desperate effort to evade being shot, Janelle plunged into the dark water. She propelled herself back up the embankment and awkwardly clawed her way onto the path. She ran, stumbling, tripping, falling, until she felt she couldn't go another step, and then forced leaden legs to continue on.

Just as her mind registered the impending collapse of her physical strength, the bushes thinned and she broke into the sunlight. Open meadow spread before her. Janelle fell to her knees, head bowed in exhaustion, arms limp at her sides. Her lungs could scarcely draw in enough air, and her heart felt near to bursting. Whoever had fired those shots might still be tracking her, but she knew with a flood of despair that her legs would carry her no farther. As it was, it was an effort even to lift her head.

The sound of pounding hoofbeats broke the quiet. Panic filled her heaving chest. Paralyzed with terror, her limbs numb from fatigue, Janelle couldn't move.

A large black stallion raced toward her, his rider bent low over the animal's neck. The horse was reined in a mere yard from where she sat. Before the huge stallion had managed to settle completely, Justin jumped from the saddle and ran to where Janelle knelt on the ground.

"Janei! My God, are you all right?" His fingers gripped Janelle's shoulders as he quickly examined her. Justin's arms wrapped around her, and she stiffened. But his grip tightened, denying the rejection.

The fierce protectiveness with which he held her filled Janelle with a surge of warmth, and a sense of sanity in a world gone crazy.

Justin rose and pulled Janelle to her feet. A tumult of emotion assaulted her as she finally leaned against him for support. She was powerless to stop him. She felt the hardness of his chest, the drumming beat of his heart against her breasts, and helplessly felt her resistance waning. Part of her welcomed the comfort his embrace offered, while yet another remained frightened, remembering the ferocity of his earlier anger and the uncertainty of his wife's plight. Fear and suspicion fought a valiant battle against longing, joy, and the growing desire to remain within the security of his arms.

"I heard shooting, and when I saw you here, practically crumpled on the ground, I . . ." He gathered her closer, forgetting the bitterness that had been in his heart for so long. With her body pressed provocatively against him, with the thought that he might have lost her forever, feelings began to stir in him he'd thought long dead. Since her return he had deliberately avoided looking at his own confused emotions, or into his heart. But a rush of desire, an urging to take her, to show her whom she really belonged to, was fast becoming too strong to ignore.

Janelle twisted slightly in his embrace. Bold passion flickered in the depths of the dark eyes that looked down at her. She knew he was going to kiss her, but felt unable to turn away. Her heart beat frantically, and then seemed to lodge in her throat as she watched his head lower toward hers. She shut her eyes, determined this time to merely endure, to feel nothing. She had been in his arms once before and found herself almost lost in the magnetism of his embrace, drawn helplessly into a kiss that had been frightening in its intensity, in its control over her. But that evening had ended in anger and cruelty. It had been a grim lesson, and not one she wished to repeat.

"Look at me, Janei," he whispered, commanding her.

Janelle opened her eyes and stared up at him. She steeled herself against him, against the kiss she knew she would not be able to resist.

What control Justin maintained over himself suddenly slipped from his grasp, vanishing the instant her face turned toward his. He was conscious only of her soft, quivering lips and how much he wanted to taste them again. Oblivious of the place, of the threat of danger that still loomed around them, he gathered her to him tightly, and with a gentle yet fierce demand, his mouth claimed hers.

She was powerless to stop her body from responding. His kiss deepened, his lips hungrily covering hers, and a wave of shuddering pleasure washed over Janelle, sweeping through every limb, every muscle. She knew she should struggle against him, break his hold of her, but her arms seemed more treacherously disposed to encircle the wide breadth of his shoulders, while her fingers ached to tangle in the thick waves of black hair at his neck. Halfheartedly she pushed against his shoulder in a feeble attempt to escape.

Justin's arms tightened, and his mouth ravaged hers with devastating intensity. Languor invaded her limbs, flooding every fiber, weakening every muscle, stoking the fire that already simmered deep within her, and she realized hazily her struggle was as much to control her own betraying emotions, her own traitorous body, as against his embrace.

As the last thin shreds of fear disappeared, Janelle became fully conscious of Justin's hard, muscled length next to hers, of the dangerous excitement being held in his arms aroused, and the drugging pleasure his mouth was wreaking on hers. His tongue forced her lips apart, filling her mouth, caressing, probing the moist, honeyed recesses. With deepening demand his mouth molded itself to hers, and all thought of escaping him, of fearing him, dissolved. She found herself responding to the touch of his hands caressing her back, her lips returning his kiss, eagerly accepting the sensual invasion of his tongue. This dark, passionate lover whose kiss was drugging her with pleasure was not the cold, rage-filled man she feared.

The sound of Tobar pounding his heavy hoof restlessly on the ground invaded Justin's drunken senses and he reluctantly pulled his lips from hers, finally remembering the peril of only moments before. The sight that met his eyes as he again gazed down at Janelle caused the corners of his mouth to curve in a smile.

If it wasn't for the unnerving effects of his own emotional upheaval, or the thought that she might have been seriously hurt in the swamp, Justin would have burst into laughter at her appearance. As it was, he stifled the urge.

Limp hair hung about her shoulders in wet, muddy ringlets, the shorter strands plastered to the sides of her dirt-smeared face. Weeds stuck to her everywhere, in her hair and dress. She was covered with grime, the bodice of her gown torn open, the skirt almost in shreds, the hems of her petticoats caked with mud, and a heel of one shoe missing.

Then he remembered just what she was. The knowledge that she had tricked him into marriage had always goaded his pride. That he had still wanted her, desired her, even after discovering her many lovers left him full of self-loathing. That she still had the power to arouse him now, to make him betray himself, infuriated him; and that she had dared come back to Delacroix, back into his life, incensed him.

Sensing the quick change in him, Janelle tried to pull away, but his steel-like grip on her arms tightened. The gray eyes, only moments ago dark with passion, were now the color of a chill winter sky and just as cold.

Without a word or another glance, Justin spun and forced her to follow him to where Tobar stood waiting. He mounted, reached down, swung her up in front of him, and settled her on his lap. Too tired, frightened, and confused to resist, Janelle sat stiffly within the circle of his arms, straining away from him, desperately trying to ignore his nearness. Remembering the scene in the swamp, the closeness of the bullets, she shivered and wearily tried to push her suspicions away.

It could not have been Justin firing at her, chasing her through the bayou. He was saving her, taking her back to the plantation house. Would he do that if only moments before he had been trying to kill her?

They had traveled only a mile before encountering Lady. The small mare was skittish and uncertain at their approach, but instantly calmed at a few soothing words from Justin and quickly fell into step behind Tobar.

"I can ride Lady the rest of the way," Janelle offered. She wished her voice hadn't quaked when she spoke.

"No."

He offered no reason, and a quick glance into his hard eyes convinced Janelle not to ask for any.

Only a few yards from the spot where Justin had found Janelle, the large gray gelding stood behind a thicket of saplings at the swamp's edge. His rider lowered the rifle slowly. Thin fingers carefully uncocked the hammer and guided it back to its resting place against the firing pin. Eyes filled with hatred watched Justin wrap his arms around his wife in visible concern.

A gloved hand pulled on the reins and the horse turned away, carefully picking its way through the grove. A gator slid from the tall reeds beside the path and the gelding shied sideways and snorted, nervously pawing at the ground with a huge forehoof. The rider calmly stroked the animal's powerful neck, whispering soothing words of encouragement while retaining a tight grip on the reins. A small piece of gold lying in the weeds beside the path caught the sun, its reflection drawing the rider's eyes.

Moments later, Sammy, seeing the riders approach, ran to take Tobar's reins. With almost angry movements, Justin slid away from Janelle and dismounted. He immediately reached back up and pulled her from the saddle. Her feet had barely touched the earth when his hand swooped behind her knees and she was roughly lifted into his arms.

"I . . . I am perfectly capable of get . . . getting to my room alone," she stammered. Instinctively she tried to draw away as he turned his head toward her.

His mouth curved in a mocking smile, a smile that did not warm the gray eyes. "But that is not how I want you, *chérie.*" He strode toward the house without glancing down at her again. Yet the feel of her warm, yielding body nestled against his chest made him almost mad with wanting her.

"Now what happened?" Marie asked, hurrying into the foyer upon Justin's entrance. She shot a vicious look at Janelle's disheveled appearance. Whatever had happened, she was certain Sara Janei had undoubtedly brought it on herself.

"I will take care of her, Marie," Justin stated as he passed. His eyes, more than his words, told Marie he would tolerate no argument. He carried Janelle directly up to her room, pausing in front of the door only long enough to ruthlessly kick it open and once inside slam it shut with a backward thrust of his booted foot.

Hearing her mumble some senseless words of appreciation for saving her, Justin brusquely ordered Janelle to remain silent. In the center of the room he released her and Janelle's lithe body slowly slid down the length of his, the movement like a caress to his hard, tautly held muscles. Cursing hoarsely under his breath he grasped her shoulders, forced her to turn away from him, and swiftly unfastened the tiny pearl buttons at the back of her ruined gown. The dress fell to the floor. He picked the few remaining pieces of bramble from her hair and gently ran his fingers through the muddy strands. Deftly he unfastened the hooks of her petticoats and urged her to step from them as they fell around her ankles. Moving around to face her, Justin pulled at the ribbon that laced the front of the thin camisole.

A shiver ran through her as his fingers grazed her flesh. Janelle drew a long, shuddering breath and moved to step away, knowing she should resist him, should fight against him, but his softly spoken command stopped her.

"No," he ordered huskily, "do not move." A smile that hinted at both depthless passion and cold cruelty creased his face.

Too weak and exhausted to put up a struggle, her emotions in turmoil, Janelle found coherent thinking totally beyond her. She gazed up at him and longing welled within her; a warm wave of desire slowly invaded her senses. In that moment, Janelle knew she wanted him, had always wanted him, and nothing else mattered.

Searing ripples of heat danced across her skin as his fingers pushed the ruffled camisole from her shoulders, exposing the gentle curves of her breasts. She had been so lost in her own thoughts, she hadn't noticed the odd smile on his lips, or the hard look in his eyes. Janelle felt a hot flush spread across her face and shivered with apprehension under his coldly appraising look. With a swift movement his fingers closed around the waist tie of her pantalettes, ripped it open and pushed them down over her hips, the ruffled leggings falling to cover her feet.

Fear instantly returned and she retreated, hands clenched tightly at her sides. There was nowhere to run, or hide. She was trapped. But the urge to flee was not as strong as the longing to stay.

"You are still beautiful, Janei, even like this." His

gaze flickered over her dirt-smudged length and his lips curved in a mirthless smile. "Maybe more beautiful."

The soft cast of late afternoon sun streaming through the windows gilded her shoulders and gave the green of her eyes the intense depth of pine woods in spring, the golden flecks becoming dozens of tiny sunbursts. She heard his sharp intake of breath, caught the spark that flared in his eyes and knew he wanted her as much as she yearned to be his. Yet, he made no move to take her or even touch her, holding his desire on a firm leash.

Gray eyes devoured her, mesmerized with the vision before him. She seemed almost ethereal. Her dark hair fell wildly about her shoulders in a halo of red-kissed tangles. Her body was slender, with just the right proportion of curves to tantalize, her legs long and graceful. For timeless moments his eyes roamed her body, drinking of its beauty, his breath trapped in his throat, his hunger for her almost choking him.

With each rapid breath, her high, full breasts rose and fell, the skin of each a crescent of whiteness, a startling contrast to the bronze of the rest of her body. For a brief moment he wondered what could have possessed Janei to reveal her body to the coloring rays of the sun, but as quickly relinquished the thought as he continued his sensual exploration. Her nipples were the pink of a dew-kissed rose, and taut, as if reaching for his touch. They swelled as he watched.

Though his features were in shadow, Janelle could feel his steady stare and her face burned crimson as she felt his gaze travel her naked form. Never had she felt so open to a man's scrutiny, so vulnerable to his power. She wanted to say something to him, but didn't know what. She wanted to go to him, but didn't know how.

Justin felt the stirrings of passion but repressed the feelings, steeling himself against the urge to throw her on the bed and take her by force, to show her by strength that she was his, to own as no one else should. Which bothered him more, he was uncertain, his wife's return, or this new power she seemed capable of wielding over his traitorous emotions.

Going to the door, Justin threw it open and called loudly for Marie.

Confused and embarrassed, Janelle quickly grabbed a batiste wrapper that lay across the bed, slipping her arms into it and holding the gown tightly closed about her waist.

The housekeeper appeared almost instantly and Justin spoke to her in harsh whispers for several minutes before turning back into the room. Without a glance in Janelle's direction, he moved to the window, his features set as he stared unseeingly at the horizon. He knew what he was going to do. He would teach her, finally, who was the master. But he would do it slowly, coolly, and leave her begging for more.

Janelle stared at the hawkish profile. His black hair glistened so that blue shadows appeared in the thick waves, and his skin glowed a golden bronze; only the jagged white scar marred the smooth concave of cheek. Strangely the scar no longer seemed a disfigurement on the patrician face, but served to further enhance the savage handsomeness.

She longed to reach out to him, to touch his sun-warmed skin, to tangle her fingers in the blue-black strands of hair and make him smile. Instead, she stood still, fighting the mad temptation, resisting the insane urge to run into his arms. Forcing her voice to remain calm, she said, "Th . . . Thank you, Justin, but now if you'll ex . . . excuse me . . ."

The door behind her flew open to a bustle of activity. Marie and Callie entered, each carrying large buckets of steaming hot water.

With an exaggerated flourish that made a mockery of the polite gesture, Justin bowed. "Your bath, madam," he said dryly.

In a flash of unexpected temper, she snapped, "I would appreciate it if you would leave my room while I bathe."

"But my dear, you wouldn't deprive your own husband the pleasure of washing that lovely back of yours, amongst other things, would you?"

All color drained from her face as she stared at him, her eyes wide with horror as she realized the implication of his words. "You . . . you can't! You wouldn't!"

He continued to smile arrogantly, making no move toward her until Marie and Callie had quietly left the room, the older woman glaring at him every step of the way.

He crossed the room with all the grace of a stalking panther. With a sweep of his arm he brushed the thin robe from her shoulders and lifted her from the floor before she could resist. His mouth captured hers, smothering her words of protest in a languorously searching kiss that seemed endless as it awakened a pleasurable longing deep within her. His lips crushed hers, his kiss hardening to a passionate demand that left her staring at him in hazy wonderment when he tore himself away, carried her across the room, and unceremoniously dropped her into the ugly green tub. Lavender-scented water splashed up to engulf her.

Sputtering angrily, blinded by spraying water and soap bubbles, Janelle flailed the air with her hands, hoping to connect with his face. Before she had a chance to recover, a flood of warm water was dumped over her head, plastering wet muddy ringlets of hair to her face and shoulders and leaving her gasping for air. Just as Janelle finished wiping her eyes, another wave of water rained down on her head.

"Damn you, Justin Delacroix, stop it! Stop it!" she screamed, not caring that the entire house might hear her.

Suddenly his hands were on hers, pushing them from her face and brushing the wet hair from her eyes. "Calm down, wildcat," he murmured against her cheek. His lips tenderly caressed the curve of her jaw. His soap-lathered hands moved across Janelle's wet shoulders and slid down the length of her arms, leaving tingling trails of gooseflesh across her skin. His mouth closed over hers again, warm and demanding. It pulled her into a world of pleasurable sensuality, drugged her senses, and ignited a flame within her body that scorched her.

For one brief moment he felt the urge to tear himself away from her, to flee the madness he felt sweeping over him, but resisted the impulse. He was too physically aware of her supple silken body, its lush golden curves and hollows, to deny himself what he considered rightfully his. He felt himself harden as his hunger for her turned to a devastating ache. His eyes darkened with passion as he moved one hand to lightly cup her breast, and after the first few seconds, when her body had tensed and tried to move away from him, heard the low involuntary moan that escaped her lips as his thumb rhythmically began to encircle the hardened pink nipple. A look of satisfaction lit his face as he felt her body arch slightly to meet his touch.

Janelle's anger began to melt the moment his seducing lips claimed hers, stopping her words of protest. She had tried to avoid his kiss, his touch, but was helplessly trapped in the big tub, with nowhere to go but into his arms if she attempted to stand. Caught in his embrace, Janelle was forced to accept his plundering kisses, the probing, seeking, darting force of his tongue curling intimately around her own, enticing her growing need of him. His hand left her breast, leaving her with a surprising sense of disappointment until she felt his fingers slide across the soft flesh of her inner thigh. Shock made her attempt to shrink away from him, but his touch was too intoxicating, his kisses sweet as wine, leaving her dazed and thirsting for more. Janelle sensed the moment her control began to slip and tried to push away from him, but his hold on her only tightened, his lips roaming across the curve of her neck before moving to reclaim her mouth and quiet her resistance.

"Ah, Janei, my wicked, Janei," he murmured. His mouth moved across her wet skin to taste the silken flesh that peeked temptingly just above the soapy bubbles. "Tonight you will forget your other lovers, Janei. I will make you forget."

Janelle twisted away from him and pushed against the cool metal of the tub's raised back. For several unnerving seconds she stared at him, too shocked by his words to respond. In the flames of her passion she had forgotten that Justin thought of her as Sara Janei, the woman he considered no better than a whore. "No! I'm not . . . I . . . I mean . . . we can't! Justin, I . . . I'm not who . . . who you think I am. I'm not Sara Janei. Pl . . . Please listen to me. I'm . . . I'm from another place, another time," she cried. "You've got to believe me."

He reached a hand toward her, firmly captured her chin, and forced her to look up at him. "It won't work this time, Janei. I warned you, remember? No games, no charades." He didn't wait for her to answer but reached for a towel from a nearby rack and rose to his feet, the cloth held between his outstretched hands.

Janelle stared at him wide-eyed, a sense of hopelessness in her heart. Why had she blurted out that insane denial? He didn't believe her, and she couldn't blame him. It sounded too incredible even to herself. Realizing she had very little choice for the moment, Janelle drew a shaky breath and stood up.

A violent and sudden onslaught of desire surged through him as he watched her emerge from within the cloud of bubbles. Rivulets of water streamed over the golden skin. Justin felt himself harden with a devastating hunger to take her, his arousal heightened by the tantalizing thrust of her breasts, tiny drops of water gleaming like diamonds on the soft mounds. With a muffled curse he held out the large towel, waiting for her.

She rose and Justin wrapped the large towel around her wet, naked length. A tremor of uneasiness fluttered through her. In one swift movement she was lifted from the tub, and once again crushed against his chest, his arms hard and unyielding as he carried her easily back into the bedchamber.

"You are mine, Janei, and tonight you shall know it," he said. He wanted to make her cry out for forgiveness for all the lies and deceit. At the same time, he wanted to inflame her with longing, caress her with infinite gentleness, and make her see that she loved him.

Janelle sensed his fury and saw the shadow that flickered across his eyes, and felt like screaming at him, and holding him. Her emotions were in as much conflict as his.

He laid her on the bed and bent to join her. She tried to avoid his kiss, but there was no escape as one strong hand moved to her face, forcing her to receive his hungrily seeking mouth. His tongue pushed its way between her teeth, darting to fill her mouth, demanding that she surrender to him.

With one hand pinioned between their bodies Janelle pushed feebly at his shoulder with the other, while she tried to twist away from him. His lips pressed savagely on hers and his hand caught her wildly flailing arm. She moaned softly, and he instantly loosened his hold on her arm.

Justin looked down at her for a long moment, at

the still-damp and tangled auburn tresses that spread across the white pillow, the passion-bruised lips trembling beneath his stare, and the green eyes—eyes filled with confusion, rebellion, and something else, something he stubbornly refused to recognize. Guilt assailed him, and he steadfastly pushed it away.

His lips left a feather light trail of warmth across her skin from the curve of her neck to the satiny soft breast, his teeth gently grazing the sensitive flesh.

Janelle was unprepared for the sudden shock of passion that swept through her as his mouth tormented her body. He aroused sensations in her she had never known existed. His free hand caressed her length, his light touch tantalizing, teasing. With a faint, strangled mew of defeat she found herself no longer wanting to resist him, but rather, for him to continue.

The tip of his tongue circled her ear and Janelle turned her head, capturing his mouth with hers. "Oh, Justin," she whispered. She was being consumed with pleasure, drowning in its exquisite swell, the increasing ache of anticipation almost unbearable as it spread through her.

His grip on her arm loosened and she pulled her hand free, moving it to encircle his shoulder, her fingers entwining in the tendrils of black hair at his neck. But Justin, his body raging with desire and need, didn't at first notice. His assault had been meant to conquer, to instill in her such passion that no one else would ever again be able to please her, to drive her to heights she had never known before, so that he could later deny her, as she had him.

His assault had begun with that intent, but her strangled sob of his name startled him. The cold anger was dissolving beneath the onslaught of sweet havoc her body was wreaking upon him merely by its nearness. His hand moved to caress her cheek and she sensed the change in him, the sudden absence of the fury that had filled him only seconds before.

Justin's lips recaptured hers, and when she didn't resist, his kiss deepened. She knew she should try to escape him, ignore and fight the frantic beat of her heart, the treacherous passion she could feel spreading through her veins like wildfire, but her defenses were too weak, the drugging pleasure of his kisses too strong on her newly awakened senses. What restraint Janelle had on her emotions quickly receded, and to her mortification she found herself responding to the feel of his body pressed on hers.

His lips moved to nuzzle the sensitive skin at the curve of her neck, and he felt her shiver of pleasure as they traveled to caress the soft swell of her breasts. His breath was ragged as he pulled away from her, pushing himself from the bed to stand silently above her.

She was beautiful. More beautiful than he had ever seen her. And softer, not cold and hard as she had been before. There was something different about her, and it touched him, awakened feelings within him that he hadn't wanted to experience ever again.

Janelle's arms felt empty. She had succumbed to him again, allowed him to incite a passion within her that hungered for his touch, and he had once again rejected her, humiliated her.

Too shaken and hurt to feel anger, a warm tear slipped from Janelle's eye, just as she felt Justin's weight return to the bed, his lean form, now devoid of clothes, moving to half-cover her body.

As if sensing what she had mistakenly thought, Justin gathered her tenderly in his arms, a new gentleness to his touch that even he did not understand.

Once again she felt the passion of his kiss, his tongue twining about hers, burning wherever it touched, like the lick of a flame as it explored the sweet darkness.

His hands roamed freely, arousing and exciting, filling her with erotic abandonment as her body arched toward him of its own will, no longer paying heed to earlier hesitations or restraints, brazenly demanding to feel his flesh against hers. Janelle felt an almost painful ache of desire, and knew she was lost to him . . . forever.

Chapter ten

JANELLE HAD KNOWN ONLY ONE LOVER BEFORE, but the sensual emotions and pleasure she was experiencing at Justin's touch were in a sense all new. So powerful were these new sensations she felt frightened, apprehensive, and yet delirious with joy, and with each new wave of pleasure his demanding mouth and caressing hands provoked, her body longed for more.

Justin's cold wrath, his need to punish her, had evaporated, leaving him with a yearning tenderness he could not control, and a vulnerability he would not acknowledge at any other time. Never before during their brief marriage had he been consumed with such a burning desire to have Sara Janei.

The other times he had made love to Janei she had been cold and unresponsive, merely enduring his touch, silently suffering his caresses, her body and heart hard and unyielding. But this time was different. There was something wild and pure about her glorious body, and perhaps its very strange combination of familiarity and newness was the intoxicant. She was all straining passion and trembling need. Justin responded to this lack of artifice or design, drawn into the welter of feelings she created, wanting only to make her feel more, to lose herself in wanton desire for him, and him alone. His lips fed upon hers, as if seeking nourishment as his hands moved over every hollow and curve of her body, imprinting each to memory. She was his, and he would brand his possession on her, enflame and enslave her desire as she had his.

Janelle arched toward him and his arms pulled her close, their bodies pressing together until her soft curves melted into his hard, muscular form. A fiery heat surged through her veins, and she cried out for him.

All Janelle felt was the excruciating joy of her body being united with his.

"Ah, love, sweet love," he gasped hoarsely.

I don't want to go back, Janelle thought dazedly, and then closed her eyes and abandoned herself to the dreamy rapture of the moment, of Justin.

They moved together, holding each other tightly, lost in the wild abandon of their desire for one another. Her mouth clung to his, her hands clawing, caressing, sweeping over his body. She matched his passion, unconstrained, unashamed, and they were melded together by their searing joining. When she tensed beneath him in a heartrending release, the explosion of his own bursting desires nearly stripped and drained him of his very soul. They catapulted over the precipice of ecstasy together. A rainbow of blinding sunbursts exploded within her as they spiraled over the cliffs of passion, fusing their lives, to become a part of each other forever.

Janelle fell asleep in his arms. Just when he slipped from her side she wasn't sure. When she awoke, the bright light of the morning sun was streaming in through the open windows, the strong scent of honeysuckle drifting in on the still air. She turned to snuggle against the warmth of Justin's body but her arms met only cool sheet. Her eyes fluttered open in surprise. He was gone. Sitting up, she looked around the empty room, her gaze stopping at where his clothes had lain on the floor after he'd hastily discarded them only hours before. They too were gone. But evidence of his visit to her bed enveloped her. Janelle nuzzled his pillow, remembering the feel and taste of him, her body still aching from their passionate joining, a warm surge of happiness in her veins. He had loved her, and she him, nothing could ever take that away from her now, or diminish the all-consuming joy it had given her. But even as she hugged that thought to her, the doubts returned.

Justin had made love to her, but had it been to her, or to Sara Janei? Did he know the truth?

A sharp knock on the door broke into her thoughts, and she turned expectantly, both hoping it was Justin, and praying it was not. In a flurry of good cheer and smiles, Callie entered the room. She carried a large serving tray set with a china pot beside a cup, saucer, and a plate of sugarcoated beignets.

She'd found herself becoming addicted to the unique plain-sweet flavor of the square sugar-powdered dough-nuts. Callie set the tray on the bedside table and poured Janelle's coffee.

"You'd best be getting ready now, Miss Sara. Michie Justin been downstairs awhile waiting on you."

"Huh? Waiting on me? For what?"

Then she remembered. She had forgotten their plans to go into town together this morning. Her heart sang. She pushed her doubts away. Justin was innocent, she just knew it. It had been someone else shooting at her in the swamp, someone else who felt threatened by what they thought was Sara Janei's reappearance. It wasn't Justin. He might have been bitter toward his wife, even hated her, but she couldn't believe he'd killed her. She wouldn't believe it! Everything was going to be all right.

He'd talk to her now. They were going into town, and it would be marvelous.

Suddenly Janelle knew what she had to do. Justin must be told the truth. It was the only way. He had to be told who she really was.

She took the cup of coffee Callie offered and slipped into a batiste wrapper. While waiting for her clothes to be laid out, Janelle walked to the open French doors and stepped out onto the gallery, moving to lean against the waist-high balustrade. The strong scent of blooms perfumed the air. Janelle smiled to herself. Everything at Delacroix was breathtakingly beautiful.

"What in God's name are you trying to do, Janei?" Justin said loudly.

She jumped from the railing, frantically grabbing at the cup that almost tumbled from her grasp.

He was standing on the lawn directly beneath the gallery, eyes burning with rage as he glared up at her. Janelle stared down at him in confusion.

Several black men, workers in the garden, were also looking up at her, some sheepishly stealing glances, some boldly staring.

She realized with sudden horror that she was dressed only in the sheer batiste wrapper. With the light from the morning sun shining directly on her, the thin material left virtually nothing to the imagination.

"I . . . I'm sorry, Justin," she muttered, a hot flush sweeping across her face as she turned and ran back into the bedroom, slamming the door behind her with a snap.

Callie had heard the altercation but feigned ignorance. She busied herself at the armoire, sorting petticoats and underthings, sneaking furtive glances at Janelle every few seconds. She was surprised at the meek response her mistress had offered at Justin's angry confrontation. It wasn't like Sara Janei not to come back with a spiteful retort, laughing gleefully at her own remarks. In fact, Callie had to admit, everything about her mistress lately was strange, she just didn't seem like the same person since her return.

Callie had seen Sara Janei do some strange things in the past, but never anything like what she had just witnessed. The batiste wrapper was no more than a whisper of cloth, its folds providing only the barest hint of modest cover and the morning sun eliminated even that. The garden workers had received an eyeful, and Callie knew that could prove very dangerous for Sara Janei. Animosity against the mistress of Delacroix was strong among the slaves, especially the men. For some the boasting threats were just that—harmless blusters and fake bravado, but Callie knew there were a few who would dare to fulfill those threats if circumstances allowed. For the mistress of Delacroix, that could prove fatal.

Sara Janei's frequent rides through the fields had always been a constant source of resentment to the workers. Her presence meant at the very least an embarrassing tongue-lashing for someone, at worst a whipping at the end of an extra-long day. The plantation's mistress enjoyed the slaves' discomfort, relishing their humiliation and fear. She delighted in the godlike power she held over them, and if she could not discover a reason for punishment, she would happily invent one. She laughed loudly as she instructed the overseer which slave to bring to the back of his house at day's end. This ritual was their secret, hers and the overseer's, Stephan O'Roarke, one they carefully kept hidden from Justin, who had yet to discover the sadistically cruel depths of his wife's personality.

It was always after the whippings that the half-conscious slave would observe Sara Janei's payment to the overseer for his part in her malicious hobby. In the open yard behind O'Roarke's small cottage, overseer and plantation mistress would claw at each other like animals, their mating barbaric and unrestrained.

Callie had never witnessed these things herself, but she'd heard the talk, listened to the hatred that spewed from the lips of Sara Janei's victims. Shaking the unpleasant thoughts from her head, Callie took a dress from the armoire, fluffing the skirt out as she turned to Sara Janei, but the room was empty.

Chapter eleven

JANELLE LEANED HEAVILY AGAINST THE DOOR of the dressing room, waves of nausea washing over her. Swallowing hard, she pulled in deep gulps of air and willed herself not to be sick. She had been totally unaware of the workers in the garden, pausing from their work to stare boldly as she stood enjoying the morning sun. It was such a beautiful morning; all she'd intended was to enjoy it.

How could she have known what would happen? She would never have gone out onto the gallery dressed only in a sheer wrapper if she had been thinking. Justin had looked up at her with disgust. Contempt for what he believed her vulgar show of exhibitionism had rung in his words.

"Miss Sara, you in there?" Callie called anxiously, rapping on the door and breaking into Janelle's thoughts. "Miss Sara?"

"Yes, Callie. I'll be out in a minute," Janelle answered weakly. How was she ever going to face Justin now? She moved to the washstand to press a cold cloth to her face.

"You all right, Miss Sara? Can I come in and help you?" Callie called again after several minutes.

"No. I'm fine, I'm fine. I'll be right out." Janelle dipped the washcloth in the water again, rubbed its coolness along her neck, slid it across her chest and brought it back up to hold momentarily on her forehead.

When Janelle opened the dressing room door, Callie's eyes were full of questions, but she remained silent. Within minutes she had helped Janelle dress and had pinned her hair into a mass of curls.

Her shoulders squared, chin set at a defiant angle, Janelle left the room and made her way downstairs to the dining room. But the room was empty and silent. Not even the servants seemed to be about.

So, he had gone to town without her. She wasn't sure what she felt more, anger or disappointment.

Justin's sudden appearance at the open French doors startled her. They regarded each other silently across the long room. Janelle backed her hands into fists in a futile attempt to stop their trembling. Her heart seemed lodged in the back of her throat, its frenzied beat so loud in her ears she was sure he could hear it too. She felt faint.

Justin made no effort to ease the tension that hung heavy in the air between them. He noticed the defiant tilt of her chin, the apprehension in the wide emerald eyes, the way she had unconsciously taken a step back when she'd become aware of his presence. In spite of his anger, in spite of the promise he'd made himself after leaving her bed, to stay away from her, he found himself admiring how the pale apricot hue of her gown brought out the reddish highlights in her dark hair, and the way the small gold flecks in her eyes flashed, like tiny slivers of dancing fire.

Remembering the feel of her silken flesh, her breasts tantalizingly crushed against his chest, her slender legs wrapped intimately around his thighs, and the sweet welcoming warmth of her body as it had received his and drawn him into her, Justin, for one long, agonizing moment, considered sweeping her into his arms and carrying her back upstairs. The devastating hunger his body felt for her threatened to overpower him. With a whispered curse he fought the maddening urge, damning his own body for its weakness.

Then he remembered the scene he'd witnessed only moments ago, her brash, arrogant disregard for propriety, and his temper flared. She had not changed. It had been another ploy after all, and he had fallen for it. But not again, he swore, never again.

He stepped into the room, and Janelle recognized his cold anger. She searched his lean, rugged face, so dangerously attractive despite the white jagged scar, but the passionate, gentle lover of last night was gone.

He halted before her. Janelle tried to speak, but nothing came out.

Justin waited, but when she made no further attempt to speak, his patience broke. "That was quite a little performance you put on for the workers this morning, Janei, but I will not have it!" He scowled, the black, arching brows drawing together in a deep frown. Any retort she would have made was sharply overridden as he continued, "I will not have you cavorting around here like some cheap trollop, do you understand?"

"But I didn't mean—"

With such swiftness the movement was felt rather than seen, Justin's hand closed around her wrist, the unyielding grip painful as he jerked her against him and snarled, "Do not bother with more lies, Janei. I am not of a mind to listen to the tales that drip so sweetly from your tongue. I do not know what it is you want of me this time, or what you hope to gain by this charade you've devised, but I warn you, never try anything like that again."

Shock at the realization that he thought she had

wantonly and purposely exposed herself to the workers quickly faded, replaced by anger. She wasn't Sara
Janei! Couldn't he sense that? Feel it? Had last night
not touched him at all? Had he merely been satisfying his lust with the body of a woman he purported
to hate?

Janelle stared up at him, green eyes sparkling with
hurt and temper. Her decision to tell him the truth, to
confide in him the extraordinary events that had thrust
her into his life was instantly reversed. The man who
stood before her now would never believe her words, or
understand. This arrogant beast most likely would not
even listen. She jerked her arm, furiously attempting to
free herself from his iron grip, but Justin's fingers held
firm, increasing their hold, biting into the soft flesh.

"You're hurting me, you big ape!" she said, trying
again to twist from his grasp. "Let me go! I didn't do
anything, if you'd only listen. I wasn't thinking, I didn't
know anyone was in the garden. And anyway, how dare
you think I would do that on purpose. What was I supposedly trying to do, Justin, seduce the servants?" Having worked herself into a fury, she hurried on, "That's
a vile thought! What kind of idiot do you take me for? I
did not mean for anyone to see me! I am not the wicked,
insensitive creature you think I am. I'm not even Sara
Janei!"

The flinty eyes, cold with suspicion and wariness,
never left her face. A derisive slant to his mouth, Justin
murmured softly, "You play it out very well, Janei, and
with such sincerity, but you forget, I have seen this act
many times before. I know you, Janei, and I know what
you are."

"No, you don't. You don't know anything at all about
me. Now let me go." Janelle yanked her arm again but
his grip only tightened, the bruising pressure causing
her to wince in pain.

"Just remember, Janei," he said through clenched teeth, "I warned you, and will not do so again. No more of your scheming. Push me too far, and you will be more sorry than you can imagine."

Always one to give as much as she received, Janelle couldn't help the angry taunting words, "By doing what? Refusing to share my bed? Or perhaps you're hoping the next time I venture from the house and get shot at, the bullets will find their mark." The minute the words were out of her mouth, she regretted them.

Justin was instantly aware of the change in her, and the indecision that had followed the harsh words. Having her so close, her body pressed to his, her golden breasts thrust against his chest, her silken skin only a touch away almost weakened his resolve. . . . almost. Furious with himself, and surprised that he could falter in his determination so easily, Justin said, "Do not provoke me, Janei. I may do something we would both regret."

They stared wordlessly at each other, waiting, neither daring to move, each painfully aware of the other's closeness. Justin shuddered at the onslaught of desire that vibrated through his veins. Knowing he would be sorry later, he gave up the struggle.

Feeling his grip on her arm slacken, Janelle tried to pull away but found herself caught within the circle of his strong arms. One hand pressed at the small of her back, while the other slid up to capture the back of her neck, his strong fingers burying themselves within the dark strands of loosely pinned hair. His grip on her neck forced her to face him, to receive his hungrily seeking mouth, and the moment his lips covered hers, she felt helpless against the aching need building within her.

It was a brutal kiss, hard and demanding, savage in its intensity, fueling rather than satisfying the impassioned emotions that had forced them together.

Anger slipped away as if never born, and she returned his kiss.

Shaken with desire, Justin was deaf to the frantic cries of denial his brain still futilely sent, until a resounding crash from the adjoining warming kitchen shattered the silence, followed by a barrage of profuse and distinct cursing.

Justin broke the embrace and moved away. Every muscle in his body was drawn tight, and he trembled from the passion she had aroused, but when he turned back toward her his eyes were cold and distant, his voice holding an edge of impatience. "If we are going to get to town before it becomes too late to conduct any business whatsoever, I suggest we breakfast and then depart."

Janelle drew a shaky breath, still reeling from the effects of his kiss, and sat down. How did he turn it off and on like that? One minute he was raging at her, then he was devastating her with kisses, and then he just as abruptly turned cold again.

Justin took his seat at the head of the table. "Ring the bell, Janei," he ordered softly.

"What?"

"If you ever intend our breakfast to be served, you are going to have to ring the bell." He nodded toward a small china bell on the table. A slow flush spread over her face. She reached for the bell, and missed the puzzled expression in Justin's watching eyes.

Marie entered, carrying a large, heavily laden serving tray. She lowered it swiftly to the table. Strips of bacon slid almost onto Janelle's lap as Marie roughly pushed the plate in front of her. Café au lait sloshed over the cup's rim and made a brown moat within the saucer.

"Sorry, Miss Sara," Marie grumbled, turning away to disappear back through the swinging door to the kitchen.

Janelle stared at the empty doorway and suddenly felt on the verge of tears. God, what kind of woman was Sara Janei to have inspired such dislike or fear in everyone? So far, from what Janelle had experienced, Janei's life seemed to be one angry, hate-filled confrontation after another, except for Gilbert Foucheau, and that was even worse. She would have preferred hatred from that little weasel, Janelle thought with a trace of bitterness. She felt Justin staring at her even before she turned to meet his gaze. "I wish Marie wouldn't act like I was Godzilla's mother!" she said without thinking.

"Whose mother?"

Another blunder. "Just an odd character I read about somewhere. A monster, I think."

Justin frowned. "That's a bit of a change for you, Janei. I didn't think reading was quite exciting enough a pastime to hold your interest."

She chose to ignore the tinge of sarcasm in his voice. "It was a long time ago, Justin, when I was a young girl."

"Not so long ago, Janei." He regretted the gentle words the moment they slipped out. He would have to be more careful. It was becoming too easy to warm to her. To care. There was something different about her, something that seemed to draw him as never before and it was taking all his strength to fight that pull. He had failed miserably last night. He'd wanted her, and damn it all, he wanted her still. The memory of their shared passion was clear and vivid in his mind, and with it came agonizing pain like a fist slamming into his gut.

Waking up this morning, finding himself in her bed, her warm golden body pressed intimately against his, Justin had, for a short time found himself believing things might just finally work between them. That is, until her little performance on the gallery. If nothing else, that show had proven to him she had not changed, she had merely fooled him once more. It would not happen again.

Watching the play of emotions on Justin's face while he concentrated on his meal, Janei felt a stab of disappointment. Each time his coldness began to thaw, the shadow of Sara Janei returned, hovering between them, reminding him, dousing the warm flame that struggled to burn.

But maybe that was better, she thought dismally. She could disappear from this house, this time, just as quickly and mysteriously as she had appeared. Why become involved with each other? It would just make it harder when the time came, when whatever brought her here took her away.

Cinder scampered into the room, jumping up and settling on Janelle's lap. The dog's presence drew her attention and she busied herself offering him bits of bacon. She was still painfully aware of Justin, of the way he was watching her, and finally, she turned to look at him.

He rose abruptly, and tossed the lace-edged damask napkin onto the table. "I've changed my mind, Janei. I think it would be best if you remain here today, at Delacroix."

Disappointment welled, almost strangling her. She had been looking forward to seeing New Orleans.

"No," she said, the stubbornness clear in her tone.

"No? What do you mean, no?" He had been moving toward the door leading to the foyer but her statement stopped him cold. Justin turned back to her, his face a study in controlled annoyance. He did not want to be near her any longer than necessary; she unnerved him, confused him, and excited him. She was dangerous. The mere thought of the long ride to town, alone with her in the carriage, her body so close to his, was nearly his undoing. He couldn't risk it. He wouldn't.

"I want to go into town, Justin. There are things I need."

"Oh, for heaven's sake, Janei, be reasonable. You'd be unescorted for the better part of the day while I attend to my business. I cannot spare the time to squire you around and I certainly do not have the time to stand here and listen to your tantrum. I'm going to be late as it is."

Tantrum? She hadn't been aware she was throwing a tantrum. She changed tactics. "Justin, please. I won't bother you while we're in town, and I don't need an escort. I am perfectly capable of seeing myself around, but I would like to go."

He glared, ready to deny her again.

"And I will go, with you, or without you," she added, holding her breath.

"Why is it so important that you go to town, Janei? What is it that cannot wait? Or is it a who?" his voice was husky with anger.

"Justin, I just want to go to town, that's all." Janelle sighed. "I want a change of scenery. I haven't been away from the plantation in days."

"I would think you had enough excitement here yesterday to satisfy you, but I can see I'm wrong. You're bored, but with you, that's not so unusual, is it?" His fingers rubbed at his temple, as if trying to massage away a headache.

She felt a brief flash of guilt, but didn't back down.

He sighed, dropped his hand and looked back at her. "All right, Janei, you can come. We'll leave as soon as Sammy has the carriage hitched. And bring a small valise, we may stay in town tonight."

After Callie helped her pack a satchel with a change of gowns, one for day, one for evening, and handed her a hat to protect her from the sun, Janelle rushed back downstairs.

She heard the clatter of the carriage wheels roll over the drive. Sammy was leading the carriage horses, his small hand wrapped firmly around the bridle bit of one, the other horse docilely moving alongside. The animals were a matched pair, strong and heavily built, yet sleek and graceful.

And they were both grays! The same color as the horse whose rider had watched her from the hillside the day Gilbert had come across her by the creek, the day he'd practically forced himself on her. She tried to push the suspicion away. It was only coincidence Justin owned a gray. Two grays. There could be others around the countryside, probably quite a few.

She turned her attention to the empty carriage, determined not to let her fears ruin the day. It was a very plain buggy, built to hold only two people, with a hood which curved up from behind to shade the seat. The carriage was black, and on each side, painted on the panel below the seat was the initial *D* in a flourish of gold and red lines, and beneath that was a single step from which hung a brass lantern.

"Where's Justin, Sammy?" Janelle called with a smile.

"I ain't sure, Miss Sara." The young groom stopped the horses just a few feet beyond the entry steps. "He told me to get the buggy hitched and bring it up to the house, and then he left the stable."

Behind her the front door opened and Justin emerged carrying a basket in one hand, a black cape with bright red satin lining in the other.

Janelle's pulses began to race. Could she dare brush this off as another coincidence? How many people wore a cape with red satin lining?

"Are you coming, Janei?" Justin asked impatiently.

"Oh, yes, of course," she mumbled. "What's in the basket?" she added, hoping her voice didn't sound as nervous as she felt.

"A few muffins, apples, and a crock of iced tea. You know Marie always packs a snack for us when we're going to town. Or don't you remember?" His tone dripped with sarcasm, and Janelle almost changed her mind about accompanying him. But it was too late. His hand was extended to assist her into the carriage.

"Of course, I remember. I was just hoping she'd made something besides iced tea, that's all. I'm not really that fond of it."

"You always liked iced tea, Janei. When did you decide otherwise?"

"Oh, I'm just tired of it, I guess." She wished she could bite her tongue off. Maybe it would be better if she just didn't talk at all. Or at least until she could decide whether she dared tell him the truth.

Once in the buggy she turned her attention to tucking the wide skirts of the dress around her legs to keep it from hanging out the side. Justin climbed up to sit beside her and all of a sudden the buggy seemed entirely too small. There was not one square inch of empty space left on the seat. She was painfully cognizant of his muscled thigh pressing against her skirts, their bodies closely wedged together, and the way his strong, corded arm brushed hers as he maneuvered the reins. Remembering the feel of those arms as they'd held her, Janelle turned away and a warm flush spread across her face.

The buggy jogged along for several miles, and they remained silent, each lost within their own thoughts. Several times, while pretending to admire the scenery Janelle allowed her eyes to stray to Justin's face, but his gaze never met hers. He seemed so aloof, almost as if unaware of her presence beside him.

But he was not unaware. Far from it. Justin's cool aloofness was merely a shield, a carefully made barrier to keep her at arm's length. Everything about her since she had returned caught him off guard, and made him question himself. But it was more than that. He should have thrown her out upon her return, disowned her. He had fully intended to do just that, but he hadn't, and now he discovered he wasn't able to. He didn't really want her to go. This newfound knowledge did nothing to improve his temper. He gripped the reins tighter and steeled himself to ignore her.

They passed other plantations and farms, crossed over small creeks and wound around knolls that forced the road to curve. In one wide field several slaves worked over cotton plants, the morning sun hot on their backs.

Uncomfortable on the small seat, Janelle shifted position and noticed a fine layer of dust settling over the orange muslin skirt. As the carriage jostled along, the layer of dust thickened. Every time they hit a rut in the road a new cloud filled the air and fluttered down on them. Janelle thought of the contrast between this ride and what she had been used to in her own time. Jumping into her mother's car and dashing off to Carson City, fifteen miles from the ranch, took her about twenty minutes. At the rate the carriage was moving, she figured they would be lucky to reach New Orleans by midafternoon.

Just as she'd made up her mind the ride was going to take forever, signs of the city began to come into view. The large plantation fields gradually gave way to smaller farms and townhouses. As they grew nearer to the evidence of the city, Janelle felt a thrill of anticipation. Much as she had known New Orleans would look nothing like what she'd seen with Cathy, she found herself unprepared for the scene which unfolded before her. It was so surprising not to see skyscrapers reaching for the clouds, along with telephone poles and utility lines, and cars zooming everywhere. On the other hand, she had expected to see a small, compact little city.

Instead, New Orleans sprawled widely, for as far as she could see. They were approaching the city from the south, with a clear view of the river. Hundreds of ships lined the shores and moved up and down the wide waterway. There were huge sailing ships, paddle wheelers, cargo barges and river rafts. With each passing mile the houses and buildings began to draw closer together and she noticed the varying types of architecture and design. Some were just plain boxes, others had fancy filigreed ironwork balconies, or thin pillars supporting airy galleries. A few landmarks jolted her with an eerie sense of recognition and she felt like a psychic who could see into the future. But, unlike a psychic, Janelle didn't need any special power to know what was to come.

They passed Chalmette Battlefield where Andrew Jackson and the pirate, Lafitte, had fought the invading British in 1815. The old plantation house on the battlefield was already falling into decay, the land having been subdivided off to tenants shortly after Jackson's victory. In later years, a future far from now, Janelle knew it would be a state park, the cannons painted and polished, hundreds of tourists roaming its lawns, children climbing over the once-deadly weapons. And the formerly beautiful house would crumble to ruin, replaced by the Beauregard House, itself saved from decay, restored, and made headquarters for the park service.

They neared the French Quarter and Janelle had to remind herself to call it the Vieux Carré, as she'd heard Justin do. She saw a small wooden sign attached to a corner building that read Rue Esplanade, and then they entered the Quarter. Justin turned the carriage onto Rue Bourbon and Janelle witnessed the 1800s' version of a traffic jam. She looked about in fascination, barely able to contain her delight. This was the future home of the famous jazz clubs, lounges, girlie shows, and all-night party bars. What a change, she mused.

Cumbersome drays and heavily laden work wagons lumbered along the narrow streets and jostled around each other for room. Between the dirt streets and the brick, wood, or in some cases, packed-dirt sidewalks were moatlike ditches filled with dirty, foul-smelling waste water. Planks or slabs of granite were laid here and there along the walk to enable pedestrians to cross over the ditches. Janelle wrinkled her nose at the disgusting odor emanating from the stagnant water. She remembered that in later years doctors had attributed the many lethal yellow fever outbreaks in New Orleans to those filthy ditches.

They turned several more corners and Justin brought the carriage to a stop. "All right, Janei, here you are. I'll meet you at the hotel in three hours," he announced. He was watching her, waiting, his eyes narrowing at her look of confusion.

She looked around quickly, not knowing where she was, or what hotel he meant. There were no street signs in sight, nothing that looked familiar. "Justin, I'm turned around. What street is this?"

"Janei, just what is the matter with you? I'm tired of this act of yours. This is the same place I have always brought you, the same area of merchants you have always patronized." Dark eyes glowered distrustfully at her frozen expression.

Chapter twelve

STARTLED INTO ACTION BY HIS OUTBURST, JAN-
elle began to scramble from the carriage. The heel of
her shoe caught on her ruffled petticoat hem and sent
her flying backwards through the air. But rather than a
brutal meeting with the hard ground, Janelle found herself in Justin's strong arms, cradled against his chest,
his face only inches from hers.

She had been so busy trying to get out of the carriage and avoid his anger that she hadn't noticed him
hastily descend and hurry around to help her. She was
disappointed as the arm beneath her legs withdrew and
her feet touched the ground. But his other arm, around
her waist, held tight.

An odd smile tugged at the corner of his mouth, softening the lean face, as dark smoldering eyes looked
into hers, searching the emerald depths. His fingers
gently traced the line of her jaw, pausing just beneath
her chin.

"Janei, I . . ." His voice, husky with emotion, broke;
his gaze was far away. The aloofness returned, and
his arm dropped from her waist. "Four o'clock, Janei,"
he said coolly, turning to remount the carriage. "Be
here."

Watching him drive away, the carriage disappearing

into the bustle of activity on the street, Janelle felt a sudden sense of loneliness that surprised her. A passing dray almost ran her down, and Janelle realized with a start she was still standing in the street. She hurried across the granite slab that spanned the water-filled ditch between road and walkway. Once on the banquette, she looked about at the various shops, trying to decide which Sara Janei would likely have patronized. Her gaze fell on a small sign. Parisian Modes by Mme Sanite.

A dressmaker. There didn't seem to be anything else nearby that looked as promising. She entered the shop. A small bell hanging above the entrance tinkled merrily, and a woman hurried through a curtained doorway in the opposite wall.

"Ah, Madame Delacroix, you are early, but no matter. I have almost finished the ball gown and only need one more fitting to touch up the final few stitches." The woman's greeting was warm and instant. Gray hair was pulled away from her face and tucked into a knitted snood, square granny glasses perched on the tip of her nose, and she had a body that could only be described as short and round.

"Oh, hello," Janelle said. "Yes, uh, that's fine, thank you." She was relieved to discover that Sara Janei had already ordered something. At least she didn't have to blunder through that situation.

The proprietress reached into an armoire in the corner and swept the mentioned gown into view. Its beauty took Janelle's breath away. The dress was made of a shimmering white satin, the neckline plunging dramatically, a long, dripping ruche of emerald green French Point lace coming together at the bodice to meet two pale pink silk roses that nestled within a swathe of pink ribbon. Tiny white pearls dotted the lace and the sleeves were full, to be worn off the shoulders.

Moments later, as the dress slid over her body, Janelle was embarrassed to find it too snug. She laughed nervously. "I'm sorry, Madame Sanite, I guess I've gained a little weight lately. You'd better let it out a bit." After impulsively calling the woman by name she held her breath, praying this was indeed the proprietress and not a hired helper. Her sigh of relief a second later was almost audible.

"No problem, Madame Delacroix. A snip here, a snip there, and it will be fine. I am afraid, though, I will not have it ready for you today. The soirée, it is next Saturday, no? I will have the gown delivered to you by Friday, no later, I promise."

"Soirée?"

"*Oui*, the annual Delacroix soirée, next Saturday, no?"

"Yes, yes. Things just seem to be slipping my mind lately."

The tinkling of the bell above the door rang out again and both women turned to see who had entered.

Janelle was instantly intrigued. The woman who walked toward them was stunningly beautiful. Her skin was a pale golden brown, lighter than that of the lightest café au lait, accentuated by hair so dark it was beyond black, echoing the ebony of the purest night sky. Her large eyes, which slanted upwards at the outer corners, were so dark as to be almost black.

She looked pointedly at Janelle. "Ah, Madame Delacroix, I am so glad to have found you. I have been hoping you would come to town soon so that we might chat." The woman smiled widely and turned to the dressmaker. "Sanite, some café, perhaps?"

The elderly dressmaker threw an uncertain glance in Janelle's direction, nodded slightly and left the room.

"Now *chérie*, let us talk without pretense, eh?" the woman said, her voice hard and cold. A glitter of loathing sparkled in the ebony eyes and Janelle's heartbeat raced. Did Sara Janei have no friends? she wondered. Since finding herself mysteriously transported to this time, she had constantly been on the receiving end of overt and sly animosity, and she had just about had it with the lot of them, including her surly husband! Or rather, Sara Janei's husband.

"I don't know. . . ."

The newcomer waved a hand impatiently through the air. "Do not make excuses and offerings of ignorance, *chérie*. Celine Gampion is no one's fool, especially yours. I have come to warn you, Madame Delacroix, stay away from Antoine. He is mine, and mine alone. You would do best to remember that. Turn your attentions elsewhere, Madame, if you value your life."

Janelle bristled. She didn't like being talked to as if she were some troublemaker. And she surely did not like threats. "I assure you, Madame Whoever-you-are, that I have no interest in Antoine, or anyone else for that matter. So you can have him."

"You insult my intelligence, Madame Delacroix. I do not appreciate that."

"Then perhaps you should get your facts straight before you accuse somebody of something that has no basis in truth."

"Do not play games with me, Madame," Celine Gampion snapped, her self-control rapidly slipping away. "If you will not listen to my warning then perhaps you need something a little stronger to convince you that I am serious. Antoine de la Reine belongs to me, and only me!" Her hand shot out from the purple folds of her skirt, an ugly little bundle of cloth and hair held between long, graceful fingers. She dropped the thing at Janelle's feet. "Now you will see," she hissed, "now you will be sorry!" Celine swung around in a whirl of silk and left the tiny shop.

The dressmaker reentered the room carrying a tray

laden with cups and a pot of hot, steaming coffee. "Oh, but where is Mademoiselle Gampion?"

"Uh, she had to leave. Something she forgot about elsewhere," Janelle mumbled, still staring at the hideous thing the woman had thrown at her feet. She didn't want to pick it up, didn't even want to touch it. For some unknown reason the mere sight of it sent a shiver of fear through her. Whatever the thing was, Janelle felt certain it was not supposed to mean goodwill.

Sanite paused, the serving tray clattering noisily to the table as she followed the direction of Janelle's gaze and saw the voodoo charm. "Oh, a gris-gris!" she shrieked, chubby fingers twisting about one another. "Where did it come from, Madame?"

"I . . . I don't know," Janelle lied. "Maybe Miss Gampion accidentally dropped it."

"*Oui,* but not by accident." The dressmaker quickly calmed. Once she realized that the evil little amulet was meant for her customer and not herself, Sanite's fear began to dissipate. "The quadroon meant the gris-gris for you, Madame. You must find a way to ward off its evil before it is too late. Mademoiselle Gampion is a very strong conjure woman, taught by the queen herself, Marie Laveau. And her own uncle is Dr. YahYah, a very powerful man. Very powerful. Some say almost as much as Marie Laveau herself. You had best take care, Madame Delacroix." Sanite bent over for a better look at the ugly charm. "That is an *ovanga,* a very evil charm. You must get help, Madame, you should go to Don Pedro. He can give you medicine to ward off this evil curse Mademoiselle Gampion has placed on you."

Janelle shook her head in disbelief. Voodoo, charms, curses? Now what had she, or rather Sara Janei, gotten herself into? "Madame, please, if you would, just throw that thing away."

"Ah, no, Madame Delacroix, you cannot do that," the

dressmaker said, her eyes wide with fear. "The gris-gris is strong medicine, evil medicine, and the *ovanga* very, very bad. You must take it to Don Pedro. He can make a conjure to protect you. You must do this, Madame, you must."

Janelle sighed and picked up her reticule. This was one argument it was best to give in to. She would take the ugly charm with her, but not to Don Pedro, who-ever he was. It would go back to Delacroix with her and into the fireplace. She drew open her purse strings and held it out. Madame Sanite gingerly picked up the gris-gris between two fingers, held it at arm's length, and dropped it into Janelle's reticule.

"Ugh, the nerve of that woman!" Janelle said, tighten-ing the strings of the tiny bag.

"*Oui*, like so many of the *gens de couleur libre,* because they are born free they take many liber-ties, no?

Later, after drinking several cups of the strong café noir and listening to the dressmaker's tales of evil voo-doo curses, Janelle was ready to try to forget the entire episode and get on with the fitting.

She stood while Sanite made alterations to the gown, and browsed through imported fabrics and dress designs. She also made some immediate purchases—several things she hadn't been able to resist. The length of her stay in this time was obviously inde-terminate, so she convinced herself she might as well be comfortable. She bought several loose-fitting camisoles, a new pair of shoes, thankfully in the right size, and a riding habit. Janelle preferred the altered slacks she'd made, but knew they weren't going to prove appropriate for anything other than riding by herself.

The riding habit she chose had actually been made for someone who had since changed her mind and, as luck would have it, the dress fit Janelle perfectly. The shop proprietress seemed shocked that Madame Delacroix would take someone else's reject, but was happy to have the purchase.

"Oh, no, I didn't bring any money," Janelle wailed, suddenly realizing she had no means with which to pay for the things.

"But madame, Monsieur Delacroix always sends me payment at the end of each month. It is not necessary to make payment now." The seamstress glanced questioningly at her.

"Oh, that's right," Janelle said, "I forget. Thank you, Madame Sanite." Mention of Justin reminded her of their meeting. "Oh, my, what time is it, please?" she asked, afraid now that she'd been much longer than Justin had stipulated. He'd be waiting, and if she had any sense of the man at all, Janelle knew he'd be angry if she were late.

But she was not, at least not yet. If she hurried it was still possible to get to the hotel on time; of course, that was if she could find it. "Madame Sanite, I would like to take my purchases home with me today, but my husband has requested that I meet him at the hotel." She didn't know if this was going to work but sincerely hoped so, otherwise she was at a loss. "I can't possibly carry everything myself. Do you think you could find someone to help me?"

"*Oui, oui,* Madame. Pierre, my nephew, will be happy to escort you to the hotel and carry your bundles." The woman disappeared behind the curtained doorway and reappeared momentarily with a young boy in tow. He was only about ten years old, with a mop of brown ringlets and huge golden eyes.

Janelle bid the dressmaker good-bye and followed the boy out the door, he carrying half her purchases, she the other half.

They had walked only a short distance when Janelle followed Pierre through the entrance of a large, elaborately adorned building. The St. Louis Hotel, which had delicate ironwork balustrades across the first and second floors, occupied the width of the entire block.

She followed the boy inside and found herself in a domed rotunda that was breathtakingly magnificent. Sunlight streamed down from the center of the dome and Corinthian pilasters that stood against the walls supported scallop-topped archways. The shouting vendors they had passed on the streets had seemed loud, but the clamor echoing within this great domed reception hall was deafening.

Over half a dozen auctions were taking place under the dome simultaneously, each auctioneer vying to outshout the others. Large oil paintings were being sold on one side of the room, slaves on another, furniture on another. Pierre noticed that she paused and did likewise, waiting patiently. She looked in the direction of the banging of a gavel just as the auctioneer's announcement came loudly: "Sold, fifteen hundred and seventy-five dollars!" Standing on a small makeshift stage beneath the auctioneer were a black man, a woman, and child. The three held tightly to one another, fear shining in their eyes, resignation evident in the droop of their shoulders.

Rigid with outrage, Janelle turned away. Soon, thankfully, there would be no more slavery.

She didn't see Justin anywhere, and hadn't the faintest idea where to look for him. An idea struck and she suggested, "Pierre, maybe Mr. Delacroix is waiting in the dining room. Could we go there?"

Pierre turned back toward the entrance doors, walking so rapidly that Janelle had to run to catch up with him, fearing he'd misunderstood. But when she repeated her request, he just nodded and motioned for her to follow. The boy led her back to the corner, turned, and reentered the hotel from another entrance.

The mahogany-paneled reception area seemed like one from an old movie, complete with a bonily thin, bespectacled desk clerk who smiled at Janelle as if he knew her. Nervous again at encountering someone else who knew Sara Janei, she hastily followed Pierre up the spiral staircase and into the hotel's dining room.

The large room was dimly lit, heavy curtains at the windows, candles on each table, and one massive brass chandelier hanging from the center of the ceiling. As her eyes became accustomed to the dimness, Janelle spotted Justin and began to move through the crowded room toward his table. He was reading something but as she neared he looked up and their eyes met. For one brief moment a smile played on his face, and her troubled heart lightened. With a controlled grace he rose from the table, handed several coins to Pierre, who was busily stacking her packages nearby, and resumed his seat.

"Did you have a pleasant day, Justin?" she asked, unable to keep a hint of sarcasm out of her voice. His aloof attitude was beginning to get tiresome.

Ignoring her question, Justin turned in his seat and raised a hand, signaling for a waiter. "What would you like, Janei?"

"I . . . I don't know. Why don't you order for me." There was no menu, and one could hardly order a cheeseburger in this elegant restaurant. It was safer to let Justin do it.

If whatever he ordered tasted as good as it sounded, she knew she was in for a treat. *Canapés de volaille, du gru aux oeufs, haricots verts en salade*, and so much more she couldn't remember what he'd said.

Silence hung heavy between them as they waited for

their meal. Justin's attention returned to the newspaper he'd spread out on the table. Janelle inspected the others in the room.

Throughout their meal she kept up a running line of chatter, keeping the topics light. She was determined not to let him retreat again behind that cold, untouchable barrier he used against her. By the time they finished, Justin had relaxed, conversing with her congenially.

"It appears I made quite a mistake in not purchasing that lot on St. Charles. Seems the Garden District is flourishing. Although I never thought the Northerners would come down here in such hordes. It is too bad. We could have done without them quite nicely."

"Do you really find them that terrible, Justin?"

"That's an unusual question coming from you, Janei. Are you not the one who has always vehemently denounced them as heathens? Or have you changed your mind?" His stare was piercing.

"Oh, I just haven't really given it much thought lately. Anyway, will we be going home now?" She desperately attempted to change the subject. It seemed that every conversation with him led to trouble.

"No, I've registered with the hotel. I'm afraid I am unable to conclude my business as quickly as I'd hoped. I have another meeting tomorrow morning and Dominic down at the bank has invited us to join him and his wife at the opera tonight. For now you may remain here at the shops if you like, but I must go to the cabildo and then over to the state legislature. I may also have to go to the docks, and I am sure you would rather not accompany me there."

"Oh, the opera, how nice," Janelle mumbled, trying to suppress the flash of panic that washed over her. Much as she'd love to see the opera, the idea of possibly being surrounded by people Sara Janei knew, and who had known her, was terrifying.

"Yes, well, Dominic's carriage will be by for us at eight. Now, I really must be going. Are you remaining here?"

"I think I'd like to take a walk in the Square, and maybe just look at the river," she enthused, anxious to see more of the Quarter.

"The Square? What Square? Oh, you mean Jackson Square." He nodded. "I am not used to the name change. It has been only a few months now, although I fail to see why, just because the city dedicated a statue to Jackson, they felt compelled to also rename the Place d'Armes."

Their carriage waited at the hotel entrance. Justin had strongly opposed her intention of strolling about the Square, relenting only at her promise to hire a coach and be back at the hotel well before darkness fell. He had also insisted on driving her there himself.

He stopped the carriage across from the cathedral, and helped her out. "You really should not be out without an escort, Janei," he said, wondering why he even cared. "Forget the coach. I'll return for you within the hour. But don't go too far. I would not want to have to search for you." He climbed back to his seat, and was gone.

The Square itself was quite different from the one she remembered visiting with Cathy. The Pontalba Apartments on either side looked the same, only newer, but the slowly waters of the Mississippi seemed much closer, at the foot of the wharves only yards away rather than behind the cement levee Janelle remembered. The trees in the Square were sparse, a few mature live oaks, but most mere saplings. Rose gardens and lawn were divided by graveled paths and in the center proudly stood the statue of Andrew Jackson, its bronze gleaming now, not yet tarnished from age and weather. As she admired the statue her gaze moved to its solid base and she smiled. Cathy's words echoed in her memory.

The citizens of New Orleans, already outraged at their city being occupied by enemy troops during the Civil War, had almost lost all self-control when the commanding Union general ordered that an inscription be placed on their beloved hero's statue. Something to do with preserving the Union, Janelle remembered, but couldn't recall the exact words. The statue's base was now bare, the fated inscription still a thing of the future.

Suddenly, someone was at her back, a hand on her shoulder, gripping it gently, but firmly.

"Ah, *bien-aimé*, what a pleasant surprise. I had just about decided you had forsaken me."

Janelle whirled around, jerking away from his hold on her. She found herself staring up into the most beautiful black eyes, which shone with a devilish spark of mischief. The stranger was at least a dozen years her senior and dashingly handsome in a rather dangerous way. A curl of brown hair fell rakishly over his wide forehead and a mustache curved upward as he smiled disarmingly at her. His brown frock coat and trousers were tailored snugly to fit every curving muscle of his tall, lithe body. Manicured hands, each bejeweled with several sparkling rings, reached out for her again. She took a step back in an attempt to put some space between them but he immediately closed the gap, his eyes laughing outrageously at her even as he moved to block her escape.

Janelle felt instinctively this was a man most women would stay away from.

"Come, *chère,* you have no greeting for your Antoine? After so long apart?" His voice was soft and teasing. Before she could protest he had wrapped his fingers around her wrist and was guiding her to the shade of an oak tree. He pulled her beneath the draping moss which acted as a partial curtain.

But the shroud of nature was not enough to screen them from the penetrating stare that came from the shadows of the cathedral nearby. As Celine watched Antoine and Sara Janei, she fanned herself furiously, her knuckles white from the pressure she exerted on the thin whalebone spines of the fan. She had warned the woman, told her explicitly to stay away from Antoine. If Sara Janei Delacroix would not heed the warning, then Celine Gampion knew she must make good her threat. There was no other way.

Janelle yanked her hand away from Antoine's, her mind racing, searching for some way to rescue herself from this situation. She had to take care. The last thing she needed was to make him suspicious of her. If she did, it might complicate her situation further, yet she did not want to find herself in his embrace either. Judging from the way he was looking at her, she knew that was just what he had in mind.

"Please, Antoine, this is neither the time nor place," she declared, hoping she sounded convincing.

"But, *chérie,* we have always met at the statue, although I must confess, I knew you were in town and was beginning to think you would not come." His hand rubbed up her arm, moved to brush her cheek, then curled swiftly around to the back of her neck to clasp her toward him.

"No." She pulled away. She was horrified by the confirmation of yet another lover. Damn, how many were there?

His arms dropped to his sides and his eyes narrowed. "Something is very wrong here, *chérie.* You have changed. I see the same Sara Janei on the outside, but what has happened to the passion, the spark on the inside?"

"It . . . it's just not the right time. I can't explain now, just trust me. Anyway, you still have Celine to warm your bed." Janelle started to turn away, a satisfied smile on her lips. She hoped her comment sounded like something Sara Janei would say.

"*Non, chérie,* Celine means nothing to me. Only you. Come, we should not concern ourselves with such foolish trivialities. They are not important."

His arms encircled her so swiftly that Janelle was pulled into his embrace before she could resist. She found herself suddenly helpless, arms pinioned, body pressed so tightly against his she could hardly breathe. Antoine's lips covered hers, smothering her protests. For a moment Janelle was so shocked and outraged she stood motionless, unable to react.

She began to twist in his arms, tearing her lips from his. Antoine's hand slid to the back of her neck, strong fingers holding her still and forcing her to accept his kiss. Tiny sounds of protest filled Janelle's throat, her free arm pushed at his chest, tore at the velvet coat that draped his shoulders, but still Antoine held tight. His mouth ravaged hers, exploring, demanding response. Finally, with one desperate shove against him, twisting her body at the same time, Janelle managed to free herself. Without thinking, or considering the consequences, she struck his face. His dark cheek reddened instantly with the imprint of her hand.

Janelle took a step back. Her heel caught on an exposed tree root and she began to fall. Antoine lunged forward, his arms grasping her waist and pulled her back to her feet. His grip remained tight as he studied her. Slowly his arms slid away.

She had tasted the whiskey on his breath, felt the iron-willed determination in his embrace, sensed the recklessness that drove him . . . and it scared her. This was not a man to anger.

His looks were almost classic, out of Greek mythology, but there was something about Antoine de la Reine that disturbed her. There was a sinister air about him, mixed with an aura of forced bravado, and yet there was also warmth. Janelle had a feeling that the world had once held great promise for Antoine, but something had gone wrong. Somehow the dream had been destroyed, or discarded.

Antoine moved toward her, a flicker of barely leashed violence within the black depths of his eyes. "What is this, *chérie*? What gambit do you play with me this time?"

Games! He'd accused her—no, Sara Janei—of playing games with his emotions. Justin had made the same accusation. Was that all the woman had ever done? Had there been no feeling in Sara Janei Delacroix? No emotion behind any of her actions? Despite her inner turmoil, Janelle's voice was calm as she answered, "This is no game, Antoine, believe me."

"Contact me when you are ready, *chérie*," he said coldly. "You know where to find me, Sara, but do not wait long, I am not a patient man."

Janelle looked up quickly, his last words all too familiar. Hadn't Gilbert Foucheau said almost the same thing?

Nodding his dark head in a mock bow, Antoine turned and strode from the park, disappearing into the shadows of a small alley that ran between the cabildo and the cathedral. As she watched his departure, Janelle exhaled sharply at noticing something that sent her heart plunging.

The Delacroix carriage had just come around the corner of the *Presbytere* and was approaching the Square. Janelle held her breath, but if Justin recognized Antoine, he gave no sign of it, and yet Janelle was certain they passed within only a few feet of each other.

The carriage stopped directly before the Square gates, the soft rays of the setting sun reflected in the burnished metal of the brass lantern that hung beneath the boarding step. Beneath the buggy's raised hood, Justin remained seated, lost in the shadows of dusk.

Janelle stood staring into the blackness of the buggy's interior, trying to see the strong, bronzed face that, against all reason and sanity, was becoming dear to her, but it was too dark. She felt a flutter of apprehension.

As Justin got out of the carriage, she saw his clenched jaw and the coldness sparkling within his eyes.

So, he had seen Antoine, and once again misconstrued her behavior. And it hurt, damn it. And because of the hurt, her anger boiled over, bubbling to the surface and consuming all reason.

Chapter thirteen

"I DON'T NEED YOUR HELP." JANELLE SLAPPED away the offered hand. Grappling with the heavy petticoats and hoop cage, she made several attempts to mount the carriage steps. The first time, her foot securely on the step, skirts held high, she almost broke her neck when she discovered, too late, the hem of a petticoat was caught under her heel. On her second attempt she just couldn't seem to get her balance going in the right direction. Finally, on the third try, jaw set in determination, she made it into the seat.

Justin climbed aboard, snapped the reins against the horses' flanks, and the carriage jerked into motion, throwing Janelle against the back of the seat.

The carriage moved through the streets at a brisk pace but it soon became evident to Janelle they were not headed for the hotel. Within moments the loud, boisterous cries of a dozen street vendors assaulted her ears and the smell of fresh vegetables, game, poultry, fish, and sweet candies mingled together and wafted through the sultry air.

An open-air market came into view. Numerous hip-roofed structures, their canvas walls rolled to the ceiling, covered the area. Among the stalls, crowds of people moved about making their purchases. Freshly caught fish lay on a long table, their blue-gray bodies glistening in the light from overhead lanterns, and beside the table a deep barrel held tiny red crawfish, their miniature claws snapping at the air as they wriggled over one another. Cocoa brown eggs were wrapped in Spanish moss to protect the delicate shells, vegetables lay wilted from the afternoon heat, sharing space with sharp-edged pineapples and mountains of fat, golden plantains. Janelle's eyes were wide with fascination as she looked at the bustling scene. Ducks and geese hung from the rafters of the poultry section, as well as quail, chickens, and turkeys. An Indian sat cross-legged beside a mound of woven baskets, a gaudy blanket draped over his shoulders, and flower sellers continually arranged their bouquets, tossing the dead or sun-wilted blooms onto the ground. Large turtles lay asleep atop barrels, hens squawked from their cages, and a dozen languages filled the air as the vendors hawked their wares.

Justin stopped the carriage in the midst of this confusion and without a word to Janelle, jumped to the ground and disappeared into the crowd. She was hypnotized by the surrounding activity. An old black woman in a gingham dress and muslin apron came up to the carriage, her scrawny arm raised to help support the large basket balanced on her head.

"Pr'lines? Yo' buy pr'lines?" she asked loudly, thrusting a large, flat pancake of candy under Janelle's nose.

She shook her head and the woman moved away, still calling out loudly to no one in particular.

"I gots a present for the lady," a deep voice said from the opposite side of the carriage.

Janelle found herself confronted by a massively built black man, a wide grin plastered on his extremely ugly face. Small lines of scar tissue beneath the dark skin curved about his cheeks, chin, and forehead in a grotesque design, and his head was covered with a huge turban of red silk, several black plumes held to the front by a large silver brooch.

"No, thank you, really," Janelle protested. She tried to stop herself from cringing against the back of the seat. He made her nervous, his huge, leering face poking into the carriage after her, one big, powerful hand rubbing at the stubble on his chin.

"Oh, you have to take it, missy. Ol' Majue be in big trouble if'n you don't."

Before Janelle could protest further, his other hand whipped out from behind his back and settled on the carriage seat, only inches from her skirt. His long fingers unfurled and moved away, leaving a small white box no bigger than one holding a ring. She looked up to tell him again that she couldn't accept it, but he was gone, vanished into the crowd as if he'd never existed.

With trepidation, Janelle reached for the box, her fingers shaking as they closed around it. She lifted the lid and caught her breath at sight of the tiny object inside. A wax heart lay on a bed of red velvet, a dozen seamstress pins stuck into its center. A soft gasp escaped Janelle's lips, and she flung the box away, sending it and its evil-looking contents flying through the air to splatter upon the hard-packed ground.

Melodious yet demonic laughter met her ears; the sound floated above the din of busy vendors. It sent a shiver up her spine, and she wished desperately for Justin to be back. Who had sent that man and his horrible little present? Celine Gampion? An obvious suspect. But how many others were there? How many enemies did Sara Janei have?

Justin returned moments later carrying a large burlap bag, tossed it into the box at the rear of the buggy, climbed to his seat, and immediately urged the large gray geldings into movement. Not once did he look at or address Janelle.

It took only a few short minutes to travel the now almost empty streets back to the hotel. Justin helped her to step from the carriage, then turned and went his way through the lobby and climbed the stairs to the second floor. Janelle hastily followed while trying desperately not to trip over her skirts. At the end of a long hallway he paused before a door, inserted a key from his pocket, and entered the room. He left the door open behind him and Janelle standing alone in the hall.

"Dominic will be by for us in an hour. I expect that is enough time for you to ready yourself," he said tersely over his shoulder. He flung his jacket across a chair and stretched out on the bed.

She entered the room, closing the door behind her, and bit her tongue on the anger simmering in her breast. There was no point in trying to tell him about the unnerving confrontation with Celine Gampion, or the incident at the marketplace. He had seen Antoine leaving the Square, and she felt certain Justin believed she had planned to meet Antoine there. He was in no mood to listen or understand. His temper would most probably spoil the evening, but she'd just try to ignore him. Drat the man!

The two gowns that Callie had put in Janelle's satchel had been unpacked, pressed, and were hanging on the back of the dressing room door, along with Justin's dress suit.

"Aren't you going to get ready?" she asked coolly, the strain in her voice evident even to her own ears.

Justin lay on the bed, his eyes closed. She knew he wasn't asleep, but he didn't answer. "Justin?" she questioned softly.

"Just get yourself ready, Janei," he said.

He was struggling with the desire to leap from the bed and take her in his arms, to feel the silken warmth of her golden skin, to again know the intimacy of her lithe body. What was the matter with him? He had every reason to want to strangle her. Instead, he dreamed of loving her.

Unable to help herself, feeling certain his anger stemmed from seeing Antoine, Janelle lashed out at him, "For heaven's sake, Justin! Nothing happened in the park with Antoine. He tried to kiss me and I told him to get lost. Now will you please talk to me?"

Instead of the angry retort she half expected, he remained silent. He made no indication he'd even heard her.

"Justin, damn it, answer me!"

"Janei, please calm down," he said quietly, still not moving a muscle. "Your actions are your own business, not mine. I would just like to enjoy the opera tonight, with or without you. It is your choice."

"Oh! You're impossible!" Janelle grabbed a gown from the hook, went into the dressing room and slammed the door behind her. Justin was fully dressed, but still fiddling with his cravat when she returned to the bedroom.

"I'm ready," she announced coldly, moving to stand at the window to await him.

He looked at her through hooded eyes, careful not to let her notice. She was a vision in white, the moonlight beyond casting her in an ethereal glow and turning her auburn curls into coils of simmering flame. Her dress was a simple white silk, the tightly fitted bodice molding itself to the tantalizing curve of her breasts, the wide puffed sleeves, hugging the edge of her shoulders. A man of strong will and control, Justin was surprised yet again to feel his body harden with desire and need for her.

A knock sounded on the door, pulling his attention from her. *"Entrez,"* Justin called loudly, his voice husky with emotion.

A thin black man, impeccably dressed, stepped into the room; a folded piece of paper lay in the center of a silver platter balanced on his hand. He bowed deeply, and backed his way out of the room after Justin accepted the paper.

"It seems our hosts are downstairs. Shall we go?" he said after glancing at the note.

Dominic Rochemore rushed to the bottom of the spiral staircase as Justin and Janelle descended to greet them profusely. The thin Creole seemed full of exuberance. Although he had beautiful black hair, the rest of Dominic was pale and colorless, his skin a sickly white and his eyes an almost nondescript light brown.

Surprisingly Justin offered Janelle his arm as they followed Dominic out the door to a waiting carriage. It proved to be a gaudily decorated landau, the passenger box completely glassed in, the driver, seated in front of the box, outfitted in a bright red livery. Mrs. Rochemore squealed a greeting as her husband opened the door for their guests.

"Oh, my dear Sara, it's sooo good to see you again. I do so hope you enjoy this opera." She fanned herself furiously. Felicity Rochemore was physically the opposite of her thin husband, and Janelle had to force herself not to stare in surprise. She was not fat, merely very ample. Heavy breasts seemed almost stuffed into and barely contained in the shallow bodice of a pale yellow gown. She was not what Janelle had expected to see with the pale Creole.

"I'm sure I will, Madame Rochemore. I'm looking forward to it. I've never been . . ." Janelle just managed to clamp her mouth shut in time, but luckily no one seemed to have noticed.

The carriage began to move and Janelle became all too aware of Justin sitting beside her.

"Dominic did tell you that we're going to the St. Charles rather than the Theatre d'Orleans tonight, didn't he?" Madame Rochemore asked.

"No," Justin said, "he did not. I am not too sure I would have accepted your invitation, Dominic, had I known that." His chuckle softened the harshness of his words.

Dominic laughed. "That's exactly why I didn't tell you, Justin. You're such a bore about these things. So what if the St. Charles is across Rue Canal, and attended mostly by the Americans, it is good to break a habit once in awhile. Anyway, you'll enjoy it, I promise."

When the carriage halted at the steps of the opera house, Janelle's eyes lit excitedly at the sight of the huge Corinthian columns and bas-relief carvings that fronted the building. The Rochemore loge was on the second floor. The decor nearly took Janelle's breath away. Catching her immediate attention was a painting on the stage curtain of Shakespeare being borne skyward on the wings of an American eagle. Gilded and carved balustrades curved about the tiers and Ionic columns rose to the high circular ceiling.

At the intermission, the magnificent gas chandelier overhead blazed with renewed light. Justin and Dominic excused themselves to stroll the gallery but Madame Rochemore made no attempt to leave her seat and Janelle felt compelled to remain with the woman, though she would have preferred to explore.

Barely five minutes after the men had left the box, Janelle discovered why Madame Rochemore had stayed put. The woman was asleep. Janelle clapped a gloved hand to her mouth to stifle a laugh. The woman's chin rested on her ample chest, and a soft but steady snoring sound had begun to echo from her nose.

"I am afraid your friend is not much company for you this night, *chérie*," Antoine whispered at Janelle's shoulder, his face so close that she could feel his warm breath on her skin.

Janelle spun around to face him. "What are you doing here?" She was stunned at his audacity.

"Enjoying the show, *ma petite,* what else?"

"Oh, Antoine, do you know the trouble you've caused me? That stunt in the Square earlier." She glanced quickly at the still-sleeping woman. "That was too much. Now go away."

He laughed softly and ran a finger down her cheek.

"Antoine, please," Janelle whispered. She could hardly restrain herself from smacking his hand away. Amorous Frenchmen she could do without tonight.

"Oh, *ma chère,* but you are so beautiful. How can I help myself?"

"Antoine, this is dangerous. Please, you must leave. Justin saw us this afternoon," she said anxiously, scanning the gallery for her husband.

"Ah, then that should make things easier, *ma petite.*"

"Easier? Antoine, please just go away. For now," she added quickly, trying to soothe the man's pride.

He blew a kiss at her. "All right, I will leave, but not for long. Remember that, heh? Not for long."

She held her breath until Antoine was well out of the area, the nervous knot in her stomach slowly dissolving. Whatever was she going to do? How many more lovers were going to come slinking out of the woodwork at her?

Mere seconds elapsed between Antoine's departure and Justin's return. He didn't say anything, but when their eyes met Janelle knew that he had seen Antoine at her side and her spirits plunged.

She leaned close to his ear and said sincerely, "Please, Justin, it's not what you think."

"I am not a fool, Janei. I know what my eyes see." He turned his back on her and engaged Dominic in conversation.

Silently cursing the day she'd landed on Justin's doorstep, Janelle stared blindly at the stage, tears stinging her eyes. She shouldn't care what he thought. She shouldn't, but her heart was feeling bruised all the same.

By the time their hosts returned them to the hotel, Janelle was having a difficult time being civil. It hadn't taken long to decide Madame Rochemore was a snob, and boring besides, and her husband was merely a pompous little dandy. Of course, she might have felt a little more generous if Justin hadn't been treating her as if she had leprosy. But as it was, her mood had turned black.

Justin paid no attention. Once back in their room he immediately disrobed, climbed into bed, pulled the covers up to his neck, closed his eyes, and turned on his side.

"Great!" Janelle swore softly. Grabbing her cloak she stormed from the room and, forgetting to lift her mass of petticoats, almost fell down the huge spiral staircase in her haste. Rushing across the lobby, she ignored the desk clerk's inquiry if he should summon a carriage and practically flew out the door. She needed to walk, to breathe fresh air, to get away from Justin for a while, to think. Not that he would be even remotely concerned if she never returned, Janelle thought bitterly. She felt more alone and helpless than ever.

The streets were deserted and the night was quiet except for the faint strains of music coming from a saloon several blocks away. Lanterns hung on ropes stretched the width of the street from rooftop to rooftop, but they proved dim lighting, casting eerie shadows over the buildings and leaving corners and niches in total darkness.

Jackson Square was beautiful by moonlight, if a bit spooky, but the darkness of night had never frightened Janelle. Back home on her family's ranch in Nevada, it had been her favorite time, and she had frequently taken long walks under a full moon, enjoying the softness the night light gave to the harsh land. However, this darkness brought no peace to her confused heart, and she no longer knew what she was feeling or thinking.

Light from the cabildo and Pontabla Apartments cast pale reflections on the newly landscaped grounds, and the bronze statue of Andrew Jackson on his rearing steed glistened under the soft light. Several riverboats docked across the levee from the Square drew her attention. Each boat had twin smokestacks, painted black, the metal feathered at the edges where the smoke billowed out. Most of the boats were white, huge names emblazoned on their sides, enormous paddle wheels dimly silhouetted against the sky. Tall piles of freight lined the docks waiting to be hauled on board; bales of cotton stood stacked five to six squares high, and wooden kegs rose in mountainous piles alongside crates of dry goods and tied bales of tobacco.

Janelle wasn't sure how long she'd been wandering aimlessly before she began to feel chilled from a slight breeze coming in off the river. Sounds of laughter broke out nearby and she suddenly realized the foolishness of her midnight walk.

"Well, lookee what we got here, Jake. Ain't she purty?"

Janelle whirled around to see two men standing behind her. She'd been so preoccupied with her own thoughts and troubles she hadn't heard them approach. An alarm rang in her mind at the realization she was alone on a desolate street, still several blocks from the safety of the hotel. Both men were filthy, their clothes covered with dirt and grease, their faces coarse and unshaven. A well-chewed but unlit cigar hung from the fleshy lips of the one who had spoken. Both were obviously quite drunk.

The one called Jake, short and stockily built, burped loudly and staggered forward. "Think she wants ta have a good time with us, Davey?"

Davey stepped up beside Janelle and grabbed her arm, his dirty fingers closing painfully around her flesh. When she twisted in an effort to get away, he grabbed the other arm and forced her to face him, his beady eyes and hooked nose, badly misshapen by one too many barroom brawls, only inches from hers. "Whatsa matter, sweetie? Don't ya wanna have fun with Jake and me? Ain't we good enough for ya?"

"Let me go," Janelle demanded, jerking her arms frantically.

Davey laughed, his tobacco-stained lips puckering together and searching the air for hers.

"Ah, c'mon, Davey, she don't wanna play," Jake moaned. He stumbled against a tree and almost fell to the ground.

"No, you go on. Me and my little sweetie gonna have us a party, ain't that right, sweetie?" Davey snickered, yanking Janelle toward the entrance gates of the Square.

"Let me go, you creep!" she yelled, stamping a heel down hard on his boot. She could only wish she were wearing spiked high heels instead of these ridiculous satin slippers.

Davey howled in pain, cursing loudly, but he didn't loosen his hold on her arms. Swiftly she brought up her knee. With another roar of agony, her would-be attacker released her and fell to the ground, screaming obscenities she'd never even heard before.

"Congratulations, Janei, that was very good," came a silky voice from the shadows.

Janelle spun around, her green eyes blazing with fury. "Justin! Have you been standing there the whole time?"

He nodded, smiling crookedly.

"And you let me fight off this jerk by myself? What kind of man are you?" She glared at the figure leaning leisurely against a street post. What little anger she had released in besting Davey returned twofold.

"A very entertained one at the moment. I was here if you needed me, but you seemed to be doing quite well on your own. I didn't think you had that type of mettle in you, Janei."

"Damn you, Justin Delacroix. No, don't come near me," she said when he offered his hand. "What good are you to me now?"

Justin shrugged. "As you wish. I merely thought I would escort you back to the hotel. One never knows how many others like this—" he gestured at Davey still lying doubled up and moaning on the ground "—could be lurking about in the shadows."

"You can escort me. I don't have to take your arm," Janelle declared, moving stiffly to his side.

All the way back to the hotel Janelle wondered why Justin had come after her. Had he thought to protect her, and found she didn't need it?

She was getting so tired of this charade, but she couldn't help her suspicions. He was the one who had withdrawn, seducing her and then pulling away, shielding himself with cold contempt and never giving her the chance to explain anything.

And tonight was no different. Once back in their room, Justin again shed his clothing and went to bed with a darkly menacing order that she stay in the room this time.

The next morning Janelle awoke to find Justin already gone. They had slept in the same bed, with at least a foot of space between them, never touching the entire night. A sense of disappointment filled her. The room seemed cold and lonely without him.

He had left a note on the dresser. His meeting would last until midafternoon. He would be back by three o'clock. It was not yet nine.

The hours passed slowly. Deciding a breath of fresh air would help clear her head, Janelle left the hotel to browse the streets of the Quarter.

She returned feeling refreshed and, for no apparent reason, slightly optimistic.

The hotel registrar called as she passed through the lobby, beckoning her to the front desk. "Madame Delacroix, *s'il vous plaît*, would you like your carriage brought around now?"

"Well, no, I have to wait for my husband to return."

"Oh, he has, Madame. Monsieur Delacroix is upstairs in your room. I assumed upon your return you would be wanting to leave immediately, but there's no rush, of course. Just let me know and I will have your carriage brought around anytime."

Janelle hurried up the stairs, pausing before the door to their room to catch her breath. Smiling, she entered. He sat in a chair beside the window, the bright light of the late afternoon sun on his shoulders. One look into his eyes alerted her to his irritation.

"I'm sorry I'm late, Justin," she said cheerfully. "Are we leaving right away?"

"It seems you have received a present while I was gone, or had you already noticed?" Justin said between clenched teeth, his voice low and hard.

A porcelain vase, glazed pink and edged with gold, sat on the dresser top. Twelve perfect roses filled the vase, their blossoms the brilliant white of freshly fallen snow.

"Oh, Justin, thank you." Relief swept through her. He

was only upset that she hadn't been there to receive his gift.

"I did not send them, Janei," he declared, watching her through narrowed eyes.

"Then . . . who?" A tremor of unease shot up her spine.

"I am sure you would know better than I."

She moved to the dresser. "But, there's no card, and I . . ."

"Pack your things, Janei, I shall wait for you in the dining room." He moved past her and snatched at the valise sitting on the bed. "I will send a porter for your things. Do not be long. It will be nearing dark by the time we are ready to leave as it is." The door snapped shut behind him.

Her gaze shifted from the closed door to the flowers. Who had sent them? And why? It had been an intentionally cruel thing to do. Whoever had done it had to know she was here with Justin. Stuffing her belongings hastily into the carpetbag, Janelle left the room and hurried down the hall. Justin was angry but there was no reason. They were going to have to talk. She was getting fed up with constantly being blamed, teased, seduced, screamed at, and threatened. Sara Janei had been one hell of a woman, Janelle thought, and that was not meant as a compliment.

She attempted to talk to Justin over dinner, but at his icy silence, and the continual stares of the others in the room, she gave up in angry frustration.

Later, in the carriage, Justin's face was a controlled mask. The scar stood out as a muscle twitched in his jaw. Janelle's heart sank. Would they never be able to look at each other without feeling suspicion? If fate, or whatever it was, left her in this time, with him, would her every movement, every utterance always be mistaken for that of Sara Janei's?

With an abrupt gesture Justin slapped the reins, and the horses bolted into movement. They were soon out of town, the horses clopping along at a brisk pace.

Janelle leaned back against the seat, resting her head on the buggy's hood. She would talk to Justin later. Or at least she'd try. After he'd had time to calm down. Maybe then he would listen. The aftereffects of their large meal and the evening's sultry warmth began to lull her senses, and Janelle closed her eyes. She only needed to rest, just for a moment, but sleep came instead.

Without warning a loud cracking sound snapped in the air.

Chapter fourteen

THE FRANTIC NEIGHING OF THE HORSES AND the sudden jerk of the carriage startled Janelle awake. She sat up, only to find to her horror that the carriage was toppling sideways. Whinnying in panic, the horses fought for control over the harness that was dragging them toward the slope at the edge of the road. The carriage bounced on its springs, shook convulsively, and then slid from the road. Someone screamed, and as she felt herself falling off her seat in a tumble of clothes and limbs, Janelle realized the sound was coming from her own throat.

The moment the buggy began to turn over, Justin, in an effort to save them both, threw down the reins, grabbed a handful of Janelle's skirts and jumped. He landed on his shoulder, the hard ground jarring his body viciously. Stunned, he lay quiet, his own labored breathing thunderous in his ears. Long moments later his fingers relaxed enough to release the thin strip of orange material.

Pushing himself to a sitting position, he immediately regretted the movement as his head filled with pain, the world spinning about crazily as he tried to look around. Justin hung his head between his knees, and waited for the dizziness to pass. He got to his feet, but fell back on his knees twice before finally being able to stand. He felt unsteady, his legs ready to buckle at any moment, his shoulder aching with pain beyond belief. A thin trickle of blood slid down past the corner of his left eye and he raised a hand to his temple to feel the skin, where his head had met the hard earth.

The buggy lay in a ditch at the side of the road, its hood crushed beneath the weight of the body, the four wheels sticking up over the rise of the road. The buggy hitch had snapped, releasing the horses, so that the animals stood nervously together at the front of the toppled vehicle. Their harness was still intact, which forced them to remain side by side, and the reins tangled in the wreckage held them prisoner.

Justin looked around the roadside but found himself alone, the thin strip of ragged orange material lying on the ground beside his feet. Panic engulfed him, and forgetting his own injuries, he ran to the carriage, slid down the sloping embankment and scrambled around the hood. Finally he saw her. She was pinned beneath the body of the carriage, only her shoulders and head visible.

He felt his heart lurch painfully within his chest, felt the breath in his throat snag, and knew fear, real, terrifying fear that he had lost her. He leaned close, and raised a trembling hand to her cheek. She was breathing, each breath shallow and ragged, but steady, her face ashen and drawn with pain. The weight of the carriage was slowly crushing her chest, squeezing ribs against lungs. His fingers caressed her face, and he whispered her name, but she did not respond.

He gripped the side of the carriage seat rail and pushed desperately, his muscles straining under the weight, but it was too heavy. Gasping in ragged gulps of air, Justin looked about, frantic. Nearby he spotted the thin trunk of a fallen sassafras tree and hurriedly broke off its dead branches. Gripping it tightly in both hands at the thickest end, he swung the dead trunk in the air and slammed it against the base of a nearby cypress. The impact almost threw him to his knees and sent tremors of aftershock into his injured arm. The thin, upper portion of the trunk broke off. He dragged the stump back to the buggy, released the harness latch, led the horses to the roadside and secured the latch and reins to the carriage seat railing. Then he urged the big grays into movement. Yelling loudly, he slapped the reins against the horses' flanks as encouragement, while his other hand held the sassafras trunk ready.

The large grays strained against the makeshift hitch and the buggy shook, raising slightly. Within seconds there was enough room between the carriage and the ground to wedge the trunk upright into the space. Justin hastily tied the reins around the seat rail to stabilize the horses' pull, and dropped to his knees and dragged Janelle from beneath the massive weight. She stirred at the movement, calling his name in a choked whisper.

"It's all right, Janei, I have you," he murmured, holding her cautiously in his lap, fearful of hurting her further. "You're safe now." Cradling her head against his chest, he pushed aside the rumpled folds of her gown and splintered remains of her hoopskirt in order to run a hand slowly up and down her legs, gently feeling each one for breaks. His fingers moved in turn over her ribcage, arms and shoulders. Nothing appeared broken, but she cried out when his hand slid over her upper arm. Pushing the torn and dirty material of her sleeve aside, he saw the long gash that ran from wrist to elbow. Blood had already started to crust on the torn skin.

Her eyes were closed, her pallor ghostly and waxen. Memories clouded his mind then, but it was the memory of a Sara Janei he had never known existed. She had been so different in his arms that night of their lovemaking—all fire and all giving without artifice or restraint. The Sara Janei who had returned to Delacroix was not the same one who had disappeared. She had changed. It showed in a dozen ways; small kindnesses to the servants, little gestures, and her kiss. Her lips didn't lie when she kissed him.

Much as he had tried to deny his changing feelings, he found himself captivated by the innocence and mystery of her. Something new was growing between them, he'd felt it, resisted it, denied it. The fierce emotions she had invoked in him since her return were unfamiliar, uncomfortable, and in a tangle of confusion.

"Janei, can you hear me?"

A smile of relief touched his lips when he noticed the faint fluttering of her dark lashes at his whispered words. Glazed eyes looked up into concerned ones.

"Thank you, Justin." She lifted a trembling finger to brush softly across his lips only a second before she slipped back into unconsciousness.

With a sigh, his head bowed against hers and Justin held her to him, murmuring soothing words that began once again to slowly rouse her from her hazy state. With fierce protectiveness he held her against his chest, heedless of the throbbing pain in his shoulder, willing the strength of his own body into hers.

He was still breathing heavily, unaware that the labored rise and fall of his chest, the steady drumming of his heart were more soothing to her than his soft words. The darkness began to clear from her mind and she stirred, lifting a hand to gently touch his bowed head.

A rush of relief choked him at her trembling touch. "Sweet God in heaven, thank you," he murmured, his words choked with emotion. "I was afraid you were going to die." He pressed his lips to her forehead. He held her for a long moment, one strong hand tenderly stroking the silken tendrils that cascaded loosely about her shoulders.

Tears welled in her eyes, and Janelle longed for nothing more than to remain in his arms, safe and warm, the terrifying event that had led up to this moment, and all the suspicions of the past, forgotten.

"I have to get you to the house, Janei," Justin said finally. He lifted her with gentle care. He shed his jacket and swathed her in its warmth before leaving to check the carriage. He climbed to the roadside where the wheels stuck upwards, one slowly spinning as if trying to ride the night air. He examined each wheel, running his fingers along the wooden spokes and sockets. When he got to the front wheel, the one that had been on Janelle's side of the carriage and was now lying partially wedged against the embankment, half-covered with grass and mud, the reason for the accident became obvious.

Two of the wooden spokes showed signs of having been sawn three-quarters of the way through, so that they would support the weight of a moving carriage long enough for Justin and Janelle to be out of town and well on their way along the river road, but not long enough to get them anywhere near Delacroix, and safety.

Incensed by the evidence his eyes could not deny, Justin's face turned hard and determined. This had to stop. He had not wanted to believe someone was intentionally trying to kill her, but he could deny it no longer. She had returned to Delacroix injured and in rags, had been chased and shot at in Bayou Tejue, and now this. Someone had deliberately, and maliciously cut the spokes, knowing the carriage would be wrecked. The conclusion left a sour taste in his mouth, and a trace of fear in his heart.

Releasing the horses from their harness, Justin led them to where Janelle lay. Bracing one knee on the soft earth, he carefully slipped his arms around her and lifted her to his chest, carrying her to the carriage and settling her on top of the badly twisted buggy. Then he urged one of the big grays alongside. Once mounted, Justin leaned over and lifted Janelle onto his lap. He wrapped one arm securely around her shoulders while the fingers of his other hand held a steel grip to the horse's long, flowing mane.

The ride to the plantation, closer by far than New Orleans, took most of the remainder of the night, with Justin keeping the horse at a steady but settled pace. Janelle's head lay against his shoulder, but whether asleep from exhaustion or unconscious from trauma, he was not sure. Fear that she might have internal injuries twisted his nerves and drove him slowly mad. He wished he could urge more speed from the horse, and knew he didn't dare.

The moon lit their way, its soft glow just enough to keep the road visible, and the second carriage horse followed close behind them. By the time the gateposts of Delacroix came into view, the morning sun was beginning to rise, bathing the treetops in a soft haze of yellow. The sky turned a misty gray blue as the day began to break. Justin sagged wearily, his entire body aching, but he did not think of releasing her. His being was wholly concentrated on getting her to safety.

Janelle had stirred several times during their slow ride, each time more restlessly than before, and Justin's grip tightened with each movement to keep them both from toppling from the back of the large horse. He didn't know if she heard him, but he whispered reassurances to her all the same.

Nearing the entry drive she awoke and pulled herself upright in his arms. She twisted slightly, her movement causing his own injured shoulder to sear with pain.

Every muscle, every bone in her body ached, but when Janelle recognized the gates of Delacroix, she relaxed and leaned back against Justin, savoring the delicious sense of wellbeing. She was so content to be in his embrace, to see the concern in his eyes.

They moved slowly down the entrance drive. The house seemed quiet, all curtains drawn against the morning light, but there was a bustle of activity coming from the stable area. As they neared, voices began to filter out on the air and Janelle felt Justin stiffen. The horses sensed it, too. Both started a little prancing dance, shying sideways and snorting. Justin's grip tightened on the reins, and he nudged their horse forward, the other unwillingly following close behind.

Suddenly Sammy burst from the stable door, his face a mask of panic.

Justin halted the gray, jumped to the ground and reached up for Janelle. His strong arms wrapped around her and pulled her into his embrace.

Cradling Janelle to his chest, Justin swung back toward the groom. "Sammy, calm down," he ordered. "Now, what has happened?"

"I don't know how it happen, Michie Justin. I don't know, I swear, I don't." Sammy's head shook violently.

"Sammy, what in thunder is wrong? Tell me," Justin demanded.

"It's Micaelai. I heard all this whinnying and snorting going on and at first I didn't pay no mind, 'cause I thought he was probably just trying to get that new little mare to pay attention to him. But he just kept on and on, so's I got up to go quiet him down. Thought maybe a little early snack would shush him some."

"So what is wrong with him?" Unconsciously Justin's arms tightened about Janelle, his muscles rigid with tension.

"It's his leg. It's all broken up. It ain't hanging right no more. I don't know what he did, Michie, and that's the truth. He must of been athrashing in that stall all by himself, maybe showing off for that mare, maybe just mad 'cause he ain't had no breakfast, but he musta been thrashing pretty good, 'cause that leg's twisted ever which way."

"Damn!" Justin's jaw clenched tightly. "Sammy, Janei's hurt. I must get her to the house. I'll return as soon as I can." He turned away.

"No, Justin, please," Janelle said quickly, "let me help." She saw the indecision, the concern for her in his eyes and spoke again before he could argue. "I'm all right, just sore. And there's no time."

She was right and he knew it. There was no time. With her cradled tightly in his arms, Justin walked directly to Micaelai's stall.

Micaelai was a huge chestnut-colored stallion, power-fully muscled, with a four-pointed white star in the center of his forehead and a mane and tail whose luxuriant tendrils resembled white silk. But the special bond between the proud stallion and Justin stemmed from much more than beauty. Micaelai had been the last birthday present Justin had received from his parents before their death. The horse was eighteen years old now, but still as beautiful as the day Carlton Delacroix had brought him home for his son.

Micaelai stood with his head held high, ears peaked, tail raised, looking squarely at his master. But Justin's heart sank when he saw the great animal's left foreleg. It hung limply, turned slightly to the right, the hoof raised a bit from the ground, as if even the pressure of resting it upon the earth was too painful. The bone had been broken in the center, between knee and hoof.

Janelle heard the intake of breath in Justin's throat, felt the racing beat of his heart, and saw the anguish in his eyes as he looked at the big stallion. Turning, he carried her from the stable area and settled her on a small bench near the open entry door.

"I'll return shortly," he said, his voice barely more than a choked whisper. He stared into her eyes for a long moment, his own full of pain. When he finally straightened and moved away from her, it was with hard resolve in his eyes, a forced rigidity to his body. "Sammy, get the rifle," he ordered quietly.

The intent of his last words did not register upon Janelle until moments later when Sammy, rifle cradled in his arms, stepped from the small storage area and moved toward Micaelai's stall. Janelle got to her feet and rushed toward Micaelai's stall, paying no heed to the screaming protests of her aching body.

In the stall, Justin moved slowly up to the horse, taking its muzzle tenderly between his hands. "You've really done it now, old friend," he said, struggling to hold back the tears that stung his eyes. He leaned his forehead against the white star, all the while talking softly, his fingers continuing to caress and soothe. He knew he was putting off the inevitable, but he didn't want to say good-bye.

Janelle paused at the stall door, her gaze riveted to the horse's broken leg. She tried to remember the things her father had taught her. Was it possible to adapt her father's teachings to this time? There were no instruments, no modern equipment, not even the right medicines and antibiotics. But she couldn't bear the pain and despair etched so clearly on Justin's strong features. She had to do something. She had to try.

Before she could move, Justin turned from the horse and took the rifle from Sammy's arms. Grim and resolved, he ripped off the leather sheath. He raised the deadly weapon and aimed it directly at the head of the majestic animal who stared back at him so trustingly.

"No! Justin, no!" She rushed into the stall and flung herself at him. She wrapped a hand around the rifle barrel and pushed it aside. Breathing heavily, her own bruised and aching body rebelling, Janelle leaned against him for just a second, but retained her grip on the gun.

"Janei, Micaelai's leg is broken, can you not see that? I have no choice. Do you want him to suffer?"

"Justin, you don't have to put him down. He can be saved."

"That's impossible. How can he ever walk again, with a leg like that? Now, stop this nonsense and let me do what I have to."

"No. Listen to me. We can save him." She turned to Sammy, who stood at the stall door. "Sammy, get me some strong rope, several bed sheets and something soft. Like cotton. Lots of it. And hurry!"

Justin stared at her, but made no further attempt to stop her.

The boy was back in a matter of minutes, dumping the requested supplies on the floor beside Micaelai as Janelle ordered.

"Now, Sammy, climb up to those rafters—" she pointed to the ceiling "—and loop these ropes over them, then toss the ends back down to Justin."

While Justin and Sammy followed her orders, Janelle busied herself with spreading the sheets on the ground beneath Micaelai's stomach. She took large bundles of cotton and arranged them at each end of the sheets, snatching her hand back hastily as the horse, nervous from his injury and the hurried movements all about him, shied away, his big rear hooves trampling the sheets' edges. Sammy threw the rope ends down as directed and Janelle ordered Justin to loop them loosely under the horse's stomach, one just behind his front legs, one in front of his hind legs. She tucked the sheets between the ropes and Micaelai's skin, placing the thick cotton where the binding touched, and then the ropes were tossed across the rafters again, their ends dangling down on each side of the injured horse.

The two men began shortening the ropes' length, Justin pulling one end, Sammy the other, and the stallion began to rise from the ground. When they had him high enough so that his hooves only lightly touched the earth, thereby preventing any pressure being put on his legs, they tied the ropes to the stall's side rails.

"Sammy, I need two flat pieces of wood, cloth strips, and some strong liniment. Can you get those?" Janelle asked.

The young groom nodded and hurried off, returning within minutes. Janelle, chewing nervously on her bottom lip, knelt before Micaelai, knowing the most dangerous part was yet to come.

At Janelle's direction, Justin secured a bridle to Micaelai's muzzle and grasped it tightly in his fist in an effort to keep the horse from attempting to rear.

When they were ready, Janelle took a deep breath. "Justin, I'll need you to hold on to his other front leg so that he doesn't kick."

Taking a firm hold of Micaelai's injured leg in both her hands, Janelle gripped it tightly around the break and began to press, straining to push the bone back into its original place. The horse thrashed wildly, twisting his body. He broke free of Justin's grasp on the reins. Justin shoved Janelle unceremoniously backwards, out of the way of the deadly arc of the hoof.

Micaelai's mane whipped the air as he shook his head, and finally quieted at Justin's soothing, persuasive voice and caressing hands. Sammy secured Micaelai's hind legs together with a leather thong and then tied its end to the stall rail. At least that way, the stallion could kick out, but not toward Janelle. With another thong, Justin pulled Micaelai's uninjured foreleg to a bent position, looped the leather strip around the horse's neck and tied it, forcing the leg to remain raised and motionless. Justin continued to talk to the huge beast, rubbing a hand over the soft muzzle and keeping his lower body wedged between Janelle and Micaelai's uninjured foreleg, the reins wrapped tightly about his fist. At Justin's brusque gesture to her, Janelle took a deep breath and returned to her position.

The broken bone slowly moved under the pressure of her fingers, sliding toward its rightful position, and she began to press harder. High-pitched screams filled the barn. Suddenly Janelle felt the bone set. Micaelai was lucky. It had been a clean break, the flesh unbroken. After rubbing the leg heavily with a thick, syruplike liniment, Janelle hastily wrapped it with strips of cloth, winding the fabric over the break and pulling as tightly as she could so that the bone would remain in place.

Micaelai calmed as she began to wrap his leg. For a fleeting moment, as Janelle looked up into those eyes, she felt as if the animal had finally come to understand that she was trying to help him. The horse reached down and docilely nuzzled against her shoulder.

Janelle rose, bone-weary, every muscle smarting. She felt like one big hurt. The disaster with the carriage and the hour of sitting on her knees beside the injured stallion were taking their toll. Justin and Sammy released the stallion and untied the thongs on his rear legs.

"Janei, will this really work?" Justin asked. Never had he heard of a horse being treated for a broken leg; it would have been the normal thing to kill the animal. Nor had he ever seen Sara Janei so compassionate, so brave. Ignoring her own injuries, she had helped Micaelai. Even with her dirty, bloodied clothes and tangled hair, shadows of exhaustion dark upon her pale face, she was the most beautiful woman in the world to him then.

"Well, he'll have to stay hung up like that for a while, and then take it nice and easy for weeks after that. I wouldn't count on entering him in the Kentucky Derby, but I think he'll be just fine, Justin, as long as no infection sets in." She smiled, proud of her work.

"What's a Kentucky Derby?" Sammy asked.

"Where did you learn this, Janei?" Justin ignored Sammy's question. He closed the distance between them, taking her arm as he noticed her sway slightly.

"Oh, I . . . I don't know." She tried to avoid his sharp scrutiny. Answering questions was the last thing she wanted, and there was really no explaining what they'd just done. The procedure of setting a horse's leg, rather than shooting the animal, wouldn't be accepted for years yet. All she wanted to do was get back to the house, take a nice, hot bath, climb into bed, and sleep the day away.

Justin watched her move toward the door, her steps crooked and unsure, and felt an overwhelming urge to take care of her. He reproached himself for his own insensitivity. She had just endured a horrible ordeal, and all he was doing was voicing suspicion again. With several long strides he was beside her, arms clasping her waist in mute invitation to lean on him for support. She stiffened at first, and Justin found himself doing likewise at the possible rejection, then with a reedy sigh she leaned into his hard length, as trusting as Micaelai had been.

Inside, he ordered Marie to prepare her bath and leave the room, but this time the big woman refused, gently but adamantly. She shooed Justin out and turned to assist Janelle in getting out of the dirty, torn clothes. Giving Janelle neither the time nor the opportunity to protest, Marie quickly set about cleansing the gash on her arm. Wrapping a clean bandage around it, Marie ushered her toward the tub that Callie had just filled, the sweet fragrance of honeysuckle floating upwards on the rising steam.

Janelle lowered herself into the hot water. She kept her freshly bandaged arm propped against the tub's high rim and laid her head against the green tin backing. She let out a contented sigh as her body finally relaxed, but came back to rigid alertness when Marie turned toward her, wide jaw set in determination, fingers splayed upon ample hips.

"Missy, I don't know what's going on here, or what's come over you lately, but something's wrong. No, that ain't what I mean. Something's different about you, mighty different."

"Marie, I'm not up to arguing now." Janelle wished the woman would just go away. There hadn't been one pleasant word between the two of them since she'd arrived, and God knows, Janelle thought, she'd tried. She had offered to help the housekeeper with the chores and gotten a quick rebuff. One morning she had even gone to sit in the kitchen while Marie worked, and attempted to draw the woman into a conversation, receiving only clipped responses. Now suddenly, when she wanted nothing more than peace, quiet, and a little rest, the woman wanted to talk.

"I ain't looking to argue with you, missy. I just come to say my piece and I'll go. There's something different about you, that's for sure, and I got to say it's for the better, too. But, I think I know why you's different." Marie let the statement hang in the air as Janelle turned to look at her, their gazes locking. "You ain't really Sara Janei, is you, missy?"

Fully alert now, Janelle gaped at her, dumbfounded, and when she didn't answer, Marie nodded and continued.

"That's what I thought. I may be only an old mammy and housekeeper, no schooling or pretty ways about me, but I don't need anything but these old eyes to show me what's been going on round here. You don't talk like her, you don't act like her, and you even looks different than her. Your voice is softer, missy, and you got a funny little sound to it. And your skin, it's got the touch of the sun to it, not all pale and white like hers. Humph, tiniest bit of sun touch Sara Janei's skin and she closed herself up in this room for days." Marie shook her head. "But it's more than that, missy. You been nice, and that ain't something Sara Janei knowed how to be. You let Tansy keep that hat, and for that I'm real thankful, and you been good to Callie and Sammy, but most of all, I can see what's going on between you and Justin."

"There's nothing going on between me and Justin, Marie." Janelle lowered her gaze to her bent knees peeping above the bubble-topped bathwater.

"No sense denying it, missy. I don't know who you really are, or where you come from, or even how come you looks just like that witch he married, and I ain't asking. But I do know two things. You ain't her, and you care about Justin. I can see it in your eyes, and the way you act when he's about. He cares for you too, child, and I ain't never been wrong about those kind of things. Never."

Janelle let out a long breath. "I wish it were true, Marie, but all I seem to do is make him angry. Everything I do is wrong." It was not as if she was admitting to being—or rather, not being Sara Janei.

"That's only 'cause he ain't figured it all out yet. It's just taking him a might longer than it took me. Every time he looks at you he sees her, but not 'cause he wants to. He just don't know what to make of you, that's all." Marie moved to leave, then turned back. "You know what first got me to thinking? It was that dumb dog. He used to follow her around all the time, faithful as an old hound. But it wasn't 'cause he liked her, no sir, he was scared of her. Poor dog would sit beside her and shake. But with you, that little thing is so happy to see you he can't control himself, bouncing all over the floor, yipping, and racing around. That's what got me to thinking, to knowing you wasn't really Sara Janei."

Janelle said nothing. Without going into the entire, incredible story of who she really was, confirming Marie's suspicions was impossible, and right now she was too tired to even try.

Marie seemed to understand. Though there were still questions in her eyes, she smiled warmly. "You stay in there long as you like, missy. Justin's still in your room, pacing like a caged cat, but he'll wait. There's a pitcher of water right beside you on the washstand to rinse your hair." With more grace and speed than Janelle thought the huge woman capable of, Marie was through the door, leaving her alone with her thoughts, which were more confused and jumbled than ever.

The hot water soothed her bruised muscles, but not her mind. If Marie had guessed she wasn't Sara Janei, would it be long before Justin did? And then what? Could she tell him the truth? She wanted to, she wanted to tell him right now, this very minute, but something held her back, some lingering thread of doubt that would not allow her to completely trust or believe in him yet. The carriage accident—which, Justin had explained, wasn't really an accident—quite easily could have proven fatal. In all probability it was meant to, at least for her. The wheel had been cut on her side. Justin had been thrown clear, not pinned beneath the heavy carriage as she'd been. But he'd saved her, Janelle's heart argued.

But had he saved her because he'd wanted to, or because leaving her there, still alive, would have been more dangerous for him?

Hurrying through the remainder of her bath, she wrapped herself in a robe of embroidered cheviot and wound a towel around her wet hair. She took a deep breath, steeling herself. After what she had done to save Micaelai, Janelle knew there were bound to be questions, she just didn't know how she was going to answer them.

Back in the elegant bedroom, Janelle felt an instant mingling of relief and disappointment.

A fire crackled in the fireplace grate, the soft light of the morning sun filtered into the room through the lace window panels, but she was alone.

Chapter fifteen

"*JUSTIN, HOLD UP!*" *GILBERT CALLED. HE URGED* his horse across the small meadow separating Delacroix from the Foucheau plantation. "I rode over yesterday but Marie said you had gone into town. Did you hear anything more on that export tax business?"

"No, it will be some time yet before we have any news." Justin reined Tobar to a halt. "Did you want anything particular yesterday?"

Gilbert looked puzzled, then smiled brightly. "Uh, no. Melody mentioned that you borrowed a couple of our better cooks to help with food for the soirée. I just thought I would see if you needed anything else. Always glad to help out, you know."

The two men talked for several minutes longer, although Justin wanted nothing more than to terminate the conversation and head back to the house. He was annoyed with himself, and he didn't know what had possessed him to ride the fields this morning. After being up all night since the fiasco with the carriage, and then Micaelai's broken leg, he was exhausted. But he knew it wasn't really any of those things that had his body in knots, and his emotions in utter chaos. He could no longer tell what was black, what was white, what was right or wrong. His world had been turned upside down by the one person he had vowed he would never allow himself to feel anything for again—except scorn. His private war still raged. Justin's mind fought for logic to use against her, while his heart surged with desire, and a love he fought to deny.

She was everywhere he looked, in his thoughts, in his blood, even in his dreams. Yet it wasn't that simple. He couldn't forget the anger he'd felt when he'd seen Antoine de la Reine with Janei the day before in the Square. A momentary desire to run his rapier through the heart of the philandering *maître d'armes* swept over him. But neither could he forget the icy fingers of fear that had engulfed him at seeing Janei pinned beneath the carriage, her face so ashen and lifeless.

Nothing made sense to him anymore. Nothing was as it should be. Waiting in her room earlier while she bathed, he'd paced the floor in a nervous turmoil, unable to stop. He'd known then he had to get out of the house, away from her. He needed time to think, to reason, to try to understand what was happening.

Whenever he was around Janei now, all Justin wanted to do was sweep her into his arms, press his lips to hers and let his hands roam her body. He needed to feel her warmth reach out to him, her sweet passion rising to match his. But he was afraid to trust those feelings. Many, many times she had deceived him. He couldn't allow himself to be tricked again. Shaking his head clear of thoughts of Sara Janei, he turned his attention back to Gilbert and told him of the carriage "accident." He made no mention of the sabotaged wheel. That was between Janei and himself.

"Pinned under the buggy!" Gilbert gasped. "My Lord, it's a miracle she's unhurt. And no broken bones? Melody and I will ride over tonight. We must call on Sara

Janei. *Mon Dieu,* she must have been scared out of her mind."

For a moment Justin eyed him suspiciously. It had never occurred to him before to look at Gilbert in any light other than friend and neighbor. Was it possible that Gilbert and Sara Janei had been more than friends? Maybe still were? Thinking of his wife as she had been during their first few months of marriage, Justin knew it was all too possible. But what of the copper-haired vixen who had returned to him? She was entirely unpredictable. If there had been something between Janei and Gilbert before, what was their relationship now? Could she have threatened exposure of their affair? Gilbert Foucheau relished his social standing and good name. Could he have feared the unveiling of an indiscretion so much that he would attempt to kill in order to prevent it?

Justin could not believe that. He had known Gilbert all his life. The man was a lover of life, and yes, probably of women, maybe even Janei. But a killer? No, he didn't think so.

They parted company, Gilbert insisting he and his wife would be over by late afternoon. Justin knew what that meant. Good manners dictated that if your guests arrived during the late afternoon hours, they must be invited to dine. He wasn't looking forward to an evening of Melody and Sara Janei in the same room. For some reason, Janei enjoyed taunting Gilbert's wife until an argument broke out, and Melody could not seem to stop herself from satisfying Janei's habit. Although the last time the women were together, Justin had been pleasantly surprised at Sara Janei's restraint.

Or perhaps his apprehension was more that his self-invited guests would interrupt what he had planned as a quiet evening with his "new" wife.

Janelle was also unable to sleep, even though her body was crying for rest. Callie brought her a glass of hot milk, and she even tried meditating and ordering her body, limb by limb, to relax and accept sleep. It didn't work.

Throwing the covers off in exasperation, she swung her legs from the bed and began to pace the large room. Somehow she had to find the answers to whatever was going on at Delacroix. Where was Sara Janei? Was she still alive? Janelle was beginning to seriously doubt that. Then she remembered her abandoned search of Sara Janei's room. She would search it again. There had to be something there that could give her an idea of what was going on. She just knew it.

She looked through the armoire, pushing clothes aside and tapping at the drawers and walls in the hope of finding a secret hiding place. An examination of the rest of the furniture also proved fruitless.

About to give up, Janelle let her gaze idly roam the room. Then she noticed the top of the armoire. The closet was at least eight feet tall, with an elaborately carved crown piece.

Pulling a chair over to the huge closet, she scrambled up to stand on it, but even then her fingers barely reached over the top edge. She piled pillows and books on the chair. It looked as if she was building the Tower of Babel, but it proved worth the trouble. Pushed into a corner of the amoire top Janelle found a leatherbound journal tied with a yellow ribbon.

Quickly replacing the pillows and books in their proper places, she returned to the comfort of the bed, excitement mounting. She untied the ribbon and opened Sara Janei's diary.

The daily accounting of the woman's life started only six months prior, in January of 1856. A month before she had married Justin. The journal seemed big enough only for a single year's writing, so Janelle knew there were other volumes, but she didn't care. This was the important one, the one that would tell her of Sara Janei's days as Justin's wife. Flipping to the first page, her jaw dropped open in shock. Written across the top of the page in bold script was Sara Janei's full name—Sara Janei Bernice Chevillon Delacroix.

Janelle closed her eyes, squeezing the lids together tightly. It was a coincidence. It had to be. But she knew it wasn't. The name was not that common, she was certain; she'd spent hours with her mother researching the family genealogy. Suddenly another thought struck. Could that be what this whole thing was about? Why she was here? Rather than merely a fluke of nature or time; was it predestined?

Laying the diary aside, she jumped from the bed and hurried across the room to the desk. The board to the secret compartment stuck slightly but she yanked it free. Scooping up the packet of pictures, Janelle carried it back to her bed and hastily tore off the ribbon binding, spreading the daguerreotypes out on the coverlet. She found him immediately, and turned the picture over to confirm his name. Bernard Louis. It was hard to compare the face of this unsmiling young man with that of her own mother, but then, there had been several generations in between. It came slowly, but as Janelle searched the face of Bernard Louis Chevillon, she began to see a faint family resemblance. Bernard, Sara Janei's brother, had been Janelle's great-great-great-grandfather. She was a descendent of Sara Janei's family!

"Is that why I look so much like her?" she whispered, not really needing an answer. She felt dizzy with the enormity of the realization, and the fate that had conspired to bring her back in time. Janelle took a deep breath and forced her attention back to the diary. The first entry was dated New Year's Day, January, 1856:

Robert was killed a year ago today. It seems like only yesterday that he held me in his arms and promised to be at my side forever. I was young, and foolish. I believed him. But for the duello. Marcel meant nothing to me. Merely a flirtation. Why did Robert have to challenge him? It was foolish pride and too much drink. Now, all our dreams and plans, hopes for the future, lost with the lunge of the rapier. Ah, but on to the living now. Justin Delacroix has asked me to marry him. He bores me terribly, but he is rich, treats me well, and is quite handsome, although not nearly as much as my dear beloved Robert was. The wedding is to be in one month. I will hate living on the plantation, though. So far from the soirées and operas. I shall miss many gala events, and my friends, but at least I will never have to concern myself with money worries ever again.

Janelle sat bolt upright. Robert! It had been his picture in the small locket she'd found in the swamp grove. Sara Janei had still been mourning her lost love, still pining for her dead fiancé while being courted by Justin, and then callously accepted his proposal of marriage. All for the sake of money. Rage at the woman's cold and calculating action crept over Janelle. Yet a part of her felt pity for the woman who had lost her first love in so brutal a manner, in being forced to marry because there was no viable alternative except spinsterhood. Janelle scanned the diary's pages until she came to a later date: April 8, 1856.

Gilbert is getting boring. He expects me to meet him every day, and when I say no, he acts like a spoiled little boy, pouting and throwing a tantrum. It is becoming quite tiresome. He also knows about Antoine and is insanely jealous. I have been trying to discourage Gilbert's attentions, but he is so insistent. I hesitate to tell him outright it is *fini*. I am not sure what he would do. Sometimes he frightens me. There is a look about his eyes whenever he is upset that is not quite right. I am afraid he could truly become violent if provoked beyond a certain point.

Janelle turned several more pages. As closely as she could figure, Sara Janei had disappeared around the middle of that same month. She looked at the last pages. Yes, she'd been right. There were no entries after April 18th.

Antoine is such a darling. Why couldn't I have met him before Justin? Everything would have been so much simpler. Of course, Mama probably would have swooned and not allowed me to marry him. Poor dear, hasn't much money of his own, at least not like Justin. Antoine's fencing academy does quite well, and the beautiful gray stallion he bought to race should help, but it is still not enough. If only I could find a way to get my hands on Justin's money, or better yet, get rid of him altogether. Then everything would be mine, and Antoine's, of course. I never thought I could ever love again, not after dear Robert, but Antoine has shown me I was wrong. Very wrong. He has pleaded with me to leave Justin and come to him, but I cannot. How can I give up all the luxuries the Delacroix money and name afford me? And Justin, that beast! He is becoming so suspicious of me. He has grown cold and hard. If I did not know better, I would think he actually knows of Antoine and Gilbert. Ah, a thought! Perhaps my little mongrel Stephan has let his lips flap a bit too much. Could the idiot have let our secret slip from his tongue? He was quite angry with me the last time when I wouldn't let him touch me. But he was too dirty, and we were expecting callers at the house. I must talk to him.

Janelle set the diary aside and lay back against the pillows. How could the woman have been so cruel? To have used so many people, with such little regard for consequences or their feelings. Especially Justin, and his love. She had never cared for him, only his money and position in New Orleans society. He had been nothing more to her than a means to an end.

All this information now posed new questions and possibilities as to what had happened to Sara Janei. It seemed more than likely that she was dead. In Janelle's mind, things were beginning to point toward murder. The evidence was circumstantial, but logical.

Sara Janei had had three lovers at the time of her disappearance. Each was a possible suspect. Gilbert had been insanely jealous and Sara Janei had written of trying to break off the relationship. Had he, in a state of jealous rage, attacked her? And what of Antoine? She claimed to love him, but love, it seemed, was not as important to Sara Janei in the end as money. Had she tried to explain this to Antoine, refusing to leave her rich husband, and then met death from the man she professed had taught her to love again? Or had she gone to confront the overseer Stephan O'Roarke as she indicated she might? Had she perhaps threatened to dismiss him for having a loose tongue, and instead found her own tongue silenced . . . permanently?

Suddenly, voices echoed through the big house, angry, loud voices that drew Janelle's attention and sent a shiver of alarm up her spine. Before she could make a move to rise from the bed, a knock sounded on the door and it flew open. Callie rushed into the room, a harried expression on her young face.

"Miss Sara, there's a . . a woman downstairs to see you. I told her you was not receiving today, and her kind ain't welcome at Delacroix anyways, but she won't go. Mama tried to throw her out, but the woman started ranting and screaming 'bout curses. I's scared, Miss Sara. You gots to come down, please."

"What do you mean, 'her kind,' Callie? Who is it?"

"I don't know who she is, Miss Sara. She won't give me no name. Just said she wasn't surprised you wasn't feeling good and that I was to come fetch you. Said to tell you if'n you don't want to be feeling worse, you'd best come down." Callie shook her head, eyes full of worry. "I don't like her none, Miss Sara. She ain't no lady. She's a conjure woman, for sure."

"All right, Callie." Janelle sighed. She had a pretty good idea who the woman downstairs was. "Help me dress and I'll go and see to our *guest*." It was the last thing she wanted to do. What she wanted was an aspirin for the headache she felt coming on, but Janelle suspected the pills did not exist yet.

Sore muscles forced her to descend the stairs slowly. She had brushed her hair back to the nape of her neck, securing it with a lavender ribbon that matched the poplin gown she'd chosen. It was a simple gown, but cheerful, the lightweight fabric cool. Long, fitted sleeves hid both the bruises she'd incurred in the carriage accident and the gash on her arm. The neckline however, was cut just a shade too low to conceal the faint purple coloring that marred the flesh above her left breast.

Celine Gampion stood at the bottom of the wide staircase, her outfit outrageously flamboyant. The vibrant turquoise hue of her gown was so vivid that it made the rich furnishings of the foyer seem drab in comparison. The edges of her massively draped overskirt were scalloped with lengths of ivory lace. She wore a matching swatch of fabric wound around her head in a turban, a huge diamond cluster brooch pinned just over the forehead to match the choker encircling her throat. A cold smile widened the woman's lips as she watched Janelle descend the stairs, and she made no attempt at courtesy.

"So, Madame Delacroix does not feel well. I warned you, did I not? The gris-gris has already begun its work for Celine. Now, Madame, perhaps you will heed my words."

Janelle came to stand directly before the woman and instantly wished she had not. She had to look up to meet Celine's smug expression. It would have been wiser to have paused on the last step.

Yet Janelle smiled politely. "Miss—" she caught herself and began again. "Mademoiselle Gampion, if that is why you rode all the way out here, then you have wasted your time. As I told you in town, I have no interest in Antoine de la Reine. If you want him, you can have him." Janelle's hands clenched tightly within the folds of her gown. As far as anyone was concerned, she was Sara Janei Delacroix, and she'd be damned if she would let this creature scare her in her own home.

"Do not attempt any more of your pretenses with me, Madame," Celine said, nostrils flaring. "You claim to have no interest in my Antoine, yet I saw you in the Place d'Armes with him yesterday. I saw you kiss him, all the while throwing your body at him. Only the whores on Burgundy Street have as little discretion as you seem to show, Madame Delacroix."

"I warn you, Mademoiselle . . ."

"No, it is I who warn you, Madame. My gris-gris is already at work against you. You are ill, your skin looks sickly. But I can help you, Madame," offered Celine slyly. "I can lift the conjure from you, but I will do so only if you promise me that you will never again see my Antoine. Promise me that, and I will make you well again. Otherwise, you will grow weaker with sickness until finally you will die."

"What?" The woman was mad. Celine actually thought her ugly little charm was responsible for Janelle not feeling well. "Mademoiselle Gampion, you are impossible. I was up most of the night. I am tired, plain and simple, not sick. You have no power over me or anyone else.

Furthermore, I threw your ugly little whatever-you-call-it into the fire this morning."

A stifled gasp came from the shadows of the foyer near the kitchen door and Janelle glanced over her shoulder. Callie huddled against the wall, her eyes wide as she stared at Celine. Beside her stood Marie, her massive bulk filling the corner. A faint trace of a smile tugged at Marie's mouth and her black eyes glistened with satisfaction. She nodded toward Janelle.

Celine suddenly began to laugh hysterically, and Callie gave another squeak of fear. Outraged, Janelle grabbed Celine's arm in a tight grip and turned the woman toward the door. Enough was enough!

Celine ripped her arm from Janelle's grasp and spun around. She raised a hand high in the air and began to mumble in some kind of a chant. Suddenly a white powder drifted through the air and a small black ball shot from the woman's hand, bouncing against Janelle's skirt and falling to the floor at her feet with a dull thud.

"You will be sorry, Madame," Celine shrieked. "It is too late for you now. You should have heeded my words when I warned you, but you are all the same, you Creole women. Always think you can control everything, have whatever you want. Well, not this time, *chérie*. No one can save you now. No one!" Cackling loudly, Celine hurled the door shut behind her as she left.

Janelle heard the crunching sound of carriage wheels on the drive. With a sigh of relief she moved to return upstairs, wanting nothing more than to retreat to the sanctuary of her room.

Marie stepped forward and gripped Janelle's shoulders. "Are you all right, missy?"

"I'm fine, Marie, thank you. I'm just tired. What in heaven's name was all that stuff she threw around?"

Marie sighed. "It was the conjure powder. She was putting a curse on you. Supposed to mean, when the powder is throwed round you that no good can come to you 'cause it can't get pass the bad of the powder."

"Oh, criminy." Janelle laughed weakly. "And that stupid little ball that didn't even bounce, what was that for, my life to bounce away?"

"The conjure ball supposed to make the spell work better. It's evil. Everybody's afraid of the conjure ball more'n the gris-gris, missy."

"Do you believe in it, Marie?"

"Me? Nah. Justin teached ol' Marie all abouts God and heaven and everything. When I's his mammy and he was just a little thing, he used to read his Bible to me. He say the voodoo all in the mind." She smiled, proud of herself. "You go on now, get yourself some rest, y'hear?"

Cinder pranced into the foyer just as Janelle turned to follow Marie's advice. The dog bounced around her skirts, begging for attention, and she stooped to pick him up.

"Come here, you little imp." She lifted him high enough to nuzzle his head against her forehead. "Where was all this barking a minute ago when I needed you? You're supposed to be out here running all these nasty people away."

Janelle carried the dog up the stairs with her, settling him on the bed before she climbed beneath the covers. This time, sleep came instantly.

The sun was slipping from the horizon when Callie entered Janelle's room again. The young maid hated to wake her mistress, but she had to. It was time to dress for dinner and they had company, the Foucheaus. At least this time, Callie thought, their guests were more pleasant, and Michie Justin was here.

Callie ran her hands over several of the dresses in the armoire before making a decision. The red dress with the black lace and tulle trim. It was one of her favorites, and she knew her mistress looked dazzling in the color.

Janelle was slow to awaken and even slower to force herself from the warmth of the bed. She was anything but pleased that they had company again, especially when she heard it was Gilbert and Melody. Janelle sat at the dressing table to apply a bit of rose petal to her cheeks as blush. She needed the color, she'd decided, after one glance in the mirror told her she looked like a ghost.

A loud crash sounded as the door burst open, slamming against the wall, and Justin strode into the room. Startled, Janelle nearly buried her finger in the jar of crushed charcoal she had been experimenting with on her eyelids.

"What is this nonsense Marie is spouting about some quadroon coming here today and putting a spell on you?" He stopped a few feet from where she sat. She had turned from the mirror at his entrance. Wrapping the fingers of one hand around the bedpost, knuckles turning white from the pressure, he continued. "Answer me, Janei. What is this all about?"

Rising, Janelle clutched the robe closed and moved toward him, unaware that the thin material, nearly transparent now from the glow of the candles at her back, left little to his imagination, and was doing much to destroy his tautly held control. She wanted to calm him, to make light of the situation Marie had obviously blown out of proportion. Janelle reached out, laying her hand on his arm.

"It was nothing, Justin. Just some silly woman who thinks I've done something I haven't. It's not important."

"Not important?" His self-restraint was almost gone, shattered by her nearness, the sweet fragrance of her wafting around him, teasing him, drawing him to her.

He grabbed her forearms, pulling her roughly toward him. "Do you realize that woman could have every black on this plantation cowering in fear if they learn of this? Her kind is dangerous, Janei. What in heaven's name did you do to her?"

"N. . . nothing," Janelle said, her voice barely audible. She couldn't think straight, couldn't concentrate on his words. Her breath was lodged in the back of her throat, her heart hammering frantically at his nearness. Concern etched his features, shining from his eyes, but whether for her or the slaves she was not certain, and at the moment did not care. He was beside her, holding her, and that was all that mattered. A lock of black hair fell across his forehead. She ached to reach up and run her fingers through the ebony strands, but could not, her arms still held in his viselike grip.

Justin groaned beneath his breath. Touching her had been a mistake. He trembled with the effort to control himself, to deny the passion already warming his blood. It took all his willpower to release her and turn away, hands clenched tightly at his sides. He had been a fool for her long enough. He hated the thought of another man's hands on her, another man knowing the passions of his wife, but he was not fool enough to pretend it had not happened, or would not happen again. "Tell me the truth, Janei. Does this have something to do with Antoine de la Reine?"

Janelle's disappointment at his words was so great she felt it as a stabbing pain deep within her chest. She looked at his rigid back and longed to reach out to him, but spoke softly instead. "There is nothing between Antoine and me, Justin. Please believe that. You are my husband. There is no one else."

He dragged her up against him, her lips only inches from his. Indignation flashed across his face, and burned within the depths of his eyes as he stared down at her.

"How can you say that? I have seen you with him. And what of the others, Janei? How many are there?"

"None, Justin, none. You must believe me," Janelle cried, even though she knew it was useless. Justin's trust in Sara Janei had been destroyed long ago.

"Marie warned me not to allow you to return, but I wouldn't listen, and now what she feared has come true. Your very presence seems to always bring nothing but trouble to those around you. Now you have brought a conjure woman, a voodoo queen to Delacroix. God help us all if the field slaves hear of this." His eyes were cold, his face hard. "Get dressed, Janei, and get downstairs. We have guests to attend to."

She felt cold and empty inside, as if a permanent chill had settled in her veins. Was it jealousy or hatred that provoked Justin? She pushed the troubling thoughts to the back of her mind. Moments later, she entered the parlor with a smile on her face, but the evening proved as disastrous as both she and Justin had anticipated.

To Justin's surprise, Sara Janei was very pleasant to Melody, trying to engage her in amiable conversation. Not once did she bait the petite blond, but it proved not to matter. Melody had arrived at Delacroix in a cool, reserved mood. Gilbert, on the other hand, was all warmth and exaggerated concern over Janei's escape from the carriage. Every now and then, when he thought no one was looking, he managed to send Janelle a conspiratorial glance or wink. But Justin was no longer playing the fool; he now suspected Gilbert had been one of his wife's lovers. He noticed every move the man made, and though it galled him to the core, he remained silent, perplexed by what seemed Janei's distaste not only for Gilbert's flirtations, but for the man himself.

By dinner's end, Melody had progressed from cool to downright hostile. Sara Janei, to everyone's surprise, played the perfect hostess. She ignored Gilbert's stares and vainly tried to placate Melody. Only once during their conversation did she seem less than poised and that was when the small blond mentioned a silver stallion.

Occasionally Janelle would turn to Justin and smile ruefully, apologetically, as though inviting him to share in the absurdity of the situation, and her humor did serve to dissipate some of the chill in his eyes. Unbeknownst to her, it also stoked the passion that always simmered in him now at her nearness.

When they adjourned to the parlor for brandy, the situation worsened as Gilbert rushed to sit beside Janelle on the double settee. Melody, left standing by the door, was most definitely not amused. Neither was Justin, who had now had his fill of Gilbert Foucheau's concern, neighborly or otherwise. He was moving toward Gilbert to forcibly remove the man from his wife's side when Melody's words stopped him.

"Gilbert, dear," she said softly, "perhaps Sara Janei would rather have her own husband sit beside her."

Before Gilbert could dismiss the comment, Janelle spoke up. "Yes, Gilbert, please. Your concern is touching, but I assure you, I am fine. Do join your wife."

Though it was obvious to all that he did not want to, Gilbert went to sit beside Melody on the opposite settee, and her cool voice again broke the silence. "Justin, did you ever talk to Antoine de la Reine? You remember, I told you he was spreading ugly little rumors in the Quarter about Sara?"

Janelle glanced anxiously at Justin, but could read no expression on his lean face.

"It really is a shame, the way your good name is being sullied like that. But I guess some women are just unlucky enough to attract that kind of man . . . and talk. Of course, when one follows the rules of proper behavior . . ."

"Rumors only become gossip when people maliciously repeat them," Janelle interrupted smoothly. She had taken about as much verbal abuse from Melody Foucheau as she could handle for one evening. "As you were told before, Melody, Antoine is an acquaintance, nothing more."

"Such a pity Antoine does not realize that."

"Perhaps he does, and is also suffering from this gossip."

"Suffering?" Melody laughed nastily. "That hardly seems likely, considering his reputation and the circumstances."

"I'm sorry, Melody. I do not mean to be rude, but it seems I have no choice," Janelle said, rising from her seat. "I will say it for the last time. Antoine is an acquaintance. If you choose to believe otherwise, that is your problem. Since you seem inclined to give advice, I shall reciprocate and offer you some. It might do you more good to pay a bit of attention to your own problems, than carrying ridiculous rumors to the table of your host. Now, if you will excuse me, I am going to retire. I'm sure you know your way out."

Melody stared, mouth agape, as Janelle, in a rustle of silken skirts, swept gracefully from the room. At the door she paused, glancing back over her shoulder.

Gilbert looked crestfallen.

Justin grinned enigmatically into his brandy glass, unperturbed.

Chapter sixteen

"CATHY," TANO WHISPERED WEAKLY, HIS LIPS trembling from the effort.

The nurse rose from her chair in the corner and moved to the old man's side, then hurried to the door and flung it open.

"Dr. Donovan, he's waking," she called in a low voice.

Kyle was across the hallway and past her before the words had died on her lips, Cathy Delacroix at his heels. Tano had been moved to the hospital the night before, at Kyle's insistence. The old man had remained in a comatose state, and yet Kyle had not been able to find anything physically wrong with him. It was as if he just did not want to wake up. At least not until now.

Quickly, Kyle checked Tano's vital signs as Cathy hovered alongside. When Tano suddenly called her name again, she practically shoved Kyle aside in her excitement to get nearer the old man.

Her face only inches from Tano's, Cathy whispered, "Tano, it's me, Cathy. Can you hear me?"

At first there was no response, then suddenly, weakly, he called out Cathy's name again. His lids fluttered open.

"I'm here, Tano," she said urgently. "I'm here."

"Bi . . . ble." Tano's bony fingers slid across the sheet, the movement slow and tentative. "Bi . . . ble, Bible, Bible."

"It's right here, Tano. I packed it for you. See?" Cathy took the worn book from the nightstand and held it up for him to see.

"Pic . . . ture. Inside." Each effort to speak caused his chest to heave for air. Kyle reached past her and gripped the frail arm, feeling for the old man's pulse.

"Picture?" she echoed, flipping the Bible's pages again and again. "Tano, I can't find a picture."

Tano had always been there, like the house, old and dignified, from another era. It was hard to think of one without the other. Cathy looked upon the old man almost as a grandfather, and a friend. She couldn't imagine him gone, but now, looking down at the tired, ancient face, she knew it could well be for the last time. Tears came to her eyes.

"In . . . in back. The c . . . cov . . . er."

Cathy searched frantically, afraid he would slip away again if she didn't find the picture.

Kyle moved to her side and gently took the Bible from her hands. "Let me," he said quietly. He took a handkerchief from his pocket and tenderly dabbed at the tears on her face. He brushed his fingers across her cheek, and was both surprised and heartened when she bent her head to his touch, cradling his hand between her face and shoulder. He leaned down and kissed her forehead gently, the urge to sweep her into his arms swelling up in him as he felt her lean into him. But he resisted the impulse. Turning his attention to the Bible, Kyle looked closely at the back cover.

A thin slit had been made in the leather near the book's spine; it was almost undetectable. He slipped a finger beneath the slit, wedging it deep into the pocket until it met with the edge of something small and hard.

Poking at it with his finger, he finally dislodged the object enough that it slipped toward the opening and dropped onto the white sheet beside Tano's limp hand.

It was a brooch, no bigger than the size of a silver dollar, exquisitely designed, its edges made of filigreed gold spun in a maze of swirls and loops. But it was the center work that held their attention.

"It can't be," Cathy whispered. Her fingers shook as she reached out toward the small pin.

Kyle wrapped an arm around her, fearing she might faint.

"Kyle, what does this mean? This is impossible. It looks just like Janelle," Cathy murmured, dazed. She sagged against him, welcoming his strength, accepting his warmth. Their gaze met for only a few brief seconds, but that was time enough for each to see the caring reflected in the other's eyes, to acknowledge the first stirrings of love. But this was not the right time, and they returned their attentions to the brooch.

The tiny painting was of a woman with vibrant green eyes and dark hair, red highlights gleaming from the cascade of curls that graced her shoulder. It was a happy face, one that seemed to radiate warmth from the miniature.

Chapter seventeen

A HEAVY SHROUD OF DARKNESS WRAPPED around Janelle, pressing close, crushing her lungs. She couldn't breathe. The pressure grew heavier. She tried to pull away, but couldn't move. It was as if shoulders, head, and neck were paralyzed. Blackness was all around, seeping into her mind, becoming warm and comfortable, beckoning, offering its deathly welcome.

She tried unsuccessfully to open her eyes. Groaning, she attempted to turn over, and found that, too, impossible. She wanted the dream to end, but it wouldn't. A faint scratching sound echoed and slowly her sleep-drugged brain alerted her that this was not a dream. Suddenly she was awake, thrashing about in the bed, arms flailing the air, legs kicking and twisting beneath tangled covers. The nightmare was real!

Something was being held over her face, the pressure intensifying. Her throat and chest burned as her lungs screamed for air. Panic began to take over. Janelle jerked convulsively, attempting to throw herself from one side to the other. Someone jumped on top of her, the sudden weight crushing her ribs and forcing out what little air she had left in her lungs. The pressure worsened. The hazy blackness returned and swirled around the shadowed edges of her mind.

Summoning every ounce of strength left in her body Janelle pushed herself upwards. There was a dull crash, and the weight across her midriff disappeared. She heaved the pillow from her face and scrambled from the bed, gasping for air. There was a scratching sound against the door, followed by a dog's whimper, and then more scratching. Janelle screamed out for Justin.

Janelle's eyes began to adjust to the darkness, and she saw, a few feet away, a shadowy blur. The hair on her trembling arms stood on end as she stared at the apparition. She could make out only a long flowing cape topped by a deep hood pulled far forward. She grabbed a crystal vase from the bureau and held it above her head like a club.

Suddenly she heard footsteps running toward her room, heavy and rapid, and Justin's voice calling her. At the same moment, the intruder turned and raced for the open French doors that led out onto the gallery.

Realizing her attacker was about to get away, Janelle jumped across the bed and scrambled to grab at the cape. She made a flying tackle she felt certain could rival any NFL lineman, and collided with the fleeing figure. A booted foot crashed down on her unprotected toes. She crumpled over in pain, but not before she grabbed a handful of the voluminous cape. There was the faint sound of fabric ripping and a thin strip of red satin came away in Janelle's tightly clenched fingers as the caped figure disappeared into the night.

A loud, thudding crash sounded against her bedroom door and a second later it flew open, slamming against the wall. The lock hung from its bolt, twisted and useless. Cinder raced into the room, scampering across the floor and barking excitedly.

Justin stood in the doorway, staring at the dishevelment. Janelle's gaze rose to meet his, and a rush of emotions swept through her so fierce, so intense that she shuddered from the impact. Relief. Joy. Love.

He wore only the black trousers he'd had on earlier that evening. His wide shoulders glowed in the pale moonlight streaming in from the open French doors, the sinewy cords of muscle on his arms taut with tension. In four long strides he was across the room, kneeling beside her and pulling her into his arms. Janelle welcomed his protective embrace, her own arms curling shakily around his neck. She laid her head against his chest and drew on his strength; the rapid pounding of his heartbeat echoed against her ear.

Tears of relief filled her eyes. Someone had just tried to kill her, but her heart was singing in pure joy. It hadn't been Justin! There was no more doubt or suspicion. She had trusted him and been proven right. Her mind may have doubted him, her heart had not. It had been the love she felt for him that had given her the impetus to survive.

Lifting Janelle in his arms, Justin carried her back to the bed. He glanced over his shoulder at the open French door. The curtains billowed in the faint breeze that blew in from the bayou, and from the darkness came the peaceful chirping of crickets, the lilting melody of the nightbirds' song.

He walked out onto the gallery. A wooden trellis supporting a vine of jasmine was secured to one of the pillars beneath the portion of the gallery near Janelle's room. When he peered over the balustrade, Justin saw that one of the top rungs of the trellis hung loose, broken. If he had been mere seconds later Janei would have been dead, lost to him forever. He shuddered at the thought. He was still confused over his undeniable need and desire for her, and the changes he saw and felt in her, but his defenses were crumbling, rapidly and steadily.

The commotion from the main house roused the servants and stablehands hurried across the lawn in alarm. Justin ordered them to begin a search of the grounds, though he felt certain it was useless. He turned and reentered the house.

Callie rushed up to the bedroom door, and stopped abruptly in her tracks at seeing the room in such a mess. Her eyes widened in fear as she looked past Justin to the swaying curtains and open doorway. At Callie's sudden halt, Marie, who was close behind her, almost trampled over her daughter.

Callie went to light a lamp.

"What happened in here, missy?" Marie asked. "You all right? You ain't hurt, is you?"

Bending to inspect the broken lock of the French door, Justin answered in a voice edged with steel. "Someone evidently broke in and tried to kill her, that's what happened. And I'm damn well going to find out who!"

His eyes glinted with repressed fury and his gaze swept the room again. He clenched his jaw tightly and the jagged line of marred flesh on his cheek seemed to jerk in tiny spasms. He had to find out who was responsible for these attacks before it was too late. His scowl deepened as he picked up the discarded pillow, and stared at it, his hands tightly crushing the soft mound of material.

Only when he looked up at Janelle did the hardness in his eyes disappear. She was safe, and his heart recognized the courage and love undisguised on her radiant face. Justin felt at once humbled, and he came to sit beside her, taking her hands and lifting them to his lips. He brushed her cheeks with his fingers, feeling the wetness of her tears on his skin, and the fear that seethed in him at how close he'd come to losing her almost overwhelmed him.

"Are you all right? I would have gotten here sooner, but I was downstairs in the kitchen when I heard your scream," he said huskily.

Janelle nodded. Her fingers squeezed his. Her heart was near to bursting. She didn't have all the answers, but she did know the most important one. Justin was the only man for her, for eternity, for all lifetimes.

His hand moved to cup her cheek, the tips of his fingers caressing the smooth flesh. A tear fell from her eye. Justin tenderly brushed it away, bent forward, and pressed his lips against the moist skin.

"Don't cry, Janei, please," he whispered hoarsely. "I'll not let anyone harm you again, ever."

Soon there would be time for other promises, but not now. "Janei, we have to find out what is happening, and why. Did you see who it was?"

She shook her head. "It all happened so fast, and it was too dark. I could barely make out where he was, let alone who it was." Her voice faltered, and Justin's arms tightened about her. "I'm all right. I thought I was dreaming at first. Having a nightmare. I don't even know why I woke up."

"Cinder," Justin said simply.

"Cinder? But he wasn't in here."

"That's just the point. After Melody and Gilbert left, he fell asleep on the chair in my study. I left him there."

"Then how did he wake me up?"

"I guess he woke up downstairs and decided he wanted to be in your room. He began barking and scratching at your closed door. That's probably what woke you, only by that time you were evidently too engrossed in fighting for your life to hear him." Justin reached to rub Cinder's head. The dog was now curled in a ball at the foot of the bed.

Janelle pulled the tiny black bundle of hair into her

lap and hugged him. "Thank you, Cinder. You've been a good friend." The dog licked her hand and yawned contentedly.

Justin glanced at Marie and Callie. "Are you two all right?"

Both nodded.

"Good. Marie, could you make some coffee? I doubt we will be getting much more sleep tonight." Justin smiled wryly.

As the two women left the room, Justin turned back to Janelle. "There are a lot of things I still do not understand, Janei. I know someone is trying to kill you. I didn't believe it at first, but I believe you now. Too many things have happened, and each attack is closer, more deadly. The shooting in the bayou, the carriage wheel breaking, and now this."

She shivered.

"Listen to me," he ordered. "I will not let anyone harm you. We will find out who is behind this, but until then you must be very careful to remain near the house. Always stay with someone, never go out alone. But there is something else." His voice became soft, ragged with emotion. "I do not understand what is happening between us. Things are so different now. Better between us. But I don't know why."

She put a finger to his lips, silencing any more words, halting his questions. "I love you, Justin, with all my heart. I have things to tell you that I'm afraid you're going to find very hard to believe. But try, promise me that, Justin. Try to understand what I'm going to say."

Once he would have jumped to the conclusion that her motive for being nice was that she wanted something of him. This time was different. This Sara Janei was different. She had said the words, finally. Sara Janei had never before said she loved him. But it was more than that. Something had changed in her. He'd recognized it, felt it, the moment she had returned, though he had fought to deny it. Now, he had to know the reason behind it.

Justin nodded in agreement.

"You agree readily, but it won't be easy. I can hardly believe it myself, but if you'll try, really try to understand, I'll tell you."

Marie returned with the coffee, and put it on a small table beside the bed, then left the room.

Janelle stared at Justin. She loved him, and she knew he loved her. They were from two different worlds, two different times, and yet they belonged together, their love a bond so strong that time itself ceased to matter. She wondered how she was going to tell him the truth so that he would understand. How was she to begin? Gazing into his eyes now, seeing the love he felt for her reflected there, Janelle prayed she could make him believe her.

Taking a deep breath, she spoke. "First of all, Justin, I am not Sara Janei. I'm not your wife."

He started at her words. "Don't try another of your plays, Janei," he said abruptly.

"No, Justin, I promise you. This is the truth. Just listen to me."

Bright green eyes pleaded with him, and he responded to the sincerity in them.

"Justin, I know it sounds like some tale from the dark side, but let me tell it. My real name is Janelle Torrance. I was born and raised in the state of Nevada. My father was a veterinarian." She saw his eyes narrow in suspicion, and hurried on. "He was an animal doctor, but Daddy specialized in horses. That's how I knew what to do when Micaelai broke his leg. I used to help my father. He ran a horse clinic on our ranch, a hospital for horses. My folks died one night on their way home from Lake Tahoe. There was a little snow left on the hills, and it was raining that night. It's believed my father lost control of the car."

"Car?" he asked, disbelief clear in his voice.

Janelle smiled. This wasn't going to be easy. "Sorry. A car is a carriage, but it doesn't need horses to make it go. I'll explain later, for now just let me tell you how I got here. My best friend at college invited me to come to her home in Louisiana for the summer, to kind of help me get over losing my folks. Justin, my friend's name is Cathy Delacroix. She is, or I guess now I should say, will be, your great-great-great-granddaughter. You see, when I went to her house the year was 1991."

There was a long silence, then Justin looked away from her to stare out the window. Worried, she watched his strong, cleanly carved profile. When he turned back toward her, the slanted smile on his lips did not warm the coldness in his eyes.

"You expect me to believe this? It is 1856. . . 1856! What kind of a fool do you take me for, Janei?"

She reached to clasp his hand. He neither drew away from her touch or returned it. Instead he watched her, the suspicion he felt clearly evident in his intent gaze.

Janelle ignored it and began again. "I started to experience strange things the minute I arrived in New Orleans. Instead of the way the streets should have looked, I began seeing flashes of how they are now, but for me that was over a hundred years' difference. Then I saw Antoine's house, but I didn't know then whose house it was. In 1991 it's a rotting mess. Whatever happens, his house does not survive the years, but Delacroix does, and when I saw this house, Justin, I almost passed out. It was so familiar, and yet I had never been here before. It felt as if I had come home, but I knew that was impossible. And these things kept happening. Then the morning after my arrival I went for a walk in the garden. I was confused, scared, I needed time to think. A storm broke and I lost my way."

At mention of the storm, Justin's features tightened as he, too, recalled the day of her return.

"The garden was so big, the bushes and trees too tall to see around, and there were so many paths that I couldn't figure out which one would lead me back to the house." She paused and closed her eyes in remembered terror, then forcing herself, continued. "I ended up taking refuge in the family cemetery, beneath a large tree. There was a tombstone there and the marble seemed to almost glow in the dark. I don't know why, but I touched it, and when I did, something strange happened. For a few seconds I couldn't move my hand away. Justin, it held me there, and then the sky literally opened up. I don't know what happened, or why. All I know is that when I finally made it back to the house it wasn't 1991 anymore. I walked across your threshold, or I should say, collapsed across it. And it was 1856."

There it was. All out in the open, as implausible as it sounded. Janelle held her breath. He had to believe her. He just had to. She couldn't stand it if he didn't.

"You expect me to believe this?" His voice was low, but hard. There was a moment of strained silence as they stared at each other, and then he exploded.

Janelle flinched. The eruption of Mount St. Helens had nothing on Justin Delacroix, except volume. He didn't shout, but his quiet, leashed anger felt more dangerous and searing.

"You must think me a complete fool. I am to accept tombstones that glow in the dark? Carriages that move with no horses? And that you are some . . . some person who just happens to look exactly like my wife, but traveled here in a storm from . . . what? A hundred and thirty-five years in the future?" Flinty gray eyes pierced her remorselessly, flaying away her defenses.

"Justin, it's the truth. I'm not Sara Janei. My name is Janelle and I was born on February 18, 1965 in Reno, Nevada."

He rose. "I will not play the fool for you again, Janei. I warned you on your return. Evidently you did not believe me. This story is preposterous. How can you sit there and tell it? How?"

Proof! He needed proof. "Wait, Justin, wait," she cried, jumping from her chair and rushing to Sara Janei's desk. She yanked out the top drawer, reaching in to pull out the secret compartment. "You want proof? All right, I'll give you proof."

Janelle had moved the locket and vial from their hiding place behind the armoire to the drawer the day before when she had discovered Callie trying to sweep behind the huge closet. She pushed everything aside hastily, pulling at the fake drawer and mumbling to herself, "If I had to be thrown into someone's place, couldn't it have been someone nice? It's not like I chose this or anything."

She didn't see the reluctant grin lifting one corner of Justin's mouth as he watched her.

Finally Janelle straightened with a look of triumph. She marched across the room, stopped a few feet from where he stood, and held out her hand.

"So, what are those things?" Justin arched a sardonic brow, but he no longer sounded angry.

"Look at them, for heaven's sake!"

"I am looking."

"They're what should prove to you I'm telling the truth. They came here with me. From 1991. Look at them. I'm sure you'll agree they didn't come from anything your world could make, or even knows about yet."

In the palm of her hand were two objects, both foreign to Justin. One was a small vial, shiny and colored, with writing all over it. The other was her locket, which he recognized immediately, until she flipped open its tiny jacket. Beneath a small oval of glass fitted over one side, numbers flashed on and off repeatedly.

"What are these things?" He frowned.

"This one—" she picked up the plastic vial and held it toward him "—is a decongestant. I have allergies and always carry one with me. You put it up to your nose, like this." She demonstrated. "And take a deep breath. It helps clear your sinuses, er, nose, so that you can breathe. Look at it, Justin, you know it isn't something from your time."

He took the vial from her hand, holding it up to the light and peered dubiously at the label. "Desoxyephedrine, methylsalicylate," he pronounced awkwardly, and glanced in her direction. "Tamper resistant, use only if imprinted plastic wrap is intact." Judging from his expression it meant as much to him as pig latin. He handed it back to her and picked up the locket. "What have you done to your locket?"

"My mother had a watch put into it."

"A watch has a face on it, with numbers, so that you can tell the time. This thing is only showing numbers. It does not have a face, or hands," he said, no longer mocking.

"It's digital, Justin. That means it doesn't need all those things to tell me what time it is, and what the day and date are. It even has a stopwatch function, and a memory for retaining a few telephone numbers."

"What kind of numbers?"

"Oh, well, forget that for now. But look at the watch. Here, push this button, see? The time disappears and the day and date come on. Then you push it again and the time comes back." All the while she watched him intently, trying to read beyond that expressionless mask of his, her heart thumping madly with the fear that he would not accept her explanation, not accept her.

Suddenly, without warning he threw the watch on the bed and stalked from the room without a backward glance. Dumbfounded, Janelle watched him leave. She'd thought she was getting through to him, but this was the last straw. She flopped down on the bed and let the tears come. All the frustration and anger she'd felt in the last few days came rushing up to engulf her, all her hopes and dreams of a life with Justin fading out of sight.

"Missy, what happen? Where's Justin?" Marie entered the room to gather the empty coffee tray. She put a comforting arm around Janelle's shoulder.

"He's gone. He stormed out."

"Good Lord Almighty, what'd you say to him now?"

"I just told him the truth."

"Then maybe you best tell me."

Heartsick and dispirited, Janelle kept it simple, assuming the woman wouldn't be able to understand half of what she'd told Justin. But Marie surprised her.

"That man is so stubborn. Just like his papa, but he'll come round, missy. Just give him time to mull it over some, and he'll be back." A chubby black hand reached out and patted Janelle's arm. "You listen to Marie. I helped raise that boy, help bring him into the world even, and if there's one thing I know, it's that he loves you. I seen it in his eyes. He didn't never look at her that way, not like he looks at you. Give him time. What you say happened, well, it's a might much to believe, but it sure is a fact you ain't her." Marie stood. "He'll be back, missy."

"Thank you, Marie," Janelle whispered raggedly. "I hope you're right."

With a snort, the housekeeper left the room, closing the door softly behind her. Janelle felt more alone that moment than she had ever felt in her entire life. There was nothing more that could be done. She had told Justin everything. Now it was up to him. Did he know how much he had come to mean to her? Did he know that since she first saw him, hostile and contemptuous, her silly heart had been lost? No, she hadn't told him that. But if he didn't believe her now, then there was really nothing else she could do, and love would not be enough.

Going to the window, Janelle looked out at the quiet night, memory of the attack of just an hour before the furthest thing from her mind. Light from her room threw an eerie reflection on the dark gardens below, scarcely penetrating the thick shadows in the heavy shrubbery. Suddenly, a movement beneath one of the live oaks caught her attention. Justin moved from beneath the large tree, brushing aside a curtain of moss with a casual sweep of an arm. Janelle stepped away from the window to stand behind the heavy drapery. She didn't want him to see her watching him. When he was ready—if he was ready—he would come to her. Stubborn pride was a bitter thing when her heart ached to call out to him, to run down the stairs and throw herself into his arms, but she couldn't, not unless he believed what she'd told him. It would never work between them if Justin continued to think of her as Sara Janei.

Suddenly, Justin walked toward the front of the house, out of her sight. Janelle returned to bed, slipping her legs beneath the warmth of the covers. Noticing the packet of Sara Janei's pictures on the bedside chest where she'd left them earlier, she picked them up and pulled the tintype of Bernard Chevillon from the stack.

"Maybe I'll get a chance to meet you, too, Grandpa. But what am I supposed to do about Justin?" she whispered, looking into the eyes of the dark young man in the old photograph.

"How about talking to me instead of a picture?" Justin

asked softly. He stood in the doorway, one hand gripping the doorjamb.

Her heart nearly stopped. She dropped the tintype and looked up into his eyes. A fire smoldered in their depths, but was it from the flames of love, or anger? She wasn't sure.

"Justin, let me try and—"

"No, you've done your talking, now it's my turn," he interrupted. A crooked smile softened his face as he walked across the room and sat on the edge of the bed. "Everything you told me sounds like something too strange for words, and yet, I—" he shook his head, paused, and then went on. "I realized almost instantly there was something different about you. A lot of the things you said and did were so out of character, but I did not understand. I still don't know if I really do. What you have said seems so unbelievable, and yet I have no other answer. I am not sure I can accept your explanation, but I know that I need to talk with you more."

Janelle could barely restrain herself from hurtling into his arms. Hope filled her heart. "Justin, all I need you to accept is that I'm not Sara Janei, and that I love you. That's all. All those things she did that hurt you, that wasn't me. I didn't do them. Sara Janei's gone, Justin, and I'm here. Look," she hurried on, "you said you saw the differences yourself. I talk differently, I know you noticed that. And all the other things. Like my feet, I had to buy new shoes. My feet are bigger than hers. And I can't ride sidesaddle. Oh, Justin. Marie believes me. Can't you?"

His smile deepened at her almost disjointed explanation. "I don't know. I want to. Oh, how I want to, but I don't know if I can. There have been so many tricks in the past, so many lies." He sighed.

"Not between us, Justin, between you and Sara Janei. But she's gone. I think she's dead."

His head shot up at that.

"I don't know all the answers, Justin, but I'm the one who's here now. I love you, more than I've ever loved anyone. I want to live my life with you, feel you beside me in bed every night, feel your arms around me. I want to ride the fields with you every morning, and walk the gardens every night with my hand in yours. I want to be the mother of your children, and I want to grow old with you, Justin Delacroix, in this house, this time. And then I want to be buried beside you, and walk the heavens with you, for eternity, if I can."

He looked long and hard into her luminous eyes. The world, his world, was in her smile, her eyes, her tears. Each breath she took was his, each beat of her heart was his. When had she come to live in that secret, innermost place of his soul? She was still a mystery to him. How much did he truly know about her? Yet this love he felt for her, these feelings, were unlike any he had known.

This woman, this beautiful creature who claimed she had come to him from another time, who declared she loved him, was stubborn, courageous, and all-giving. Everything he had looked for in Sara Janei and not found. And this woman was offering it all to him. Part of his mind still cried for caution, but his heart paid no heed. She was his, his love, his life, and he would never let her go. A smile tugged at the corners of his mouth. His hand came up and cupped her chin and then slid gently down the soft skin of her neck, coming to rest on the curve of her shoulder. "I love you," he whispered as his head lowered toward hers.

Janelle pulled back slightly, gazing unblinkingly into his eyes for a long moment. The faint pressure of his hands on her back sent a flush of warmth spreading across her skin. The rapid flow of blood racing through her pulses was a roar in her head, the sound blending with the frantic pounding of her heart. She felt his strength enclose her, an incredible aura of masculinity, will, and determination reaching out to pull her into a haze of passion and longing.

When she finally spoke, her voice was no more than a whisper. She blinked away tears, and unconsciously swayed forward. "Would you . . . would you say that again?"

"I said I love you." His voice was husky with emotion.

Eyes glowing with happiness, Janelle returned his smile. "I love you, too, Justin, more than anything in life. I love you."

The warmth of his lips against hers stopped further conversation. He raised a hand and placed it at the back of her neck, his thumb caressing the hollow at the base of her head. She pulled away from him and looked directly into his eyes. A shadow flitted across her face, a strange vulnerability that plucked at his heart.

"Are you sure you love me for who I am, Justin? Who I really am?" Fear twisted like a knot in her stomach, and she held her breath, waiting for his answer.

He stared down at her for long seconds, a grave expression on his handsome face. When he finally spoke, a smile playing at the corners of his mouth, Janelle felt herself almost faint with joy.

"I have loved you for yourself, Janelle Torrance, since the first time I kissed you." The words surprised even Justin himself, for until he had spoken them, he had not realized just how true they were.

"What did you call me?" she asked, almost unable to believe she'd heard him correctly.

"Janelle Torrance. That is what you said your name is." He laughed, and pulled her further into his embrace.

"Then you believe me?"

"I have to. I knew Sara Janei never loved me, and she never could have said the things you just did with any conviction. I thought, at first, she and I had something special, but I discovered soon after the marriage ceremony that the only thing she found special about me was my money. But that is in the past. I do have one question, however. When I came back into the room you were talking to that picture and calling it Grandpa. What was that all about?"

"Bernard Chevillon was . . . is . . . was my great-great-great-grandfather. For several years before my mother died she'd been researching the family genealogy, tracing all our ancestors so that she could needlepoint a family tree. I got roped into helping her. Now I'm glad. See, I didn't know about Sara Janei because she wasn't directly related to my mom. Or if I did, I've forgotten. So she wouldn't have been a big part of our research, but Bernard was. There is definitely a family link, and that explains why Sara Janei and I look so much alike."

"Janelle, I do not know if I can ever truly accept this, about you being from the future, but I do know you are not Sara Janei. And I know I love you. No matter where you are from, or who you are, I need you with me. Share my life, Janelle." He smiled then, and her heart leapt with wonder at the happiness she finally saw on his face as his lips lowered toward hers.

Marie, standing in the shadows of the hallway just a few feet from Janelle's bedroom door, smiled to herself. She didn't make a habit of listening in on Justin's conversations, in fact she couldn't remember ever having done so before, but she had felt it a necessity this time. She liked the girl. Justin could be happy with her, she wasn't like the other one. Thank heavens that one was gone for good. Or was she?

Chapter eighteen

THE EBONY BLACKNESS OF NIGHT TURNED A hazy orange-yellow, and the silver glow of stars faded into the brightness of morning as the sun crept over the horizon. Justin's lips on hers were warm and possessive, the taste of an after-dinner brandy still clinging to his mouth. Gently his tongue coaxed Janelle's lips apart, seductively tasting and demanding, igniting her passion.

She trembled as the flames of desire burst to life in her. Slowly the clenched hands that had been gripping each other in nervous tension uncurled and moved to glide over the sinewy band of muscle that embraced her. She swayed toward him, wild exultation like a cresting wave sweeping over her, and though she had lost all sense of perspective and time, she was vibrantly conscious of her body, of Justin's.

He was losing himself to her, and he didn't care. The past was no longer part of his life, only now, only Janelle. He wanted her, needed her, and he loved her. She was everything he wanted, had ever dreamed of, and she was his. Tomorrow he would search for the answers, he would find a way to keep her beside him.

There was a feeling of sudden freedom in her chest,

as if a caged eagle had been set free to soar the heavens. An unbidden moan deep in her throat escaped as Justin folded her even closer to his aroused body. Not a space separated them. Her body melded to him; her slim legs fitted between his.

They had fallen into each other's arms before, allowed their bodies to take command and join them together, but this time was different. Each touch was slow and tantalizing, each caress titillating. Her senses were intoxicated with pleasure, her flesh burning as his lips skimmed the silken surface. The ache building in her body intensified. Her hand slid across his chest and slipped through the short curls of black hair. She pressed her lips into that satin forest, drinking in the taste and scent of him, rewarded by the groan of desire that escaped Justin's lips as his mouth moved to recapture hers.

She felt as if she had loved him for so long, an eternity. Had it really been only mere days? Moreover, she would continue to love him whatever their fate; whether it be together, or a hundred years apart, Justin Delacroix would forever be a part of her, living within the sacred, perhaps secret, confines of her heart. Suddenly Janelle drew away, and as she looked up at him, she was both shocked and deeply aroused by the passion so evidently stamped on his taut features. Her heart gave a strange leap, then she jerkily averted her face.

"Justin, I might be sent back," she whispered. Tears stung the back of Janelle's eyelids and she swallowed hard to stop the sob that threatened to spill from her throat. "We have no way of being sure we can have a life together, or that I'll even be here tomorrow. That's not fair to you."

Strong, warm fingers cupped her chin. With soft pressure he forced her head to turn, his eyes burning into hers. "No one has any guarantees in life, Janelle, you know that as well as I do. Our situation may be riskier than most, but I can live with that. I am willing to take the chance. I love you. I need you in my life, for however long we have."

"But what if tomorrow never comes for us? What if . . ."

He pressed a finger to her lips, cutting off the rest of her words. "We cannot spend our lives worrying about something that may never happen. You may be taken away from me at any moment. I'll live with that fear every day, but I will also treasure every second that we are together. If you are ripped from my side I will spend the remainder of my life wondering why and cherishing memories of the love we shared." He brushed his lips across hers, his touch gentle and featherlight. "But it may never happen, and I pray it does not. I want you beside me, Janelle, as my wife, and the mother of my children. I can take the risk, if you can."

"But it might . . . happen years from now, after we've had children, while they're still young. What if I'm gone from your life then?"

"Then I will raise our children alone, the best I can, and I will never regret my decision." He gently held her face in both his hands and his words struck away her fears. "I will tell them all about their mother, where she came from, what happened to her, and how much she loved them. I'll tell them how special she was, and I will live. Just as you will live, my love. And I'll tell them how much I love her, and miss her. In our hearts we will be together always. Fate has given us this chance, Janelle, and it'll not be so cruel as to take it from us. Trust in me, trust in our love, and all will be as it should."

Her eyes misted with tears and his features blurred momentarily. Janelle didn't know whether her heart was bursting with too much love or breaking at the threat of losing it, she only knew that she could not bear the thought of being without him.

Justin gently brushed away the tears that slid down her cheeks. Janelle Torrance might look like his missing wife, but there the similarity ended. He had married Sara Janei in the belief that he loved her, that she was perfect. He had quickly discovered his error. Now he was learning the real depths of his own passion from this wondrous woman who claimed to be from over a hundred years in the future. She had been able to forgive him his callous treatment of her, his suspicion, his anger. A sensual promise of a lifetime of love glowed from her eyes as she gazed up at him. God, how he had misjudged her! He vowed then that he would treasure this new beginning, this priceless love. And woe to the fiend who dared to harm her.

"I'm afraid," she whispered, her hands resting against his chest. His heart pounded beneath her fingers, echoing the racing beat of her own pulses.

He pressed his lips to her forehead, his warm breath fanning the curled wisps of hair at her temples. "Janelle, love has nothing to do with how long we live, or where, or how. Our love can transcend time. It can survive, whether we are together or apart. We have proven that. You say you have traveled a hundred and thirty-five years to find love with me. Do not be afraid to commit to it. Listen to your heart, *chère,* and do what it tells you to do. Let us begin again, my love, together."

Janelle looked up into his face. The love she saw mirrored in his eyes took her breath away and caused her heart, soaring with happiness, to beat in thumping, somersaulting rhythm. "Oh, Justin." She wrapped her arms around his neck, her fingers losing themselves in the soft black curls at his nape.

His gaze roamed her face, drinking in her beauty, memorizing every curve and line of the delicate features; green eyes luminous with tears and framed by a wet fan of auburn-tinged lashes, high cheekbones hollowing to cheeks a pinkish hue, the pert curve of her nose, and her mouth lush and full, smiling its invitation, her lips moist and slightly swollen, an irresistible temptation for any man.

"Love me, Janelle Torrance, for whatever time we have, that is all I ask," he said huskily, pulling her tightly against his warm body.

She met his eyes for a long moment, the love she had for him surging through her and she promised, as solemnly as taking an oath upon hallowed ground, "Yes, I love you, Justin Delacroix. Till my last breath I shall always love you."

They slept, bodies entwined, until midmorning. He awoke to the sun on his face, and lay quietly for long moments, staring down at the still-sleeping Janelle, her head resting in the cradle of his arm. His gaze traveled over her lovely features and he knew that the fates had finally blessed him. An impulse to once again taste the sweet warmth of her lips beneath his possessed him. He lowered his head and his mouth gently covered hers. Lush lashes fluttered as she stirred beneath his touch, her lips hungrily responding to the questioning pressure of his.

"I think we've missed breakfast," he mumbled, his fingers making light circles on her shoulder.

"Ummm."

He laughed. "Is this what I am to expect? A wife who wallows in bed half the day after wantonly seducing me for most of the night? And then cares not if I have food to replenish my waning strength?"

She turned her face toward him, propping her chin on

his shoulder. "Is it so bad, the seducing part, I mean?" A teasing sparkle lit her eyes.

But as he moved to take her lips again, Justin caught the faint frown that marred the delicate features, and he pulled back.

"What is it, *chère?* What has brought the worry back into those beautiful eyes?"

"I'm not your wife, Justin. Sara Janei is, and we don't know where she is or what's happened to her."

"God has made you my wife, Janelle, as you are my life. But you are right. Our lives will always be threatened by the possibility of Sara Janei's return. We must discover the truth of her disappearance now, and of the attacks on your life."

Janelle sat up, hugging the pillow to her body and unconsciously blocking his view of her naked form. "Justin, what do you think happened to her? Could she have run off with someone?"

"Possibly. I knew she had lovers. I always knew. But was never sure of whom or when. By the time she disappeared, I didn't care."

"Antoine was her lover. And Gilbert," Janelle said softly, holding her breath as she waited for his reaction. She didn't really know what she expected him to do, or say, only now that the time of truth was upon her she felt a small, niggling thread of fear. Everything was so wonderful between Justin and her, he was as perfect a lover, in every sense of the word, as she could ever want or hope for; but there was so much that could go wrong, that could destroy what they had found together.

"Umm. Antoine, I suspected. But Gilbert? No. I admit I occasionally considered him, but as easily dismissed the idea. I always thought him too intelligent to succumb to her schemes. Evidently I was wrong."

"And O'Roarke," she added. "He was one of her lovers, too."

"That I would never have guessed."

"What about us, Justin? What if she did run off with someone? That would mean she's still married to you."

Moving swiftly, he removed the pillow she still clutched and pulled her into his arms, enveloping her with the warmth and passion of his body. "You are my wife, Janelle," he vowed, his voice a hoarse whisper in her ear. "Before God, and in my heart, you are my wife, my true wife. And I will move heaven and earth to make you my wife in the eyes of the law and Church. Trust me, *chère*. Trust me."

It was well after the noonday meal was ready and cooling on the sideboard when Justin arrived in the dining room. A few minutes later, Janelle entered. Justin's gaze, alight with love, followed her as she moved toward him. Gone was the cold-eyed man of the days before; the anger he had worn like a protective cloak to hide his feelings, his pain, was nowhere in evidence. Instead he radiated warmth, his eyes gleaming with passion. His smile touched her heart and sent a wave of pleasure tingling throughout her body.

He could only wonder and marvel at how this wonderful woman had come into his life, a second chance offered by fate, one that he had nearly destroyed with his own bitterness. But never again, he vowed, would he give her cause to doubt him, to fear him, or to regret accepting his love, and giving hers in return.

They had stayed in bed, talking of their pasts and planning their future together. That future was endangered by the attacks on Janelle's life. They discarded several plans of action before finally agreeing on one. The upcoming soirée would have in attendance all Sara Janei's friends. What better time to search for the truth and lay a trap?

After seating Janelle beside him at the long dining

table, Justin rang the bell that summoned Marie to serve.

"Marie, has all the food been prepared for Saturday night?" Justin asked, aware of his housekeeper's knowing smile. He grinned, acknowledging her approval.

She nodded emphatically. "I seen to all of it myself."

"Good, good. We'll be going out for a ride. Please bring iced coffee to the study when we return."

"Yes, Michie. We already cleaned in there today."

Marie's hint about their lateness in rising was not lost on him and he chuckled softly. "I've been told that I have a hard head, Marie. It would appear that you've known a lot more about what has been happening here than I did."

A satisfied smile widened the housekeeper's generous cheeks. "This one's too nice. It gave her away. And I saw how she watched you. Scared sometimes, but drawn, too. It wasn't like before, with the other one. That one didn't have no heart for nobody. Only cared about herself." Her smile deepened at the glowing look Justin exchanged with Janelle.

He rose and moved to stand before Marie, affectionately hugging her big body to his. "But this *is* Janei, Marie. You understand? For all intended purposes, from now on, this *is* my wife."

"As long as you two is happy, and it's peaceful around here, that's all I care about. Her and I had our talk while you was still fuming and strutting about." She moved to stand before Janelle. "Don't matter none to me who you are, or where you come from, missy. He loves you, and I can see you love him. Nothing else matters. Leastways, nothing I care about."

"Thank you, Marie," Janelle said softly, touched.

When they rode from the barn the midday air had already turned sultry, humid waves of heat drifting across the horizon. Janelle kept Lady alongside Tobar, the great height of the big stallion putting Justin's shoulders well above her head. She had to lift the wide brim of her hat and raise her head to actually see his face.

It felt wonderful to be out, riding beside him, no secrets to hold them apart. Her eyes drank in the lush landscape, and she breathed deeply of the sweet, almost overpowering fragrance of sugarcane that filled the air. But her attention always returned to Justin, a sensuous glow warming her from the inside, spreading through her as their eyes met and held. This would be her home for the rest of her life, God willing. And she would be by the side of this magnificent man, to love him and be loved, as she had never dared dream.

Coming to a cotton field where a group of slaves were busily cultivating the earth beneath the prickly plants, Janelle started at seeing the overseer ride toward where she and Justin had reined in.

Stephan O'Roarke greeted Justin affably, and his attention seemed concentrated on his employer, but Janelle began to feel uncomfortable as the man's gaze drifted to her whenever Justin turned away. She would have ignored it, or simply smiled, but for the lust she saw sweep across his features each time he faced her. Justin leaned down to speak to one of the field workers and O'Roarke, staring at her, winked, the fleshy pink lips curving in a lewd smile, his hand moving to rub suggestively at his crotch. He seemed not at all perturbed by her aloof expression.

She exhaled deeply in relief as she and Justin rode away.

"I'll fire him as soon as I locate a replacement," Justin said quietly. "It won't solve the problem of their antagonism toward you, but it will help." There was no recrimination or condemnation in his tone, only the warmth and cherishing of a man who would see her happy and loved. He leaned toward her, and she raised her mouth to receive his kiss.

They rode for another hour before coming within sight of the cypress grove. The hair on the back of Janelle's neck rose as they neared the dense growth. They had come to look for Sara Janei, agreeing a search of the grove was the most logical step to begin their pursuit of the truth.

Tying the horses to a bush, Justin led the way along a narrow path that wove between the thickly grown trees. The hot afternoon sun was instantly blocked off and only an occasional stream of light pierced the dense growth. He stopped frequently, bending down to run his fingers through a clump of grass or beneath a fallen log. The silence in the grove was deafening, the sound of their steps on the damp ground the only noise except for the infrequent chirrup of a bird or croak of a frog. Finding nothing, they were about to turn back when Janelle screamed and clutched frantically at Justin, her eyes dilated as she stared at the ground a few feet before him. He chuckled and wrapped an arm round her shoulders. A young alligator, no more than four feet long, slid from the bank where it had been basking in a thin stream of sunlight that shone through the trees. The ridge-backed reptile slipped quietly into the murky water.

"It's as scared of you as you are of it, probably more," Justin soothed as they headed out of the swamp.

"I rather doubt that," she said weakly. "I just thank my lucky stars I didn't see it when I was in here alone. I don't know what I'd have done, probably turned around and run smack into a bullet." It was a feeble joke, but she felt infinitely better with his arms around her. She did not see the worry that came into his eyes at the mention of the attack on her.

Moments later, Janelle waited beside the horses while

Justin searched the edge of the grove where she had collapsed after being shot at. When he finally came out he held something in his hand, a thoughtful expression on the dark, handsome face.

She asked anxiously, "What did you find?"

He held his hand out toward her. A small bit of gold chain, caked with mud, lay in his palm.

"Can you tell if it's from Sara Janei's necklace? The one I told you I found—and lost?"

"It could be, but I can't be sure."

They rode back to the house slowly, each deep in thought, pondering what their next step in solving the mystery of Sara Janei's disappearance should be. Near the entrance drive to Delacroix, the Foucheau carriage turned onto the main road and blocked their entry. The driver pulled to a stop as the petite blond in the open carriage leaned forward and tapped his shoulder with her fan for emphasis.

"Janei, Justin, how fortunate! I was so disappointed not to find you home. I was calling, Janei, to see if you would join me. I'm going to town." Melody's gaze remained locked on Janelle as she smiled. For the first time Janelle recognized fully the hatred that simmered beneath the woman's calm facade and a chill ran up her spine.

Janelle tried to smile. "Thank you, Melody, but this afternoon Justin and I have to see to the preparations for the soirée. Maybe another time."

"Isn't it a bit late in the day to be going to town, Melody?" Justin inquired.

"Ummm, maybe. It was a sudden decision, though I'll most probably spend the night in town. Dear Gilbert is off on another of his business trips until tomorrow and I am utterly bored. I had hoped I might entice you into accompanying me to the opera."

Melody said good-bye and urged her driver to proceed, then abruptly turned back to them instead. "Oh, Janei, I noticed something the other night while we were calling on you. I meant to comment on it then, since it has always been such an obsession with you, but it slipped my mind. You haven't been wearing your locket lately. Did you lose it? Perhaps in that horrid carriage accident?"

Janelle's hand rose to her throat, her gaze moving to Justin for help.

"We are having it repaired, Melody. The clasp broke," Justin drawled silkily.

"Oh, that really is too bad. But you're lucky it wasn't lost. It really is sweet of you to do that, Justin. I mean, everyone knows that Sara Janei carries an old beau's portrait in her locket. Most men wouldn't be so understanding of such a thing. Aren't you just the tiniest bit jealous?"

Justin's mouth thinned, and his eyes became hooded, but not before the two women caught a glimpse of the iciness beneath. A muscle throbbed in his taut jaw, and the scar on his cheek whitened. He had never liked Melody Foucheau. He liked her even less now.

Melody immediately began to pale and fidget, visibly backing away from Justin's penetrating gaze. She did not wait for an answer. She issued a brusque order to her driver, and the carriage was instantly jerked into motion.

"She wanted nothing more than to confirm that you were here, at Delacroix," Justin said, his drawl more pronounced.

"And to make sure I was not with Gilbert," Janelle stated flatly, her mind working along the same vein as Justin's.

Chapter nineteen

JANELLE STEPPED ON JUSTIN'S FOOT FOR THE hundredth time and groaned loudly. "I'm never going to get the hang of this. How about if we just pretend I broke my leg and I'll sit the evening out?"

"No. You cannot 'sit the evening out,' as you put it. Sara Janei loved to dance."

"Just my luck." She rolled her eyes. "Let's try it again. I guess I'll get it sooner or later."

He made as if to hobble. "Sooner would be nice."

She glared and raised a fist at him and he chuckled again, then he pulled her back into his arms and began to hum aloud. Lifting the voluminous skirts in one hand, Janelle tried to follow his lead, peeking down at his feet every few seconds. They had managed a waltz with no trouble, a polka, a schottische, and a quadrille, the dance that would open the soirée. But this last dance he was trying to teach her was proving a challenge, to them both. The galloping cadence of the Roger de Coverly was meant for only the very graceful and quick footed.

After several attempts they both collapsed exhausted on the settee, breathing heavily from their efforts. Justin rested his head on the carved rosewood edging of the seat while Janelle used him for a pillow and lay against his shoulder.

"Oh, my aching feet. I'll have to have Sammy make me a pair of metal covers for my toes before Saturday," Justin teased.

"Why, you . . ." She laughed, slugging his shoulder with a fist. "Get off that lazy rump of yours and let's try it again."

"I have a better idea." He lunged for her. A wicked smile curved his lips. His arm snaked between her body and the seat's cushion, pulling her to him, and she came eagerly, her hands sliding up over his arms, relishing the feel of hard muscle that rippled beneath the linen shirt. Her lips burned from the pressure of his as they brushed the corners of her mouth, igniting the flames that awaited only his touch to be kindled. At first tender and soft, his kiss slowly grew demanding as passion intensified. Her lips parted without hesitation and she welcomed the hot, moist joining of their tongues, each tasting the essence of the other. With a low moan deep in his throat, Justin drew her closer. His tongue flicked about hers, teasing, sliding down its length and then moving to probe the sensitive hollows of her mouth. All coherent thought fled her mind.

He pulled her to lie across the wide breadth of his chest and she felt the hammering of his heart pounding against her breast. Her own beat an accelerated rhythm in answer. She threw back her head, her breath deep and ragged as Justin trailed a fiery path of kisses down the gentle curve of her neck to the pulsating hollow at the base of her fragrant throat. His lips savored the taste of hers, and a quick, feathering flick of his tongue brought a soft cry of pleasure from her. His hand spread over her ribcage, moving to cup her breast. Even through her gown Janelle could feel the heat of his touch, the slow, steady circling motion of his thumb over her nipple. She clung to him, her fingers buried in the crisp black curls of his hair.

With the inert speed of a man drowning in his own pleasure, Justin's mouth sought to claim hers again. He was consumed with desire as she responded to his hands and tongue. This was all new and wonderful to him, the feeling of receiving total love, the wanton abandon he felt flowing from her, enveloping him, hungering for him. In her giving and love, she was pure and whole, loving him as he had never been before. Realization of the depth of her love brought forth a surge of desire within him.

A soft knock on the door brought them both instantly upright, Janelle almost tumbling from his lap to the floor. Cheeks flaming, she swung around on the seat, quickly adjusted her skirts, and brushed at the strands of hair that had come loose. Justin moved to stand beside the fireplace. When she was composed, though her flush deepened at his gleaming eyes, he called to whomever was waiting to enter.

The door swung open and Marie carried a pitcher of lemonade and a tray of sandwiches into the room. She placed them on a table in front of the settee. "Got kinda quiet in here, so I thought I'd serve refreshments," she said, her effort at being subtle a dismal failure.

On a mischievous impulse Justin quickly moved to Marie's side, taking her in his arms and whirling the startled woman about the room. Janelle giggled with delight.

They made such an odd couple; the tall, handsome Creole and the short, round, black housekeeper. Even in his presently casual but rumpled state of dress, Justin cut a devastatingly handsome figure. Black broadcloth trousers held tight to his long, lean legs and a white linen shirt stretched taut across muscular shoulders.

He wore no cravat, and the neck of his shirt was unbuttoned, a swirl of curly black hair peeking out from the *V* of pristine whiteness.

Cinder pranced into the room and on seeing the whirling couple, became excited. He ran between their legs, yipping happily. Janelle called to him to come to her but it did no good, the tiny dog was too caught up in the frenzy of the moment to pay her heed. Justin stumbled over the small body, but caught himself instantly. Cinder jumped against Marie's skirt and the big woman lost her balance. She shrieked and tottered, her arms swinging at the air. Justin tried to catch her. His hands grabbed at the voluminous folds of her sleeves, but it wasn't enough. They both went down, Marie landing on the generous padding of her rear end, Justin straddling her lap. Cinder, after pausing for just a brief moment to scrutinize the damage he'd done, wiggled beneath the low-slung secretary beside the fireplace. Only the faint glimmer of staring eyes gave evidence of his presence wedged into the dark cavity.

"I'm gonna kill that dog!" Marie howled, puffing furiously as she tried to get up. "That mutt's gonna be the death of me yet! Always under my feet, getting in the way, yapping and whining. Ought to cook him for dinner, that's what I ought to do."

Janelle rushed across the room to help them. Justin was back on his feet before she reached him. He put a hand under one of Marie's arms, Janelle took the other, and together they hoisted the large woman to her feet.

An hour later the galloping steps of the contredanse were conquered. Justin and Janelle moved as one, in enviable grace and fluidity, their bodies attuned to each other, to each step and sway.

Janelle's lessons continued at the table as Justin explained the food to be served at the soirée, but halfway through the meal she waved her hands in surrender. "I give up, Justin, I can't remember all this. My smattering of high school French is rusty, at best. I'll just have to fake it."

"How?" he challenged.

"I don't know. I'll just do it, that's all. I'll nod and smile, and flirt if I have to, whatever it takes. Now, is there more?"

"We have just begun."

"Great!" She sighed.

"All right, now in the reception line . . ."

"Wait, I've got a better idea. Let's turn the soirée into a costume party and I'll come as Batwoman, that way no one will recognize me and I won't have to learn all this."

The somber expression on his face stopped her laughter. "Okay, never mind. Bad idea, anyway."

But half an hour later, while she listened to him recite all the things she still needed to learn, the idea began to look even better. Her heart sank. Three days, that was all the time she had in which to learn how to be Sara Janei Delacroix under close scrutiny. So far, she'd managed to bluff her way through short encounters, but the soirée would last for hours and she would be on center stage the entire time.

With endless patience Justin coaxed and soothed and taught: how Sara Janei used her fan to flirt, the names and histories of the guests, the correct way to greet and introduce them, who Sara Janei liked and who she didn't. There were people whose friendship she cultivated merely because of their position in society, and others she snubbed remorselessly. Janelle had to learn how to talk like the missing woman, what words she always used in French, her mannerisms, and most importantly, she had to learn who her own relatives were. Janelle's heart leapt at that last instruction.

"You mean they'll all be here? Bernard will be here?" she cried in excitement. "I'll get to actually meet him?"

"Yes, but remember, he's not your ancestor now, he's your brother." His tone held a warning note. The whole charade they'd concocted for the soirée weighed heavily on his mind. He looked at her, sitting there so calm and trusting.

"Stop worrying, Justin. Everything will work as we planned. We've agreed that Sara Janei was probably murdered and most likely by someone very close to her. It's the only logical explanation for her disappearance. This is our chance to prove it. The guilty person will undoubtedly be at the party."

"That is exactly what worries me. This person is trying to kill *you* now." He jumped up from the table and began to pace the room. "This little . . . plan of ours is not foolproof. What if it does not work? It is so dangerous, *chère*. There will be too many people here."

Janelle rose and moved to his side. "Justin, it will work. It has to. It's the only real chance we'll have. If we don't lay a trap for him now, I'll be at his mercy until he decides to strike again, and we won't know when or where that will be. At least this way we're picking the time and place, so we'll be prepared."

He knew she was right, but he still didn't like it. There were too many things that could go wrong.

"Justin, listen to me, you'll be with me all evening, and both Marie and Sammy will be alerted to watch for anything suspicious. If anything happens, you'll know. We'll all know."

He reached for her and in the fiery haze of his eyes, she saw her image reflected. His arms pulled her into a tight embrace, crushing the air from her lungs with its urgency.

Her hands slipped around his waist.

"I couldn't bear to lose you, Janelle," he whispered, brushing his lips across hers, the light touch instantly stirring a tingling deep in her breast.

She hungrily returned his kiss, waking his passion and sending it surging through his body to engulf every nerve, every cell. Without thought or hesitation, he lifted her into his arms and carried her up the stairs to her room, not pausing until he stood beside the large poster bed.

They loved each other long into the night, until finally, their desires sated, their bodies content and exhausted from the long day and tiring dance lessons, and lacking sleep from the previous night of loving, they snuggled close and fell asleep in each other's arms.

They were seated across from each other at the large oak table in the warming kitchen, having a very early cup of coffee.

"What were you doing outside?" she asked.

"I woke up and couldn't get back to sleep. I didn't want to wake you, so I went down to check on Micaelai."

"How is he?"

"Pretty good, thanks to you. He did not flinch once when I examined his leg."

Over a second cup of coffee Justin talked of the coming harvest and his plans for the plantation, but as he expanded on his ideas he became aware of a shadow slowly passing over her face.

"What is the matter, Janelle?"

"I don't know what's going to happen, Justin, to me, to us, but there are things I have to tell you. Things you should know so that you can prepare for them." Janelle sighed. Too bad she hadn't been carrying an American history book with her when she'd been thrown back here, but, she thought wearily, nothing's ever that easy.

"Justin, there's going to be a war, a bad one. This business with the slaves, it's going to cause trouble and everyone will suffer, but mainly the South. You've got to prepare for it."

He nodded. "I've thought as much, the way things have been going. When will it start?"

"In 1860. No, 1861, April, I think. The South, the Confederacy, fires on Fort Sumter in South Carolina. The war between the North and South will last about four years, until Robert E. Lee surrenders to General Grant at Appomattox Courthouse in Virginia."

He closed his eyes for a minute, rubbing a hand through his hair. When he finally looked at her again she saw the resignation and infinite sadness in his expression. "I have wanted to ask you so many questions, Janelle, about where you're from, what the world will be like in the years to come, but I just couldn't bring myself to do it. Maybe I was afraid of your answers."

For the next hour she told him about the twentieth century, about her family and her life before. When she finally spoke of the Civil War, the shadow returned to his features, and worry creased his handsome face.

"What can we do? Can we prevent it?" he questioned.

"No, Justin, we can't change history. It's impossible. All we can do is prepare for it."

"And us?" he whispered, stroking the soft flesh of her wrist with his thumb as he held her gaze.

"I don't know." She sighed.

"It's the possibility of leaving you that scares me, Justin, the thought of never seeing you again, having to live my life without you. I'm afraid to start a life with you because I fear I'll lose it."

He grasped her hand and lifted it to his lips, kissing the point of each knuckle and then turning her hand over, the warmth of his mouth pressed against her palm.

A shiver of pleasure ran through her, and Janelle trembled. She reached out her other hand to touch his scarred cheek, her fingers moving lovingly over the marred flesh and then sweeping up to lightly brush aside the waves of black hair that curled at his temples, the short stubble of beard on his jaw scratching against her palm.

"We have to take the chance, *chère*, we have to," he said huskily. He leaned across the table to press his lips to hers. She could smell the warm, moist essence of his body, and her own responded instinctively to his strength and virility. Her hands slid over the rolling muscles of his shoulder, enclosing his neck, entwining in the satiny blackness of his hair as her lips greedily answered his demand.

Suddenly the kitchen door swung open and Marie came into the room, mumbling to herself, and stopped in her tracks when she saw Justin and Janelle at the table. They pulled away from each other at her entrance.

"Lord, I didn't know you two was up already. Just had some boy from town deliver a note. He said it was only for Miss Sara, but I told him no one was up yet, I wasn't getting them up, and he wasn't waiting." She placed the note, which was folded about the stem of a single rose, on the table between them and looked down at it with distaste.

Justin tensed. Janelle released the ribbon and pulled the note free. For a long moment she studied the short message, each written word a flourish of swirls and exaggerated lines. "Until Saturday night," she said softly, reading the words aloud, "but there's no signature. From one of my admirers, I presume?"

Chapter twenty

BY FRIDAY AFTERNOON, THE DAY BEFORE THE soirée, the Delacroix household was in a state of complete upheaval, every available hand busily preparing for the coming party. Marie spent the entire day going between the cookhouse and the main house, supervising the baking, cleaning, polishing, and furniture arrangements. There were to be thirty guests staying for the night in the main house and another twenty young men in the *garçonnière*. These guests had traveled too far to be expected to return home after the soirée. Several other couples were staying with the Foucheaus, but the majority of the two hundred guests would be returning either to their own plantation or to a New Orleans hotel. And some had homes of their own in the French Quarter.

Justin left the house early that morning, wanting to check the fallow acreage in the northern section of Delacroix. He was already planning strategy against the hardships that, as Janelle had explained, would arise in the coming years due to the impending war and its aftermath.

Janelle offered to help Marie with the preparations for

the soirée, and after much arguing finally managed to squelch the housekeeper's protests. Begrudgingly the black woman put her to work cutting flowers and greenery from the garden and arranging them in large vases that had been strategically placed throughout the main-floor rooms, and within moments their aromatic fragrance filled the house.

Later, having just finished with her last trip to the garden, a basket of fresh cut flowers hanging from her arm, Janelle stood on the gallery and looked to see if she could spot Justin approaching the house. He had been gone since early morning and had not returned for the midday meal. She tried to block the glare of the sun from her eyes as she studied the horizon.

A figure moved toward Janelle from the side of the house. Feeling assured no one else was around, he drew nearer.

Janelle was unaware of him until she heard the sound his heavy boots made when he stepped from the grass onto the crushed shells at the bottom of the entry steps. She turned quickly, her nose wrinkling at the stench of a bad cigar that filled the air. Stephan O'Roarke grinned at her, feet spread wide apart, hands on hips, leer in his eyes.

"Well now, you didn't think you was getting rid of me that easy, did you, sweetie?" he asked nastily, his eyes roaming her body blatantly from head to toe.

The overseer took a threatening step toward her but Janelle refused to draw back. She realized instantly the man was angry, and more than a little drunk. A wave of disgust rose in her throat at his strong physical odor blended with the cheap cigar smoke. His thin blue work shirt clung to his body, the fabric wet with perspiration, the front hanging open to reveal a chest heavily matted with fading red hair, already streaked with gray. His thick waist bulged in a generous roll above the waistline of his baggy pants, a round swell of flesh protruding between bright red suspenders.

"What do you want, Mr. O'Roarke?" Janelle said coldly, her revulsion of him clearly evident.

"I want my job back, that's what I want. And you're going to get it for me. That dandy of a husband of yours done fired me, and I ain't standing for it." He jerked the cigar butt from his mouth and threw it forcefully on the ground. "You get me my job back, darlin', or I'm likely to tell that high-and-mighty fop about the little party games you and me been playing out back of my house."

"You've been fired, Mr. O'Roarke. I suggest you leave before Justin returns and finds you still here. I'm sure that would not please him."

"You bitch! You can't do this, I'll tell him!" he threatened, raising a clenched fist menacingly.

"Get out, Mr. O'Roarke," Janelle said. She refused to be intimidated.

Neither had heard, nor seen, Justin's approach.

"You'll be sorry, darlin'," O'Roarke snarled, taking a step toward the staircase. He caught a movement in the shadows of the gallery out of the corner of his eye and paused suddenly midstride.

"My wife ordered you to leave, O'Roarke, as I myself did several hours ago. I think you should do so now, without further delay," Justin said, his voice as cold and sharp as a rapier blade. He stepped forward to stand beside Janelle, his arm sliding protectively around her waist.

After dinner that evening, Justin brought up the subject of O'Roarke again.

"It all seems so clear now, Janelle. I suspected something was going on, but I could never put all the pieces together. The blacks hated Sara Janei so much, but still,

I find this all hard to believe. It's worse than I ever imagined." His fist slammed down on the dining table.

"You can't blame yourself for what O'Roarke and Sara did."

"But I must share the guilt. The blacks are my responsibility, they're my people. I should have protected them better."

"They don't blame you," Janelle insisted softly, trying to ease the pain she knew he felt.

"No, but they blame you. They believe you are she. How can I protect you against every slave on this plantation? How do I even know which ones to protect you from?" He was frustrated with guilt at finally realizing the full scope of Sara Janei's cruelty to the slaves, and panicked at the thought that harm could come to Janelle because of it.

"In a few years the South will be forced to free all of its slaves, Justin. Perhaps if we start now, slowly, a few at a time, we can win their trust, and maybe even their loyalty."

He nodded but remained silent. The thought was so alien to him. How could the plantation cope without them? Who would harvest the cotton, and the sugarcane? Where would the freed slaves go? How would they live? They were uneducated, unskilled. But they could be trained, his mind argued. They could be paid a wage to work the plantation, given their cottage and a parcel of land to sharecrop. It could be done, he reasoned, but he would have to start preparing immediately.

Janelle began her personal preparations for the soirée immediately after breakfast the next morning with a long, lilac-scented bath, a strong cup of café noir, and a flaky pastry roll. She passed another two hours lazing on the gallery, back to the sun, her damp hair spread over her shoulders. But, by late afternoon several of the overnight guests had arrived and Delacroix quickly became a bedlam of genteel confusion.

Half a dozen maids scurried about the house, their mistresses issuing a constant stream of orders and demands. Justin entertained the husbands in his study while the women prepared themselves for the soirée. Small trays of food were sent to each room for their guests since there was to be no formal dinner before the soirée, but rather, several buffet tables presented midway through the evening's festivities. Janelle ignored her tray, too nervous and excited to eat, but Cinder wasn't, and profited nicely from her nerves.

Janelle sat at the dressing table wearing only her thin cheviot wrapper, belted at the waist, and stared into the mirror. Callie began to brush her hair and spent what seemed to Janelle an endless amount of time twirling hair around the hot tongs, holding it in place, releasing it, reheating the tongs and repeating the process on another handful of hair. Then she began sculpting a waterfall of curls that cascaded from the top of Janelle's head to the nape of her neck and draped over the left shoulder. Callie secured a spray of tiny flowers, made of the same shimmering white satin as the ballgown, behind Janelle's left ear, weaving it into the mass of curls.

"It's beautiful, Callie, you've done a marvelous job. Thank you," Janelle exclaimed in wonder at her reflection in the mirror.

The girl smiled shyly and immediately busied herself opening several jars of face paint. Shyly admonishing Janelle to sit perfectly still, she began applying the powder to her mistress's face, finishing with a rose petal rubbed over cheeks and lips for pinkness.

When Janelle rose to dress, she found her stomach fluttering with nervous tension. A dose of fresh air would cure that, she thought. She went to the French doors and drew them open. A wave of sultry night air wafted into the stuffy room and she stepped out onto the gallery, and wrapped her arms about herself in wonder, unable to believe she felt so happy. The long entry drive below was lined with torches, their flames already licking at the darkening sky and creating shadows that danced merrily on the sweeping drive.

She gazed out at the magnificent landscape and a surge of emotion caught in her throat and stung her eyes. This was her home now, where she wanted to be, where she prayed she would remain for the rest of her life. She loved it here, as she did the man who ruled Delacroix. It was a beautiful night, and one she would remember always, whatever the outcome. It was as if all the forces of nature had cooperated to make this night special. A thousand stars surrounded a golden full moon, sparkling amid the Cimmerian blackness of the night sky. The massive live oaks stood tall against the horizon, ragged drapings of moss curtaining their wide girth as dark leaves reflected the pale moonlight, turning the deep green foliage to a thousand tiny spots of shimmering silver. The saccharine fragrance of a late-blooming magnolia blended with that of a nearby jasmine and drifted up on a light breeze to tease her senses. Everything would work out tonight, she thought, willing it to be so. Our plan must work.

Half an hour later, stepping onto the landing at the top of the grand staircase, her gaze met Justin's and Janelle warmed at the look of appreciation she saw there.

Justin felt suddenly mesmerized by her beauty, drunk with the glorious exhilaration that she was his. In the bright candlelight from the foyer's chandelier, ablaze with the flames of several dozen candles, Janelle's white silk gown shimmered with life. Tiny pearls embedded within the dripping folds of French Point emerald lace caught the light in their nacreous sheen and reflected it back in a rainbow of colors. His gaze moved from the plunging neckline where the soft mounds of her breasts swelled tantalizingly amid the green lace and pink ribbon to the tiny waist, and back up to her face. His eyes drank of her beauty, and then thirsted for more.

She raised her hands and placed them in his, and as she paused on the bottom stair he leaned forward to brush warm lips across her cheek.

"You are a vision of beauty, *chère*," he whispered huskily, all too aware of the stares of a few guests who'd arrived early. He fervently wished they were alone.

She flushed with happiness at Justin's warm appraisal. "You don't look too bad yourself, handsome," she said, smiling broadly.

His black hair glistened richly beneath the candlelight, rivaling the darkness of the broadcloth coat stretched tautly over muscled shoulders. A blue-gray silk cravat was at his neck above the stiffly starched white ruching of his shirt. She slipped an arm through Justin's and walked beside him to the entry door. "Humm, looks to me like there are more than a few women here already who wouldn't mind doing me in just to take my place on your arm," she teased.

Justin looked down sharply. Her lightly spoken words reminded him with stabbing clarity of the threat hanging over her, and the so very real danger she was in.

An hour later, all the guests had arrived and the ballroom, as well as the other receiving rooms were teeming with activity. Several gentlemen had migrated to the study, their voices loudly raised in conversation, and a group of young girls were gathered outside the study door, giggling while eavesdropping on their elders. One of the parlors had been set up as a card room, while the adjoining room was reserved for the entertainment of the younger children whose parents were staying the night at Delacroix, and there was a continual flurry of activity on the staircase and second floor as three bedrooms had been reserved as convenience rooms for the ladies and one for the gentlemen.

The huge grandfather clock in the foyer was just striking nine when Justin led Janelle out onto the ballroom floor and began the grand march, formally opening the soirée.

"I think I've scandalized our guests," Justin said, with a soft laugh.

She looked at him questioningly, and missed a step.

"We have no dance cards tonight. A sure disgrace. I thought it best to dispense with the tradition. We need to leave you available to all of our guests in order for our plans to work."

After that first dance she found herself continually in the arms of others. It did not take long, however, to discover that the attitude of the male guests toward her differed severely from that of the females in the room. Most of the men were merely politely pleasant, some openly flirtatious, but a few had to be practically peeled from her body when their dance ended. The women who found themselves forced to talk with Janelle were coolly polite, while others quickly turned their backs, and hid behind fluttering fans.

Breathless from participating in a succession of energetic dances, Janelle declined the next request and sank wearily onto a blue damask ladies' chair, content for now merely to sit and watch the evening's activities. The room seemed a blur of dazzling color as one gown after another passed, orange, blue, green, red, pink, and yellow. She stared, momentarily spellbound, at the romantic vision before her, while desperately trying to ignore the nagging feeling of danger that lurked just beyond the fringes of the innocent scene, waiting for the right moment to strike. The game of cat and mouse was more wearing than she'd anticipated.

The room had grown hot and stuffy, the open French doors to the gallery and the cooler night air beyond an inviting lure, but Janelle knew she could not venture outside the ballroom. She was only truly safe with Justin nearby. Their plan would work, but she could take no chances.

She spotted Justin standing near an open French door. He was deep in conversation with several other men but, as if feeling her gaze upon him, he slowly turned and met her eyes, the distance between them seeming to disappear.

Suddenly a hush fell over the huge room. Antoine de la Reine stood in the doorway, a quick snap of his arm sweeping the red satin-lined cape from his shoulders and relinquishing it to the butler standing alongside. The Creole's swarthy good looks were complemented by the excellent tailoring and blue-black color of his suit. A diamond stickpin in the center of his wide cravat caught and reflected the chandelier's candlelight.

Janelle took a quick breath. One of their prime suspects had finally arrived. She could hear the whispered comments of outrage filling the room, see the shocked stares of many of their other guests, and could not help but notice several women hurry away from the entry door to the small groups of men clustered across the room, as if seeking safety. Antoine de la Reine was not considered respectable, and therefore not a proper guest. But his presence had been necessary to their plan.

Janelle moved to make her way across the wide room to greet him, but was rudely intercepted by an older woman whose name she could not remember.

"What in heaven's name is he doing here?" the matron asked loudly of no one in particular.

Before Janelle could answer, several other women moved to stand beside her, each offering her opinion of the recent arrival.

"Imagine him daring to come here."

"Some people don't know their place!"

"A murderer, that's what he is. No honest man stands a chance against him in a duel."

"Definitely not one of us," the older woman who had initiated the conversation said, lifting her nose in the air.

Janelle couldn't stand it any longer. "Antoine is a guest at Delacroix, ladies," she said stiffly. "I would appreciate it, and expect that you treat him as such." Not waiting for a response, she continued on her way, leaving the shocked group gaping at her retreating back.

"Well! It's no surprise *she* would welcome someone like him into her home," came a nasty whisper as Janelle moved past another group of women.

She ignored them, not even glancing in their direction. Snobs had always infuriated her, and gossiping snobs were the worst kind. Actually, she didn't understand herself why she had defended Antoine. For all she knew, he could very well be the one who posed a threat to her, who had murdered Sara Janei, if that assumption was correct. But somehow she didn't think Antoine was the threat. Stephan O'Roarke would have been her first choice, but she wasn't sure the creepy overseer had the nerve. That left Gilbert, and he was an excellent suspect. Gilbert Foucheau reminded Janelle of a sneaky weasel, and she could easily imagine him in the role of murderer.

As she neared Antoine, Janelle breathed a sigh of relief to see Justin weaving through the guests in her direction from the opposite side of the room.

At her approach, a trace of a smile curved Antoine's

lips. Janelle felt herself blush, painfully conscious that it was most likely common knowledge that Antoine was one of Sara Janei's lovers.

Thank heavens Justin knew the truth, she thought.

Justin moved up beside her and placed a hand on her back only a few steps before they reached Antoine. "Careful, *chère*," he whispered. "Remember our plan, get him angry, but stay within my sight at all times."

"Ah, Antoine," Justin said affably as they paused before their newly arrived guest, "I see my wife has surprised me yet again."

A look of cold amusement swept over Antoine's face as he studied Justin. "And evidently many others," he finally answered, his smooth voice polite, but completely devoid of warmth.

Despite the congeniality of their words, hostility and tension hung thick in the air between the two men. Antoine bowed slightly, took Janelle's hand in his, and brushed his lips across her fingers.

"May I have the honor of this dance with your wife, Monsieur?" he said, his gaze never leaving Justin's.

"I believe my wife can decide that for herself," Justin answered, the words as well as the tone razor sharp.

"Spoken like a true gentleman," Antoine said mockingly.

Justin gritted his teeth. He wanted nothing more than to vanquish every possible threat to Janelle, and Antoine de la Reine was at the top of his list. "Well, I shall leave you in the capable hands of my wife. I have other guests to attend." Turning away, Justin moved to join a group of men nearby who had been intently watching the brief exchange.

Their plan had begun.

Janelle placed a hand on Antoine's arm and accompanied him onto the dance floor. Once amid the moving couples, he took her in his arms, holding her closer against his tall length than was proper, oblivious of the disconcerting stares and whispers of disapproval.

Beyond the open French doors, dark eyes, aflame with fury, watched Janelle glide across the crowded floor, held securely in Antoine's arms. Jealousy sparked a simmering fire of hatred and clenched fists tightened, sharp fingernails biting unnoticed into tender flesh.

Something would have to be done, tonight, before it was too late. He would thank her some day for saving him. He couldn't see it now, the Delacroix woman had tricked him, just like she had all the others, but Celine would save him. She loved Antoine too much to stand by and see him become a pawn of Sara Janei's. No, she wouldn't let it go on any longer.

"The house is almost finished, *chérie*. Are you ready?" Antoine said, his dark, intent gaze holding Janelle's.

"Ready?" she repeated.

"To leave him."

"Leave him?" Janelle echoed weakly, then caught herself and tried to instill a teasing note in her tone. "Oh, Antoine, dear, you didn't really think I would *leave* Justin, now did you?"

She saw the hurt in his eyes, felt the anger as his fingers tightened around hers, and his graceful steps became stilted and forced.

"You have decided to stay with him." It was an accusatory statement, in no need of an answer.

"Well, of course I'm staying with him. He's rich, handsome, and allows me my freedom, Antoine. What more could a woman want?" Lord, she hated pretending to be Sara Janei. She felt so cruel and heartless, but it was necessary to lure her attacker, and most probably Sara Janei's murderer, into the open.

Antoine remained silent for the remainder of the

dance, his handsome face now cold and hard. When the music stopped his grip on her waist did not lessen. "We must talk." He forcibly turned her toward the open French doors.

Although the coolness of the night air was inviting, Janelle resisted.

Antoine stopped and glanced back at her. Black eyes, gleaming with unleashed fury met hers, and she was instantly aware of the fire seething beneath his calm, cold exterior. A shiver of fear raced up her spine. The plan was working all too well.

"Until later, *chérie*," he said, turning on his heel and stalking across the room to disappear into the crowd.

Confused, Janelle stood and stared at his retreating back. Why had he given in so easily? Feeling a need to escape the stares being directed her way by some of the more curious guests, Janelle left the ballroom to check the activity in the parlors but found herself instantly detoured as she passed the cloakroom. Slipping into the small enclosure, she hurriedly examined the heavy capes in search of Antoine's. Finally she found it—at least she thought it was his. Lifting the hem, she inspected it quickly, searching for a rip, but found none. The thin slice of red satin she had torn from the cape of her attacker several nights before had not come from this cape. Turning to leave the cloakroom, her gaze suddenly fell on several other capes hanging nearby. All black, and on closer examination, several proved to have red satin lining. One had a small strip of torn hemline. Unfortunately there was no way to identify the owner of the cape. All she had managed to accomplish was to confirm that the person they sought had indeed come to the soirée.

Returning to the ballroom Janelle saw Justin near the musicians' dais and went to stand at his side, slipping her hand within the crook of his arm. She suddenly felt the need to feel his strength, his warmth, the protective shield of his presence.

"Where have you been? I was almost frantic with worry."

"I wanted to check the cloakroom, to see if any of the capes were missing that little strip of satin," she whispered.

"And?"

"It's here, but who it belongs to is still a mystery."

Justin sighed heavily. He hadn't liked her plan and had vehemently argued against it, but in the end he'd come to agree with her. There was really little alternative.

"Just be careful, *chère*," he whispered. "And for heaven's sake, do not wander off again without telling me."

Janelle couldn't answer. She wanted to, but her throat had frozen and her tongue was paralyzed. She stared at the tall figure who moved to stand beside Justin.

"Sara, my dear, how have you been?" Bernard Chevillon smiled, his handsome face creasing in amusement at her reaction to his presence. "Come, come, Sara, my attendance here tonight cannot be that much of a shock," he chided. "I realize I told everyone I was leaving for San Francisco last week, but I decided to wait and enjoy your hospitality before departing. I guess I forgot to send you a note." He laughed heartily, as if amused at his own absentmindedness.

"Oh, uh, it doesn't matter, really. I'm pleased you could come after all," Janelle stammered. A sense of unrealness assailed her. He was standing in front of her and she couldn't believe it. Her own great-great-great-grandfather, and Sara Janei's brother, Bernard Chevillon. She remembered reading about him in the mounds of paper her mother had brought home from the Historical Society in Reno, and Janelle said a silent prayer of thanks for her mother's interest in family genealogy. Looking at Bernard, Janelle could see traces of her mother—the high cheekbones and full bottom lip. Tears threatened the corners of her eyes.

"Come now, Sara, don't get sentimental on me," Bernard said teasingly, leaning over to kiss her cheek as Janelle hastily brushed at her eyes. "Once I settle out West, you two can come visit me, eh?"

"I'd like that, Bernard. I really would," she said.

He stared at her for a long moment. Something was definitely different. This rush of sentimentality was completely out of character for Sara. And her voice, there seemed to be a flatness to it rather than the lilting drawl he knew so well. When she'd disappeared he hadn't bothered to worry. His sister had always possessed a rather wild and defiant streak. Bernard merely assumed there had been a spat between husband and wife and Sara Janei had decided to teach everyone a lesson by running off for a while and giving them all cause to worry. It was just like her.

"We will definitely come and visit you, Bernard," Justin said. He wrapped an arm around Janelle's waist and pulled her close. He could see how emotional this moment was for her.

A woman of medium height, her dark brown hair braided into a wide coronet suddenly appeared beside Bernard. "Sara, *ma petite,* I must commend you, this is a marvelous party." The gleam in her eye as she looked at Janelle was anything but friendly, and judging from the sarcastic tone of her voice the complimentary words were as sincere as her forced smile.

Janelle knew instantly who the woman was—Annabelle, Sara Janei's elder, and much-disliked sister. Justin's description had been perfect.

"Annabelle, behave yourself," Bernard said sternly, giving his sister a hard glare.

"But I am surprised, Sara," Annabelle continued

haughtily, ignoring Bernard. "I mean, inviting Antoine de la Reine, of all people. Don't you think that was in rather bad taste, my dear? Or are you merely flaunting him in everyone's face?" Without waiting for a response Annabelle turned her attention abruptly to Justin, flapping her long dark lashes at him in what was presumably a flirting gesture. "By the way, dear brother-in-law, has my lovely sister explained where she has been for the past few months? Another naughty escapade, perhaps? Like the one she pulled after Robert died?" She touched his arm in a consoling manner. "Oh, but then you don't know about that one, do you, Justin, dear?"

"I'm sure the entire city knows that story, thanks to you, Annabelle," Janelle said sharply, finding a bit of pleasure in her role as the nasty-tongued Sara Janei. This woman was a viper!

"Janei and I have no secrets from each other, Annabelle," Justin said, a beguiling smile softening the pointedly spoken words.

They were interrupted by Melody Foucheau. She advanced on Janelle, a malicious smile on her face.

Chapter twenty-one

"JANEI, YOU HAVE MY COMPLIMENTS. THIS IS the most interesting soirée I've attended in quite awhile," Melody said. She wore a gown the exact shade of her blue eyes, the pale ivory lace trim closely matching the hue of her blond hair.

Not for the first time, Janelle was struck by the thought that Melody Foucheau seemed the vision of an ice princess.

"Thank you. Now if you'll excuse us we were just going to get something to drink," Janelle said, thankful she had an excuse to escape the woman.

A few minutes later, drink in hand, Melody approached again, seemingly intent on pursuing a conversation. "Justin, your patience never ceases to amaze me. Most men in your situation would never consent to such a thing." She smiled sardonically. "I mean, allowing Antoine de la Reine to attend your party. Isn't that a bit out of character, even for you? After all," she continued quickly before either he or Janelle could respond, "didn't you just protest to me the other day that the man was merely an acquaintance, and not a welcome one?"

Janelle felt an immediate urge to slap the woman's face, but before she could speak, Justin answered.

"Did I say that, Melody?" He refused to rise to the

argument. "Then it must be true. But what is this situation you think I am in?"

"Come now, Justin, surely you've heard the talk." She smiled sweetly in Janelle's direction, but her eyes were as cold as the winter's frost. "Of course, I'm sure none of it is true, nevertheless. . . ."

"Melody, I don't pay much attention to gossip. I believe I mentioned that the other day."

Janelle interrupted. "If Antoine's presence bothers you, Melody, try to ignore him." The nasty tone was Sara Janei's, but the angry words were Janelle's. Because of Gilbert, she had tried to feel compassion for Melody, but the woman's sharp tongue quickly dispelled further effort in that direction.

"At least I stay in my own bedroom, which is more than I can say for some people. And even if I were interested in a little something extra I would steer clear of *him*. He's just too, too handsome. I always felt there was something wrong when a man was that good-looking. Now take you for example, Justin. I used to think that of you too, but I don't anymore. Ever since Janei here ripped your face open with that rapier at your wedding reception, you must admit, it does rather mar the profile."

"It was an accident," Justin said quietly, even as Janelle gasped at the cruel words. It was all she could do not to strike out at Melody's spiteful face.

"Of course it was, although most women do not pick up a rapier during an argument with their husband and take a slice out of the poor man, especially only a few hours after the wedding ceremony. I never did find out why you did that, Janei," Melody said coyly.

Janelle looked helplessly at Justin. They had never discussed the events that had led up to that incident. He slipped an arm protectively about her waist, a gesture not unnoticed, but his cold eyes never left Melody's.

"We had a disagreement, Melody, if it is any of your concern. It is in the past now, and we have both elected to forget it." His words were strained, his expression grim, and Janelle could feel the coiled tension in him.

At that moment, Gilbert joined them and Janelle had to look away and count to ten to keep from laughing. He reminded her of someone out of an old Errol Flynn movie. The perfect dandy. In stark contrast to current fashion, his shirtfront was covered with ruffles, as were his cuffs, and the lapels of his gray jacket were satin. Janelle could hardly believe Sara Janei had taken this man for a lover. She sighed softly. It was time to put the Gilbert phase of their plan into action.

Gilbert was expounding on the success of an experimental crop of something or other when Janelle turned back to join the conversation and almost choked.

He'd snatched a bejeweled fan from Melody's wrist and was furiously waving it in front of his face.

"Melody, I think I'll steal your husband," Janelle said. "For a dance," she added, seeing Melody's start of surprise.

Many of the other guests, having finished eating, had also returned to the dance floor. The room was a rainbow of color, the silks, satins, and lace of the women's gowns blending into a swirl of bright hues as the couples moved to the lilting strains of a waltz. A low hum of laughter and conversation mixed with the music.

Janelle felt uncomfortable in Gilbert's arms, though she tried not to show it. His hand on her waist held a firm grip, his other securely clasped her fingers. They whirled about the ballroom, Gilbert's every step graceful, his timing perfect. He moved effortlessly, guiding her to the music.

"Did you like the flowers, *bien aimée*?" he asked, a wicked gleam in his eye as he stared down at her.

"Flowers? You sent the flowers?" she said, knowing instantly how to enact her plan with him. "You should have signed the note, Gilbert, I wasn't quite sure."

"Who did you think sent them, Janei? Some other lover, perhaps?" he asked angrily.

She shrugged. "You are my favorite, Gilbert dear, but how was I to know, really?" Janelle felt a tickle of satisfaction with herself. Getting their suspects angry with her was proving easier than she'd thought. Perhaps the right one was, or soon would be, angry enough to attempt something and they would catch their culprit. Then she could breathe easier.

Gilbert made no further attempt at conversation, seeming to draw into himself as they finished the waltz, and once, when she looked up at him, she glimpsed something in the depths of his dark eyes that sent a shiver through her. A ruthlessness that he kept well masked, a trace of cruelty neatly disguised, or a calculated dislike that masqueraded as desire? She wasn't sure which.

The music ended and Janelle made as if to move from Gilbert's arms, thankful that the dance was over, but he refused to release her hand. Instead, he guided her toward the open French doors, gently but insistently.

Janelle looked about frantically. She knew his grip was too tight to break. Relief flooded her when she saw Justin standing several feet ahead, directly in their path.

"Well, Gilbert, I see you have brought my wife back to me safe and sound. Thank you." Justin took Janelle's hand from Gilbert's. "If you will excuse us, my friend, I think I will dance with Janei now."

As they moved away, Janelle glanced back and was witness to the fury that swept over Gilbert's taut features. Turning around, he strode out through the French doors, disappearing onto the dimly lit gallery.

"We can do nothing more but wait," Justin said, when their dance ended. Janelle nodded and moved toward a nearby group of guests. It was better now, they'd agreed, to remain apart and give their plan a chance to work.

Neither noticed the swift flash of movement at the nearby French door, or felt the glare of hatred emanating from the beautiful raven-black eyes.

Her throat parched with dryness from dancing, Janelle made her way to the punch bowl.

Justin, meanwhile, noticing Janelle talking with Dr. Allard, stepped out onto the gallery for a breath of fresh air. With a foot propped on the balustrade, he pulled a thin cheroot from his jacket pocket and striking a lucifer against a nearby pillar, cupped both hands around its tip as flame touched tobacco. Surveying the landscape and the peaceful night, he found it hard to imagine that a killer lurked within his house, waiting for an opportunity to strike again.

He puffed absently on the slender cheroot, watching the white wisps of smoke curl up and fade into the darkness of the night air. Suddenly, a rush of stars exploded in his brain. The cheroot dropped to the ground and his body began to sag and fall forward. Knees buckling, he felt a pushing sensation at his back just as darkness enveloped him, and he toppled over the balustrade railing, falling several feet to the ground below. The cloth of his jacket snagged on the boxwood hedge that bordered the raised gallery, snapping off several branches as his weight plummeted past. He fell on his back, unconscious, between the bottom of the thick hedge and the house, his body partially obscured from sight.

Inside the ballroom, Janelle was standing beside the punch bowl, scanning the crowd in search of Justin when she noticed Melody walking toward her. She grimaced. Just what she needed, another confrontation with Miss Personality.

"Janei, dear, your husband asked me to give you this. He said it was very important." Melody pressed a small piece of folded paper into Janelle's hand. "He's probably found some other form of entertainment for the evening, eh?" the blond said nastily before she turned away and disappeared back into the crowd.

Janelle unfolded the note and read the bold script. "Darling, everything is all right. Have discovered all. Am with Micaelai. Meet me in the stables in ten minutes. Will explain then. Love, J."

A rush of relief swept over her. It was over, the threat hanging over her was gone. Placing the glass of punch on the table, she paused as a waltzing couple swirled past so close that the woman's swaying skirts struck Janelle's. The rigid hoopskirts collided and threw each woman slightly off balance. The note slipped from Janelle's fingers and fluttered to the floor as she grabbed at the table to steady herself. At that moment she caught sight of Antoine standing in an alcove on the far side of the room, deep in conversation with a girl who looked young enough to be his daughter. A servant moved up beside the girl and began to talk to Antoine. Toward the center of the room, Gilbert was on the dance floor, deeply engrossed in the charms of his partner. Melody was beside the dais, talking to Annabelle and Bernard.

Turning to leave, Janelle didn't notice when, seconds later, Antoine excused himself from the young woman's attentions and left the room, Annabelle sidled through the French doors to the gallery, and Melody left the house by way of the foyer's rear entrance.

Gilbert's attention turned away from his partner, his dark gaze following Janelle's swift progress toward the door to the foyer.

She crossed the entry hall and hurried toward the front door just as Marie, arranging and porcelain *glacière* filled with sugarcoated iced fruits on the ballroom buffet table, called out to her. But Janelle didn't hear the housekeeper, and before Marie could get her ample frame from behind the wide table and into the foyer, Janelle was gone. A sense of worry nagged at the back of her mind, and Marie turned back toward the ballroom, intent on finding Justin.

Only an occasional torch had been placed on this side of the house and none at all on the pathway leading to the stables. The only light Janelle had to guide her through the garden was that of the moon overhead, but halfway to the barn she hesitated.

A twig snapped nearby. Moments earlier the music drifting on the night air from the ballroom had stopped, so that now the distinct snapping sound in the silence startled her. She listened for further movement, but nothing came. Sighing, Janelle decided that it had only been a small night animal. Still she couldn't seem to shake the feeling of being watched.

"That's ridiculous," she mumbled to herself. Justin's note said it was over, everything was all right now. She approached the stable, swinging the heavy door back on its hinges and stepped inside.

A lantern hung from a far pole, its weak flame shedding a small circular spot of light at that end of the stable, but leaving the rest in total darkness. She could hear the soft, scuffling movement of horse hooves as the animals shuffled nervously in their stalls, unused to late-night visitors.

"Justin?" she called softly. A feeling of unease came over her. Something wasn't right. Justin wouldn't hide from her.

A figure stepped from one of the empty stalls, and

Janelle started, realizing how foolish she'd been to leave the house alone, and suddenly knowing, without doubt, the note had not been from Justin.

The dim light played upon the person's silhouette, but the features remained in shadow. The outline of a cloak, full and capacious, swayed with the slightest movement. Janelle instinctively took a step back. She closed her eyes and willed herself to remain calm, not to panic. The first thing she saw when her lashes fluttered open was the muzzle of a gun, pointed directly at her chest. Flickering lantern flame reflected off cold polished steel.

Forcing her gaze to move from the gun Janelle looked up into the face of her captor and almost fainted. There was no doubt in her horrified mind that the eyes she met were glazed with insanity, and totally beyond all reason. She took another tentative step backward and realized with dread that there was nowhere to go. The door had swung shut behind her, blocking any attempt at a hasty retreat. The only other exit from the stable was on the opposite wall, and her assailant stood between her and the other door.

"What's the matter, Janei? Surprised?" Melody's voice, highpitched and quavering with excitement, broke the silence.

Janelle looked back into those crazed eyes, trying to think of something to say, anything to keep the woman calm, and prevent her from pulling that trigger.

"Mel . . . Melody," she croaked, her voice barely above a ragged whisper. "Why?"

"Why? How can you ask me why?" A vengeful sneer disfigured the perfectly carved lips, and hatred gleamed unmistakably from the vivid blue eyes, turning the beautiful face ugly and hard. Her tone dripped with venom. "All I have is my husband and our land. I have no children. There is only Gilbert, useless as he is. But he's mine. You tried to take him from me, Janei. I've seen you, throwing yourself at him, meeting him in the fields, or in town. You're disgusting. You have no morals, no character. You go after everything you want with no regard to anyone else. Did you actually think I'd let you have him? My husband? I've watched you, Janei, you and Gilbert, when you two were so absorbed in mauling each other you weren't even aware of me. You are vile! Do you know that? You and Gilbert doing that filthy act!" She was screaming now, her voice cracking with hysteria, eyes dilated and wild as her fury mounted. The gun began to shake in her hand.

"Listen to me, Melody, I'm not Sara Janei. She's dead."

Melody threw back her head and laughed. "Then you must be her ghost, come back to haunt me." She laughed again, crazily. "But, I'll just kill you again. I don't understand though, I thought you were dead enough last time. There was so much blood. I cleaned it all up, it was hard, but I managed. How did you get out of that swamp, Janei? I saw you sink. And that alligator slipped into the water just as I turned to leave. I figured if there was any thread of life in you after you disappeared beneath the surface, it wasn't going to be for long. How did you do it, Janei?" she asked with almost childlike curiosity, and Janelle's heart skipped a beat at her smile, so sweet, so insane.

Suddenly a groan came from a black heap that lay next to a nearby haystack.

"Who is that?" Janelle asked, both fear and hope lodging in her throat.

"Why, Antoine, of course. He's going to murder you." She smiled again. "Well, not really. But he'll be blamed for it. I found your locket the other day when I followed you into the swamp. I sent it to him tonight with a note, from you, naturally, beckoning him here. Poor fool, he's so besotted with you he didn't even hesitate to come running." She chuckled. "Now you two will have a lovers' quarrel and he'll kill you, and then himself, when he realizes what he's done."

"Melody, please, you've got to listen to me. I'm not Sara Janei. You did kill her. She's still in the swamp. My name's Janelle."

"You can't trick me any more, Janei. This time I'm going to make sure you stay dead."

Melody began to raise the gun to take better aim, and Janelle felt a surge of panic she fought desperately to control. "Melody, I don't want Gilbert, he belongs to you. I love Justin. Please, don't. . . ."

"Love Justin? Sara Janei, my dear, you don't know what love is. You're hard. And greedy. How many lovers have you had?" The soft voice rose again in jealous rage. "Five? Six? Eight? A dozen? But you will not have my husband any longer. Sometimes I watch him when he's home. Do you know what he does? Sits and broods over you." The soft voice rose again in jealousy.

Janelle inched toward one of the stalls. If she could unlatch some of the gates and find a way to panic the horses she might have a chance of getting away in the confusion. Keep her talking, calm her down, don't provoke her, she repeated to herself, nerves shredded and near to collapse at the madness she was confronting.

"Stop moving, Janei," Melody shrieked, "you're not going anywhere, except maybe to hell. Oh yes, I'm certain that's where you'll be going. But tell me, dear, how does it feel to seduce another woman's husband? Do you feel enriched? You're like a roaming conqueror, going from one conquest to another, leaving a trail of destruction and waste behind. I know Gilbert asked you to run away with him, I heard him. That's when I knew I had to kill you."

Antoine groaned again, and moved slightly. Melody jerked in his direction but as Janelle attempted to take another step toward the stalls she quickly turned the gun back on her. "Stand still, Janei! I don't have much time. He's going to wake up soon." The gun wavered slightly. "Gilbert's affairs never bothered me, you know. Although I wish he would take a *placée* rather than bedding all our friends' wives. Less gossip that way. The quadroons are accepted, but this wanderlust he has is so troublesome. I always have to watch out for him. Heaven knows, I don't want him killed in a duel because some outraged husband discovers him in bed with his wife."

Janelle saw a shovel leaning against a stall. If she could just get to it.

"Are you listening to me, Janei?" Her voice was calm again, cold, and calculating. There was no feeling in the words, only ice. She smiled nastily as Janelle looked back at her and their eyes met. "That's better. Now where was I? Oh yes, dear Gilbert's indiscretions. You must be the tenth, yes, that's it; the tenth."

"Then why kill me?" Janelle whispered, stalling for time, for Justin to discover her missing, to find her.

"Because, my dear, you are the only one that he's ever really cared about. The rest were dalliances, little flirtations to prove to himself he was still desirable. But with you he began to think of leaving me. I couldn't have that. I won't allow it. I can't seem to change his feelings for you, so I have to get rid of you. He'll forget you in time and things will be the way they used to. Now, enough talking." She raised the gun, her arm held straight out, the muzzle pointing toward Janelle's heart. In one terrifying moment, staring into those merciless eyes, Janelle knew Melody Foucheau was going to shoot.

"Melody, no!" Gilbert screamed, rushing past. He accidentally grazed the side of Janelle's gown and nearly knocked her over. "Don't do this!"

He grabbed his wife's outstretched arm. His fingers wrapped around her wrist and he tried to wrestle the weapon from her grip, the gun trapped between their struggling bodies. His taller form blocked Melody from Janelle's sight, but only for a moment. Face contorted with hatred, Melody shrieked with outrage, kicking at him with her feet, and jerking her body from side to side. They stumbled about the center of the stable, Melody frantically trying to pull away, Gilbert, in a frenzy of determination, maintaining his grip on her arm. Grotesque shadows danced on the wall within the dim circle of lantern light.

Antoine, beginning to regain consciousness, tried to struggle to his feet, only to be forced back to the floor by the blinding pain in his head, but Janelle, rooted by the macabre specter of the grappling couple, did not notice.

Gilbert groaned in pain as Melody rammed an elbow into his ribcage, but he didn't release his grasp on her. She raked her nails across his face, while screaming at him to release her. Gilbert's hand swept up, struck the side of her face and sent Melody's head jerking backward. The gun discharged, its deafening sound filling the barn.

Through a daze Janelle heard the panic-filled screams of the horses, the crashing of hooves against fence rails. The stall gates strained from the impact of strong, muscular legs pounding against them, and hinges tore loose.

In his stall, Tobar reared in the air, his huge form rising high above the plank walls. His front hooves returned to the hard ground and his powerful rear legs instantly rose in the air, kicking out with all their force. The stall gate shot from its hinges and the lock shattered, falling to the ground in a cloud of dust. Tobar burst from the confines of his cubicle, lunging about the center of the stable, frantically searching for an escape.

Janelle shrank against Lady's stall as Tobar lunged past. The horse whinnied loudly, and stood near the closed entry door, pawing at the ground.

Janelle turned back to Melody and stared in shock at the huddled figure on the ground. Her pale blond hair hung limp about her shoulders, and her cheeks were streaked with tears. Crooning, she rocked back and forth on her knees, the gun still gripped tightly between her fingers.

Chapter twenty-two

CATHY SAT IN THE GAZEBO. SEVERAL YARDS away, in the center of the lawn, two male peacocks strutted proudly, their colorful tails spread widely as they vied for the attention of a lone female bird standing at the garden's edge. Not until one shrieked, its mating call piercing the silence, did Cathy notice their presence.

Kyle Donovan stepped from the gallery and made his way across the lawn toward her. "Cathy, I've brought out some lunch." He placed the tray on the table between them and sat down. How long would it have taken for him to realize he loved her if all this hadn't happened? He shook his head in wonder. She was watching him, a sad smile on her lips.

"How's Tano?" she asked softly.

"He's resting. The thought of coming home, and the ride from the hospital tired him. He hasn't recouped his energy yet."

She nodded and turned her gaze back to the gardens beyond the gazebo. "Where is she, Kyle? Why haven't they found something?"

"I don't know." He reached across the table and took her hand in both of his, softly caressing her fingers with his thumb.

"If I just knew that she was safe, but I keep wondering . . ." Kyle felt his heart ache with longing, and the need to comfort her, to right all the wrongs of the world for her and protect her from any more pain.

"They haven't given up looking, Cathy. The sheriff is still hopeful." The words sounded pathetic even to his ears. In almost two weeks the authorities had come up with nothing. Not one clue to what had happened to Janelle.

"When can I talk to Tano, Kyle?" Cathy asked suddenly, her eyes lighting with hope. The old servant knew something about Janelle's disappearance, Cathy was sure of it. Several times while in the hospital he'd mumbled something about Janelle, but his words had been incoherent and broken. Now Cathy was alive with impatience and a desperate need to talk to him.

"He'll sleep for a few hours more, then we can talk with him," Kyle said. "Don't build your hopes too high, sweetheart. Tano may not really know anything, but I'm sure the sheriff will hear something soon."

Cathy sighed. "What would I have done without you?" she asked, her eyes warming with love. At least one good thing has come out of this, she thought, feeling slightly guilty at the rush of happiness that surged through her breast as Kyle's lips claimed hers.

Chapter twenty-three

MARIE SPOTTED THE SMALL PIECE OF FOLDED paper immediately. It lay on the floor beside the long table that held the punchbowl. She bent to pick it up and shoved it into the pocket of her skirt before hurrying from the crowded room. Back in the foyer she drew the paper from her pocket, unfolded it and studied the handwriting, but the words meant nothing to her. Marie couldn't read.

She returned to the ballroom to stand at the edge of the swirling dancers. She had to find Justin. Marie always prided herself on her sixth sense, and at this moment it was working overtime. Something was definitely wrong—very, very wrong.

Justin had included her in their plan and requested that she help keep an eye on several of the guests. Now she noted with a feeling of dread, except for Annabelle, those they'd been watching were also missing from the room. And she didn't see Justin's tall figure anywhere, either.

Marie plunged onto the dance floor, weaving her way through the crowd, and trying not to collide with the swirling couples. Nearing the open French doors, she looked out. The gallery was empty. She began to turn away, her anxiety growing, when something caught her attention. Smoke! It was only a thin trail, a faint stream of white cloud drifting up from beyond the edge of the gallery. Rushing forward, Marie peered over the short railing and gasped in horror. Shock held her immobile for a long minute, then Marie fled to the end of the gallery, down the steps and back around the house. Tearing the large muslin apron from her waist she beat at the boxwood hedge, trying to smother the small burst of flames eating at the plant.

She dropped to her knees, grasped Justin's limp, outstretched hand, and tugged on it. Nothing happened. She didn't have enough leverage to move him. Frenzied, the housekeeper dug her heels into the soft grass, yanking, pulling, straining to drag his body from beneath the smoldering bush.

Justin moaned and Marie felt him begin to stir. Thank heavens, he was alive! She pulled harder, grunting loudly from the unaccustomed physical exertion.

Justin tried to return the grip her fingers had on his hand but his limbs weren't receiving the message from his still fog-shrouded brain. He felt helpless and inert. Struggling against his own weakness he bent his knees and pressed them into the ground, forcing himself to crawl toward her. The stiff branches of the hedge scraped at the back of his head, sending a shower of pain raining through his skull. His shoulders cleared the plant and Justin attempted to push himself upright, but the thick limbs at his back prevented it, snagging on the silk of his evening jacket.

Marie grabbed the waistband at the back of his pants, took a deep breath, jerked on the fabric, and yanked him clear of the smoldering bush.

Unsteadily, Justin pulled himself into a sitting position and raised a shaky hand to the back of his head where the throbbing was centered. He touched the swelling lump with the tips of his fingers and another shot of pain slammed through his head. Lowering his hand, he looked down at his fingers, staring at the crimson rivulets of blood slowly streaming into his palm. He ran his hand through the thick blades of grass, wiping his fingers dry. What the hell had happened?

"Justin, you all right?" Marie asked anxiously, puffing heavily as she rose to her feet.

Justin had to blink several times to focus his vision. Panic suddenly seized him. He was on his feet instantly, but the pain in his head caused him to stumble awkwardly. Everything blurred, and he swayed, grabbing onto Marie to steady himself. "Where's Janelle?" he asked.

Marie handed him the note. "I seen Miss Melody give her this paper, then missy left the house." Marie's worried eyes sought his. "Most everyone else we was watching is gone, too."

He only needed to glance at the note and its familiar handwriting to confirm his suspicions. Why hadn't he put the pieces together before this? Now it was all so clear. It wasn't Antoine who was a threat to Janelle's life, or even Gilbert, or O'Roarke, it was Melody! Melody, whose jealousy and insecurity had blinded her to all reason, obscuring any rationality, pushing her to an act of desperation. Now he saw how it had always been Melody who baited Sara Janei with gossip and innuendos, Melody who nearly fainted at seeing Janelle, and Melody who had mentioned the missing locket. She had even gone into town a few days ago, and could have arranged the so-called accident with the carriage wheel. And it had been Melody who, just moments ago in the ballroom, looked at Janelle with hatred flashing in her blue eyes.

Justin yelled for Marie to get help, and started for the stables. He stumbled several times as he tried to rush down the slope from the house. Each movement brought a new onslaught of dizziness and pain, but he fought it, grasping at trees and bushes to help him remain on his feet and moving.

Tobar stood at the edge of the gardens grazing on the healthy manicured lawn. Startled by Justin breaking through the bushes, the big horse shied away, calming a few seconds later at a few soothing words from his master. Seeing Tobar loose set Justin's heart to a frantic pace. A dim light shone from the open stable door, but no sound came from within. He approached cautiously, saw someone lying on the floor toward the rear of the stable, and the breath rushed out of his lungs as though from a physical blow.

No. Janelle had come so far to be with him. It couldn't be! He hurried into the barn, intent only on the still figure on the ground, and knelt beside the body.

It lay twisted to the side, the face turned away from him, half in shadow. Justin touched the shoulders of the lifeless form.

Gilbert Foucheau's head rolled toward Justin, eyes open, staring blindly. His lips were parted, as if he had cried out at the instant of death, attempting to deny it. The dead man's chest was covered with blood, and a small, dark hole, just to the left of his heart, was burned through the brocade vest. Justin placed his fingertips on Gilbert's eyelids, closed them, and then rose to his feet, quickly surveying the area. There had been a struggle; the hard-packed dirt floor showed deep scuff and gouge marks. Tobar's stall gate was shattered, its lock in pieces on the ground. Micaelai swayed upon his makeshift sling, eyes wide with alarm while the other horses skittered nervously.

Marie and Sammy rushed into the stable. "She ain't at the house, Justin," Marie gasped, her chest rising and falling heavily as she sucked in air.

Eyes dark with pain and fear, grooves of exhaustion slashed around his lips, Justin began issuing orders frantically. "Marie, get Callie and the maids, and search the house again and all the outbuildings. Sammy, go to the cabins, get some men and start searching the grounds. Hurry!" He looked bleakly out into the darkness. Where are you, Janelle? Where are you?

Janelle had stumbled backwards out of the stable, horror-stricken at the sight of Gilbert lying dead on the ground. Melody knelt beside her dead husband, crooning loudly and swaying on her knees. Suddenly she turned wild eyes back on Janelle, her intent clear. Frantically, pushing her way past Tobar, Janelle fled into the thick foliage of the formal gardens, running blindly. Once in the midst of the heavy greenery she slowed her pace, moving cautiously, trying to keep her steps quiet. She had to get back to the house, to Justin, to safety.

Several hundred feet of open and unobstructed ground stretched between gardens and house. Easy enough to run, Janelle thought, but she couldn't risk it. She'd be a perfect target.

A rustle of leaves sounded to her left, and she ran, crouched low, to her right, then paused, and tried to get her bearings. Time seemed to stand still. Janelle thought she could hear the music from the ballroom, but it was so faint. The plaintive wail of a screech owl broke the silence just as something skittered across the ground at her feet. She nearly screamed in fright. Like a hunted animal she crept low amidst the trees and bushes, intensely alert to every sound, every movement. Her limbs ached from the tension and awkward, bent-over position. The beautiful white ball gown snagged several times on thorns and broken branches and she was starting to get stiff, every muscle screaming to stretch and relax. Inadvertently, she had moved deeper into the gardens, putting even more distance between herself and the lights of the house. Was it safe to turn back now?

Suddenly, before she could decide, the sky split open. A blanket of gray clouds rolled in front of the moon, blocking out its light and plunging the gardens into fathomless blackness. Deafening rumbles of thunder filled the air. Streaks of lightning broke through the clouds, lighting the sky, their jagged arcs momentarily brightening the darkened gardens.

The storm was just like the one before, the one that had brought her here. Was this it, then? Was this the end? She wanted to scream a denial, to call out for Justin. And then she heard it, a sound that turned the blood in her veins to ice, and enveloped her heart with terror.

Laughter—insane and hysterical, rising madly. Janelle couldn't tell from which direction the horrible sound was coming; it seemed to surround her, to echo in the gardens and blend with the crashing of the storm. Another streak of lightning cut through the darkness, striking a branch at the top of a nearby oak. She turned from it and ran deeper into the gardens. Rain began to pelt the earth, heavy drops of water that pounded at her head and shoulders and began to turn the earth beneath her feet to slick mud. She groped through the thick foliage. The hem of her gown was saturated with mire, her satin slippers covered with heavy clay earth. Wind slashed at the trees, pushing their outstretched limbs about crazily, tearing and whipping the leaves.

Janelle brushed at a heavy curtain of moss that draped across her path, but as she bent and rushed past it, she suddenly stopped.

She stood in the center of the cemetery, surrounded by the gravestones of long-dead Delacroix. The gate stood open, a faint creak sounding as it swung easily on its hinges when caught by the wind. She had come here several times since her arrival, but each time, though she'd wished for it, cried for it, had felt nothing.

This time was different. Janelle instantly felt the pull, icy fingers reaching out, encircling her soul, dragging it into the darkness. The harder she resisted, the more the strange force wrapped her in its shroud. The wind lashed at her heavy skirts and threw her off balance. She took a step back and bumped against a tombstone, stumbling sideways to fall to her knees. A stream of moonlight broke through the clouds and the pink tombstone appeared before her, translucent, the image wavering and unclear, but definitely there. It began to glow, the cold marble slick and shiny from the rain, glistening in the soft light.

Janelle stared at it in horror. The gravestone hadn't been there a minute ago. Her mind whirled in a frenzy of panic, refusing to accept what her eyes saw. Weeds grew everywhere, entwining about the rusted, broken spears of the fence. She was falling back, back into her own time, and for a moment it was as if she was gazing at a double exposure—the mossy, eroded tombstones superimposed over the well-kept graves of Justin Delacroix's time.

"No, no, no, no!" she cried. She raised a hand toward the tombstone that was engraved with Sara Janei's name, and forced her fingers to touch the pink marble. It was cold and streams of rain trickled from the stone onto her trembling fingers. The pull became stronger and her mind filled with thoughts of Justin, her ears heard the sweet rumble of his voice saying her name and she felt a surging will to fight the pulling force.

She clawed at the earth, stumbled to her feet, fell, and rose again. She felt as if her feet were weighted to the ground, each step a straining, leaden effort. Strands of hair hung in her face, and stuck to her cheeks. A streak of lightning hit one of the metal spears of the fence, and sparks flew through the area; a loud sizzling sound filled the air as the hot metal curled. She was almost at the gate, but the next step sent a shock of blinding pain through her leg as her ankle twisted in the mud and she fell to the ground.

Suddenly, out of the darkness a figure loomed, and she screamed, terrified.

"Janelle, my God, are you all right?" Justin ran to her side and knelt down, his strong arms wrapping about her shoulders and pulling her to him.

She looked up at him, joy rushing through her, flooding her with relief. His beloved face was harsh and lined with pain and anguish.

"Thank you, God," she sobbed softly. She was with him. She hadn't left. She laid her head on his shoulder and realized for the first time that the pulling sensation and the storm were both completely gone. As suddenly as the storm had erupted and the strange force begun, both had ceased. The sky was once again calm, the moon nestled high amid the velvety blackness, and a thousand stars twinkled brilliantly like sparkling diamonds.

Justin rose to his feet, and helped her up. He looked down at her wan face, and knew instinctively how close he'd come to losing her. Pain stronger than that of his injuries lanced through him. Holding her face between his hands, he kissed her tenderly, then savagely, pulling her body to his, until heart beat against heart, the frantic beats melding to become one.

Reluctantly Justin tore his mouth from the sweetness of hers. "Come, *chère,* it is not safe out here. Melody is still on the grounds somewhere."

His words were like a splash of cold water bringing the events and danger of the evening back in a sudden rush, and with it her fear. "Justin, she's mad. She told me she killed Sara Janei. And tonight, she lured Antoine to the stables to blame him for killing me, or Sara Janei, again. When Gilbert tried to stop her, she shot him."

"I know," he said softly. "It was her jealousy."

"Gilbert, is he? . . ."

Justin shook his head slightly. "He's dead."

"Oh, God! He was trying to save me." Janelle shuddered and leaned into his warmth as his arms tightened about her.

"We have to get out of here, Janelle. Now!"

They were nearing the edge of the dark gardens when a tall figure stepped from the shadows and blocked their path. He stood with feet spread wide apart, hands on hips. The dim light behind him turned his figure into a dark silhouette, giving him the advantage of seeing them clearly, while they remained puzzled over both his identity and his intent—until he stepped forward.

Chapter twenty-four

WITHOUT A WORD JUSTIN PUT HIMSELF BE-tween Antoine and Janelle, but the proud *maître d'armes* gave him only a flickering glance, his gaze quickly returning to the woman he believed to be Sara Janei. He noted her disheveled appearance, but decided now was not the time for questions. "Sara Janei has informed me that she cannot do without your money, Monsieur," he said flatly, "so that leaves me no choice. You will meet me on the field of honor?"

"No," Janelle said, the word little more than a gasp.

"Your honor has not been slighted, Antoine. There is nothing to settle between us that demands a duel," Justin said.

Antoine's hand swept up and connected with the side of Justin's face. "Perhaps now, Monsieur? Or would you prefer that I challenge you in front of your guests?"

Justin sighed softly. "That will not be necessary."

"Good, then let us dispense with formalities. We need no seconds, nor do we need to delay. We will duel tonight, there." He pointed to a clearing toward the opposite side of the formal gardens. "In thirty min-utes."

"I agree, but I believe it is my choice of weapons."

Janelle gripped Justin's arm. "Justin, please, stop this," she whispered.

Both men ignored her plea.

"And you want pistols?" Antoine goaded. A sly smile creased his face.

"Rapiers."

Antoine nodded and turned away, satisfaction gleaming in his eyes. He turned to Janelle. "It is better this way, *chérie*, you will see." A second later he was gone.

She turned to Justin. "You can't do this."

"I have to. I have no choice."

"Why?" She felt on the verge of panic.

"Because that is the way we live." He pulled her into his arms. "And Antoine will not be satisfied until I face him."

She wanted to argue with him, but remained silent. It would do no good.

He urged her toward the house. "I want you to stay in the house. You'll be safe there with Marie. Sammy and some of the men can search for Melody."

They went up the back stairs, out of sight of the guests. Justin went to his room to get his rapier; Janelle hurried to the cloakroom and grabbed a cape, slipping it around her shoulders to cover the torn, dirt-smudged ball gown. She found Marie in the warming kitchen, pacing.

"Marie, Justin's going to duel Antoine. We have to stop him." She ran toward the back door.

"Oh, Lordy." Marie's hands twisted about each other. "Ain't nothing going to stop them now, but you shouldn't be there, missy. It ain't right."

"I don't care. I don't want Justin killed." She ran out the back door, pausing on the gallery. Music from the soirée in the ballroom drifted out on the night air, their guests oblivious to what was happening with their host. It was an ironic contrast—the laughter and music inside the house, the madness and death outside.

Justin came through the doorway behind her. "Janelle, go back inside. It's not safe for you out here."

She turned to him. "Justin, please, call this off."

He wrapped one arm around her waist and pulled her against him. "I can't, *chère*. It would disgrace my name." He touched his lips lightly to her forehead. "We will only fight until first blood is drawn. Don't worry, it will be all right. Now, go back inside. I'll return shortly, I promise."

"No. I'm going with you."

Marie and Sammy appeared on the porch. Without a word they followed Justin and Janelle to the clearing where Antoine waited. Dr. Allard stood nearby. Several torches had been placed around the outer edges of the clearing to light the area.

Justin and Antoine walked to the center of the clearing and faced each other, swords held at their sides.

Dr. Allard said something, and each man raised his sword and assumed a stance of readiness.

Janelle watched in horror and fascination. They lunged, their movements graceful and deadly, the thin rapiers swiping the air, clashing, metal sliding against metal. She held her breath, terrified.

Justin lunged, Antoine parried, a thrust, another lunge. And on and on. Antoine's rapier stabbed through the sleeve of Justin's shirt, but drew no blood. Several seconds later, the tip of Justin's rapier sliced a gash in Antoine's trousers, and still no blood.

Antoine laughed loudly. "So, my opponent is worthy of the duello after all."

"More than you know, Antoine," Justin countered.

Their fighting continued, as did their sporadic, and insane, conversation.

"Your teacher?" Antoine called out, parrying a swift thrust.

"Pépé Lulla, who else? He's the best."

"Was the best." Antoine laughed, his rapier slicing through the air and barely missing Justin's chest.

Suddenly, and it seemed effortlessly, Justin stepped to the left, avoiding the sharp steel of Antoine's blade as it bore down on him. Justin raised his own and brought it down in one swift movement, the gleaming rapier slashing across Antoine's extended arm and catching his outstretched thigh. Blood instantly spurted from both wounds. The white linen sleeve, hanging open where the sword had cut, turned red. Stunned by Justin's defeating maneuver, Antoine dropped his rapier.

"It is over, Antoine," Justin said.

"*Non*, we go on." He bent down and picked up his rapier, but his hand, now covered with dripping rivulets of blood, lost its grip on the blade's handle, and again it fell to the ground.

Janelle ran forward and threw her arms about Justin's neck. Then she remembered Antoine, and turned to look at him.

"Antoine, please, you have to listen to me."

"There is nothing more to say, *chérie*. I have failed. There is no alternative now but for me to leave New Orleans."

"Will you please stop being so pigheaded and listen to me?" She closed the distance between them and softened her tone. "I am not Sara Janei. My name is Janelle. Sara Janei was murdered, Antoine. She's dead. Do you hear me? I merely look like her, but I'm not her. I know you don't understand this, neither do I, but you have to believe me. I'm from . . . somewhere else. I am not Sara Janei. Melody killed her."

Antoine looked at her for a long moment. A sadness

came into his eyes, and at the same time the light that made Antoine so vibrant, so alive, died.

His voice was low and hushed, full of resignation and sorrow when he answered. "Janei, there is no need of such lies. You do not love me enough to leave him. That is all there is to be said."

"Antoine," Janelle pleaded, "how can I convince you I'm telling the truth? There's no need for you to leave New Orleans."

He shook his head slowly. "Go back to your husband, Janei. That is where you chose to remain."

With a sigh of frustration, Janelle went to Justin.

"In my own time, Justin, I saw Antoine's house. The one he's been building a few miles from here. It had fallen into ruin, left to rot away through the years. It made me sad then, but I didn't know why. Now I do. He shouldn't have to leave New Orleans, Justin. There's no reason for it."

"You can't stop him, *chère*. He is a stubborn man." Justin stroked her hair lovingly, and smiled at her courage.

"I know, but I have to try, at least one more time."

He nodded in understanding. Her warmth and compassion were just a few of the reasons he had come to love her so deeply, so completely.

Janelle turned to face Antoine, but as she walked toward him and he looked up, she froze in renewed terror.

Grasped in his hand, fingers curled tightly around the glistening pearl handle and black metal, was a small deringer, pointed directly at Justin's unsuspecting back.

Janelle wanted to run, to scream, to fling herself on Antoine and deflect his shot, to turn and push Justin from the path of the bullet, but she couldn't. Her body seemed paralyzed. A strangled cry burst from her parted lips, the sound so low and muffled that no one heard it. Clenching her fists, she forced the air from her lungs. A loud scream pierced the night.

Justin whirled around. At the same instant Janelle managed to scream, Antoine's finger tightened on the small gun's trigger and an explosion of noise filled the air. A faint cloud of white smoke filtered out from the short gun barrel. Antoine remained in place, his arm rigidly held forward, thumb on the firing pin, ready to recock if necessary.

Justin remained standing, his tall, solid form facing Antoine unscathed.

Another scream filled the air, wilder and more desperate than Janelle's, and then the clearing became quiet. Suddenly, the bushes behind Justin shook violently and the thick foliage parted. Blue silk, the color of a clear mountain lake, appeared between the separating leaves, a thin outstretched hand clawed at the air and white-blond hair swirled about the protruding branches.

Melody Foucheau pitched forward, her body twisting in midfall, the voluminous red satin-lined cape spreading out beneath her on the ground. She lay perfectly still, the last gasp of air having burst from her lungs when she screamed. Justin stepped to the prone figure and knelt down. The bodice of Melody's gown was stained red, her lifeblood ebbing from the small bullet wound on her left breast to soak through the fine blue silk and lace. The gun that had killed Gilbert remained clutched in her thin white fingers, lying limp alongside the flowing skirts.

Janelle, filled with a mingling of relief, horror, and confusion, turned back to look at Antoine, her eyes questioning and puzzled.

"She was going to kill you," he said simply, a sad smile creasing his handsome features.

For the first time she realized how deeply Antoine

loved the woman whose place she'd assumed, the woman who had caused hurt and pain to so many, and who had left behind such a wake of sadness and death.

"You saved my life, Antoine," she said softly.

He shrugged and looked away. He had saved the only woman he had ever loved from a bullet, but he had saved her only so that she could remain in the arms of another.

Justin moved to stand beside Janelle. "I am indebted to you, Antoine. You saved Janelle's life." He offered his hand.

Antoine shook his head, glancing first at Justin's outstretched hand and then back into his steel gray eyes. He had heard Justin call her Janelle, but refused to accept the meaning, stubbornly rejecting the idea that her earlier words held any possibility of truth.

"I saved the woman I love from a bullet, but I cannot save her from herself, Monsieur. She has come to believe that money is all-important to her way of life." Antoine's eyes grew cold as he continued. "I am not a wealthy man, and I have failed in the duello, so I will honor her decision to remain with you."

Justin lowered his hand. "That is all we can ask, then."

"Antoine . . ." Janelle began.

Celine Gampion stepped from the shadows. Her gown, a deep midnight purple of gossamer satin, blended well with the night, enabling her to have stood so near, and yet remain unnoticed. Her black hair was covered by a tightly wound turban, the same fabric as her skirts. She moved to stand beside Antoine.

"Come, *chérie*. Let's go home," she whispered softly. She gazed up at her lover, a pleading look on her face. He was the only man she had ever loved, he was her life, but the look in her eyes was one of uncertainty now.

"You have a carriage?" he asked huskily, as they turned away and began to move from the small clearing.

Janelle rushed after them and they paused as she called out, "Antoine, please, you don't have to leave New Orleans."

"I must." He turned to look at her for the last time. For an instant Janelle saw the fire that smoldered beyond his dark eyes, the tenderness and passion he held for Sara Janei. And then it was gone, as if a cloud had passed between them. "I should have left long ago, *chére*, but I was foolish. Celine and I will go north, or perhaps to France, where we can live in peace together."

"No, wait, you don't have . . ."

Celine swung around, hatred burning in her dark eyes, "Haven't you done enough, Madame Delacroix? Antoine is—"

"Celine! Silencieux!" Antoine ordered.

The beautiful woman turned instantly to face the man who had ordered her silence and in that split second, her gaze locked with his, all defiance left her. Celine lowered her head, and turned to accompany him.

Justin came to stand beside Janelle, and together they watched Antoine and Celine slowly move down the drive toward the entry where their carriage waited.

"Why can't they live in peace here, Justin?" she asked sadly.

"It is against the law, *chère*. A quadroon cannot marry a white man. She can only be his *placée*."

"What's that, like a mistress?"

"Yes. But Celine is light enough to pass for white. They can go north or to France and marry, and no one will ever know. In time, as their children grow and have children, it will most likely be forgotten even by their own family that Celine was ever anything but white."

"I wish they didn't have to leave their home."

"Someday things will change. Maybe after this war that is coming. Maybe then it will be different."

Janelle sighed heavily. "No, unfortunately that's one thing that doesn't really change."

Chapter twenty-five

February 22, 1857

JANELLE STOOD IN THE CENTER OF THE RIVER-
boat's spacious main salon and couldn't believe what
she saw. Huge baskets of flowers lined the walls; the
heady fragrance of gardenias, jasmine, roses, honeysuckle, camellias, daisies, orchids, and even some hot-
house magnolias in early bloom filled the room. Three
crystal chandeliers hung from the ceiling, a blaze with
candlelight, their teardrop prisms sparkling like diamonds. Dozens of tables, their tops covered with white
linen, had been decorated with additional wreaths of
flowers and tall white candles set in crystal sconces.
White and green ribbons of silk decorated the baskets,
curled around the wreaths, and wove within the intri-
cately carved filigree woodwork that adorned the walls
between each window and across the ceiling. Rosewood chairs, their thickly padded cushions covered in
a rich, red velvet, lined the walls between the windows and flower baskets, and more were set around
the tables. The center tables held the food, enough for
the entire assemblage of passengers. Stuffed turkeys,
quails, hens, and hams crowded one table, rice, stews,
jambalayas, crabs, crawfish, and oysters the next, and

beside them were *glacières* brimming with iced fruits and flavored ice creams. Beignets, custards, cakes, creams, pies, and pastries of every fabulous pattern and color vied for attention as they surrounded a massive white cake with edges trimmed with real violet blossoms.

Her wedding cake. She was so delirious with happiness Janelle still had to pinch herself occasionally to make sure she wasn't dreaming.

The great riverboat had been plying the water for eight hours but they were not yet halfway upriver to Natchez, Mississippi. In the last few months, since the night of the soirée, she and Justin had planned this trip, praying they'd be allowed to make it. Their wedding date had been set for six months from that evening. They had decided that since no one else knew of Sara Janei's death, and most already assumed she *was* Sara Janei, the only way they could marry would be to remarry, on Justin and Sara Janei's wedding anniversary, February 22nd.

Holding the ceremony aboard the *Belle Isle* had been Justin's idea, and one that Janelle had instantly embraced with enthusiasm.

The steamboat pulled from the docks of New Orleans at ten o'clock that morning, and their wedding ceremony was scheduled for seven-thirty that evening in the grand salon. One hundred of Justin's closest friends and business associates were on board, all guests for the wedding, announced as a repledge of their troth.

The sound of voices suddenly broke the silence and Janelle turned toward the salon door. Marie, Sammy, and Callie entered the room.

"Michie's waiting on deck for you, missy," Marie said as she approached. The others had instantly begun inspecting the tables, to check each last detail for perhaps the tenth time.

Janelle left the salon and stepped onto the dimly lit

veranda. Justin emerged from the shadows beside the door to join her. "Happy?" he asked softly, nuzzling her ear.

"Ummm, more than I can ever say," she murmured in answer.

They strolled across the deck, pausing at the white railing to watch the slowly passing horizon, a ragged silhouette beneath the setting sun.

A soft breeze blew up from the churning waters and whipped several strands of hair about Janelle's face. Tears momentarily blurred Janelle's vision as she watched the sun begin to sink beyond the horizon, its fading rays casting a golden orange glow on the river and boat, as if surrounding them with an ethereal haze. The distant shoreline, its high banks thickly covered by trees and shrubbery, turned to black shadow and the smell of the Mississippi, greenery, and gourmet cooking from the ship's galley, wafted up to tease her nose. But the tears were of joy, for Janelle was so filled with happiness and love, she still found it hard to believe it had all actually happened.

The silence of the night was suddenly broken by a blast from the *Belle Isle*'s whistle, and another riverboat passed on its way downriver. Light flowed from every window of its three decks, and the sounds of laughter and piano music drifted out from its gambling saloon.

Beside her Justin was silent, staring out into the quickly darkening sky, a slight smile tugging at the corners of his mouth, his eyes warm and alive with love and hope. "It is time to ready ourselves," he whispered, brushing the windblown hair from her face with the tip of his finger.

She slid her arms around his shoulders, and urged him to bring his lips down to meet hers.

When they drew apart, the timbre of Justin's voice

was filled with emotion. "The next time I take you in my arms, *chère*, you will be my wife."

Janelle stood on tiptoe to brush her lips across his again. "And you, my love, will be my husband."

"Do not disappear on me, Janelle," Justin teased. His tone was light but the fear behind those words was always in his heart. It was something he had lived with for the past six months, and would continue to live with. He only prayed the fear would never become reality.

"Not a chance," she said softly. Months ago Janelle had forced herself to stop worrying about the time warp. It had not happened at the cemetery the night of the soirée, even though the pull had been so strong. It would not recur, she felt certain. And hopeful.

Only the minister caught the change of names as Janelle spoke her vows, pronouncing herself Janelle Ann Torrance rather than Sara Janei Chevillon as he'd expected, but he brushed it aside.

He pronounced them man and wife, and the tears Janelle had been desperately holding back spilled over. Happy tears, joyous tears, tears of rapture and bliss. She turned toward Justin, her eyes shining like emeralds, her breast tight with the love and happiness she felt flowing through her. She went into his embrace eagerly and when she looked up into his face, the expression she saw in those steel gray eyes caused her heart to ache with a sweet, swelling joy.

He would remember her always like this, creamy white blossoms of honeysuckle woven into the satiny curls of her dark hair, her eyes afire with love, her delicate features alive with happiness. She was a vision of loveliness, her shimmering white gown trimmed with green lace an exact copy of the one destroyed the night of the soirée. His arms tightened around her waist, and as his head lowered toward hers he murmured thickly, "I will love you, Janelle, for as long as I live. You are my life." His lips claimed hers with an urgent tenderness that held all the promise of a love that would last through all the years to come, and beyond.

Nine months to the day! He couldn't believe it. Justin nervously paced the foyer, stopping every few seconds to look up at the empty staircase. Just when he thought he was about to go mad with worry, the house suddenly filled with the cry of new life. His child! His child was born. He was a father!

But before he could bound up the stairs, Callie quickly descended and cautioned him to wait, explaining it was the doctor's request.

Another twenty minutes passed, and Justin paced the floor, wringing his hands with each step. Just when he thought he couldn't wait another second, Marie appeared on the second-floor landing. A small swaddle of white blanket was cradled in her arms.

"You have a son," she announced proudly, placing the baby in Justin's arms. She pulled the blanket aside and he was surprised and delighted to discover the infant awake.

Silken strands of brown-red hair covered his tiny head and his heavily lashed dark eyes appeared to have a greenish tinge to them. A small hand reached out and flailed at the air, wrapping around Justin's finger as they came in contact.

Pride swelled in his chest. "Marie, how is Janelle?" he asked hoarsely, his eyes never leaving his son's face. When she didn't answer immediately alarm surged through him. His head shot up, but Marie was gone. Callie, who stood nearby, smiled and pointed to the top of the stairs.

"I had to go back and get the other little fella," Marie

said, grinning widely as Justin stared, too shocked to respond.

Callie took the first infant from Justin's arms as Marie handed him the second one. "They may be twins, but they sure don't look nothing alike." She laughed as Justin stared at his second-born son.

The baby's head was covered with a mass of black, curly hair, short silky brows framing eyes of bluish gray that rose to meet the almost identical gaze of his father's.

"Good Lord, they're beautiful," he mumbled, his heart surging with love and pride. He handed the infant back to Marie and bounded up the stairs and into the bedroom.

Janelle lay in the center of the big canopied bed, her eyes closed, her hair fanning out across the pillow like a silky auburn cloud. She was sleeping lightly. He sat on the edge of the bed, watching her, reassuring himself that she was all right, not releasing the breath he was unaware he held until, at last, she opened her eyes. He took her hand.

"Are you all right, *chère?*" His eyes drank in her frail beauty, ascertaining for himself she was indeed well. She was pale, and obviously weak from the long hours of labor, but at this moment she had never looked more beautiful to him, more cherished and loved.

She gave a sigh of contentment and smiled. "Oh, yes, my love," she whispered weakly, reaching out for his hand.

A beaming Marie slipped into the room and quietly placed the babies in their cradle near the fireplace.

"They're going to be a handful." Janelle sighed, a teasing note to her voice.

Justin had a mischievous gleam in his eye as he looked down at Janelle. "Don't think you're going to disappear on me now," he said with a laugh. A shadow passed over his face as his words, meant only to be teasing, hung in the air, threatening, menacing. In a shaken voice he murmured, "Janelle, I love you more than anything, more than life itself. If anything ever . . ."

She reached up to wrap her hands about her neck, her eyes warm and soft with love. His mouth lowered toward hers, and as their lips met Janelle whispered softly, "I love you, Justin Delacroix, so very, very much."

Epilogue

July 14, 1991
Delacroix Plantation

ALTHOUGH STILL WEAK FROM HIS DEVASTATING bout with pneumonia, and only home from the hospital one day, Tano insisted on the family gathering in Leland's study that evening. Kyle Donovan and Sheriff Thiebault were also requested to attend. Almost four weeks had passed since Janelle's disappearance and there was still no sign of her, or any hint as to what had happened. Clues seemed nonexistent.

Paul and Cathy helped the frail old man into the study and onto the sofa, where his long thin body sank into the thick cushions. Cathy sat on his left, Paul on the right. The others were scattered around the room. None of them knew what Tano wanted, or was about to say, but all had been waiting impatiently for hours, ever since that morning when he had informed Cathy of his demand for the meeting. It was that insistence, so unlike the old butler, that had them nervous and expectant.

Tano turned toward Cathy, his hand reaching out to grasp hers. Gnarled, bony fingers wrapped around her soft white ones. "What I'm gonna tell you, Miss Cathy, is gonna be hard for you to believe, but you gotta try. And remember, the one thing she wanted was that you be happy for her. So don't you be sad."

Cathy looked at him in confusion. Almost a century of living reflected behind his eyes creased his face and edged the timbre of his quaking voice.

Everyone in the group tensed at his words, their attention riveted on the frail old man.

"She?" Cathy questioned, hesitatingly.

"I knew her as Miss Janei." He smiled, a faraway look in his eyes as he remembered other times, long ago. "You knew her as your friend Janelle."

Paul opened his mouth to speak, catching the retort in his throat at a quick motion for silence from his father.

"I . . . I don't understand," Cathy stammered.

"You will," he murmured softly, patting her hand. "You will."

It took well over an hour before they returned to the study. Tano had insisted on going to the attic; he stubbornly refused to explain, and staunchly refused to allow anyone to accompany or assist him other than Cathy and Paul.

Once they'd entered the large cavern of dimly lit space, Tano made his way deftly through more than a century's worth of stored furnishings, crates, and trunks to a small, well-hidden closet. He took a key from his pocket and opened the door. Propped against one wall was a crate, at least six feet in height and several inches thick, and beside it a small metal box sat on the floor, layers of dust covering its once-shiny black surface.

Paul carried the crate into the study and propped it against Leland's desk. Cathy placed the small box on the coffee table in front of the sofa where she and Tano sat.

The old man motioned everyone to quiet and gestured for Cathy to open the box. "This will answer all your questions, Miss Cathy," he said softly.

The tension in the room was almost palpable as all eyes stared at the small, dust-covered box. Cathy lifted its lid. An old journal lay inside, its once-soft leather binding now old and cracked with age, frayed at the edges and corners. She carefully lifted the journal out, placed it upon her lap, and with trembling fingers opened the leather cover and began to read the words written on the yellowed pages.

"Dear Cathy, I know this will be hard for you to believe,"
Janelle had written.

For over two hours all sat in rapt attention, listening to her read the words that had been entered in the journal over one hundred and thirty years before, by a friend who had only disappeared from their home four weeks earlier.

Tears blurred Cathy's vision, and her hand trembled uncontrollably as she turned the last, brittle page. "She was my great-great-great-grandmother?" Cathy said, turning to Tano. Astonishment and disbelief edged her voice.

The old man nodded and reached back into the box. When he held his hand out to her, a small red velvet bag lay in his outstretched palm. "She wanted you to have this, so you wouldn't question that her journal was real. This box been locked upstairs for almost eighty-five years, Miss Cathy, since the day before she died. No one ever knew it was there except me and her."

"Janelle's locket watch!" Cathy gasped, as the ruby and diamond locket fell into her hand from inside the upturned bag.

"But how? She had it on a few weeks ago."

Tano shook his head. "There's some things in this world that just can't be explained," he said softly. He rose from the sofa and slowly made his way across the room to the crate. When he began to struggle with the twine that held the large box sealed, Kyle moved to his side to help.

The old burlap and paper covering fell to the floor and the painting came into full view. Suddenly, as all her doubt subsided, Cathy felt a surge of joy for Janelle. She gazed once more into the face of her friend.

Janelle stood beside Justin, the Creole she had lovingly described in her journal. Her auburn head barely reached his broad shoulder. A gray cravat at his neck was the exact color of the smoldering eyes, and the scar on his right cheek enhanced, rather than marred, the man's aristocratically handsome features. Justin's arm was wrapped possessively around Janelle's shoulder, holding her close, the fingers of his other hand entwined in hers. She looked radiantly happy in a gown of shimmering white silk, the voluminous hoopskirt billowing out around her, and folds of emerald lace, accentuating the brilliance of her green eyes, dripped from the low-cut bodice. At the couple's feet, sitting together on a small marble bench, were three children. The two boys looked about eight or nine years old, one possessing the dark Creole coloring and features of his father, the other strongly resembling his mother, and between them perched a little girl of no more than four. Her black curly hair swirled across her tiny shoulders in lustrous waves as she looked out at the world with rich, gold-speckled green eyes, a mischievous little smile tugging at the corners of her mouth.

Below the painting, secured to the wooden frame, was a small brass plaque:

Justin and Janelle
Morgan, Catherine, Travis
Delacroix
May, 1867

Cheryl Biggs currently lives in California. She previously owned and operated a personnel agency for three years before turning to writing. This is her first published book.

📕 HarperPaperbacks *By Mail*
BLAZING PASSIONS
IN FIVE HISTORICAL ROMANCES

_UIET FIRES by *Ginna Gray* ISBN: 0-06-104037-1 $4.50

..he black dirt and red rage of war-torn Texas, Elizabeth Stanton and Conn Cavanaugh discover the ..ssion so long denied them. But would the turmoil of Texas' fight for independence sweep them ..art?

..GLE KNIGHT by *Suzanne Ellison* ISBN: 0-06-104035-5 $4.50

..ced to flee her dangerous Spanish homeland, Elena de la Rosa prepares for her new life in primi- .. Mexico. But she is not prepared to meet Tizoc Santiago, the Aztec prince whose smoldering gaze ..tes a hunger in her impossible to deny.

..OOL'S GOLD by *Janet Quin-Harkin* ISBN: 0-06-104040-1 $4.50

..m Boston's decorous drawing rooms, well-bred Libby Grenville travels west to California. En route, .. meets riverboat gambler Gabe Foster who laughs off her frosty rebukes until their duel of wits rip- ..into a heart-hammering passion.

..MANCHE MOON by *Catherine Anderson* ISBN: 0-06-104010-X $3.95

..ter, the fierce Comanche warrior, is chosen by his people to cross the western wilderness in ..rch of the elusive maiden .. would fulfill their sacred ..phecy. He finds and cap- ..s Loretta, a proud golden- ..ed beauty, who swears to .. her captor. What she ..sn't realize is that she and ..ter are bound by destiny.

..STERDAY'S SHADOWS ..*Marianne Willman* ..N: 0-06-104044-4 ..50

..tiny decrees that blond, ..r-eyed Bettany Howard will .. the Cheyenne brave ..d Wolf Star. An abandoned .. child, Wolf Star was ..d as a Cheyenne Indian, ..reams of a pale and lovely ..r Woman. Yet, before the ..ion promised Bettany and .. Star can be seized, many ..much touch and tangle, .. and blaze in triumph.

MAIL TO: HarperPaperbacks,
10 East 53rd Street, New York, NY 10022
Attn: Mail Order Division

Yes, please send me the books I have checked:

☐ QUIET FIRES (0-06-104037-1) $4.50
☐ EAGLE KNIGHT (0-06-104035-5) $4.50
☐ FOOL'S GOLD (0-06-104040-1) $4.50
☐ COMANCHE MOON (0-06-104010-X) $3.95
☐ YESTERDAY'S SHADOWS (0-06-104044-4) $4.50

SUBTOTAL .... $_____
POSTAGE AND HANDLING .... $ 1.00
SALES TAX (NJ, NY, PA residents) .... $_____
　　　　　　　　　　　　　　TOTAL: 　$_____
(Remit in US funds, do not send cash.)

Name _____

Address _____

City _____

State _____ Zip _____　Allow up to 6 weeks delivery.
　　　　　　　　　　　　　　　Prices subject to change.

H0031